Tree-House Comix Proudly Presents

DOG MAN
LORD OF THE FLEAS

WRITTEN AND ILLUSTRATED BY DAV PILKEY
AS GEORGE BEARD AND HAROLD HUTCHINS
WITH COLOR BY JOSE GARIBALDI

graphix
AN IMPRINT OF
SCHOLASTIC

THANK YOU TO A DEAR FRIEND, RACHEL "RAY RAY" COUN, WHO WAS THERE FROM THE START

Library of Congress Control Number 2017963497

978-0-545-93517-3 (POB)
978-1-338-29091-2 (Library)

10 9 8 7 6 5 4 3 2 1   18 19 20 21 22

Printed in China   62
First edition, September 2018

Edited by Anamika Bhatnagar
Book design by Dav Pilkey and Phil Falco
Color by Jose Garibaldi
Creative Director: David Saylor

CHAPTERS

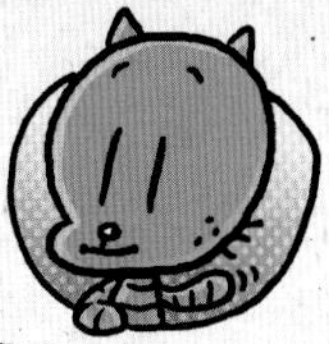

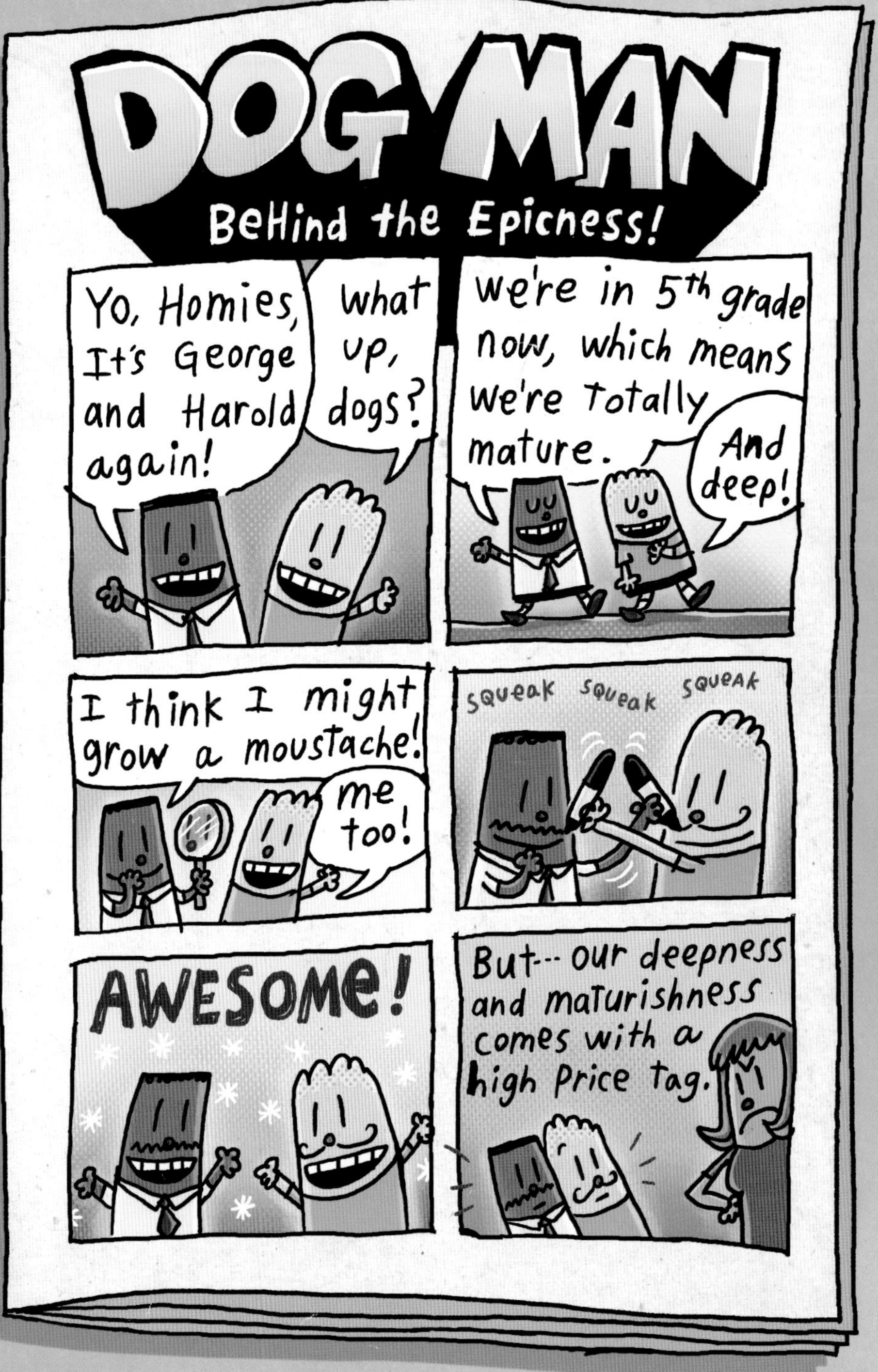
DOG MAN
BeHind the Epicness!
Yo, Homies, It's George and Harold again!
What up, dogs?
We're in 5th grade now, which means we're totally mature.
And deep!
I think I might grow a moustache!
me too!
SQUEAK SQUEAK SQUEAK
AWESOME!
But... our deepness and maturishness comes with a high price tag.

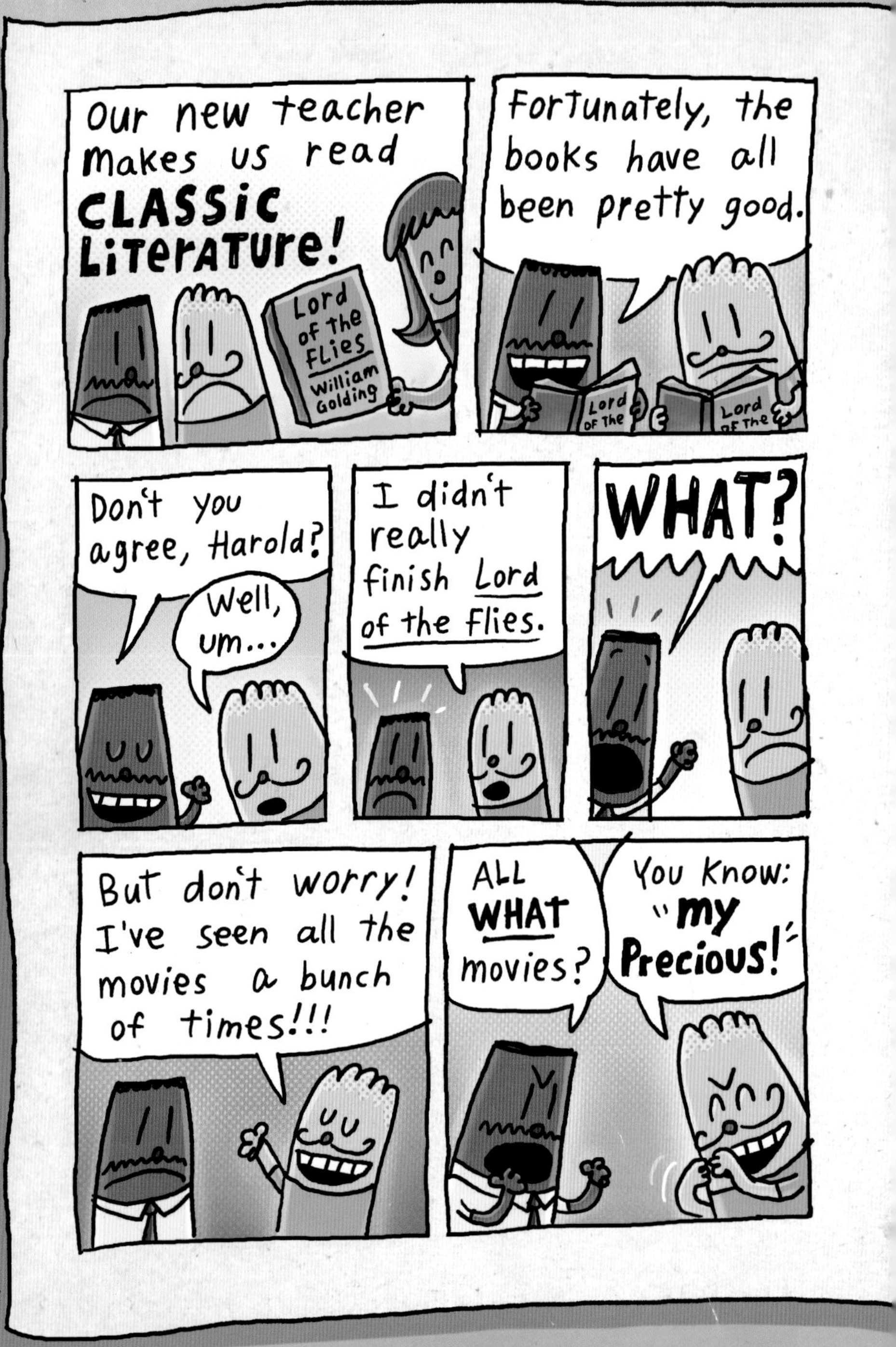

Our new teacher makes us read CLASSIC LITERATURE!
Lord of the Flies William Golding
Fortunately, the books have all been pretty good.
Lord of The
Lord of The
Don't you agree, Harold?
Well, um...
I didn't really finish Lord of the Flies.
WHAT?
But don't worry! I've seen all the movies a bunch of times!!!
ALL WHAT movies?
You know: "my Precious!"

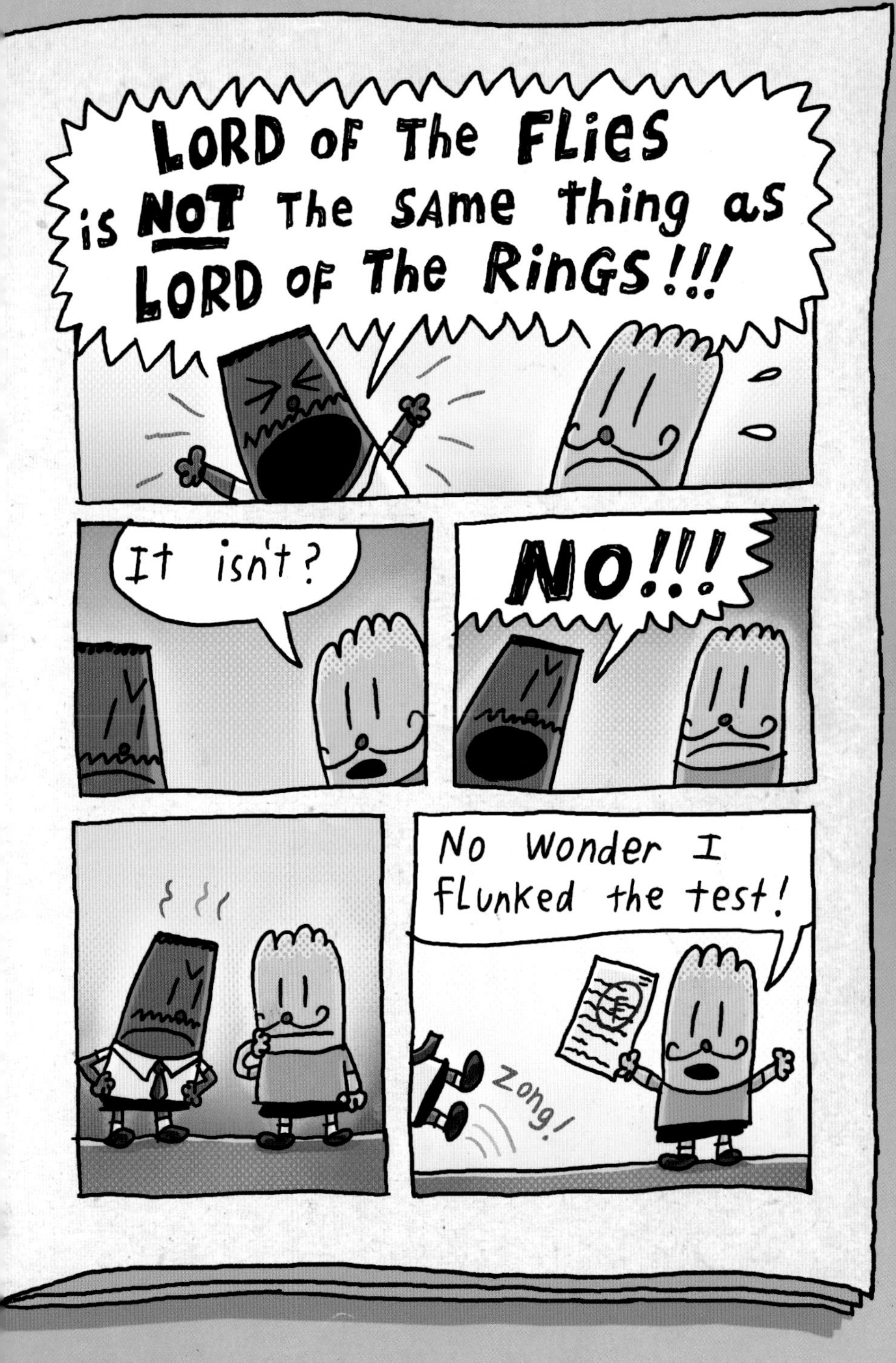
LORD OF The FLIES is NOT The SAME thing as LORD OF The RINGS!!!
It isn't?
NO!!!
No wonder I flunked the test!
Zong!

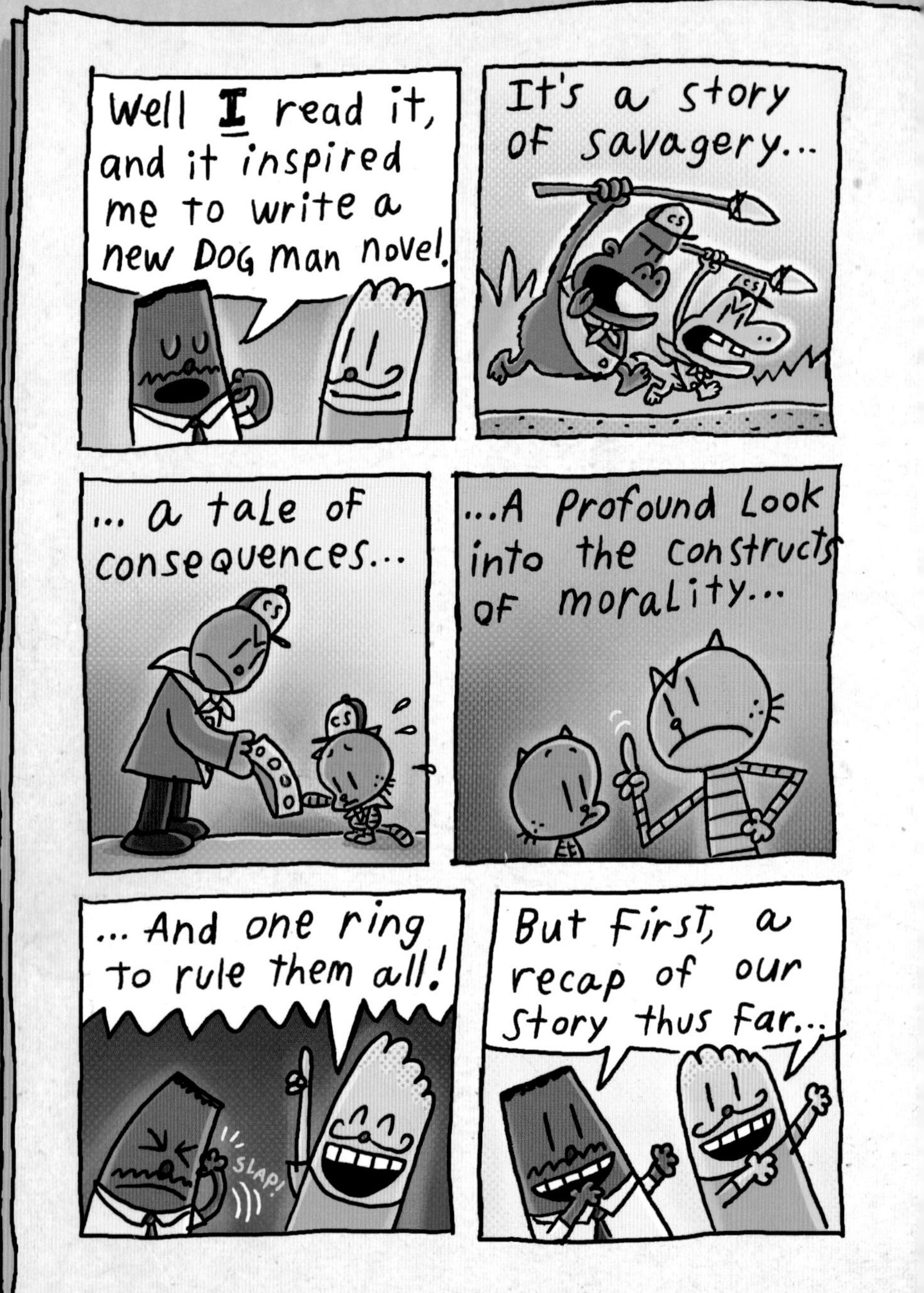

Well I read it, and it inspired me to write a new DOG MAN novel!
It's a story of savagery...
CS
CS
... a tale of consequences...
CS
CS
...A profound look into the constructs of morality...
... And one ring to rule them all!
SLAP!
But first, a recap of our story thus far...

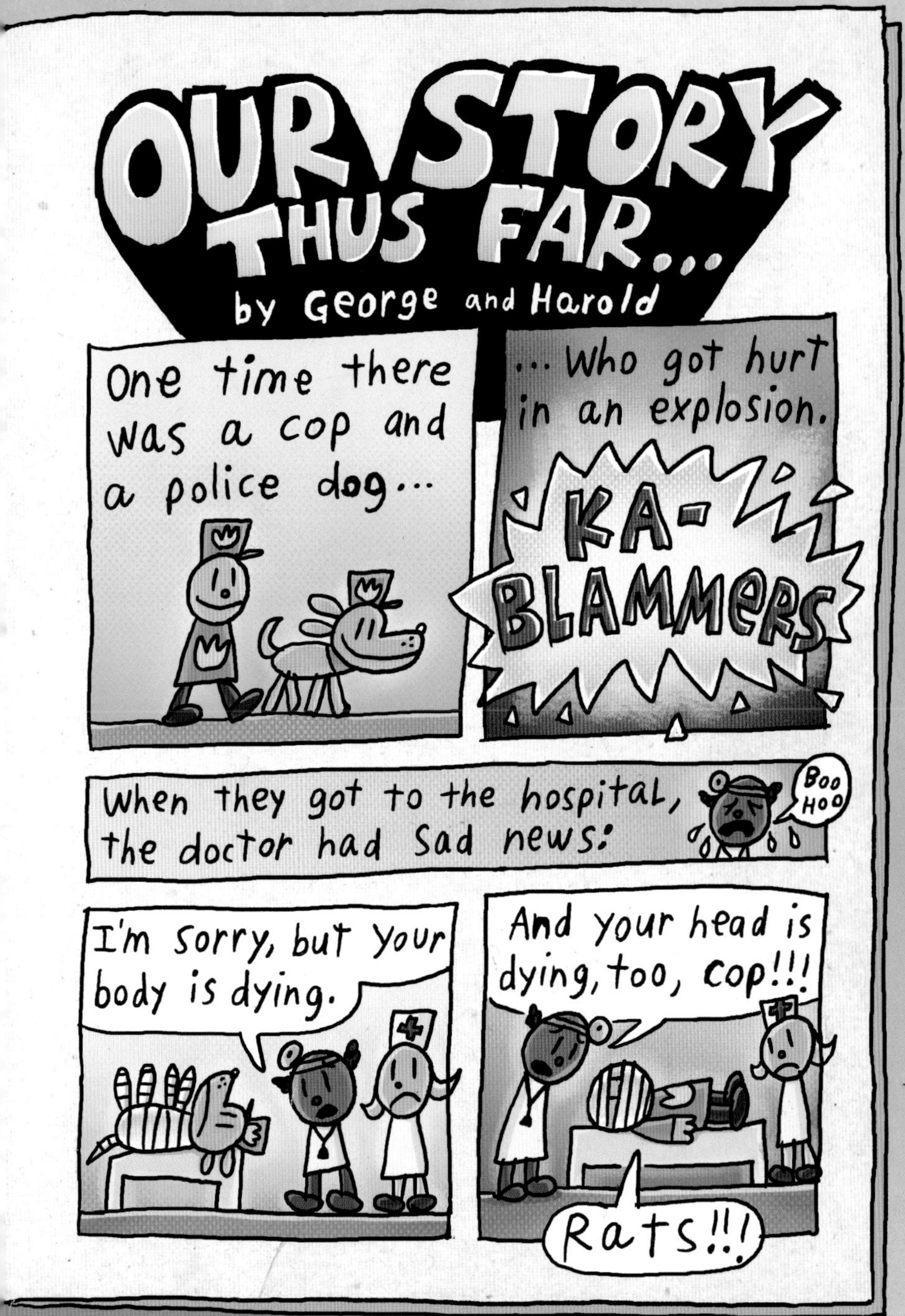
OUR STORY THUS FAR...
by George and Harold
One time there was a cop and a police dog...
...Who got hurt in an explosion.
KA-BLAMMERS
When they got to the hospital, the doctor had sad news:
BOO HOO
I'm sorry, but your body is dying.
And your head is dying, too, cop!!!
Rats!!!

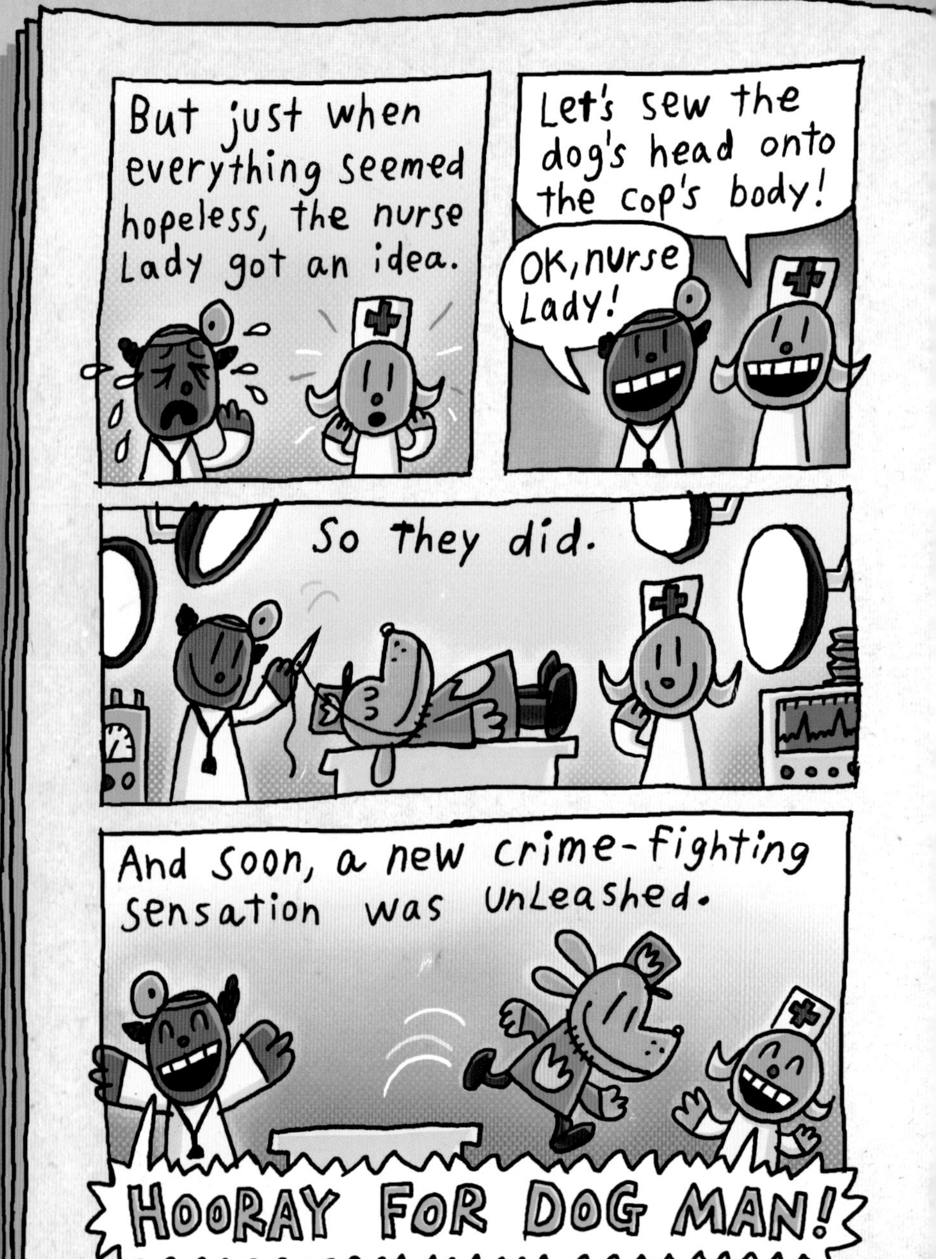

But just when everything seemed hopeless, the nurse Lady got an idea.
Let's sew the dog's head onto the cop's body!
OK, nurse Lady!
So they did.
And soon, a new crime-fighting sensation was unleashed.
HOORAY FOR DOG MAN!

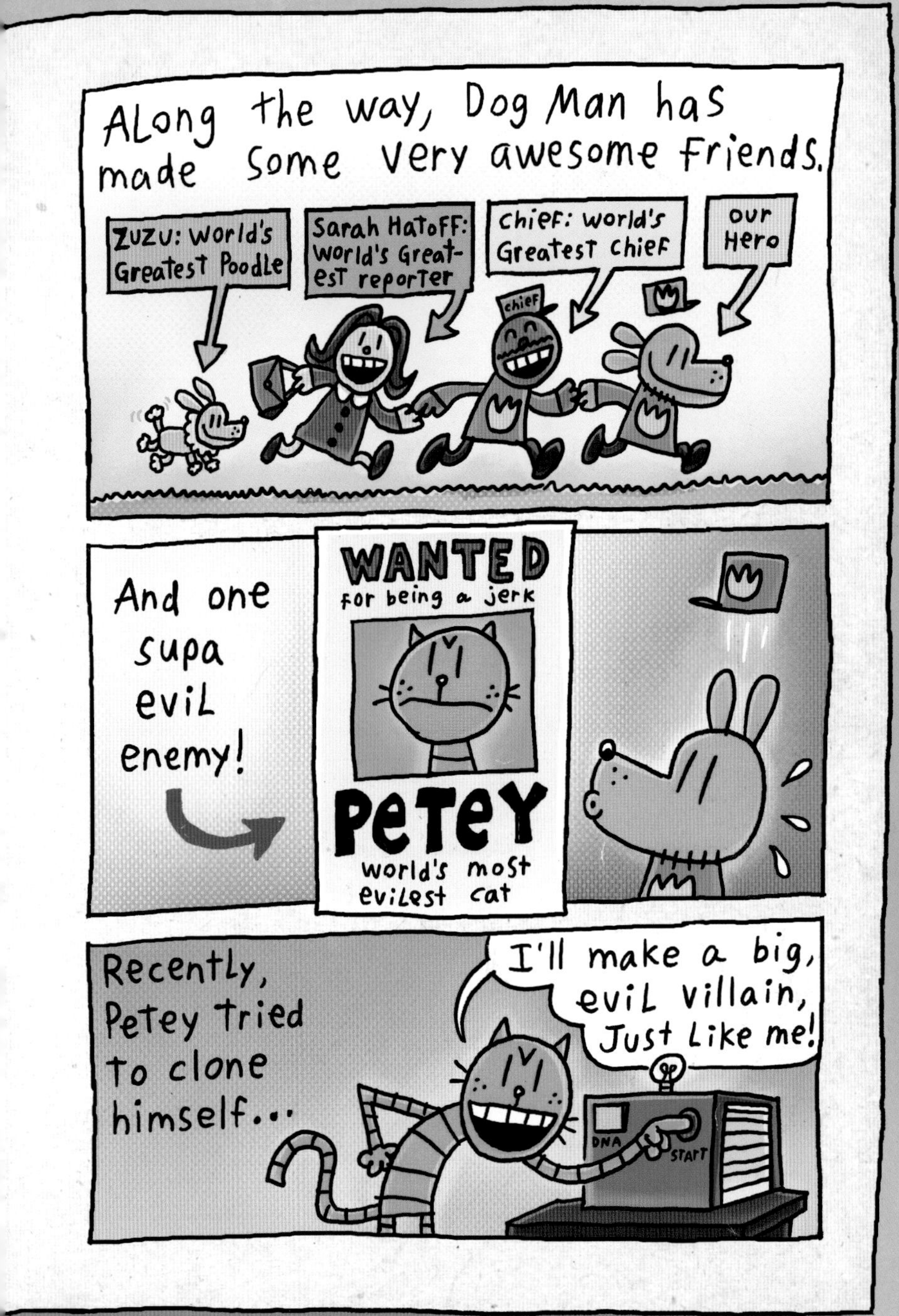
Along the way, Dog Man has made some very awesome friends.
Zuzu: World's Greatest Poodle
Sarah Hatoff: World's Greatest reporter
Chief: World's Greatest Chief
chief
Our Hero
And one supa evil enemy!
WANTED
for being a jerk
PETEY
world's most evilest cat
Recently, Petey tried to clone himself...
I'll make a big, evil villain, Just Like me!
DNA
START

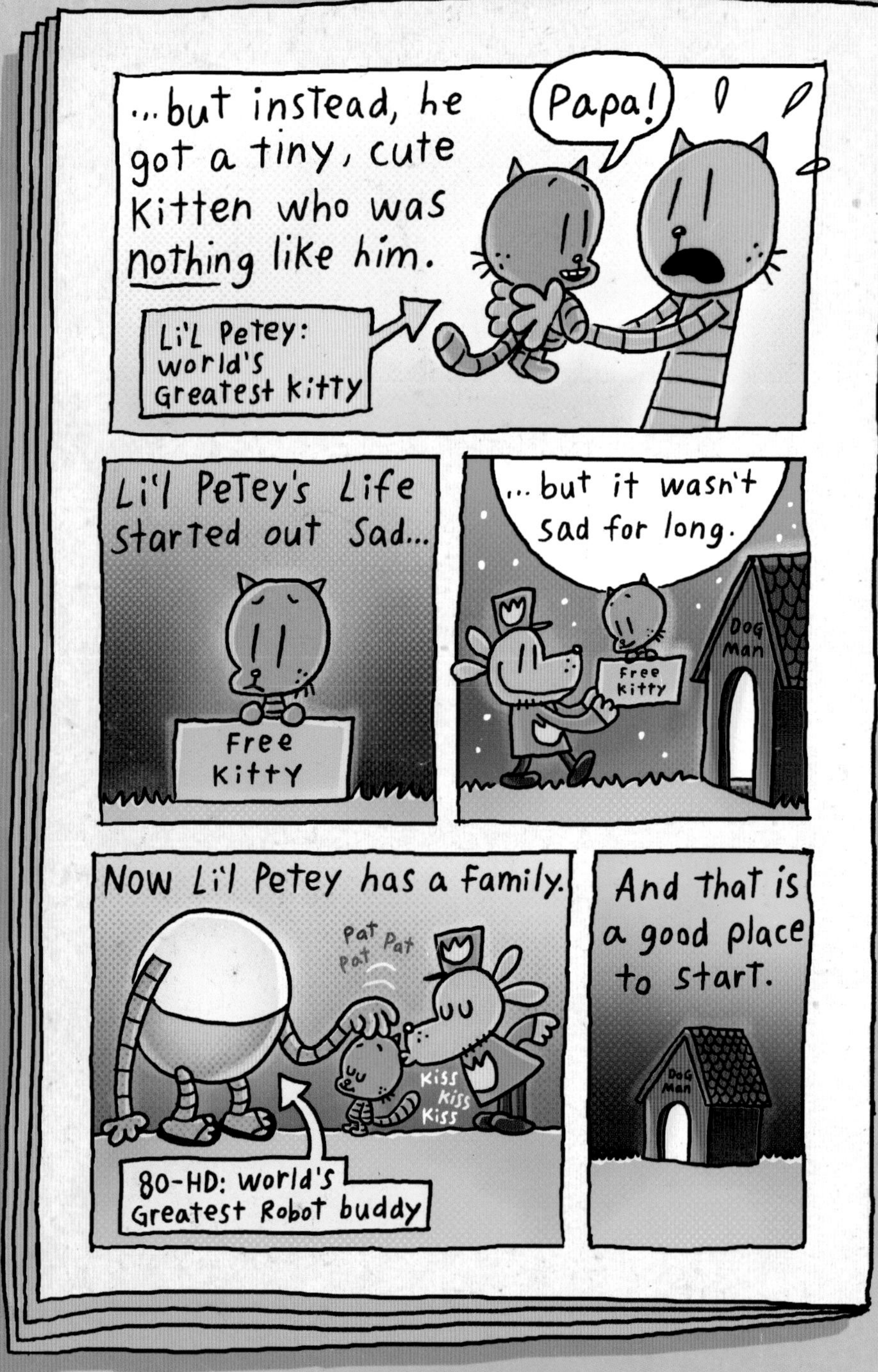
...but instead, he got a tiny, cute kitten who was nothing like him.
Papa!
Li'L Petey: world's Greatest kitty
Li'l Petey's Life started out sad...
Free Kitty
...but it wasn't sad for long.
Dog Man
Free kitty
Now Li'l Petey has a family.
Pat Pat Pat
Kiss kiss kiss
80-HD: World's Greatest Robot buddy
And that is a good place to start.
Dog Man

Tree-House Comix Proudly Presents

Chapter 1

A Visit from Kitty Protective Services

DOG Man

By George and Harold

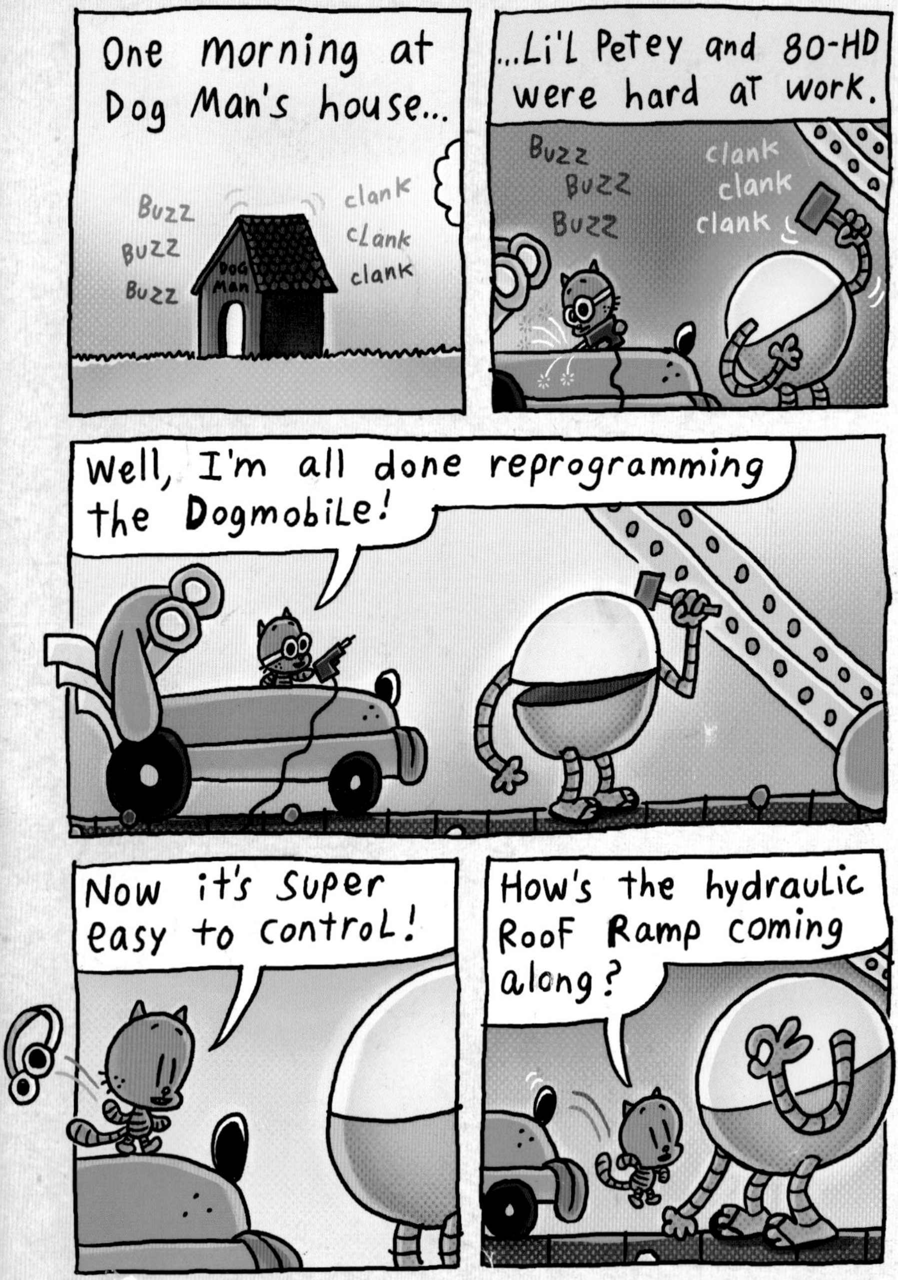
One morning at Dog Man's house...
Buzz
Buzz
Buzz
DOG MAN
clank
clank
clank
...Li'l Petey and 80-HD were hard at work.
Buzz
Buzz
Buzz
clank
clank
clank
Well, I'm all done reprogramming the Dogmobile!
Now it's super easy to control!
How's the hydraulic Roof Ramp coming along?

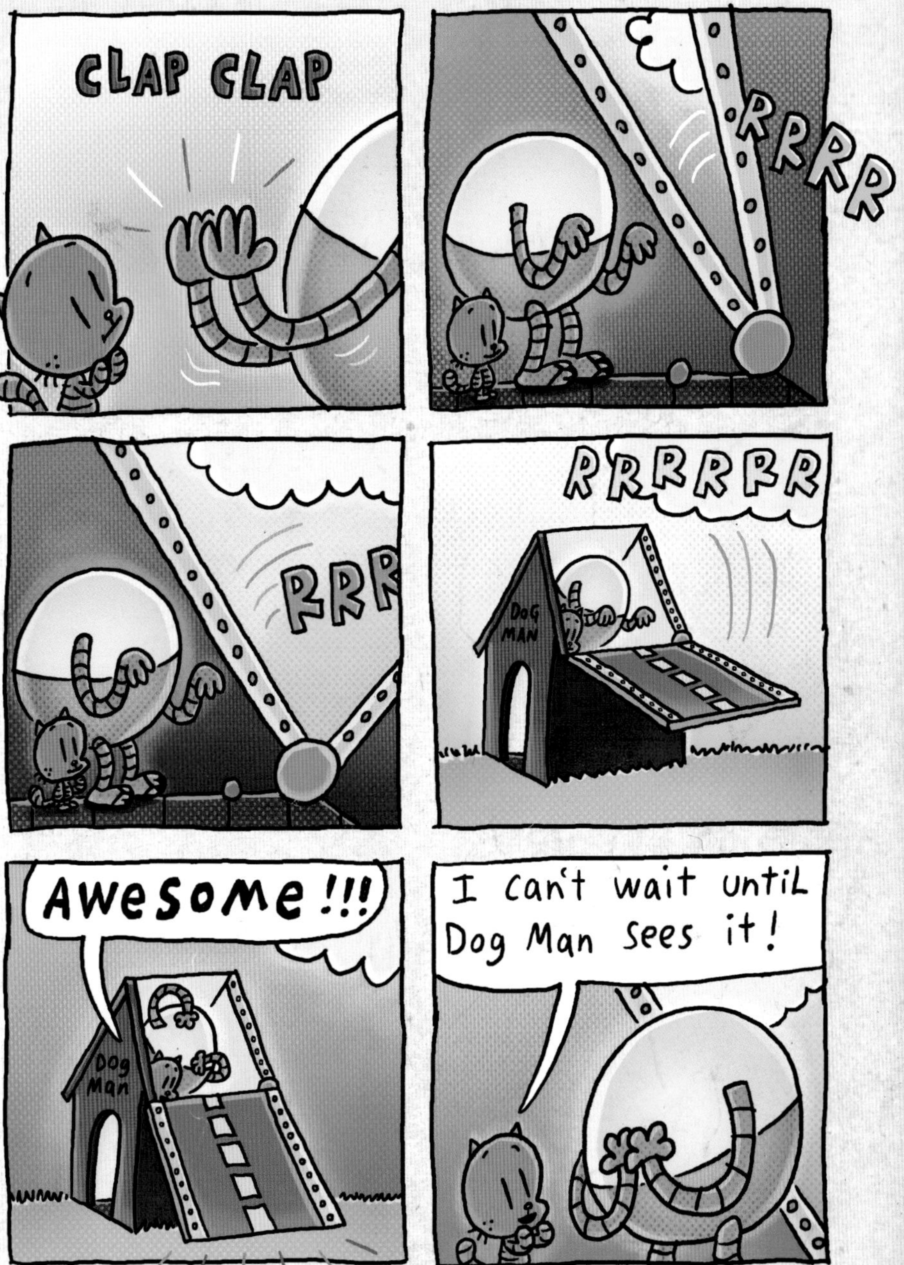
CLAP CLAP
RRRRR
RRR
RRRRRR
AWESOME!!!
CLUNK!
I can't wait until Dog Man sees it!

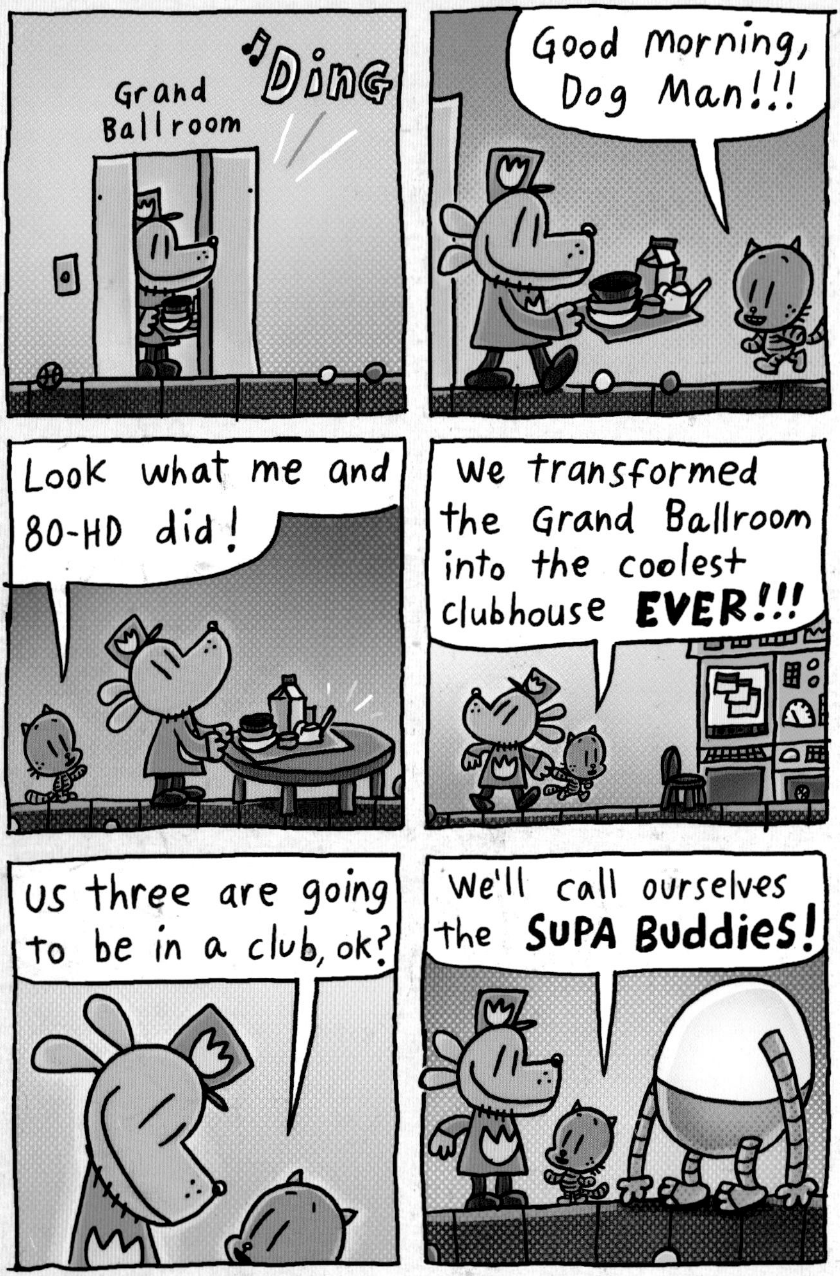
Grand Ballroom
DING
Good Morning, Dog Man!!!
Look what me and 80-HD did!
We transformed the Grand Ballroom into the coolest clubhouse EVER!!!
Us three are going to be in a club, ok?
We'll call ourselves the SUPA BUDDIES!

Most of the time, we'll just be our regular selves...

...But when danger rears its ugly head...

...We'll be super-heroes!!!

Look—I even made a cape for 80-HD!

And I made him a Flip-o-Rama mask!

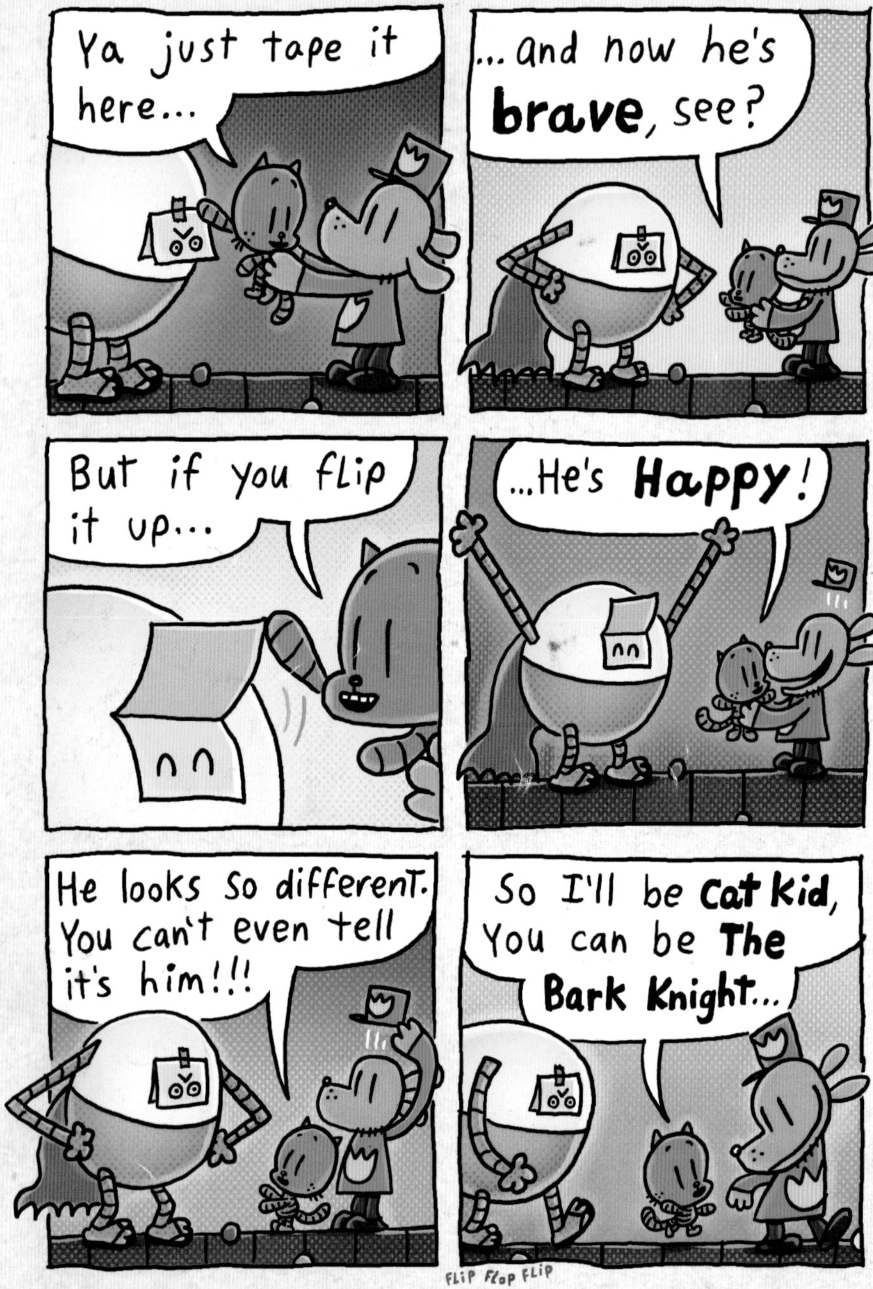
Ya just tape it here...
...and now he's brave, see?
But if you flip it up...
...He's Happy!
He looks so different. You can't even tell it's him!!!
So I'll be Cat Kid, You can be The Bark Knight...
FLIP FLOP FLIP

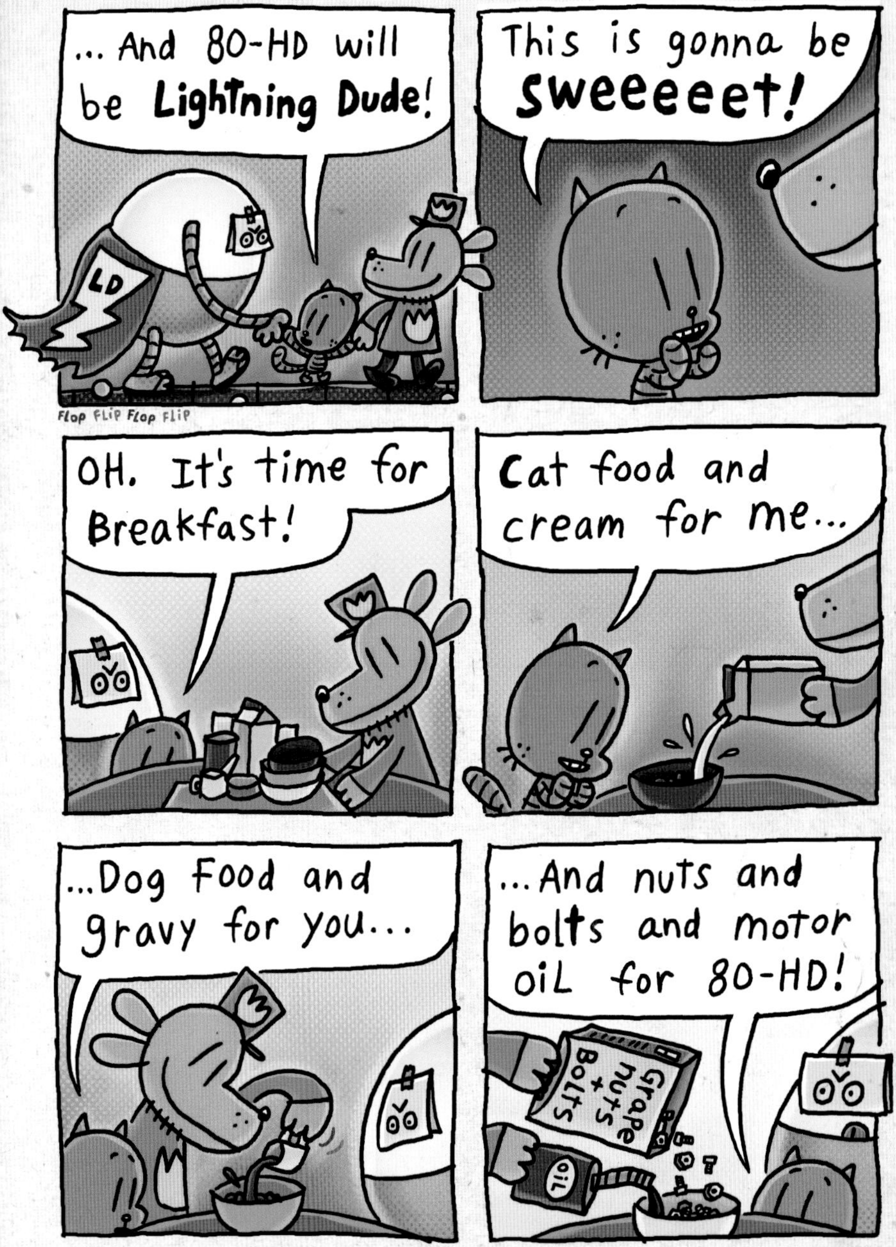
...And 80-HD will be Lightning Dude!
LD
FLOP FLIP FLOP FLIP
This is gonna be sweeeeet!
OH. It's time for Breakfast!
Cat food and cream for me...
...Dog Food and gravy for you...
...And nuts and bolts and motor oil for 80-HD!
Grape nuts + Bolts
OIL

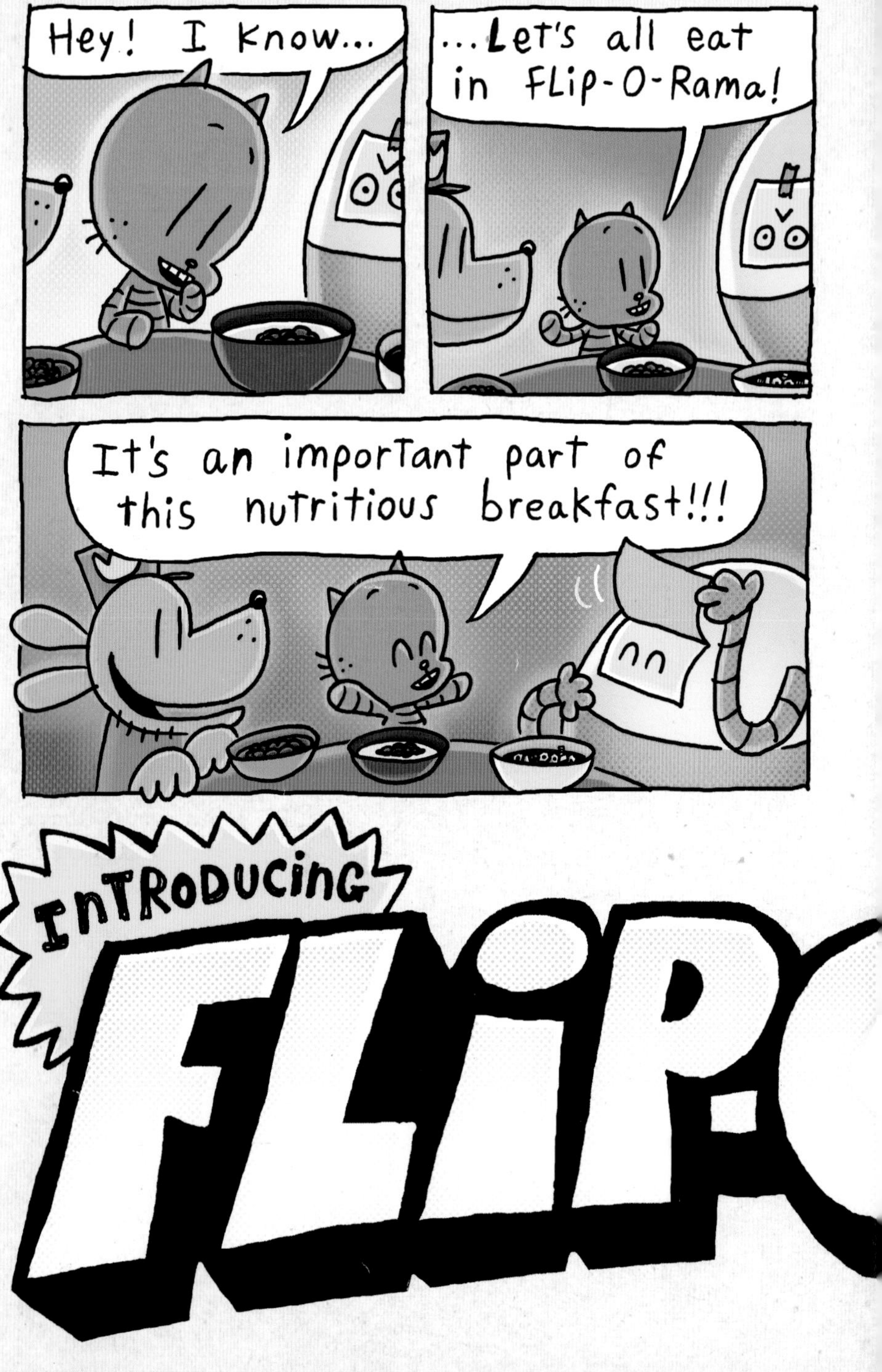
Hey! I know...
...Let's all eat in FLIP-O-Rama!
It's an important part of this nutritious breakfast!!!
INTRODUCING
FLIP-

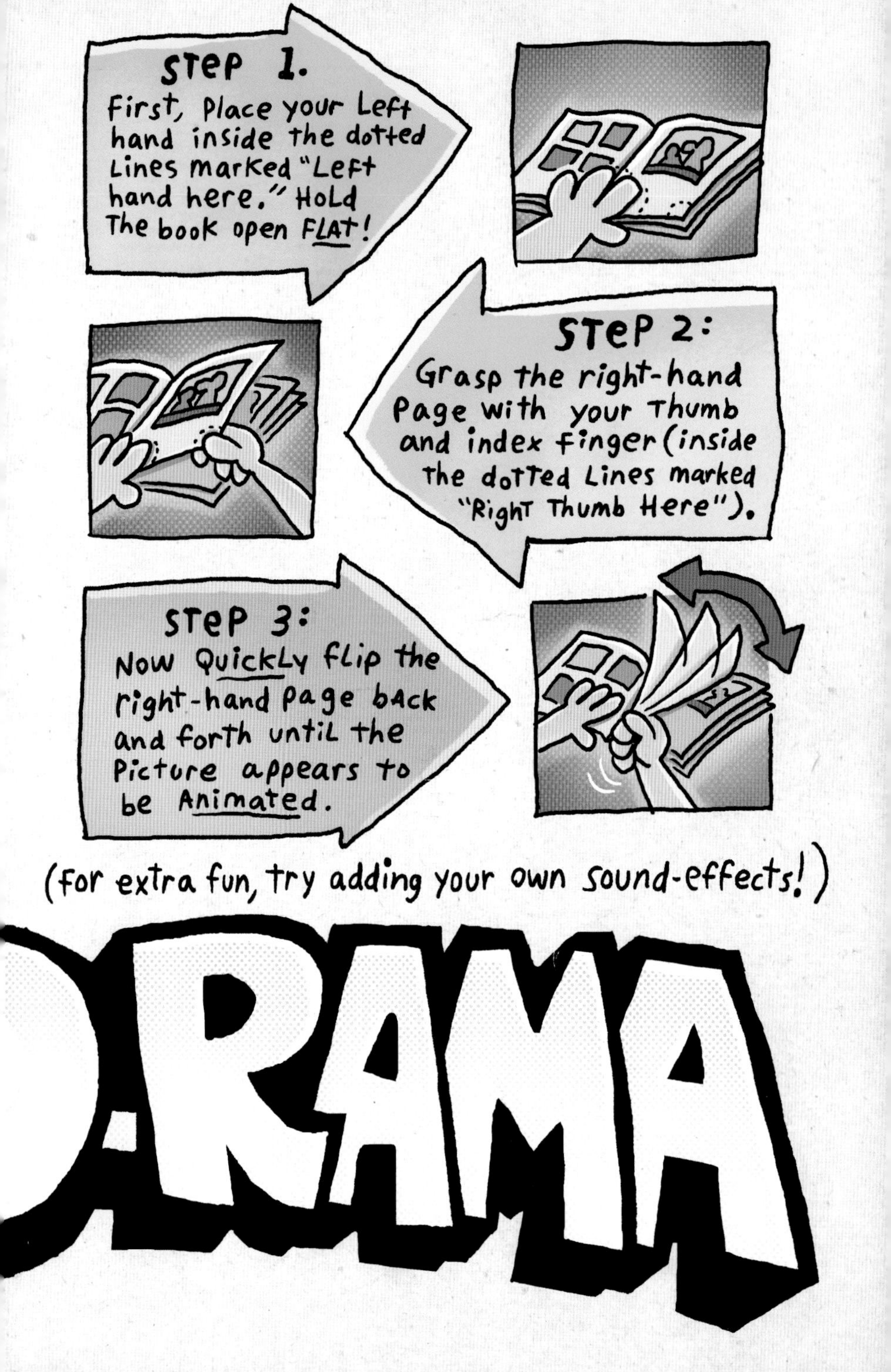
STEP 1.
First, place your left hand inside the dotted lines marked "Left hand here." Hold the book open FLAT!
STEP 2:
Grasp the right-hand page with your thumb and index finger (inside the dotted lines marked "Right Thumb Here").
STEP 3:
Now QUICKLY flip the right-hand page back and forth until the picture appears to be Animated.
(for extra fun, try adding your own sound-effects!)
RAMA

Remember,

while you are flipping,
be sure you can see
The image on page 23
AND the image on page 25.

If you flip quickly,
the two pictures will
start to look like
one **Animated** cartoon!

Don't forget to
add your own
sound-effects!

Left
hand here.

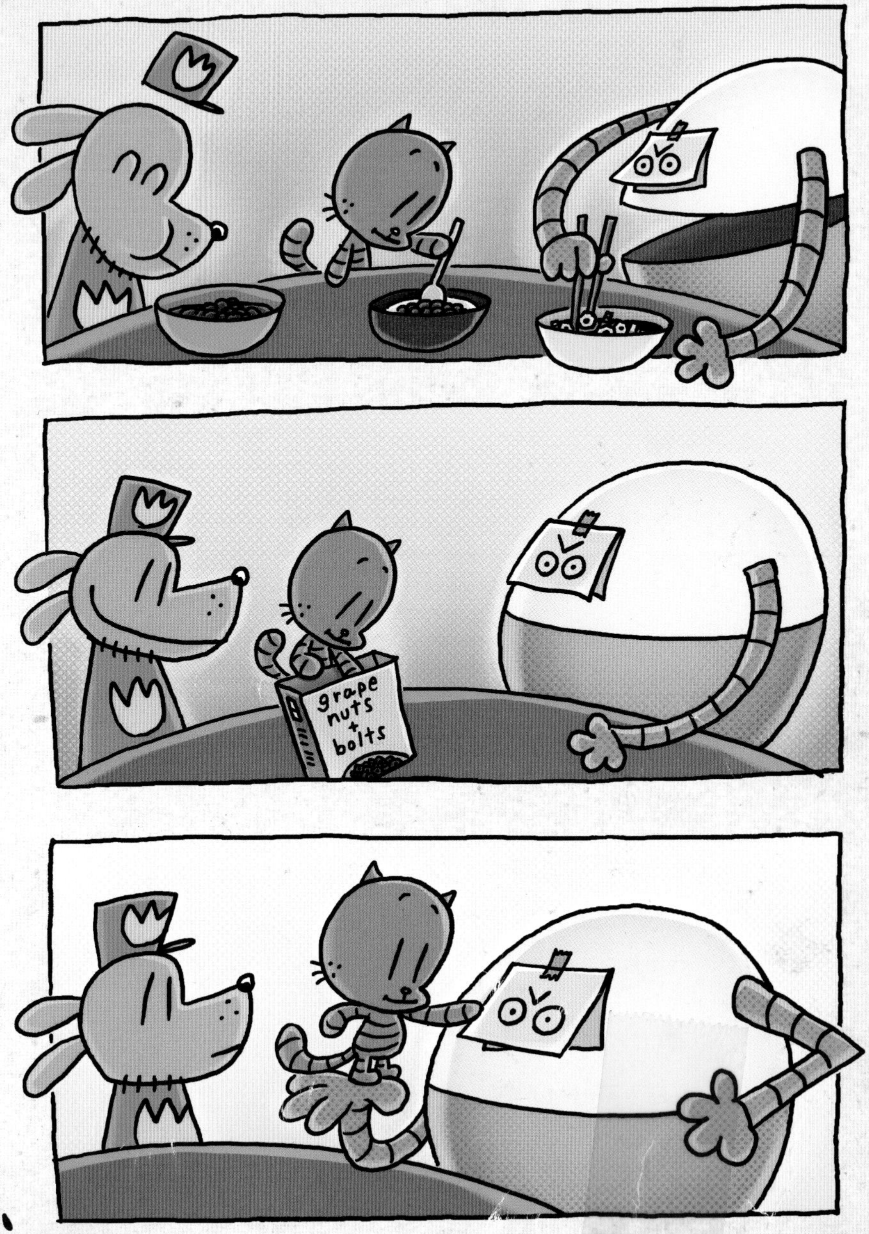
grape
nuts
+
bolts

Right Thumb here.

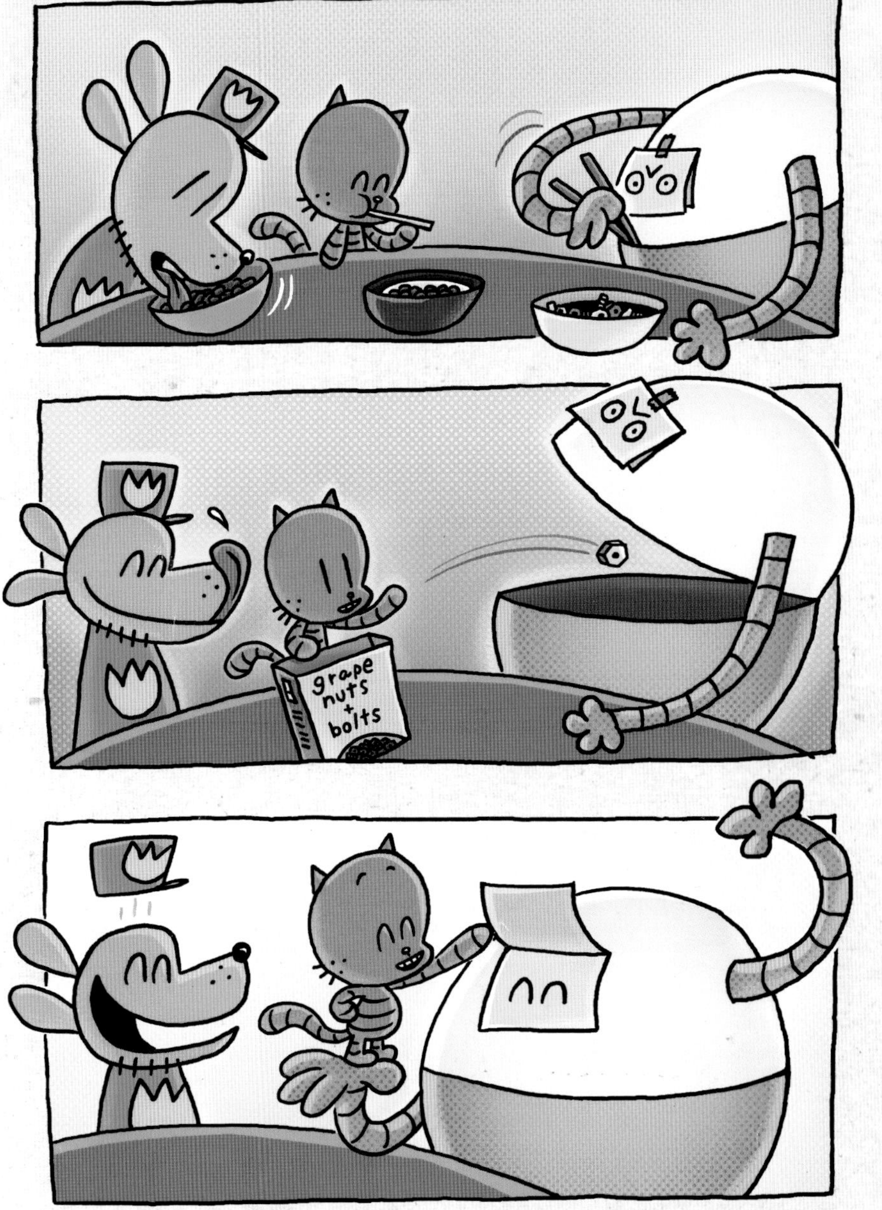
grape nuts + bolts

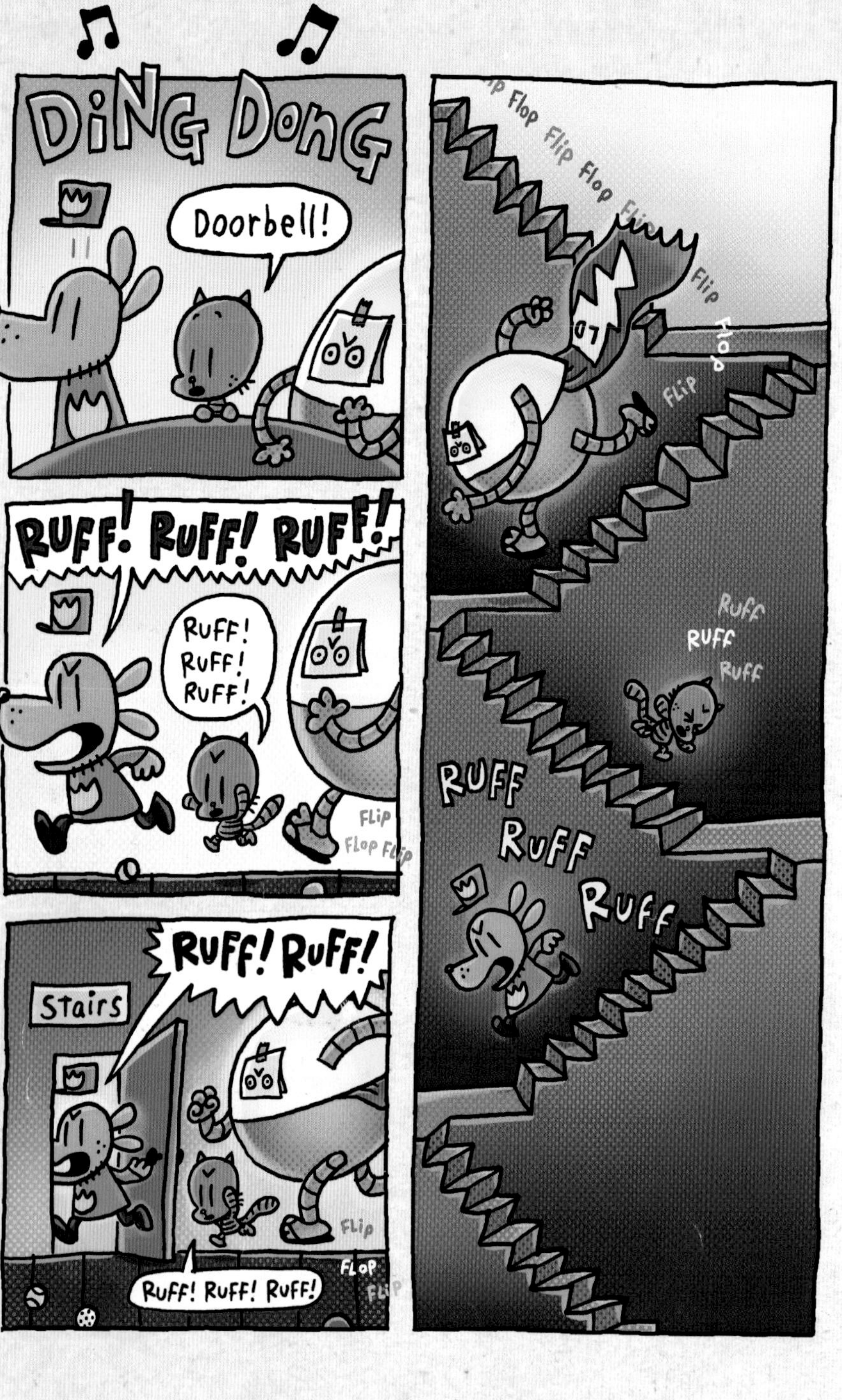

DiNG DoNG
Doorbell!
RUFF! RUFF! RUFF!
RUFF!
RUFF!
RUFF!
FLIP
FLOP FLIP
RUFF! RUFF!
Stairs
RUFF! RUFF! RUFF!
FLIP
FLOP
FLIP
Flop
Flip
Flop
Flip
Flop
FLIP
Ruff
RUFF
Ruff
RUFF
RUFF
RUFF

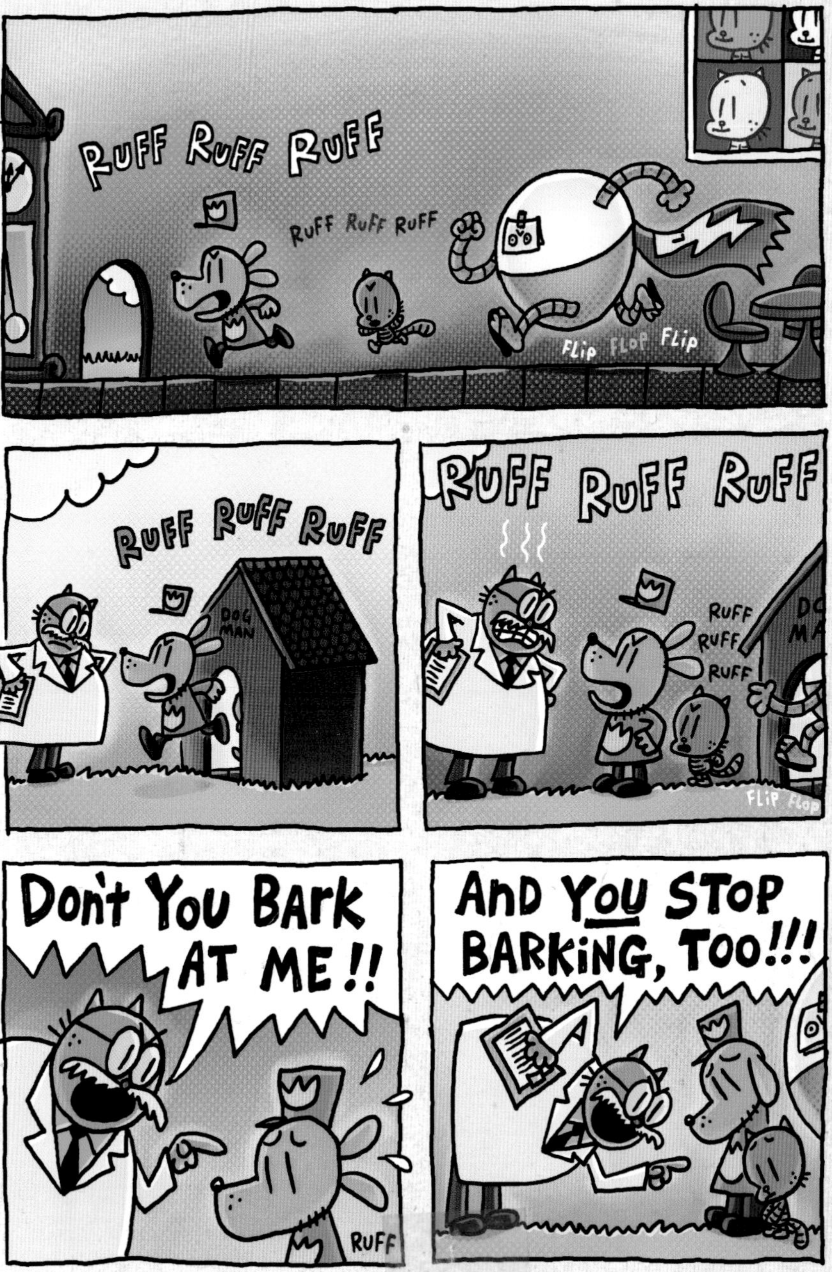
RUFF RUFF RUFF
RUFF RUFF RUFF
FLIP FLOP FLIP
RUFF RUFF RUFF
DOG MAN
RUFF RUFF RUFF
RUFF
RUFF
RUFF
FLIP FLOP
Don't You Bark AT ME!!
RUFF
AND YOU STOP BARKING, TOO!!!

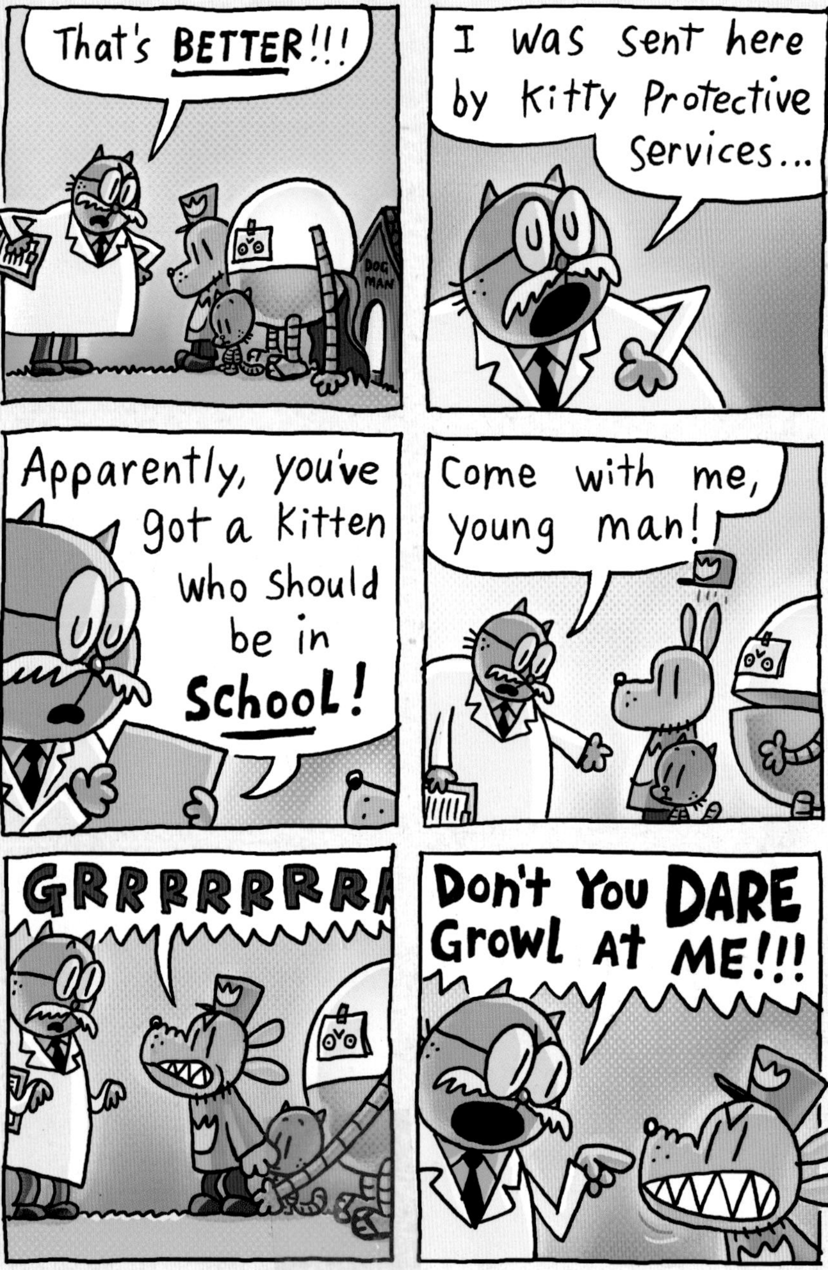
That's BETTER!!!
I was sent here by Kitty Protective services...
Apparently, you've got a kitten who should be in School!
Come with me, young man!
GRRRRRRR
Don't You DARE Growl At ME!!!

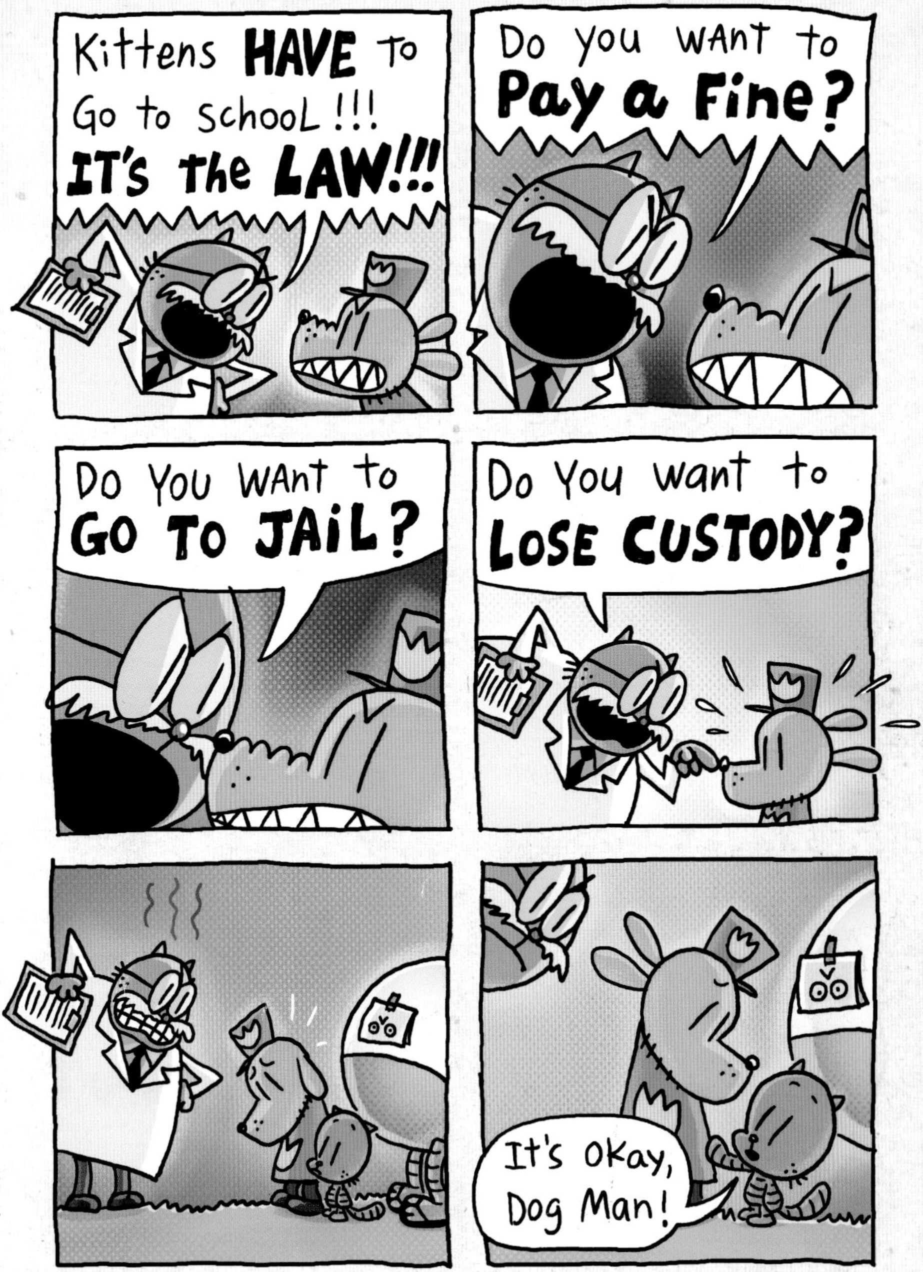

Kittens HAVE to Go to school!!! IT'S the LAW!!!
Do you WANT to Pay a Fine?
Do YOU WANT to GO TO JAIL?
Do You want to LOSE CUSTODY?
It's Okay, Dog Man!

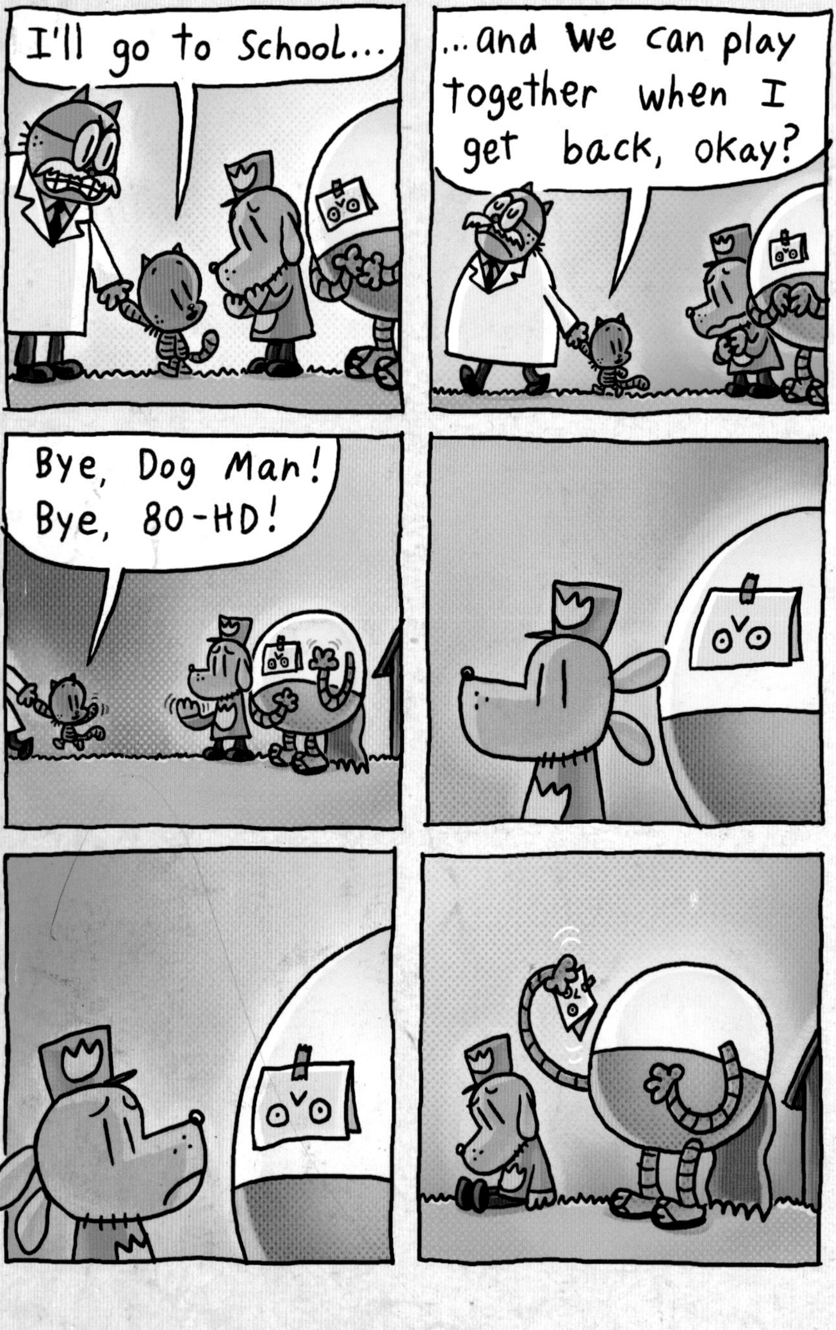
I'll go to School...
...and We can play together when I get back, okay?
Bye, Dog Man! Bye, 80-HD!

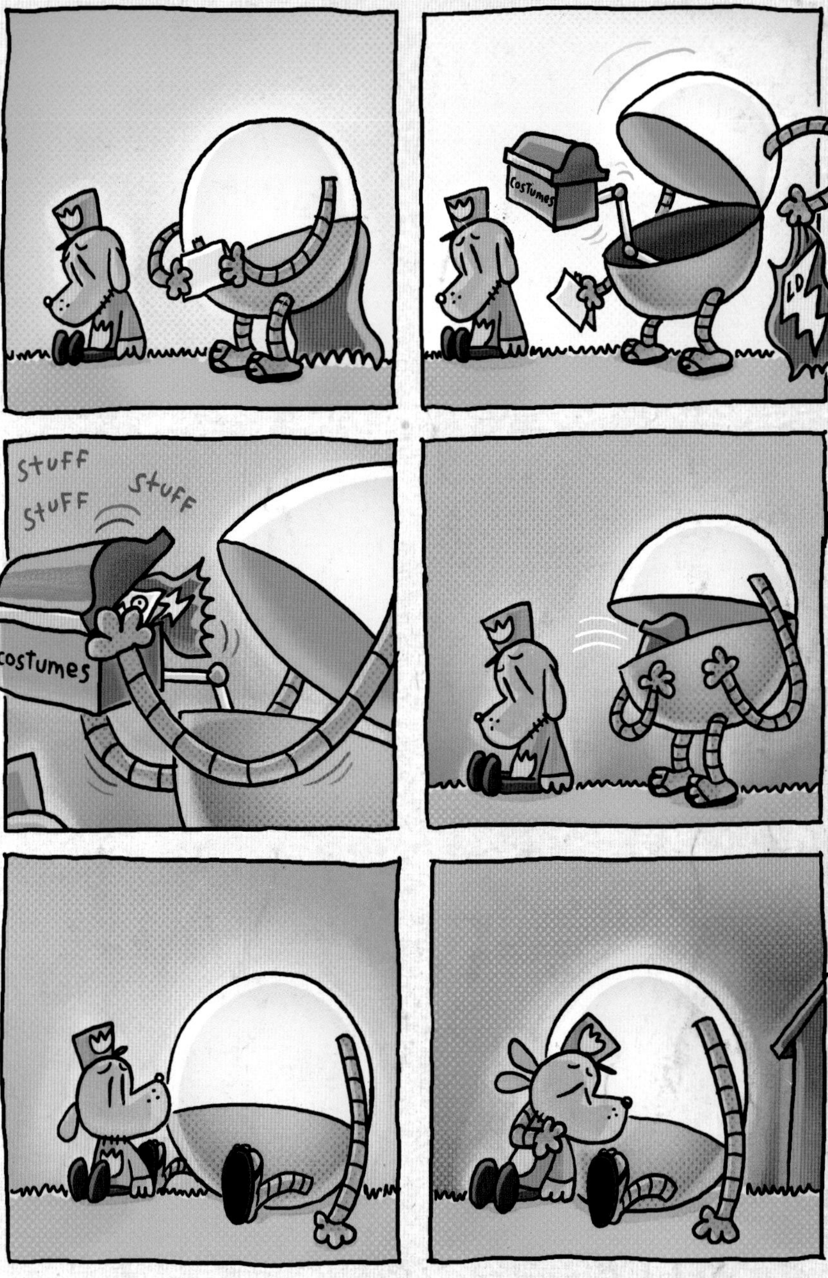
Costumes
LD
STUFF
STUFF
STUFF
costumes

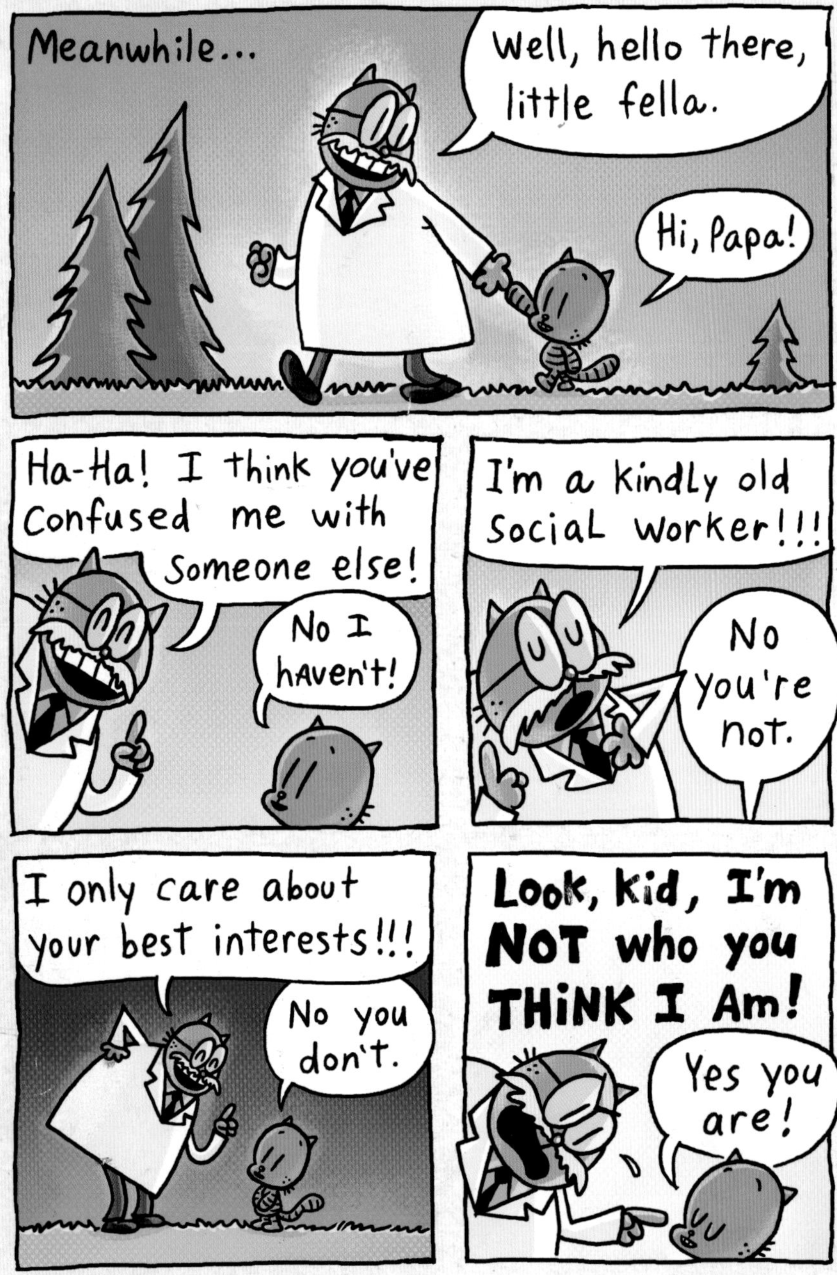
Meanwhile...
Well, hello there, little fella.
Hi, Papa!
Ha-Ha! I think you've confused me with someone else!
No I haven't!
I'm a kindly old social worker!!!
No you're not.
I only care about your best interests!!!
No you don't.
Look, kid, I'm NOT who you THINK I Am!
Yes you are!

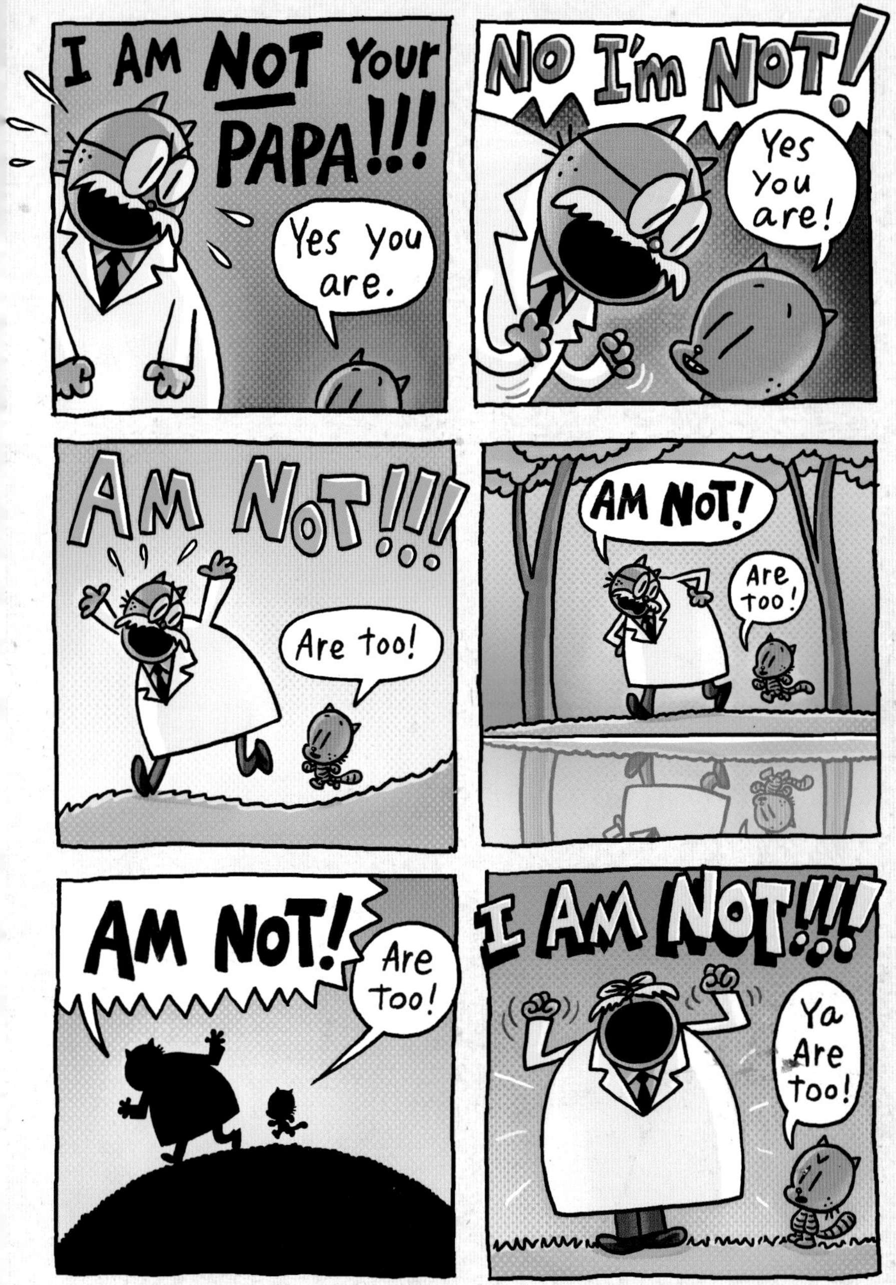
I AM NOT Your PAPA!!!
Yes you are.
NO I'm NOT!
Yes You are!
AM NOT!!!
Are too!
AM NOT!
Are too!
AM NOT!
Are too!
I AM NOT!!!
Ya Are too!

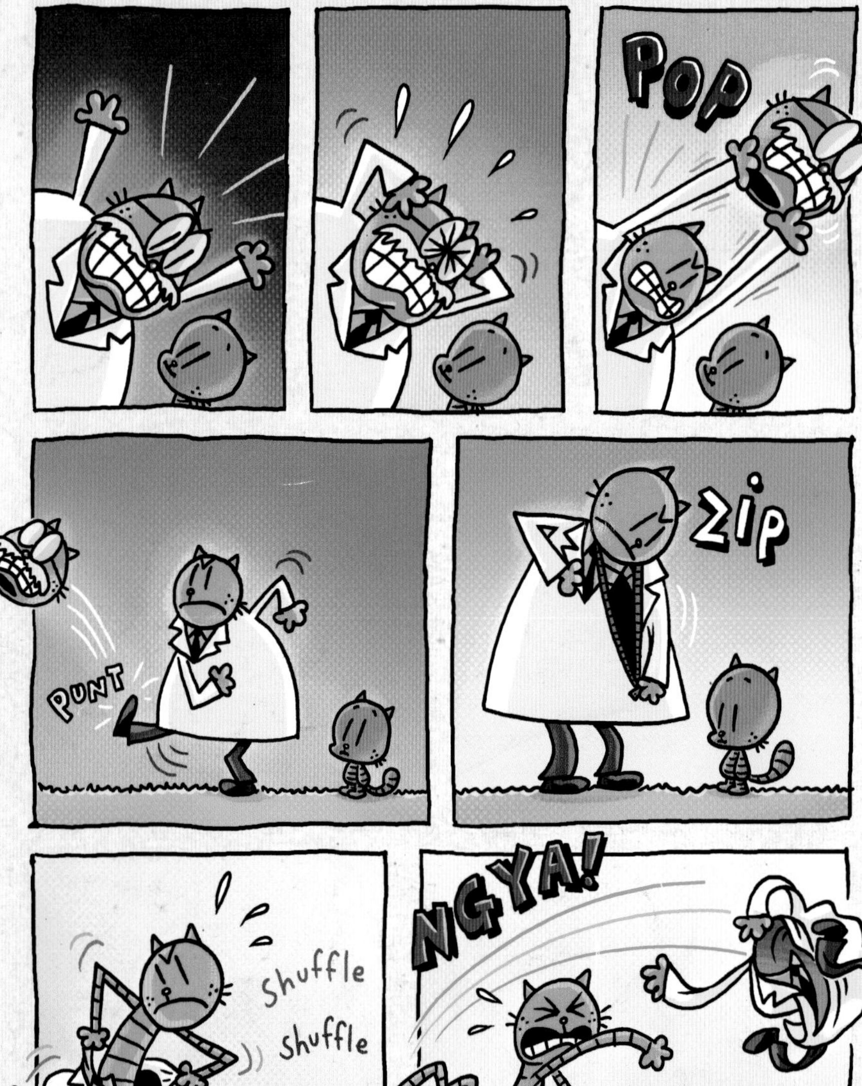
POP
PUNT
ZIP
shuffle
shuffle
NGYA!

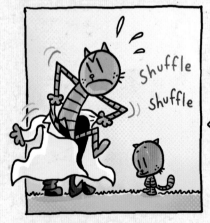

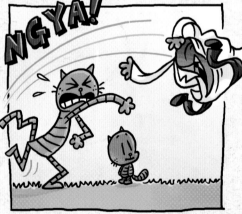

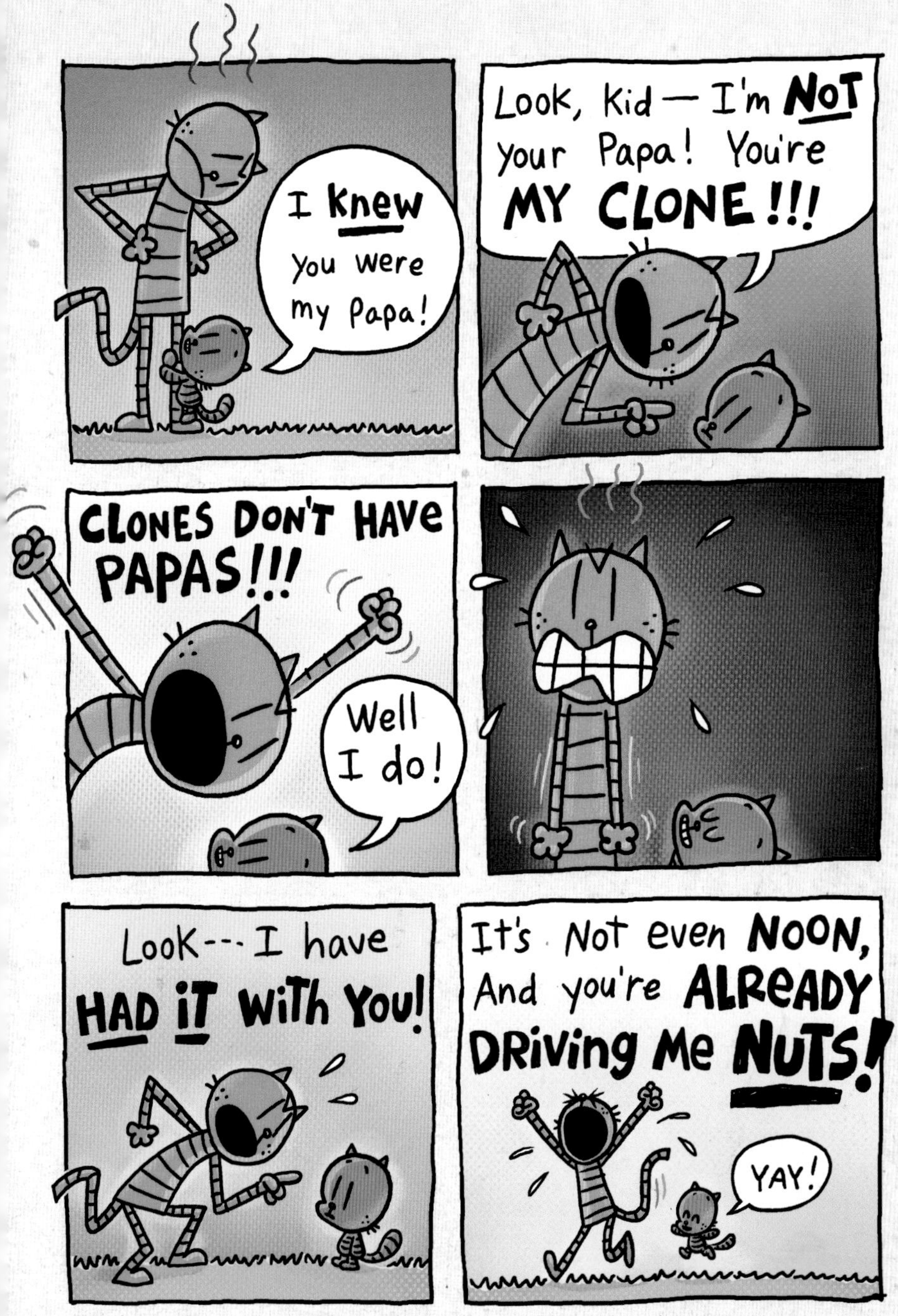
I knew you were my Papa!
Look, Kid — I'm NOT your Papa! You're MY CLONE!!!
CLONES DON'T HAVE PAPAS!!!
Well I do!
Look--- I have HAD IT WITH YOU!
It's Not even NOON, And you're ALREADY DRIVING ME NUTS!
YAY!

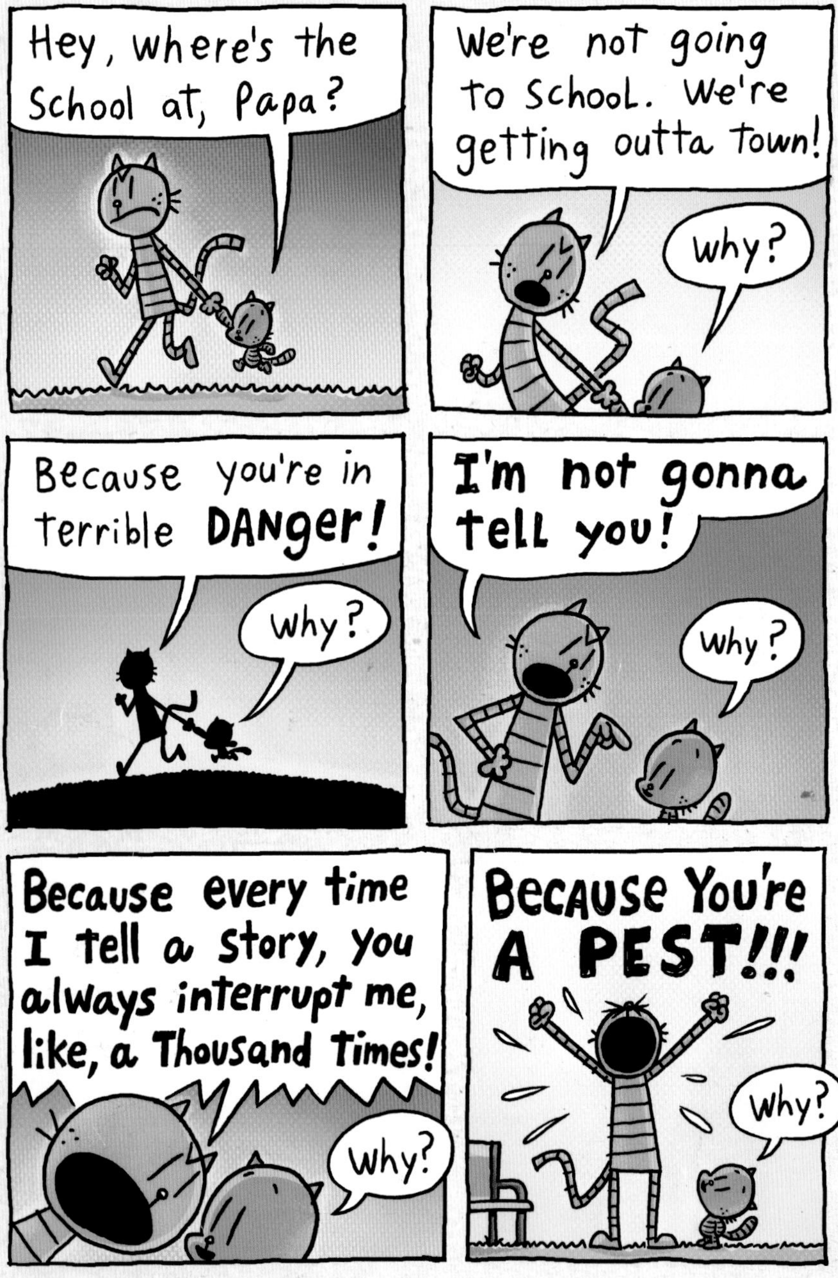
Hey, where's the School at, Papa?
We're not going to School. We're getting outta Town!
Why?
Because you're in terrible DANGER!
Why?
I'm not gonna tell you!
Why?
Because every time I tell a Story, you always interrupt me, like, a Thousand Times!
Why?
BECAUSE You're A PEST!!!
Why?

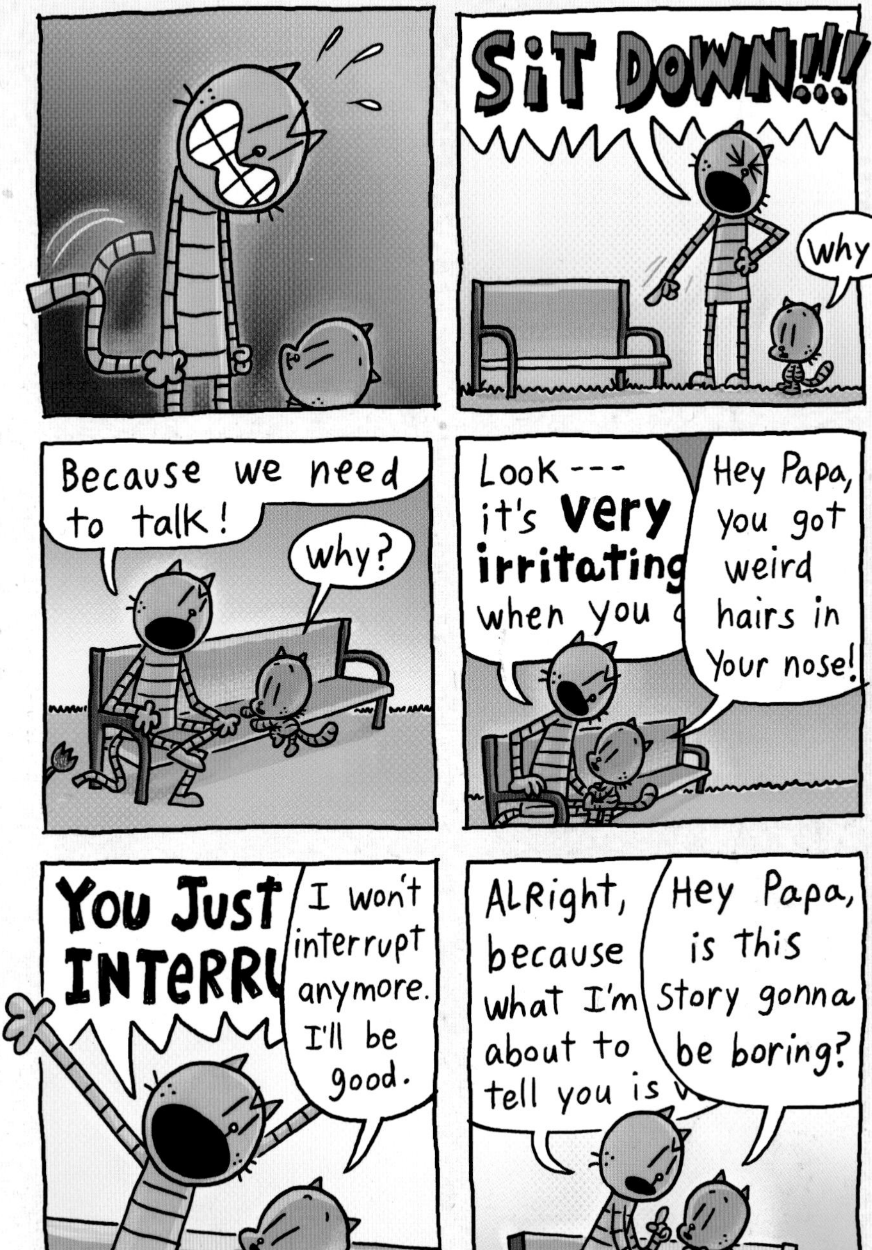
SiT DOWN!!!
why?
Because we need to talk!
why?
Look --- it's **very** **irritating** when you
Hey Papa, you got weird hairs in Your nose!
YOU JUST INTERRU
I won't interrupt anymore. I'll be good.
ALRight, because what I'm about to tell you is
Hey Papa, is this Story gonna be boring?

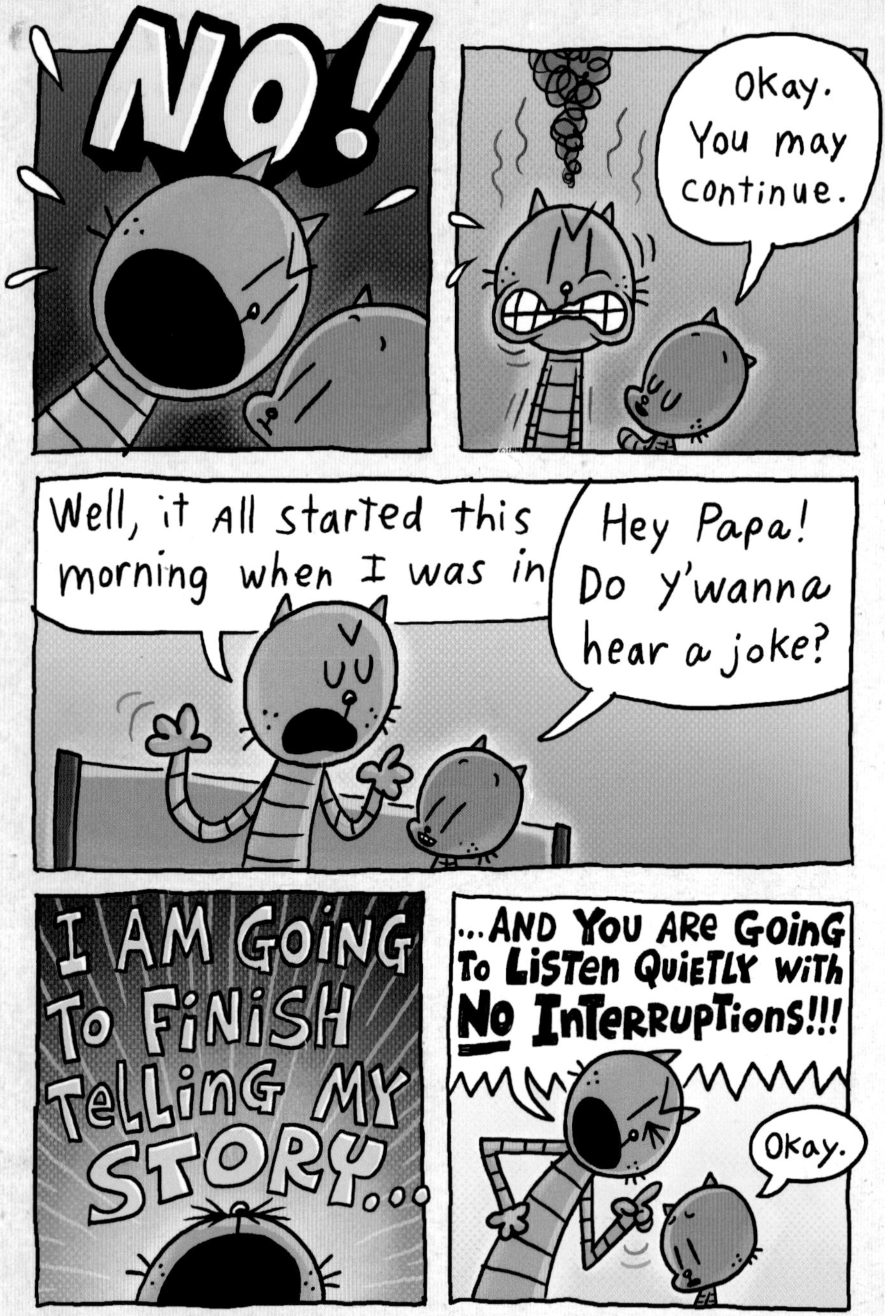
NO!
Okay. You may continue.
Well, it all started this morning when I was in
Hey Papa! Do y'wanna hear a joke?
I AM GOING TO FINISH TELLING MY STORY...
...AND YOU ARE GOING TO LISTEN QUIETLY WITH NO INTERRUPTIONS!!!
Okay.

CHAPTER 2

Petey's Story

(With Many Interruptions)

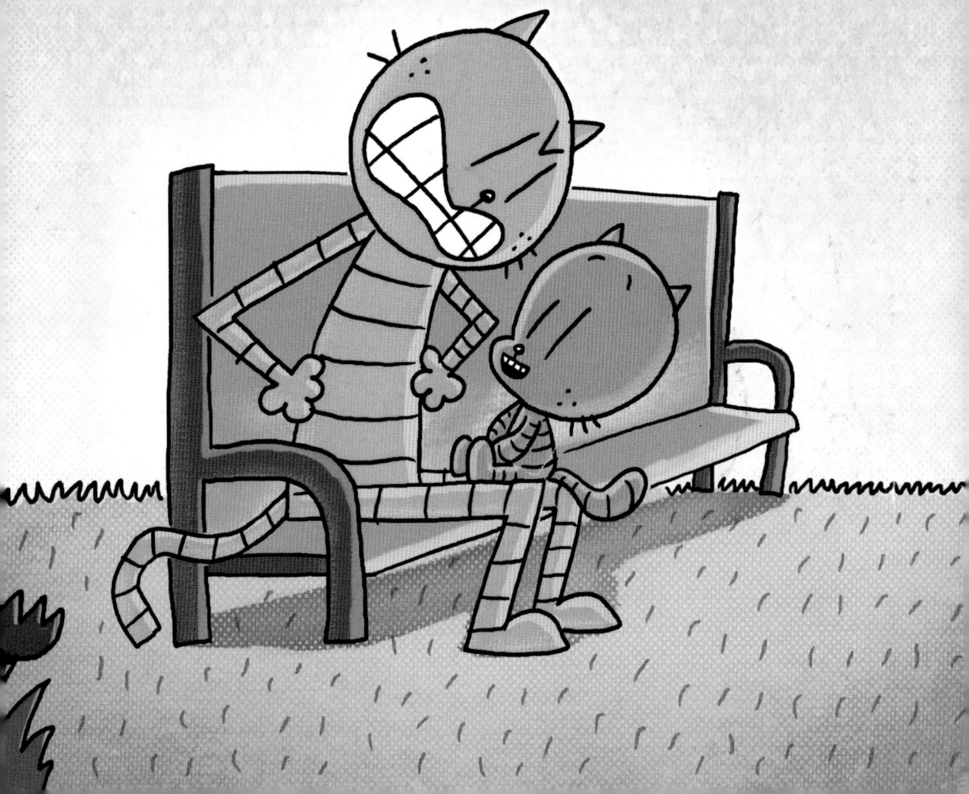

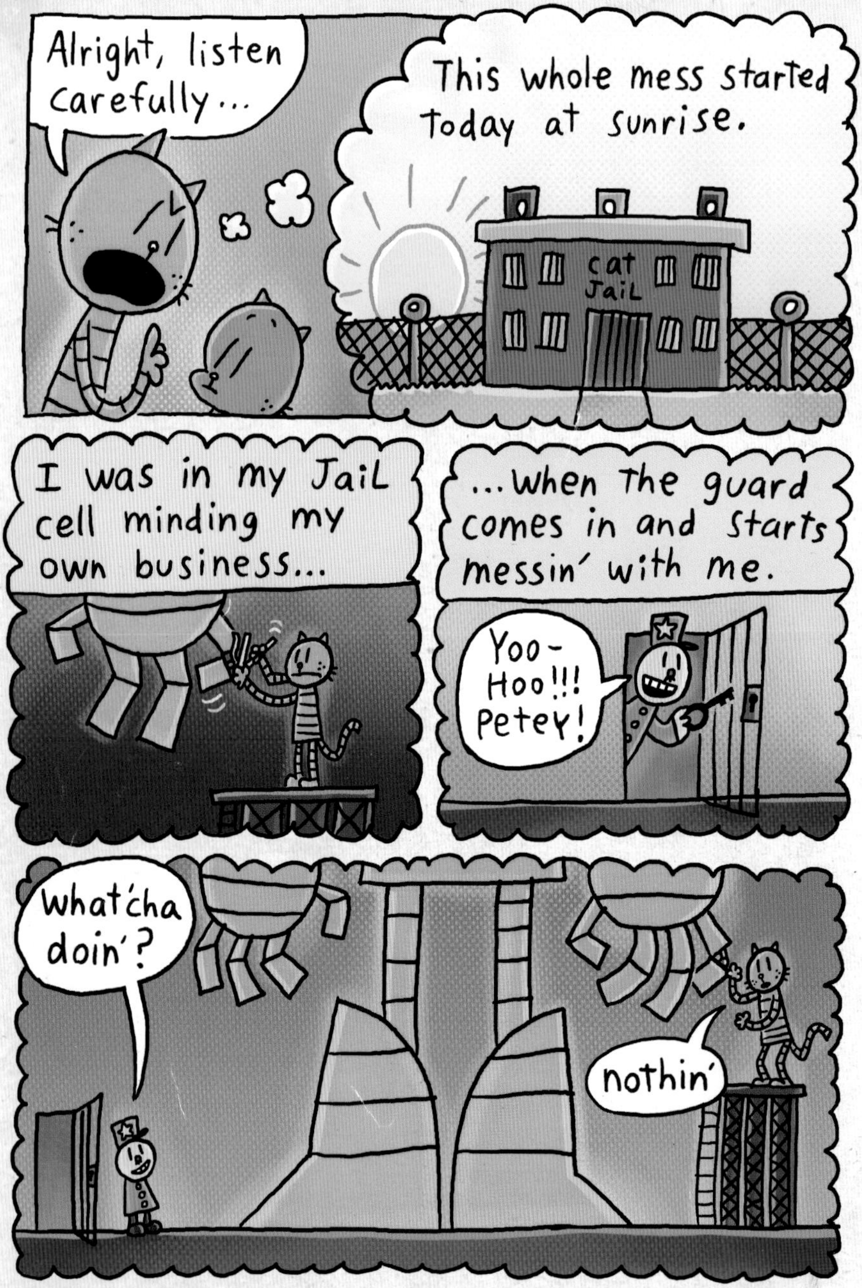
Alright, listen carefully...
This whole mess started today at sunrise.
cat Jail
I was in my Jail cell minding my own business...
...when the guard comes in and starts messin' with me.
Yoo-Hoo!!! Petey!
What'cha doin'?
nothin'

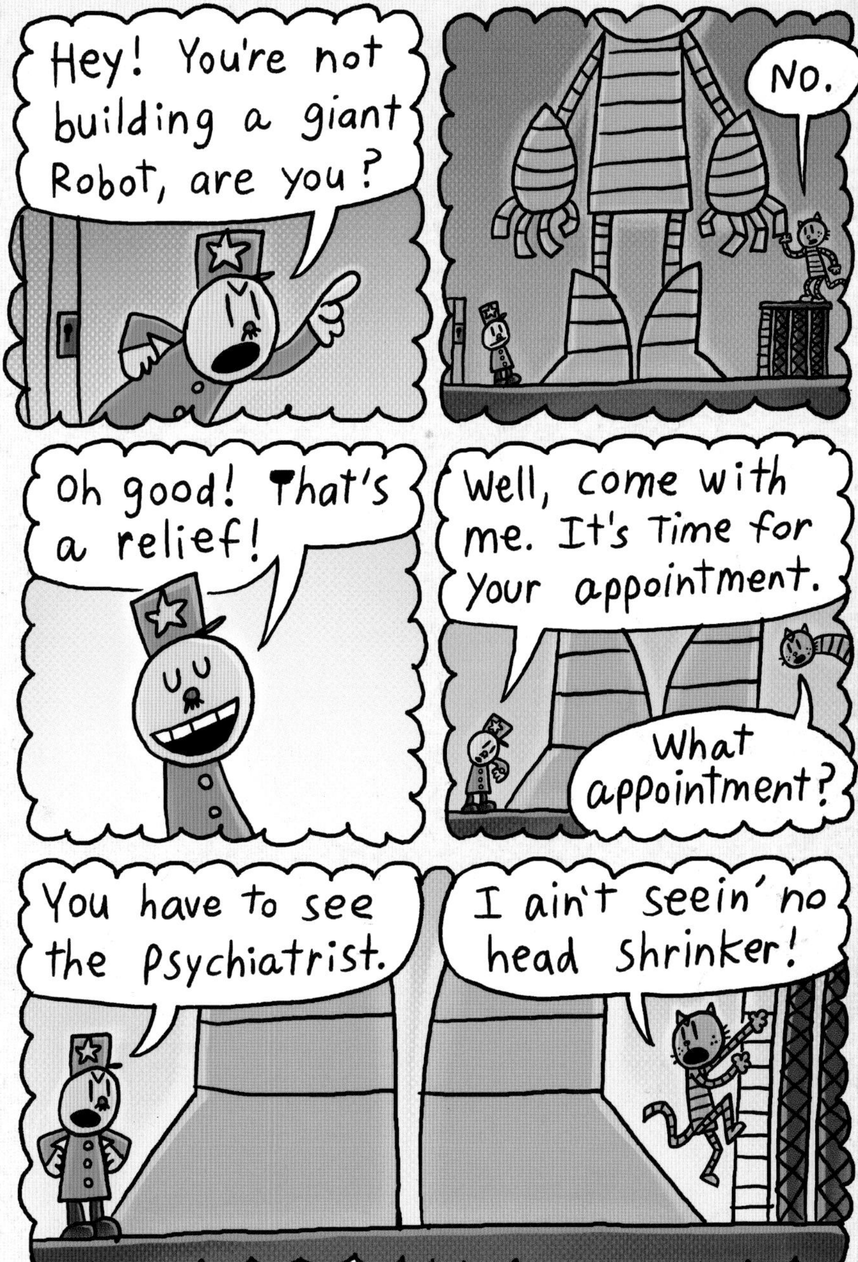
Hey! You're not building a giant Robot, are you?
No.
Oh good! That's a relief!
Well, come with me. It's Time for your appointment.
What appointment?
You have to see the Psychiatrist.
I ain't seein' no head shrinker!

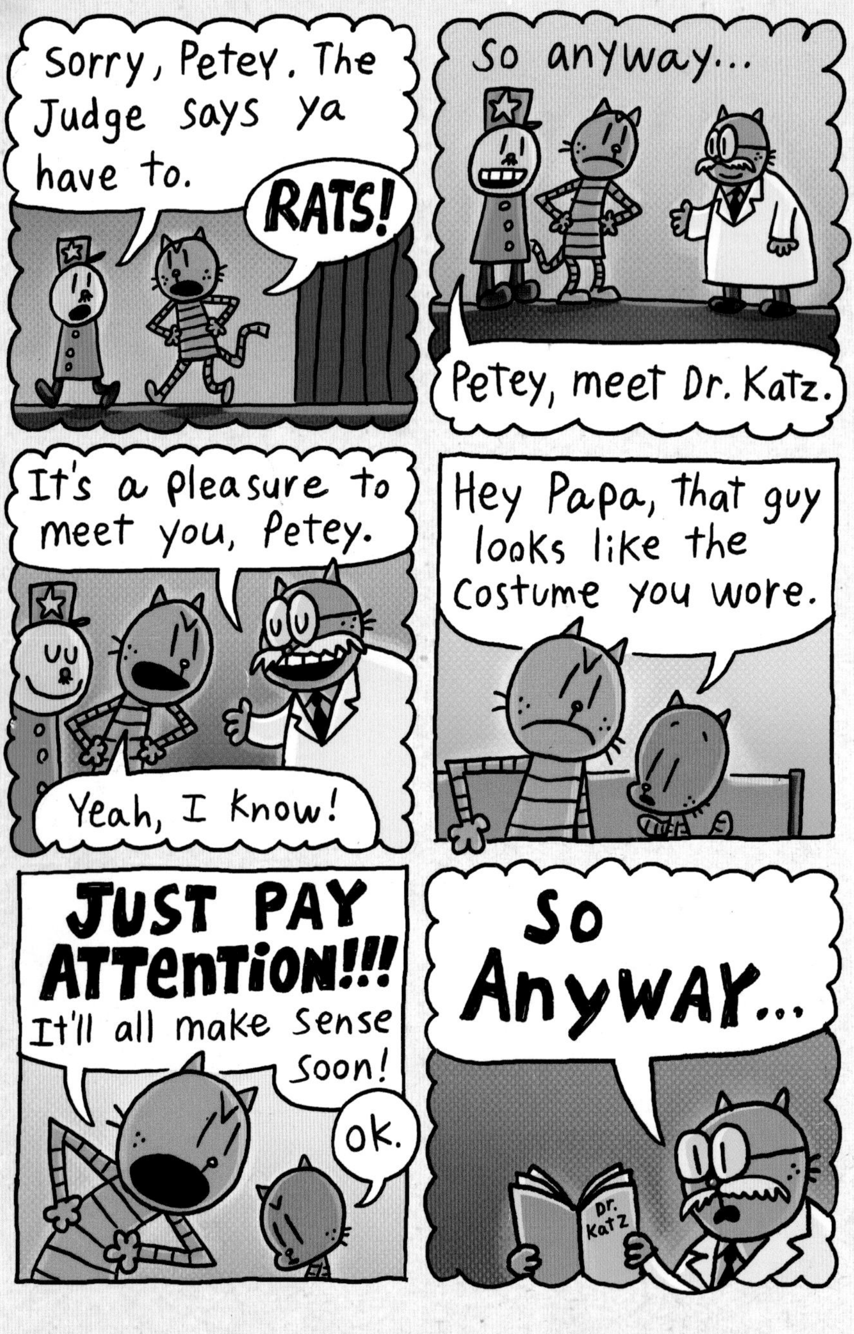
Sorry, Petey. The Judge says ya have to.
RATS!
So anyway...
Petey, meet Dr. Katz.
It's a pleasure to meet you, Petey.
Yeah, I know!
Hey Papa, that guy looks like the costume you wore.
JUST PAY ATTENTION!!! It'll all make sense soon!
OK.
So Anyway...
Dr. Katz

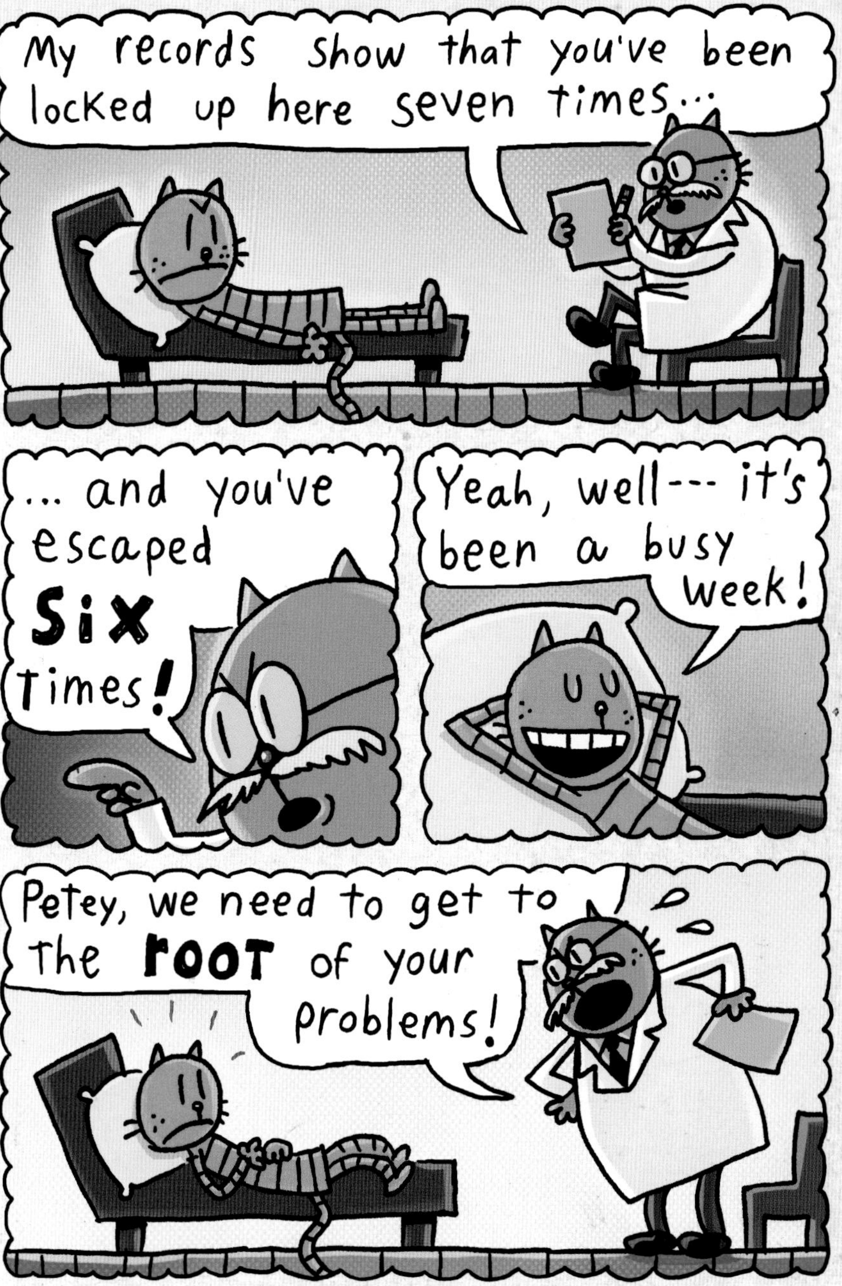
My records show that you've been locked up here seven times...
... and you've escaped SIX times!
Yeah, well--- it's been a busy week!
Petey, we need to get to the ROOT of your problems!

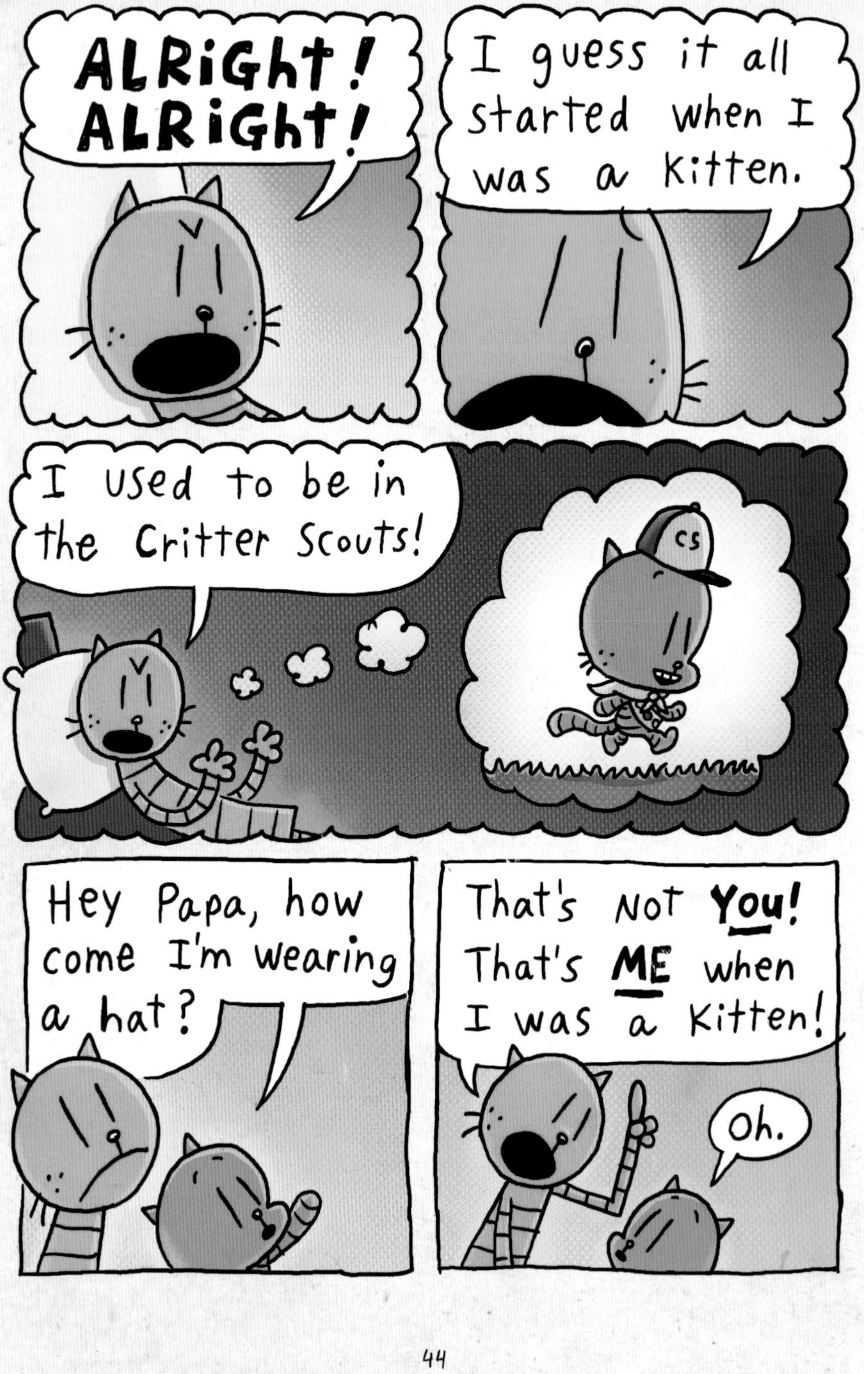
ALRIGHT! ALRIGHT!
I guess it all started when I was a kitten.
I used to be in the Critter Scouts!
CS
Hey Papa, how come I'm wearing a hat?
That's NOT YOU! That's ME when I was a kitten!
Oh.

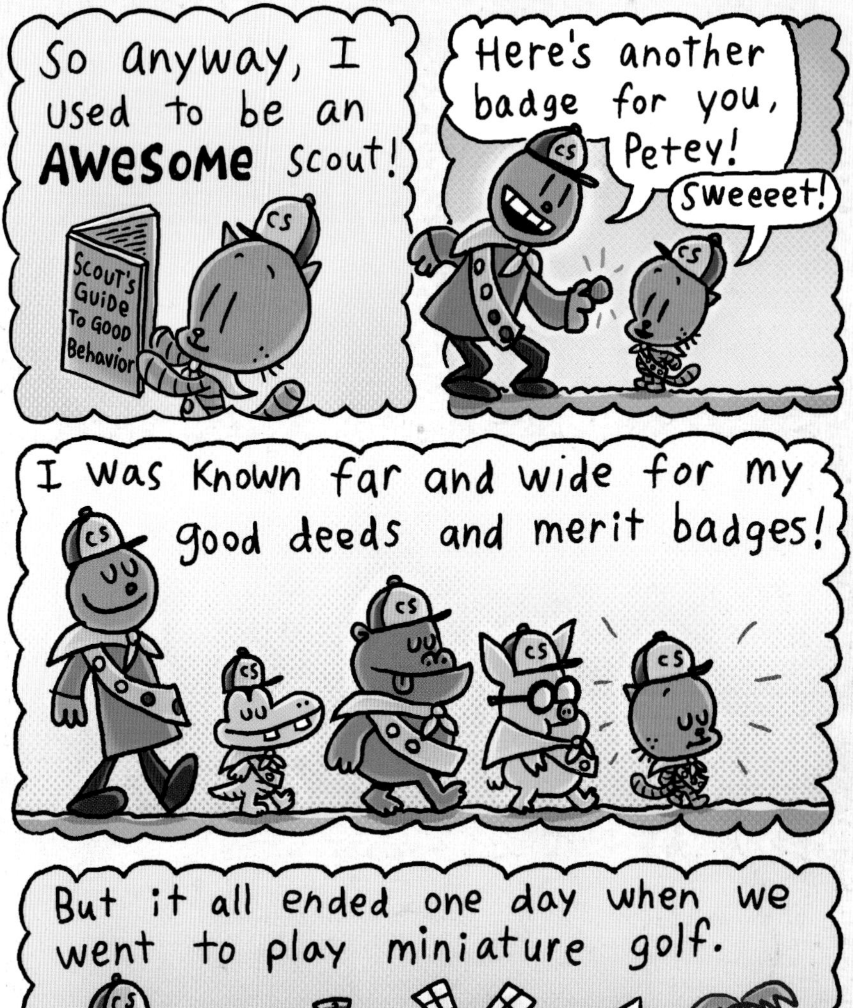
So anyway, I used to be an **AWESOME** scout!
Scout's Guide To Good Behavior
CS
Here's another badge for you, Petey!
Sweeeet!
I was known far and wide for my good deeds and merit badges!
But it all ended one day when we went to play miniature golf.
5
PUTT PUTT ISLAND

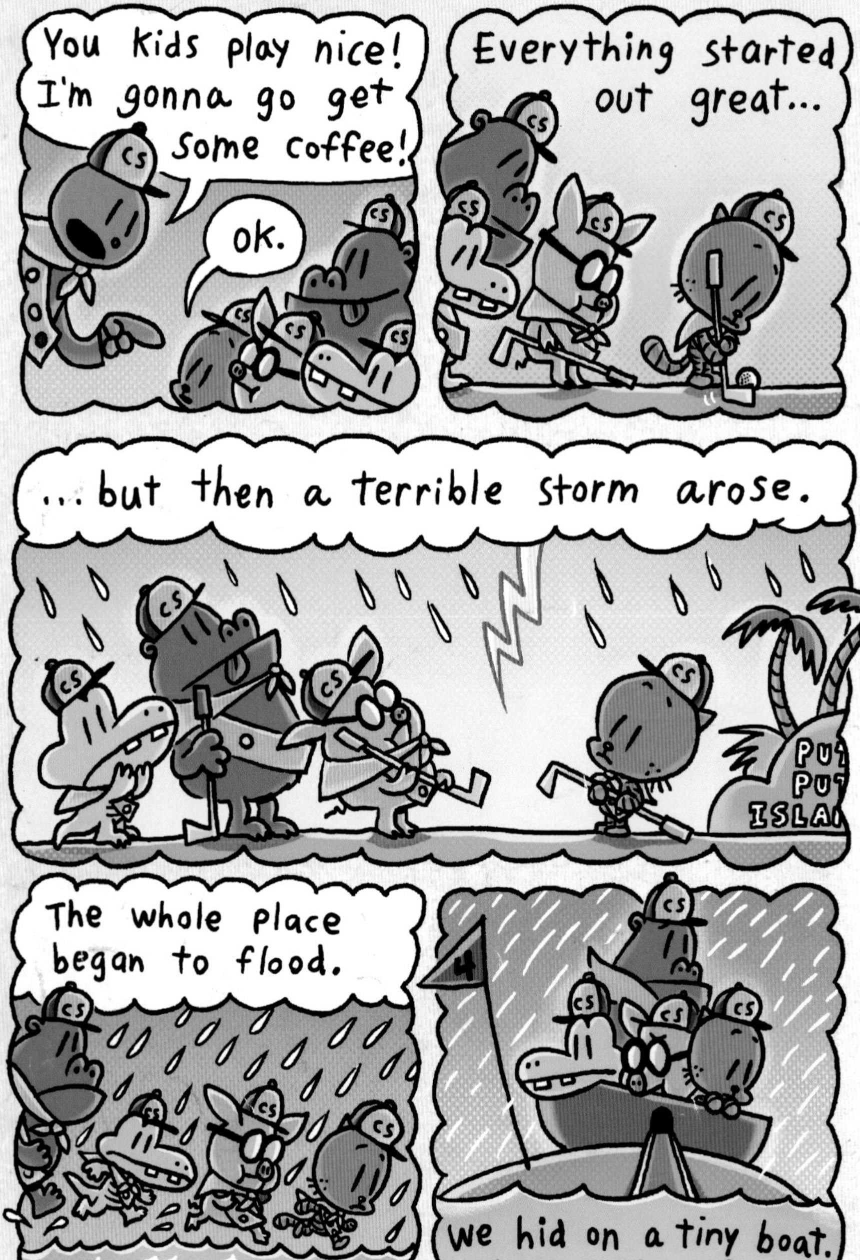
You kids play nice! I'm gonna go get some coffee!
OK.
Everything started out great...
...but then a terrible storm arose.
PUT PUT ISLA
The whole place began to flood.
4
We hid on a tiny boat.

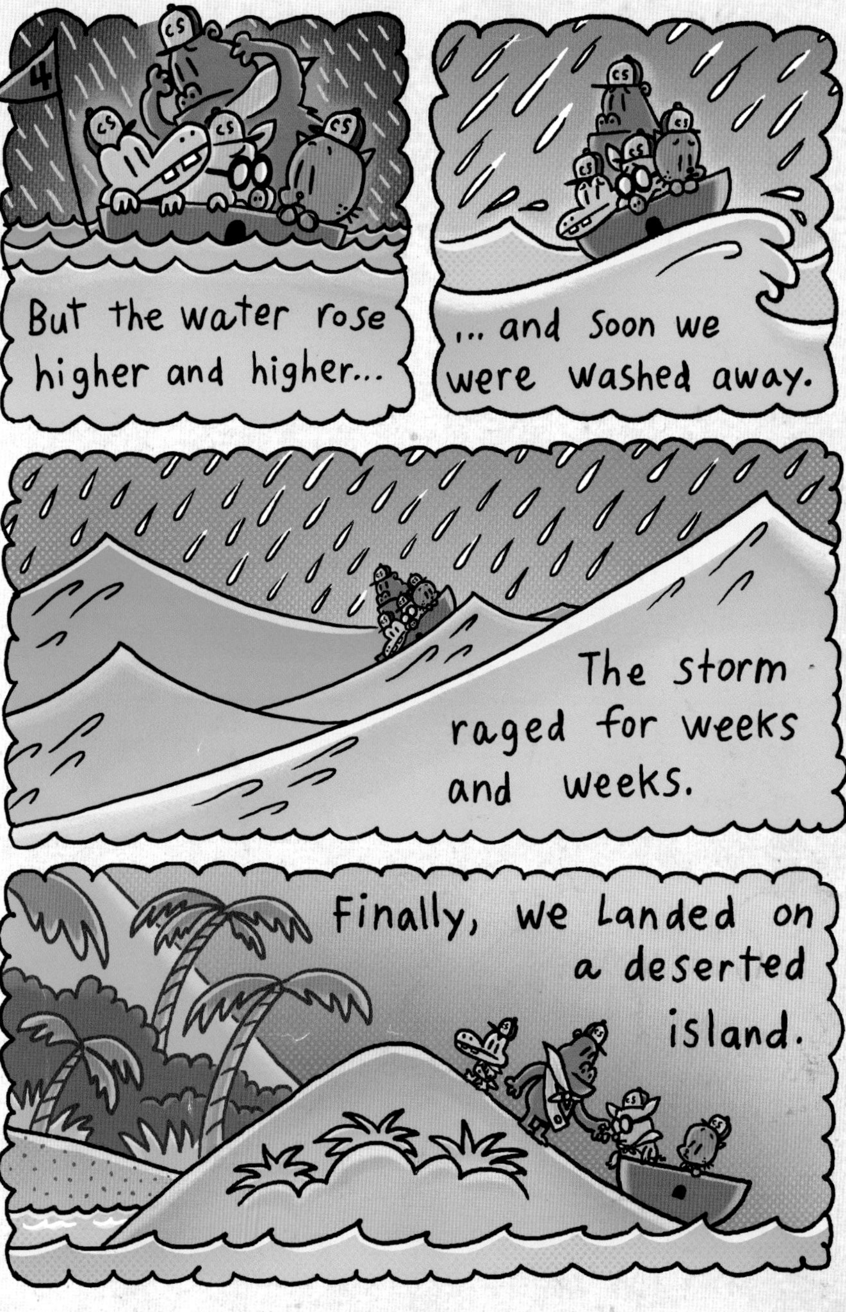
4
CS
But the water rose higher and higher...
... and Soon we were washed away.
The storm raged for weeks and weeks.
Finally, we Landed on a deserted island.

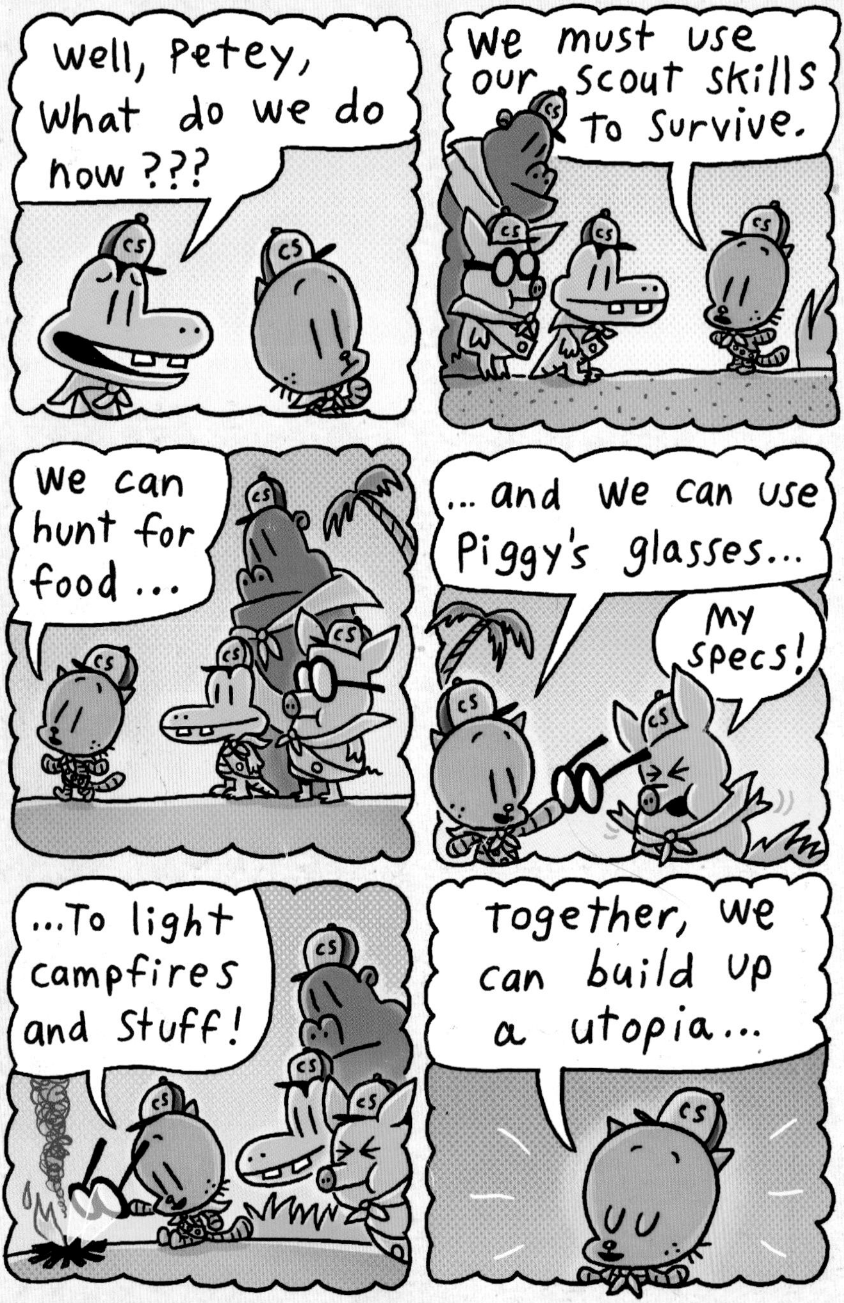
Well, Petey, What do we do now???
We must use our Scout Skills To Survive.
We can hunt for food...
...and we can use Piggy's glasses...
My specs!
...To light campfires and Stuff!
Together, we can build up a utopia...

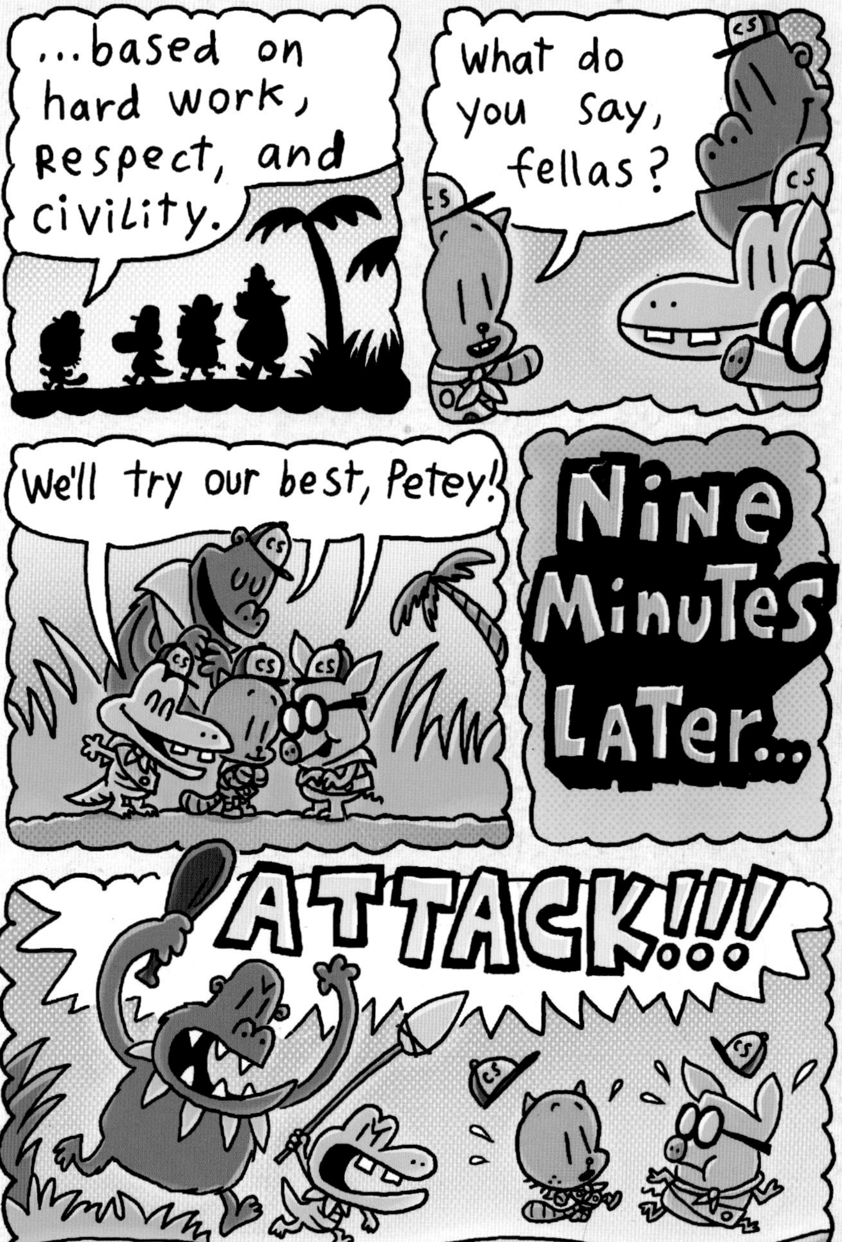
...based on hard work, respect, and civility.
What do you say, fellas?
We'll try our best, Petey!
Nine Minutes Later...
ATTACK!!!

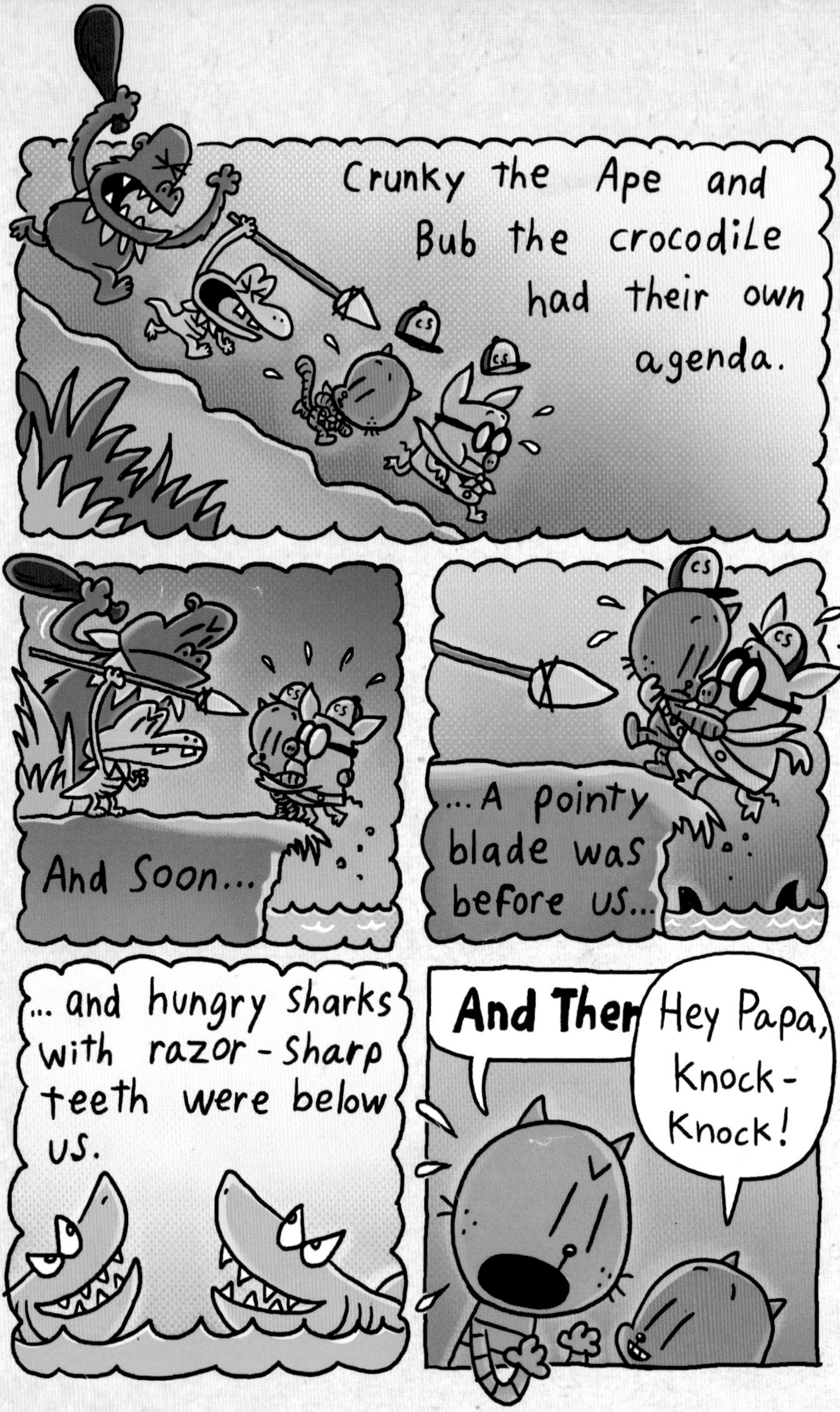
Crunky the Ape and Bub the crocodile had their own agenda.
CS
CS
And Soon...
CS
CS
CS
CS
...A pointy blade was before us...
... and hungry Sharks with razor-Sharp teeth were below us.
And Then
Hey Papa, Knock-Knock!

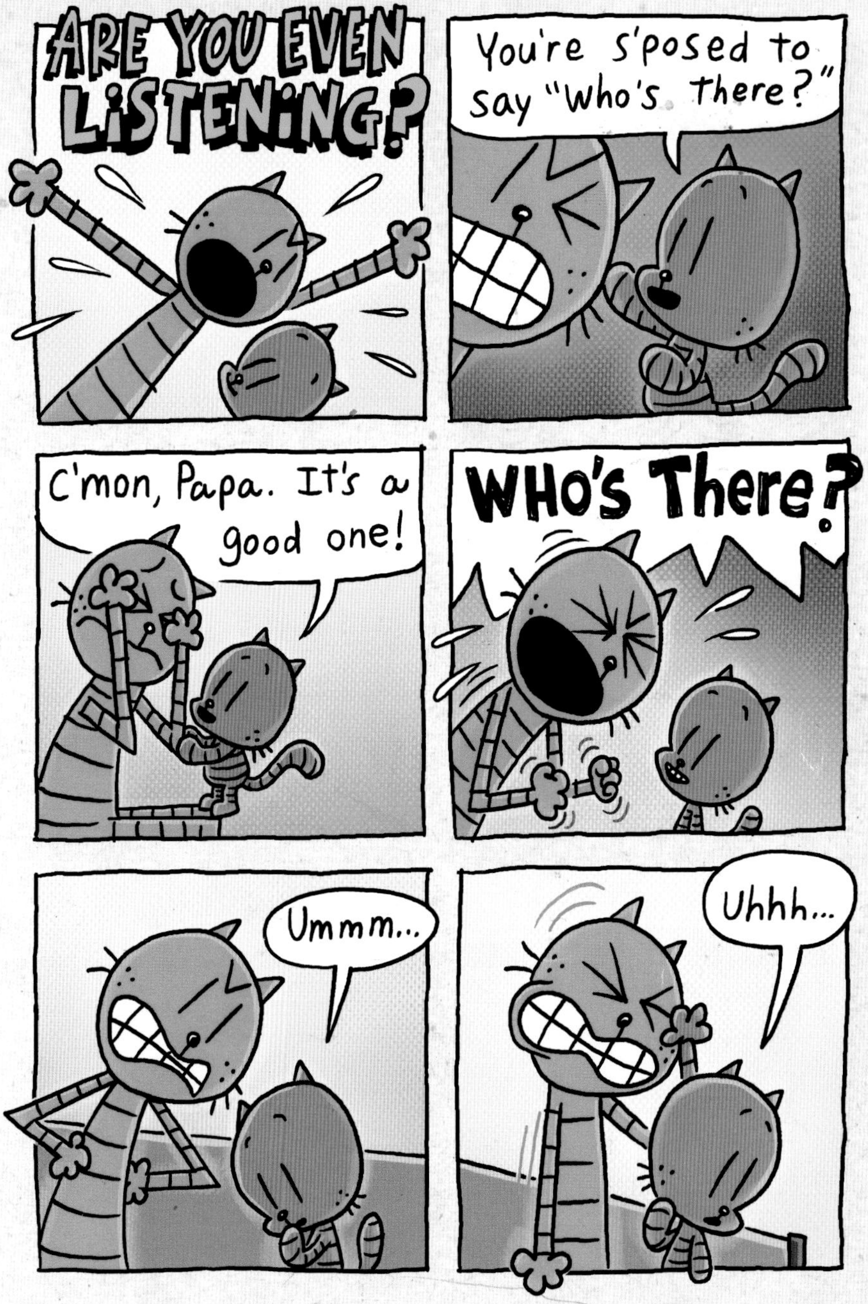

ARE YOU EVEN LISTENING?
You're s'posed to say "who's there?"
C'mon, Papa. It's a good one!
WHO'S There?
Ummm...
Uhhh...

54

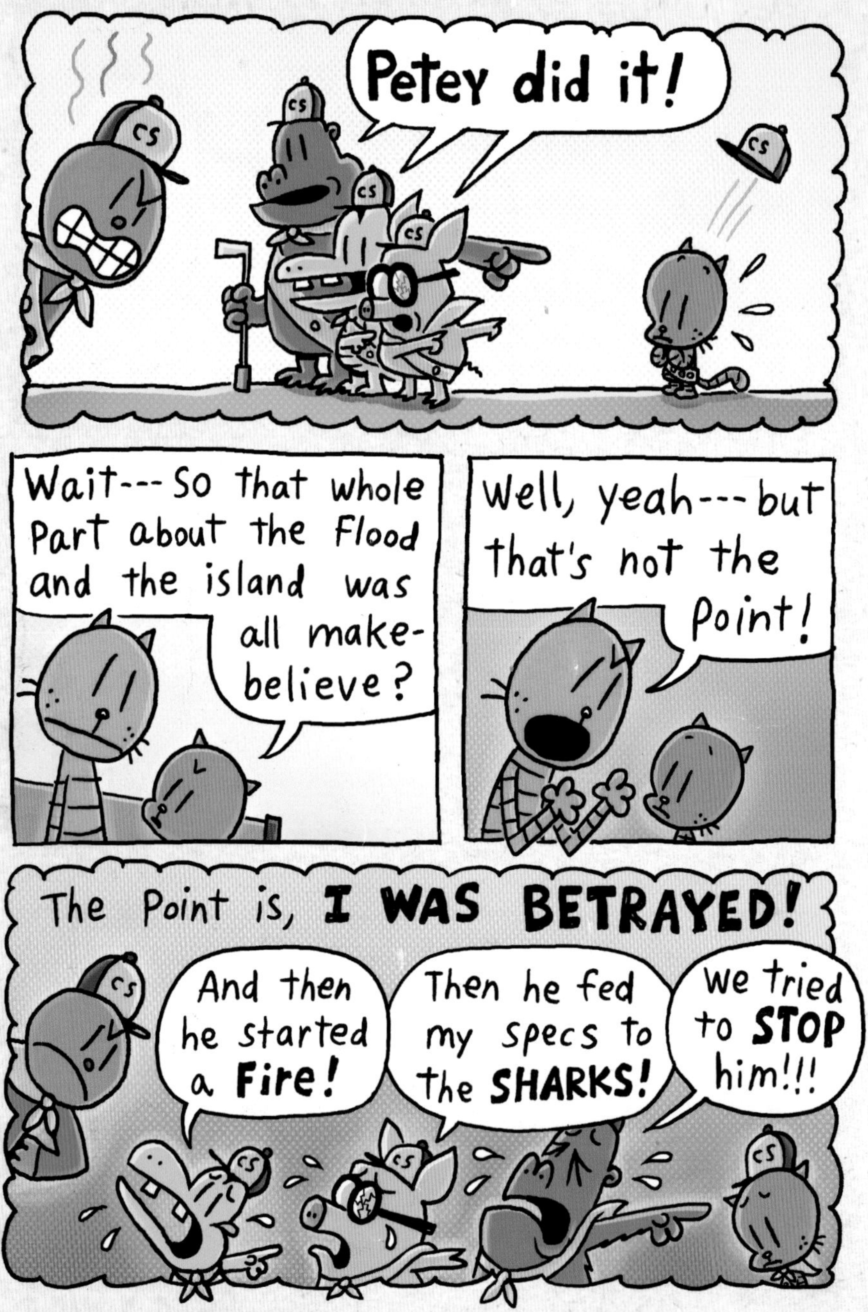
Petey did it!
Wait---So that whole Part about the Flood and the island was all make-believe?
Well, yeah---but that's not the Point!
The Point is, I WAS BETRAYED!
And then he started a Fire!
Then he fed my specs to the SHARKS!
We tried to STOP him!!!

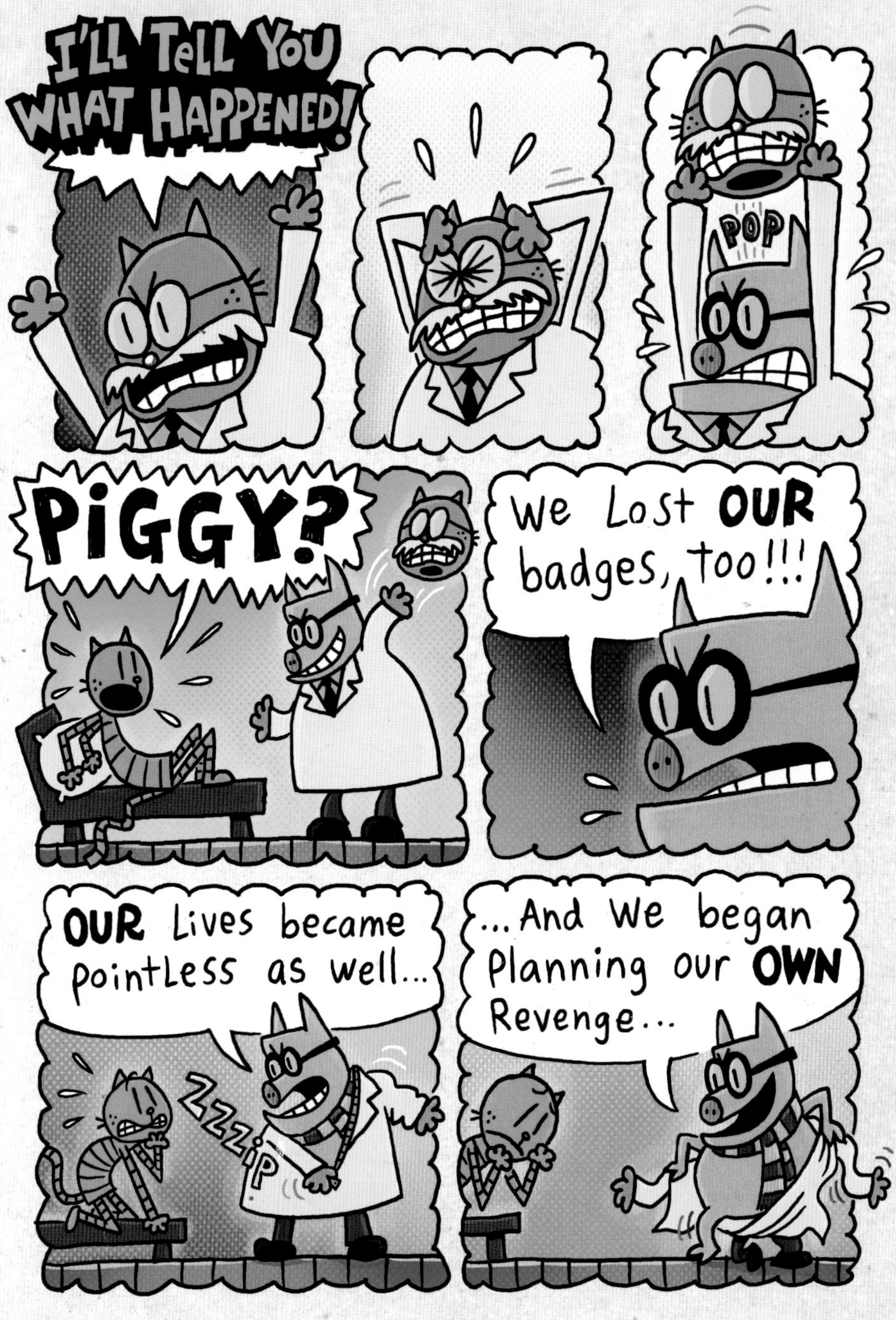
I'LL TELL YOU WHAT HAPPENED!
POP
PIGGY?
We Lost OUR badges, too!!!
OUR Lives became pointless as well...
ZZZIP
...And We began Planning our OWN Revenge...

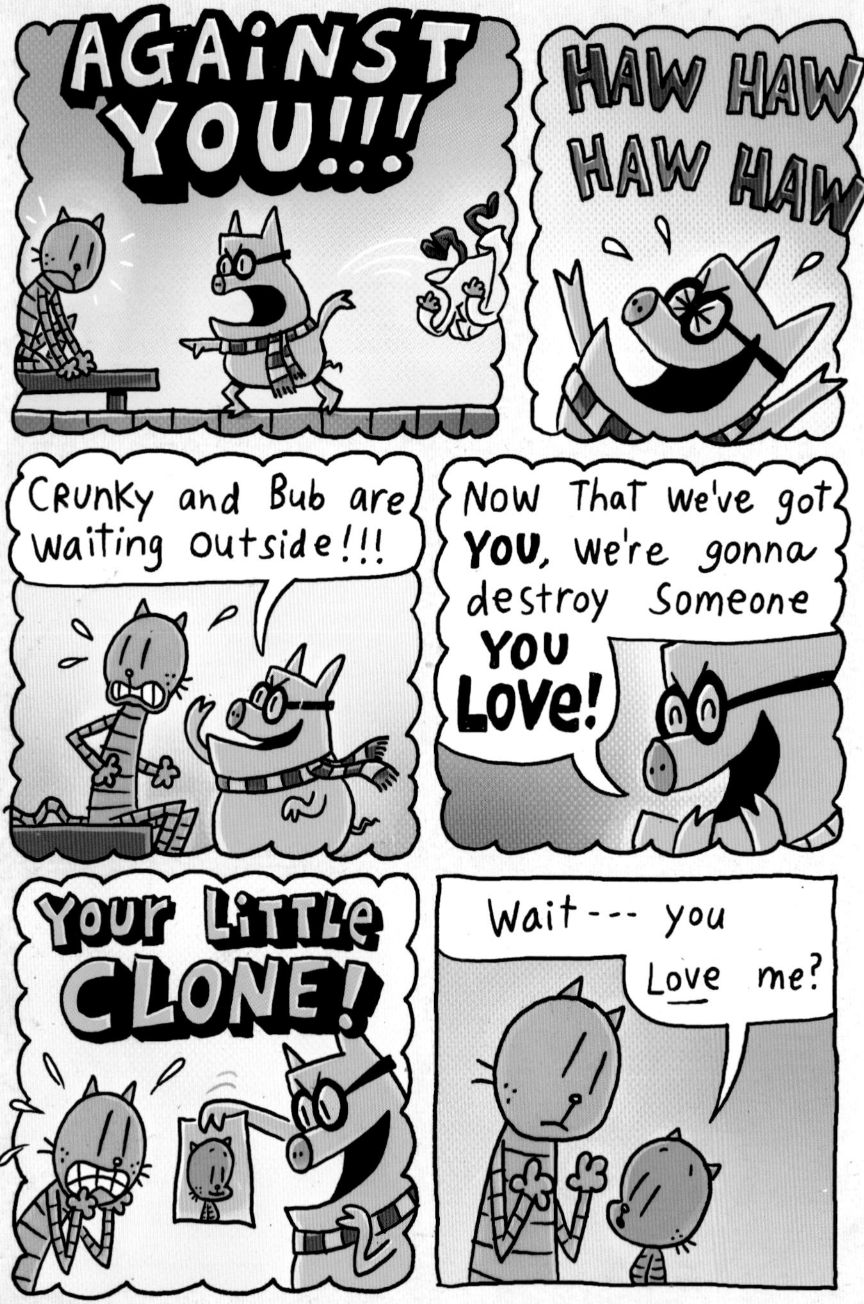
AGAINST YOU!!!
HAW HAW HAW HAW HAW
CRUNKY and Bub are waiting outside!!!
Now That we've got YOU, we're gonna destroy Someone YOU Love!
Your LiTTLe CLONE!
Wait--- you Love me?

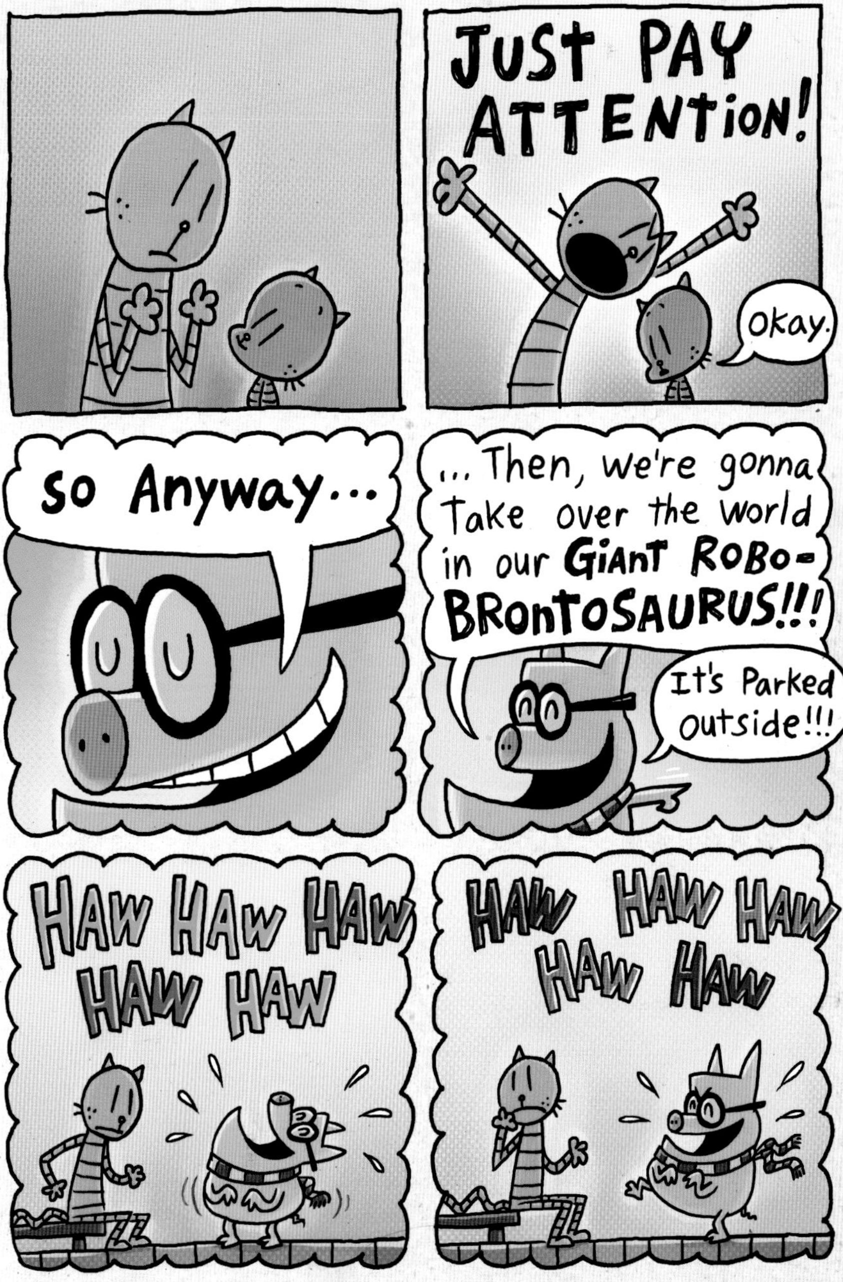
JUST PAY ATTENTION!
Okay.
So Anyway...
... Then, we're gonna Take over the world in our GIANT ROBO-BRONTOSAURUS!!!
It's Parked outside!!!
HAW HAW HAW HAW HAW
HAW HAW HAW HAW HAW

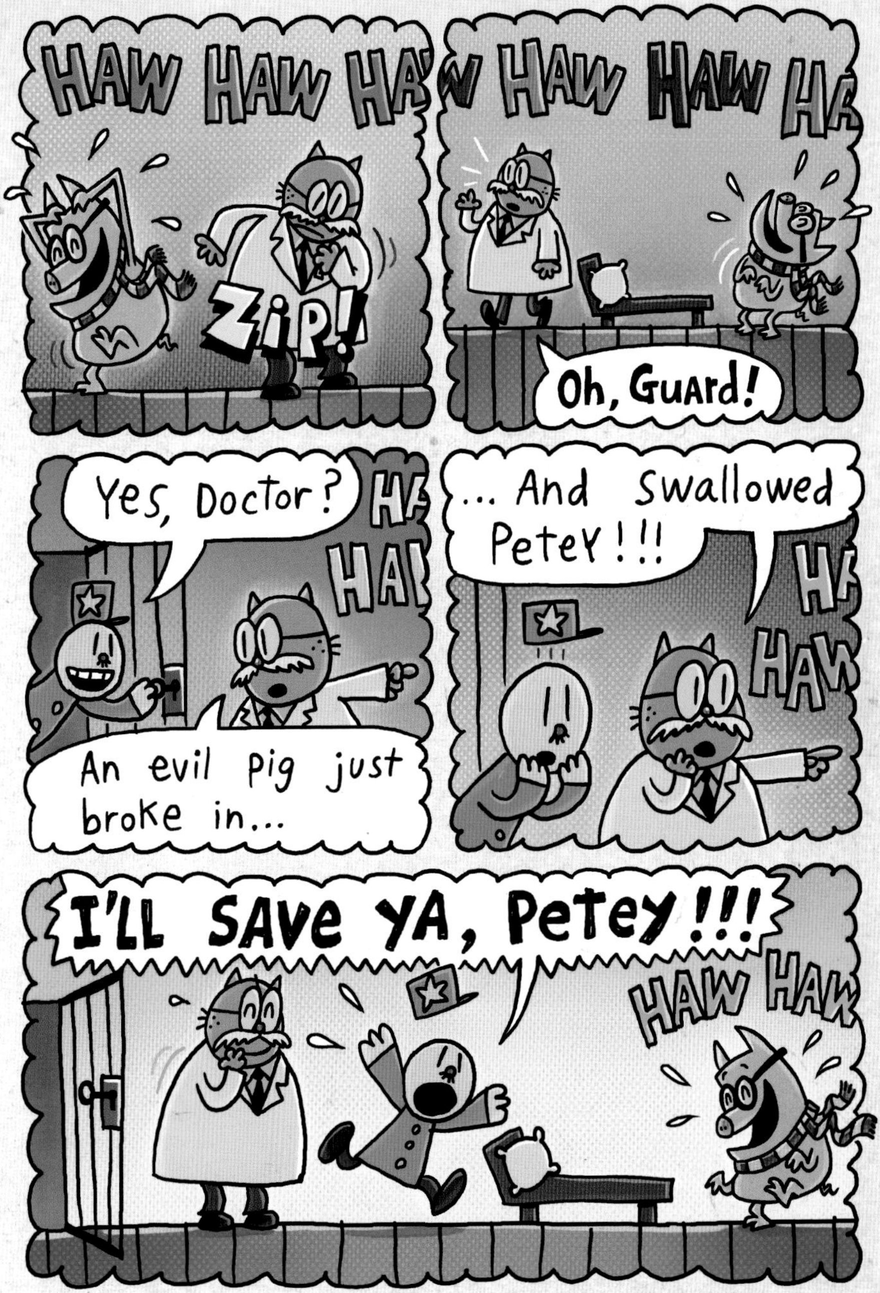
HAW HAW HAW HAW HAW HA
ZIP!
Oh, Guard!
Yes, Doctor?
HA HAW
An evil pig just broke in...
... And swallowed Petey!!!
HA HAW
I'LL SAVE YA, Petey!!!
HAW HAW

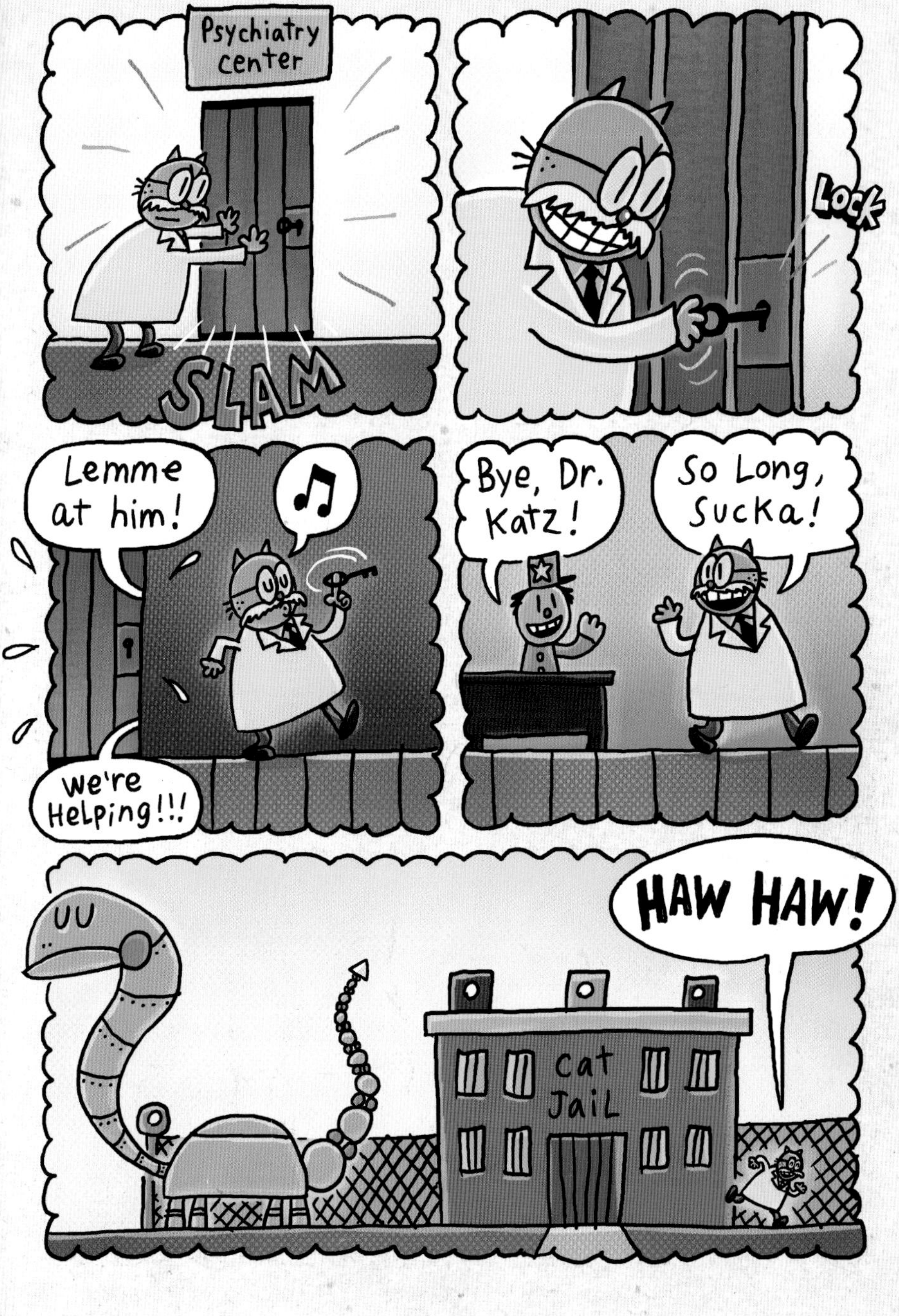
Psychiatry center
SLAM
LOCK
Lemme at him!
♫
We're Helping!!!
Bye, Dr. Katz!
So Long, Sucka!
HAW HAW!
Cat Jail

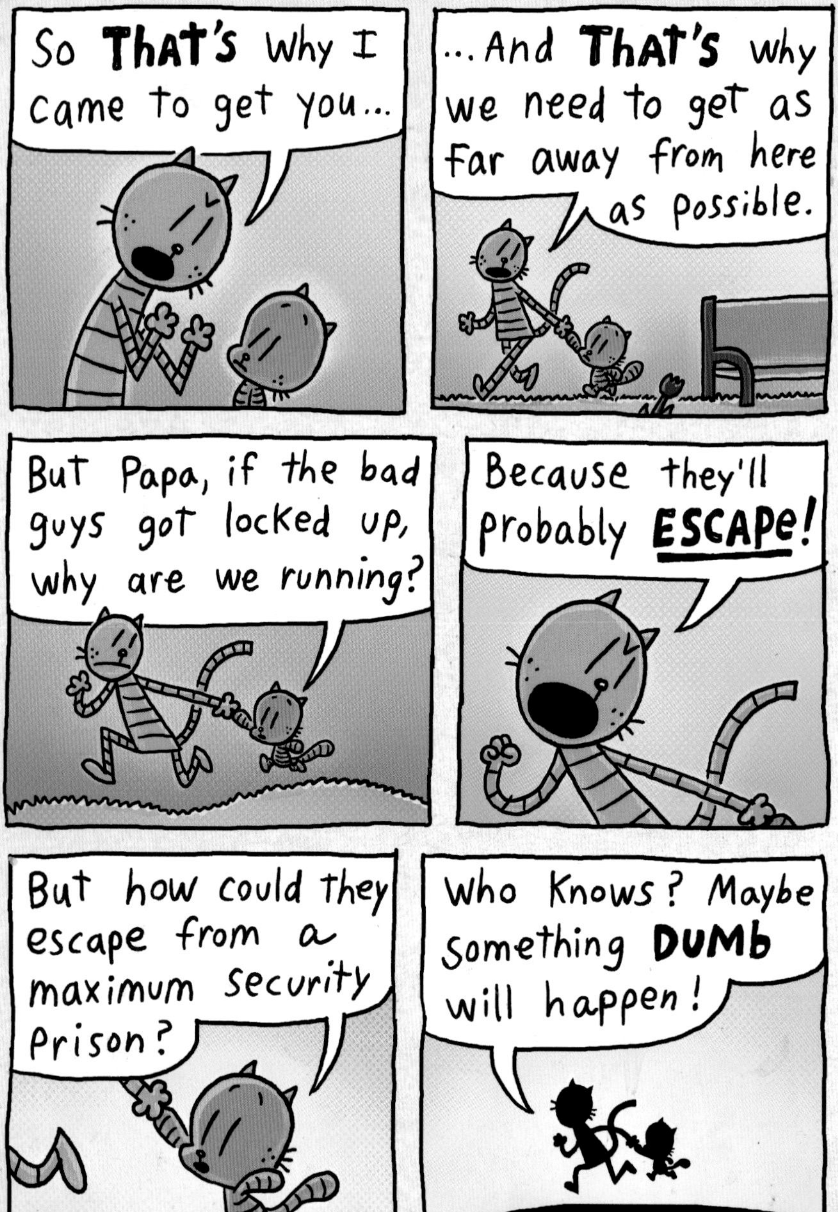
So THAT'S why I came to get you...
...And THAT'S why we need to get as far away from here as possible.
But Papa, if the bad guys got locked up, why are we running?
Because they'll probably ESCAPE!
But how could they escape from a maximum security prison?
Who knows? Maybe something DUMB will happen!

Tree-
House
Comix
Proudly
Presents

Chapter 3

Something Dumb Happens!

by George Beard and Harold Hutchins

Meanwhile...

COPS

Ring-Ring

Hello?

chief

Help! There's been a Jail escape!!!

chief

Where?

at the Jail.

Oh!

chief

I'll put my best man on it!!!!!!!

chief

Oh, DOG MAN!

chief

Dog Man is Late for work again, Chief!

Beep
Beep
Beep
Beep
Beep

DOG MAN! we Need your help!

Meet us AT The JAiL in Ten Minutes!

DO MA

AND DON'T GeT DiSTRACTeD!!!

69

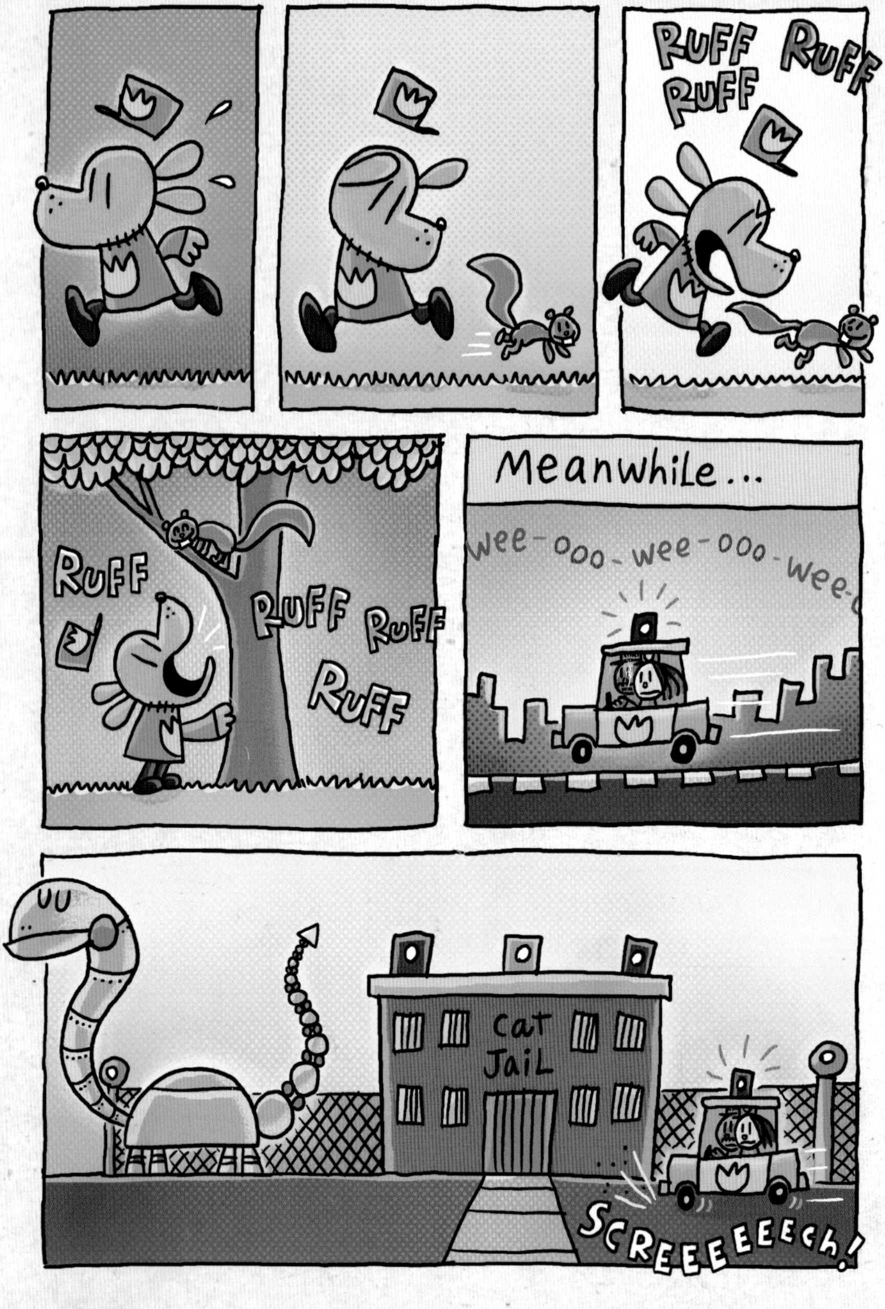
RUFF RUFF
RUFF
RUFF
RUFF RUFF
RUFF
Meanwhile...
wee-ooo-wee-ooo-wee-
Cat Jail
SCREEEEEECH!

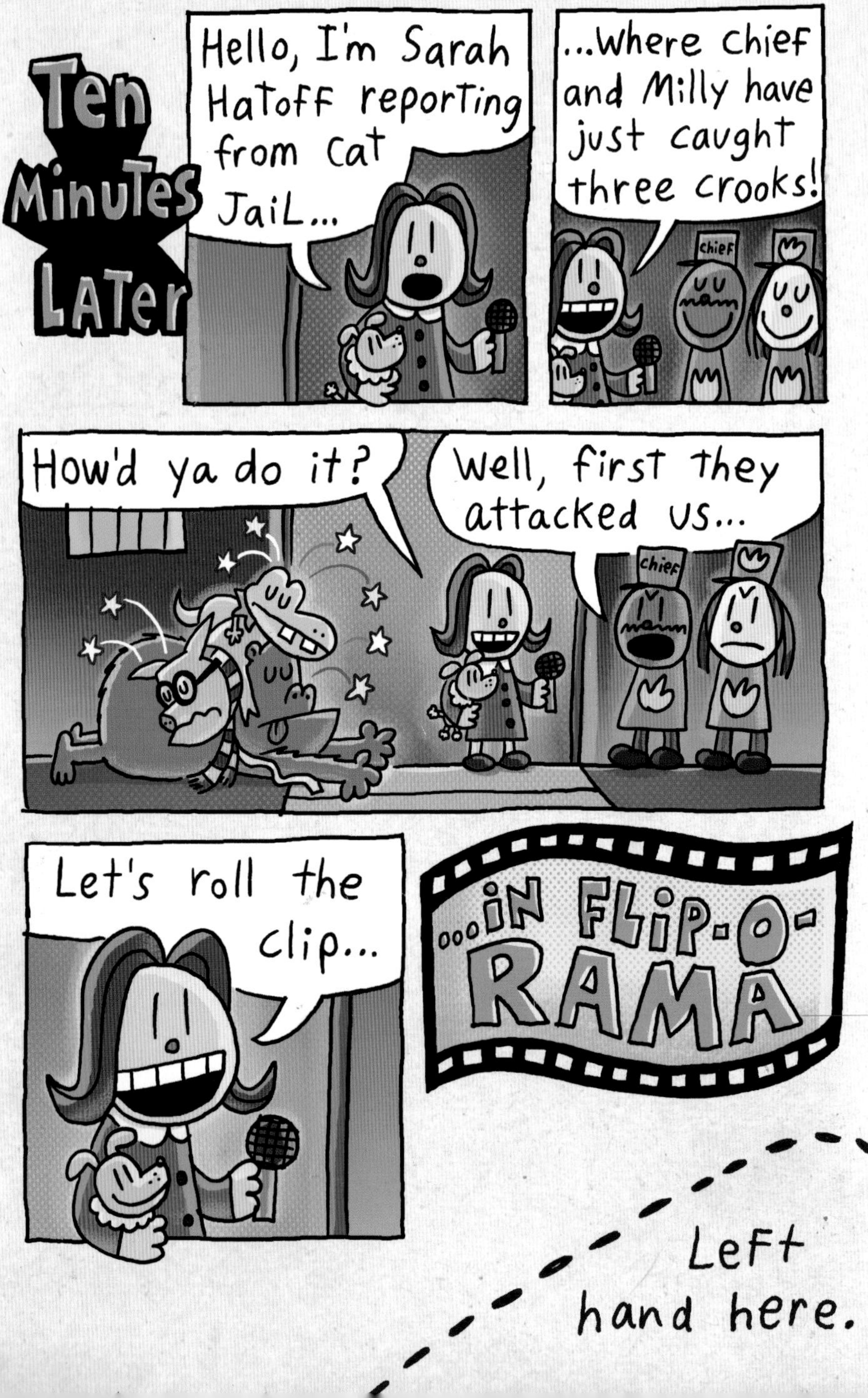
Ten Minutes Later
Hello, I'm Sarah Hatoff reporting from Cat Jail...
...Where Chief and Milly have just caught three crooks!
Chief
How'd ya do it?
Well, first they attacked us...
Chief
Let's roll the clip...
...in FLIP-O-RAMA
Left hand here.

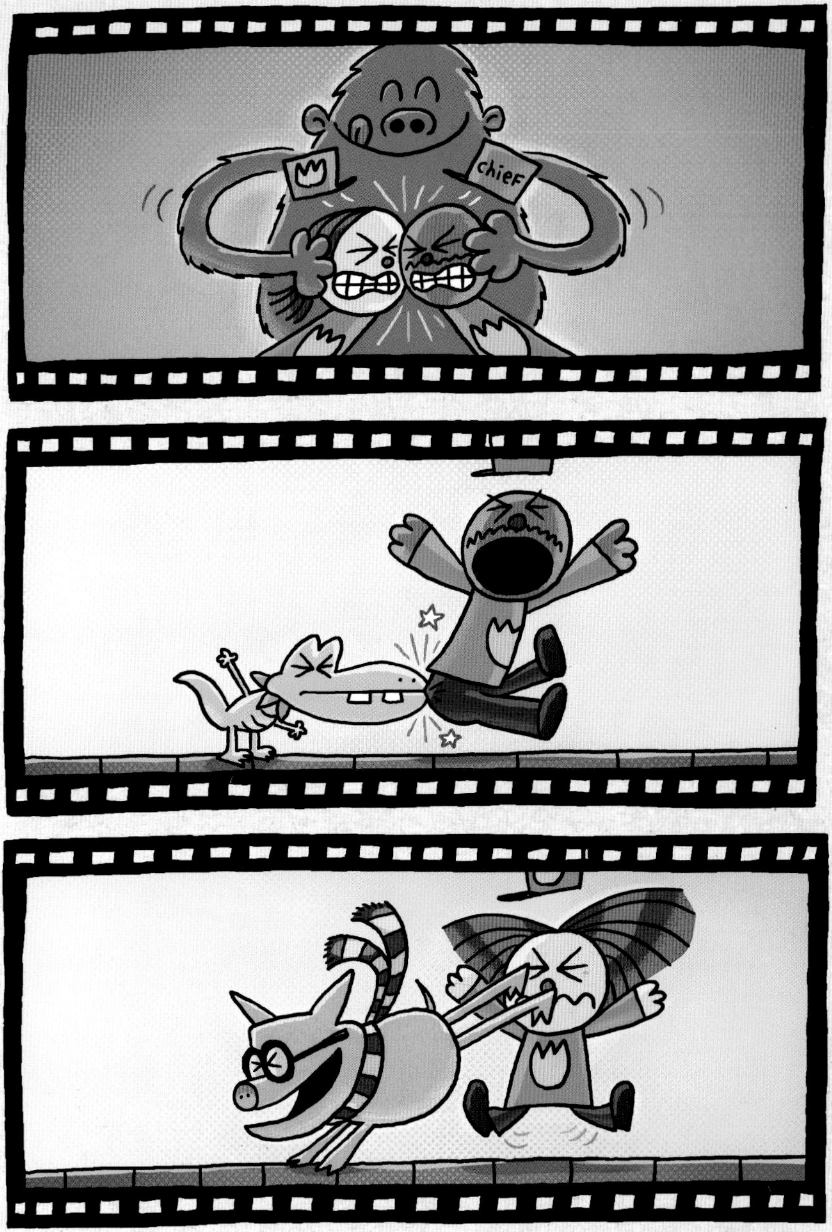
chieF

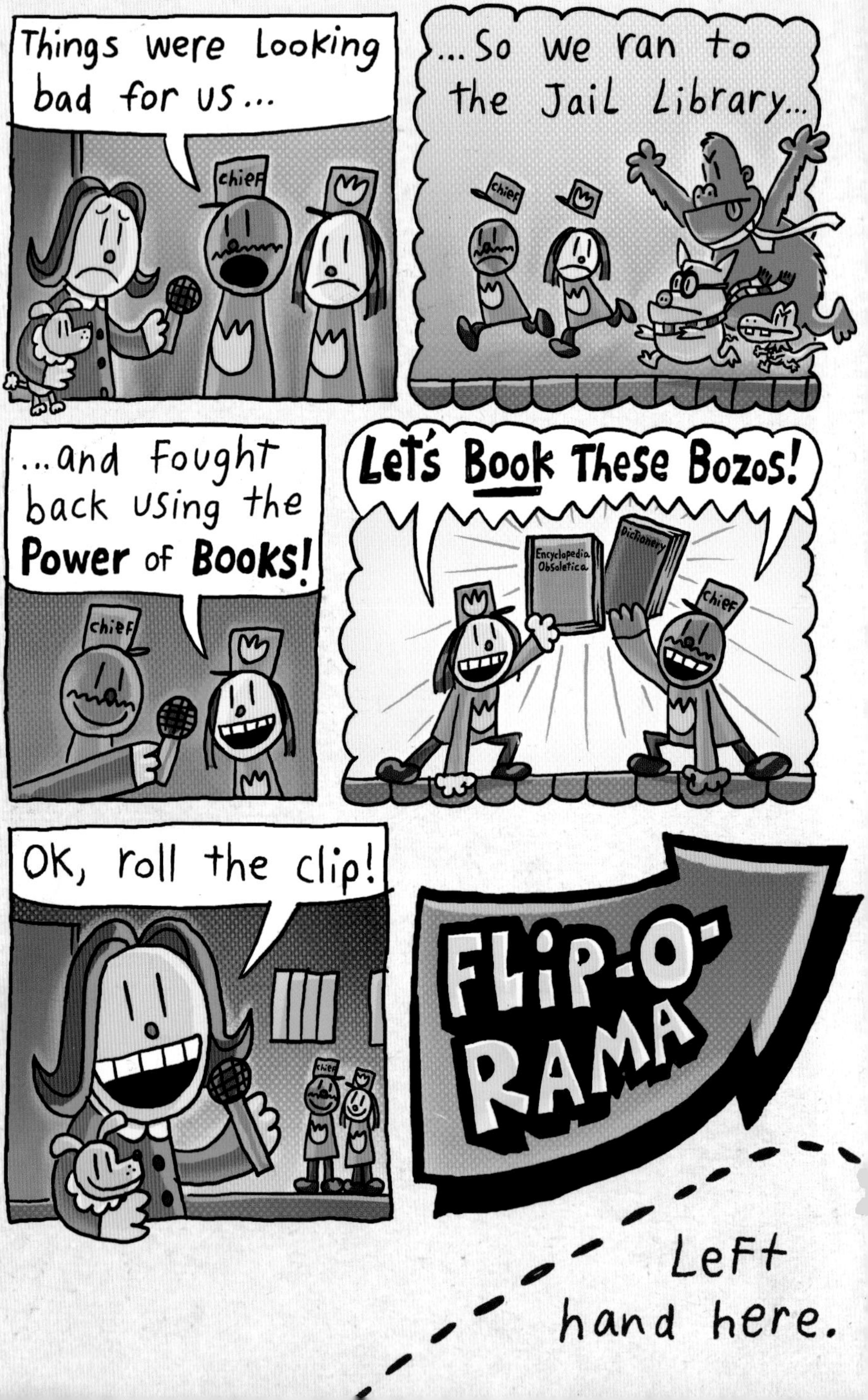
Things were looking bad for us...
...So we ran to the Jail Library...
chief
...and fought back using the **Power** of **BOOKS!**
chief
Let's Book These Bozos!
Encyclopedia Obsoletica
Dictionary
chief
OK, roll the clip!
chief
FLIP-O-RAMA
Left hand here.

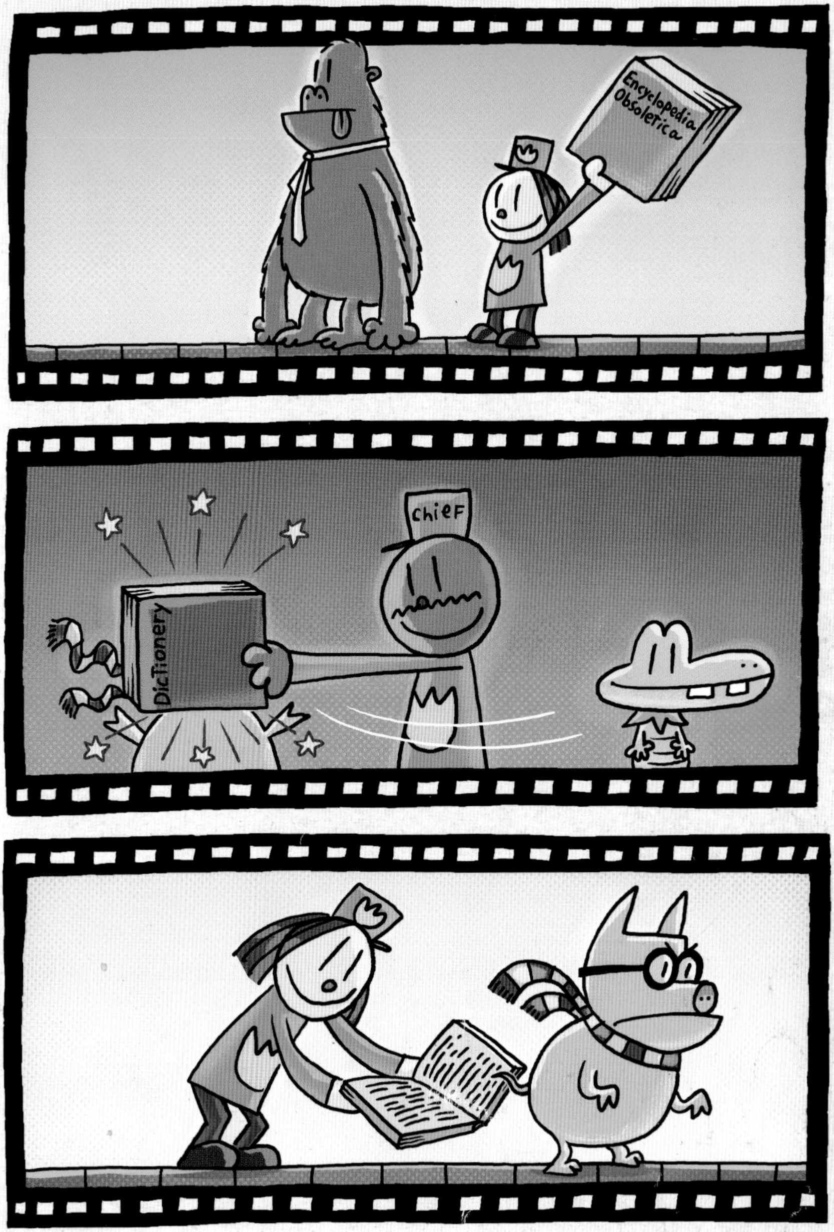
Encyclopedia Obsoletica
Chief
Dictionery

Right Thumb here.

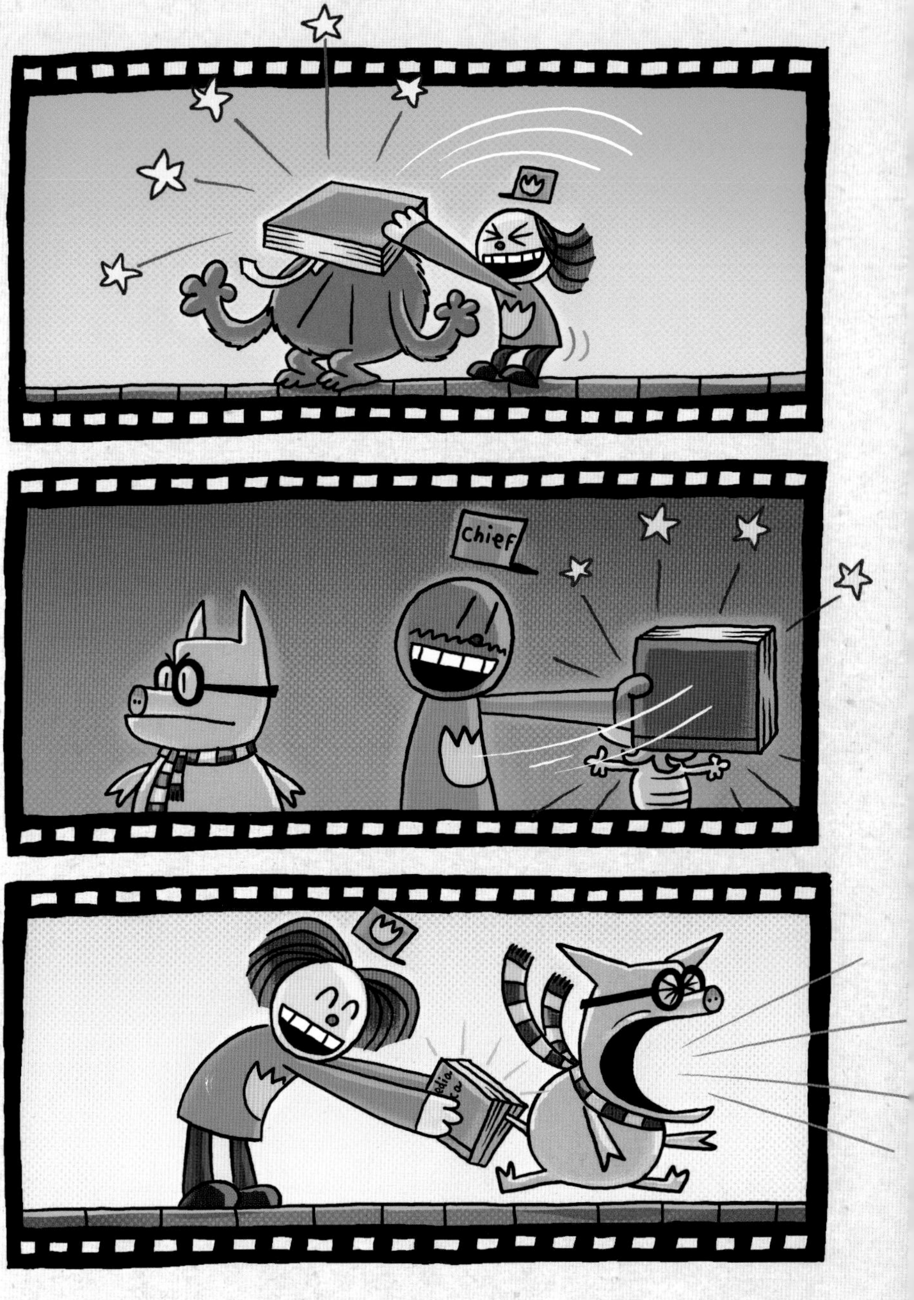
chief

Come on, Zuzu! Let's follow them!

DOG MAN, Those Guys escaped because of YOU!!!

GO HOME!

But Chief—

Sorry, Milly, He's gotta Learn his Lesson!

...And WE'VE gotta catch those crooks Again!

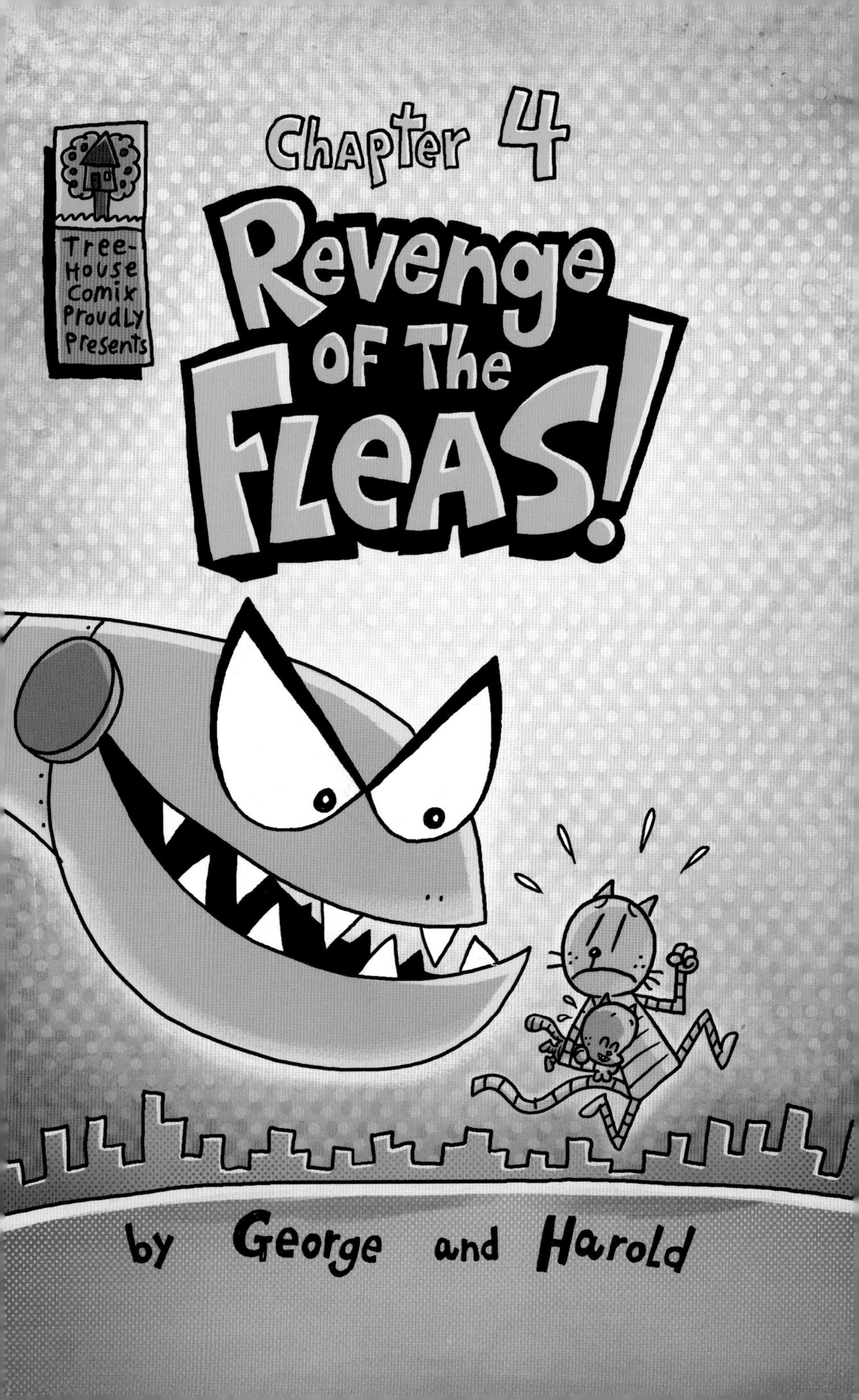
Tree-House Comix Proudly Presents
Chapter 4
Revenge of the Fleas!
by George and Harold

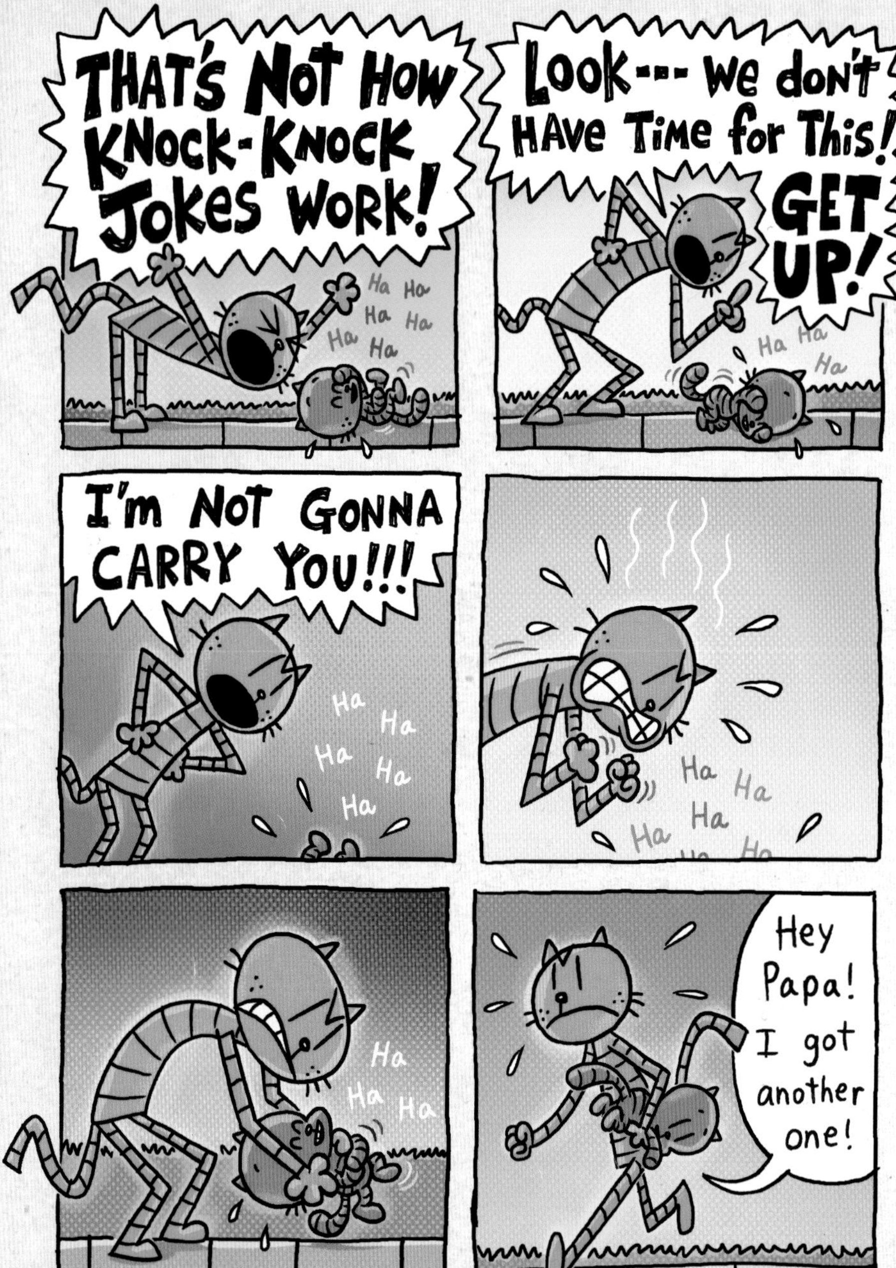
THAT'S NOT HOW KNOCK-KNOCK JOKES WORK!
Ha Ha Ha Ha Ha Ha
LOOK--- we don't HAVE Time for This!
GET UP!
Ha Ha Ha
I'm NOT GONNA CARRY YOU!!!
Ha Ha Ha Ha Ha
Ha Ha Ha Ha Ha
Ha Ha Ha
Hey Papa! I got another one!

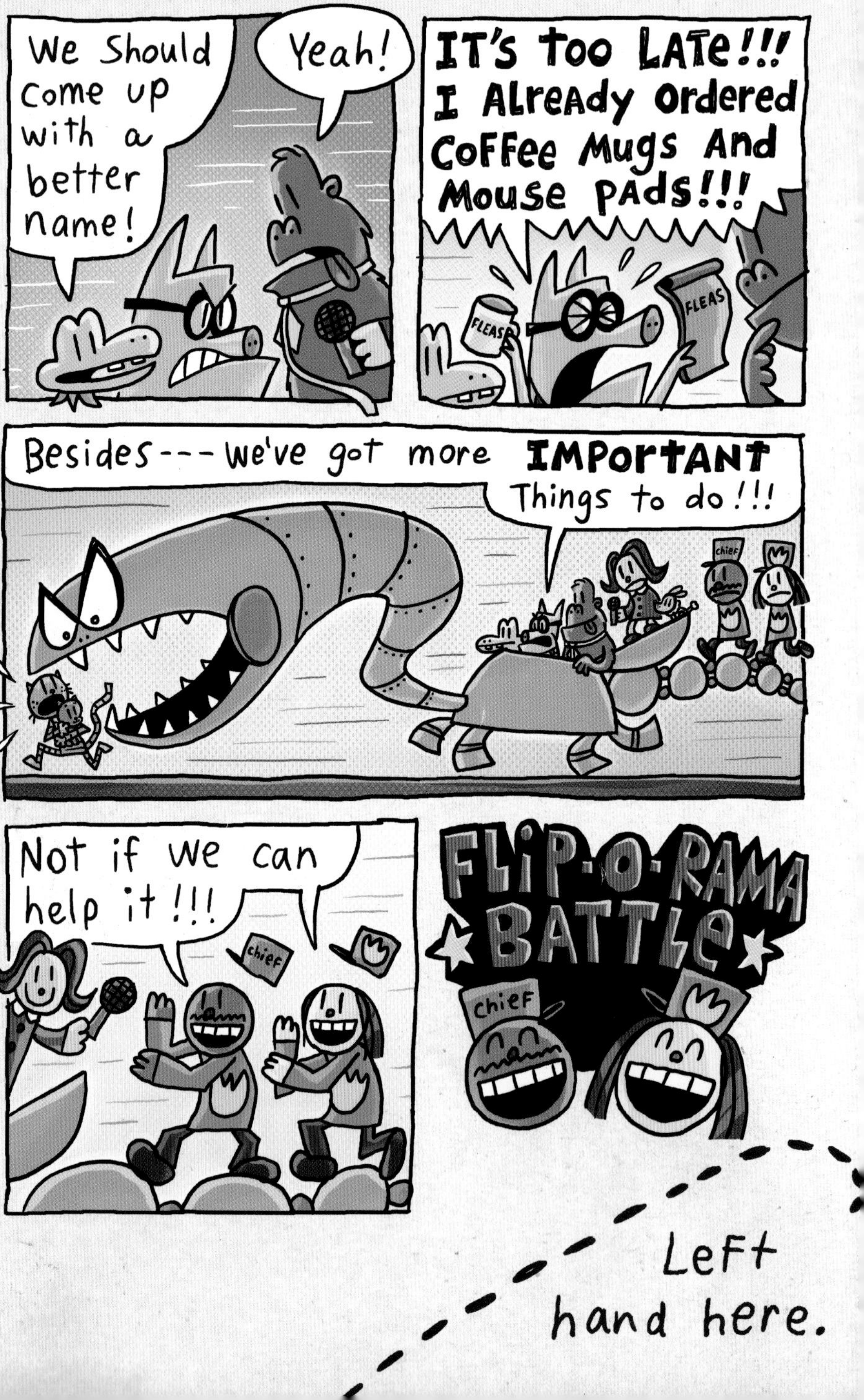
We Should come up with a better name!
Yeah!
IT'S TOO LATE!!! I Already Ordered CoFFee Mugs And Mouse PAdS!!!
FLEAS
FLEAS
Besides--- We've got more IMPORTANT Things to do!!!
chief
Not if We can help it!!!
chief
FLIP-O-RAMA BATTLE
chieF
Left hand here.

Right
Thumb
here.

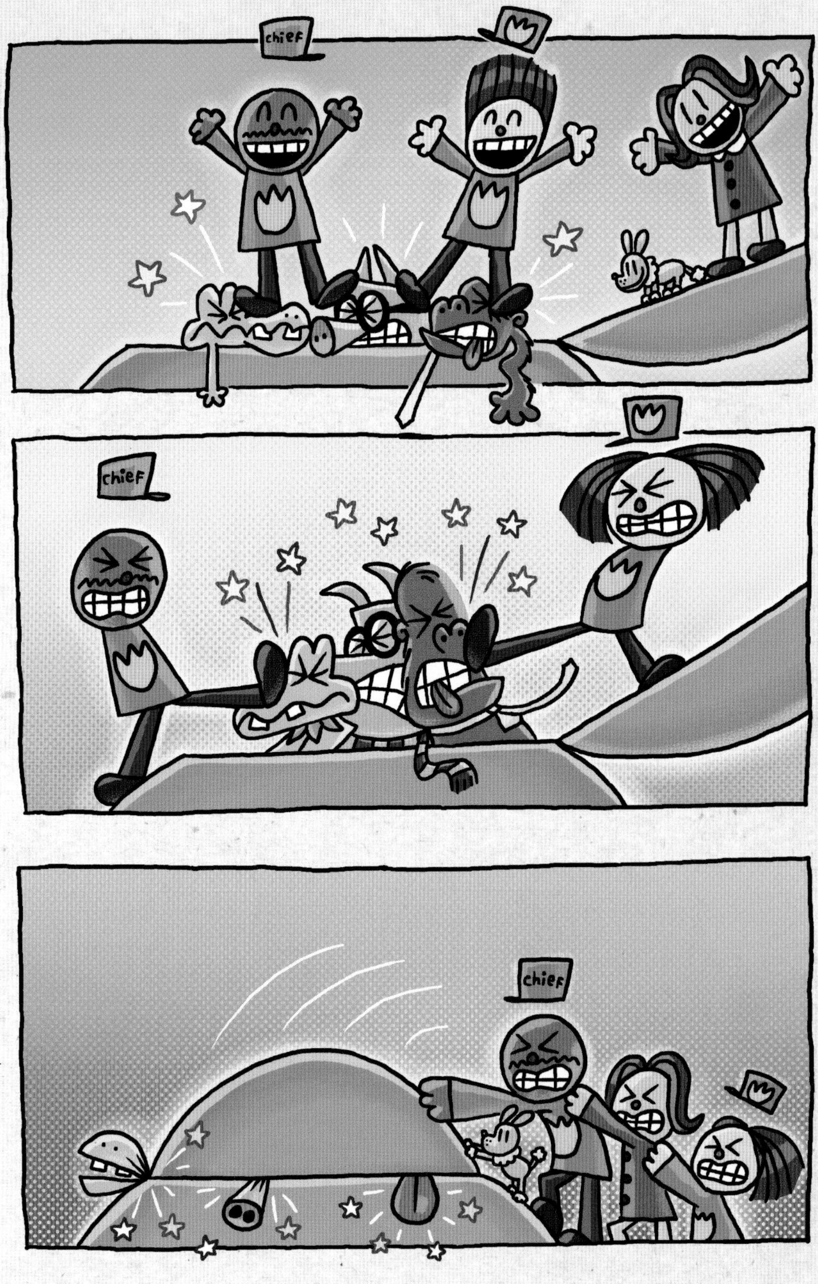
chief
chief
chief

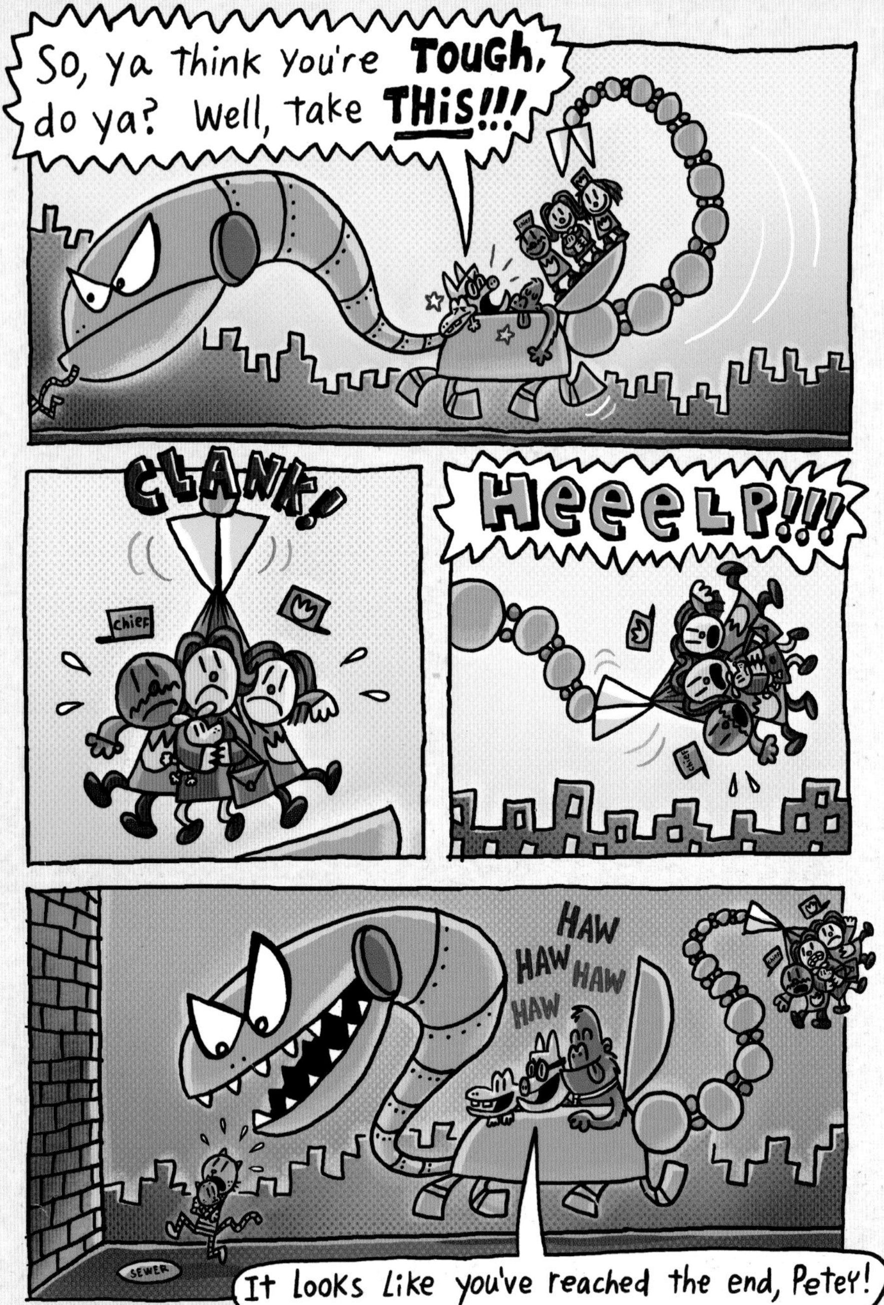
So, ya think you're TOUGH, do ya? Well, take THIS!!!
CLANK!
Chief
HEEELP!!!
HAW
HAW HAW
HAW
SEWER
It looks like you've reached the end, Petey!

Hey Papa,

What?

Knock-Knock!

No, seriously! This is the best one ever!

This is not the time or the place for that!

ALRight, who's There?

Ummm...

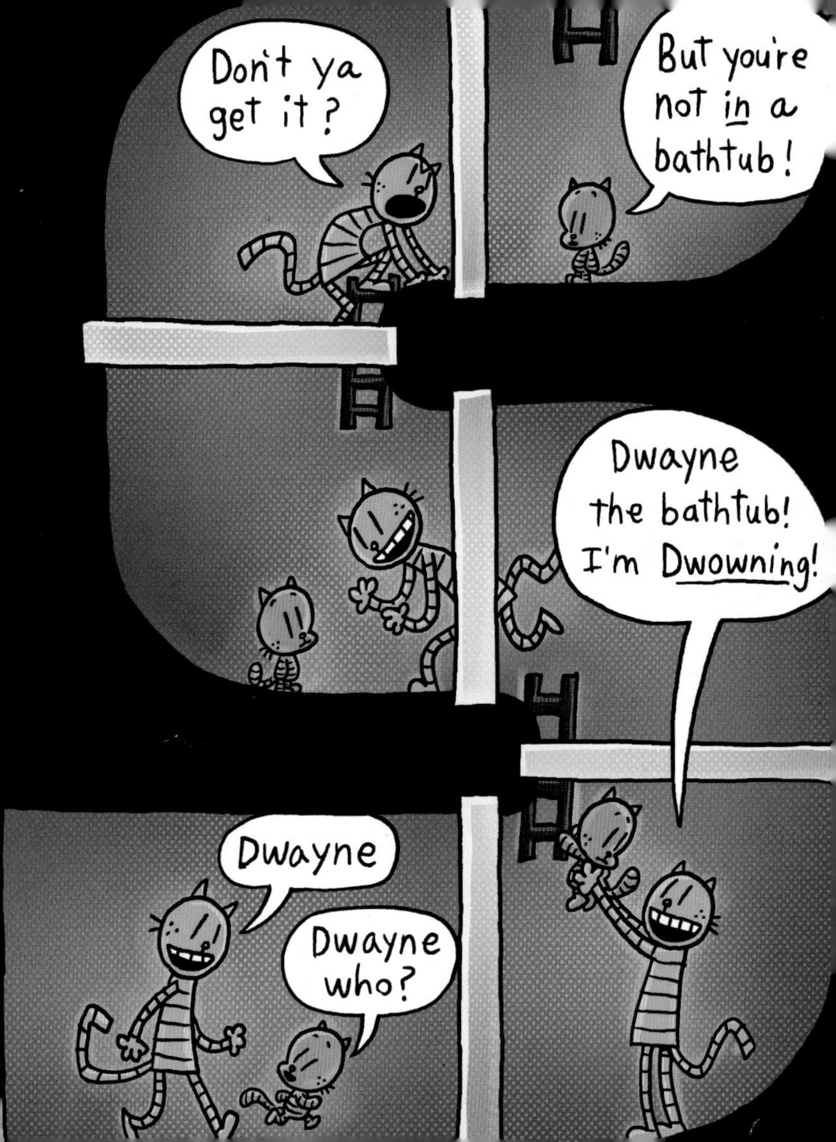
Don't ya get it?
But you're not in a bathtub!
Dwayne the bathtub! I'm Dwowning!
Dwayne
Dwayne who?

That's Not the point!

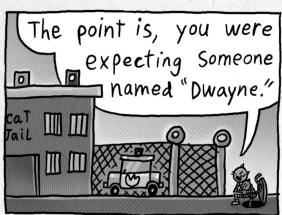

The point is, you were expecting someone named "Dwayne."

But I switched it around!

That's why it's funny!

It woulda been funnier if the bathtub pooped on your head!

WHAT IS IT WITH YOU AND POOP?

Ha Ha Ha

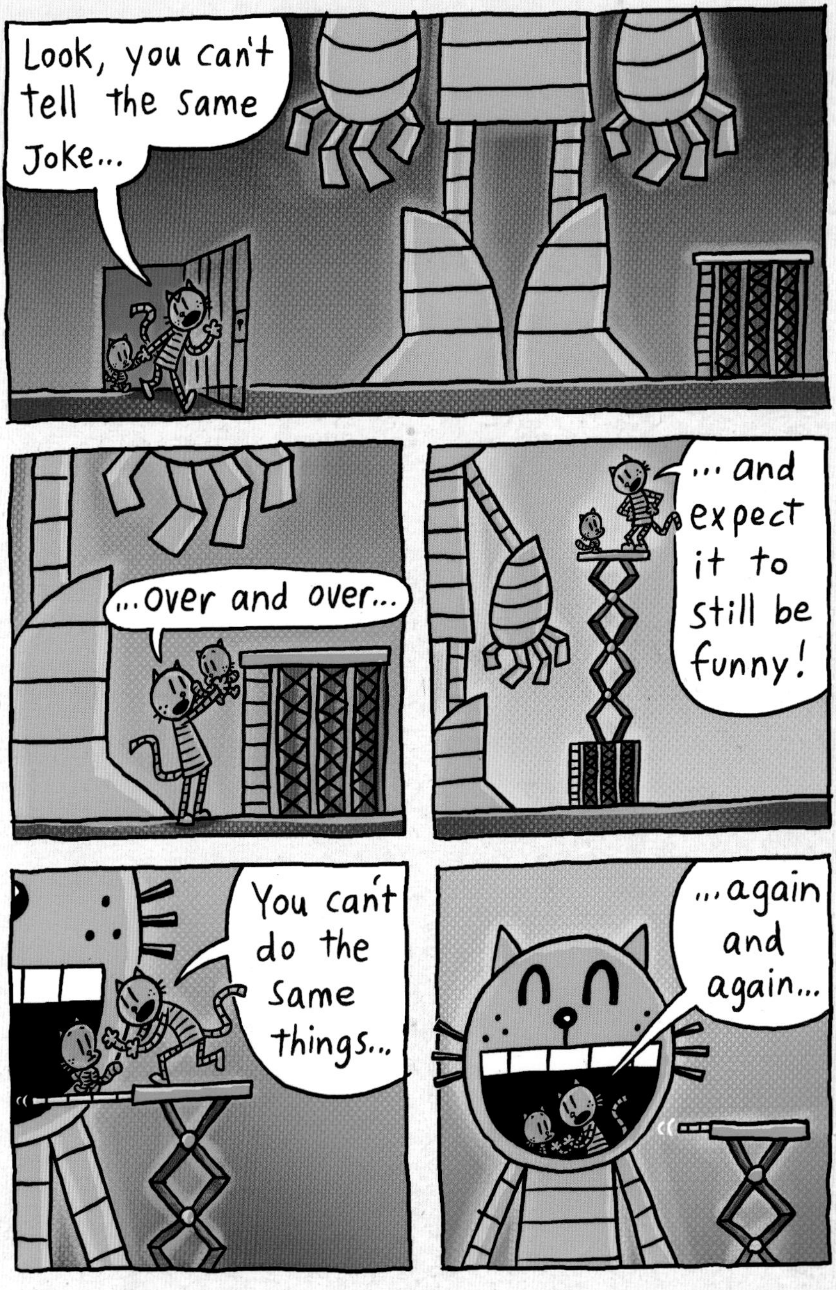
Look, you can't tell the same Joke...
...over and over...
...and expect it to still be funny!
You can't do the same things...
...again and again...

...and expect to get a Laugh!

Ya gotta avoid repetition...

... Shun redundancy...

...eschew reiteration...

...resist recapitulation...

...And also, stop telling the same Joke over and over!

Chapter 5

A Buncha Stuff That Happened Next

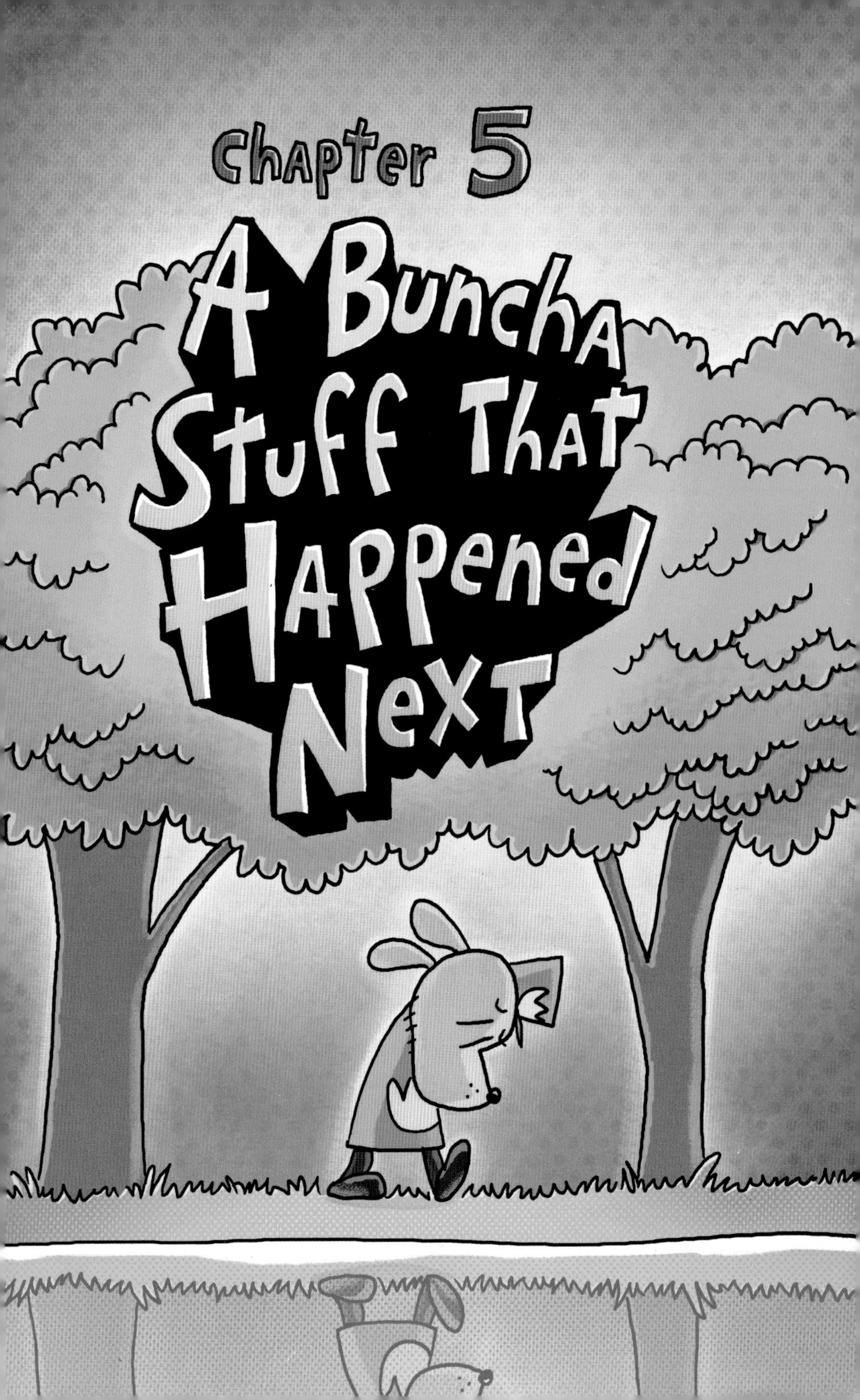

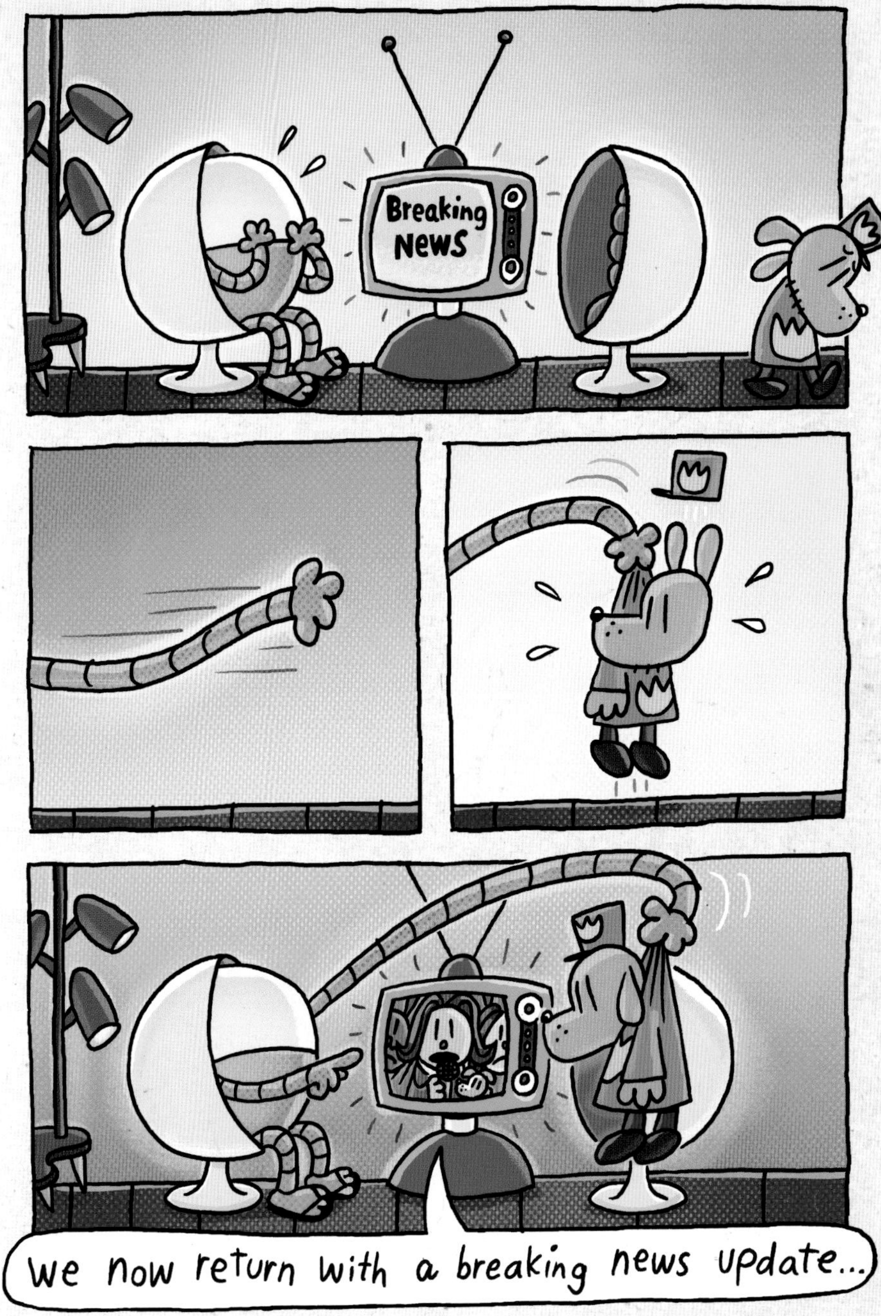
Breaking News
We now return with a breaking news update...

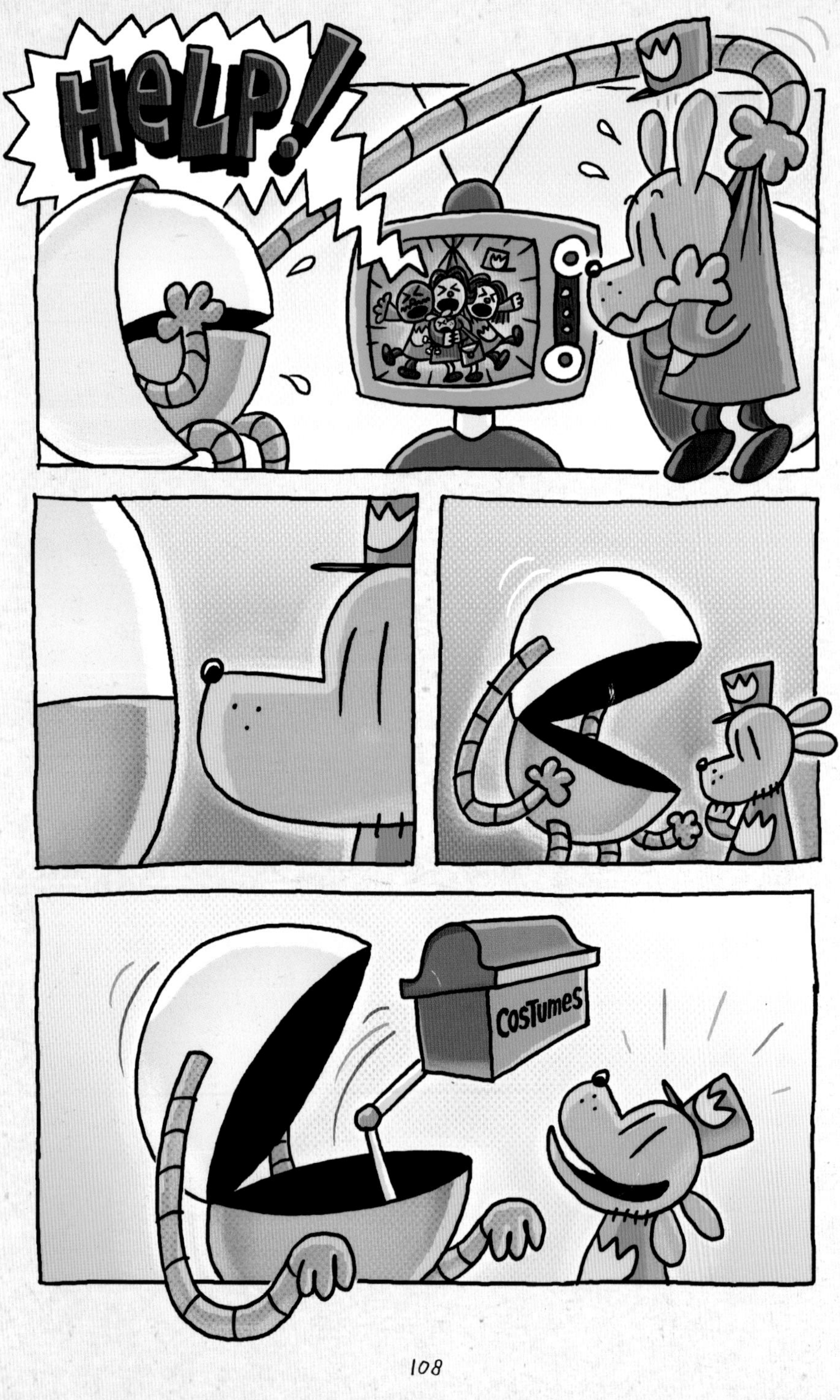
HELP!
COSTUMES

CLICK
D

LD

FWOOOSH!

Squeee!

FLOOOP!

FLiP FLoP FLiP FLoP FLiP FLoP FLiP FLoP FLiP FLoP FLiP FLoP FLiP

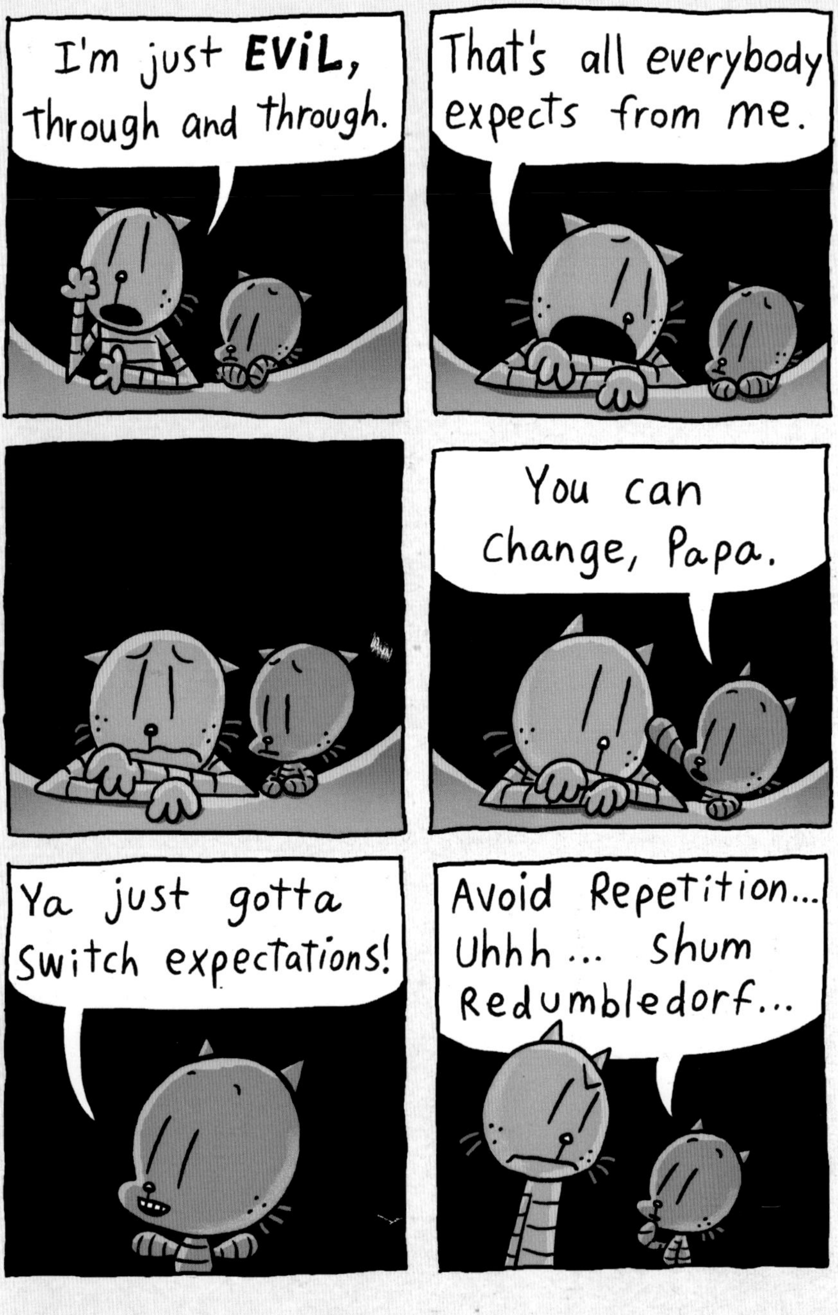
I'm just **EVIL**, through and through.
That's all everybody expects from me.
You can change, Papa.
Ya just gotta switch expectations!
Avoid Repetition... Uhhh... Shum Redumbledorf...

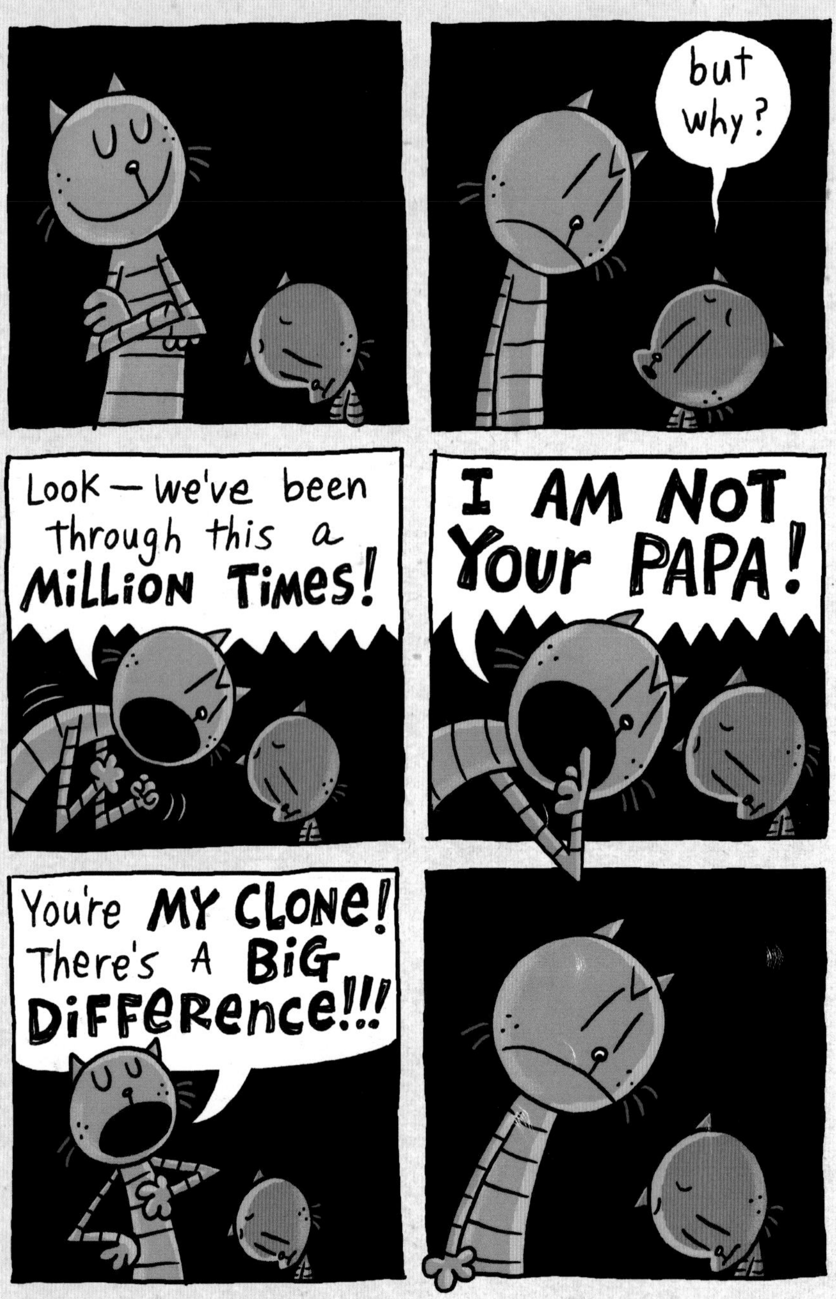
but why?
Look—we've been through this a MILLION TIMES!
I AM NOT YOUR PAPA!
You're MY CLONE! There's A BIG DIFFERENCE!!!

Meanwhile...

Stairs

CLOP FLIP FLOP FLIP FLOP FLIP FLOP FLIP FLOP FLIP

CLAP CLAP

RRRRRRR

RRRRRRRR RRR-

THUNK!

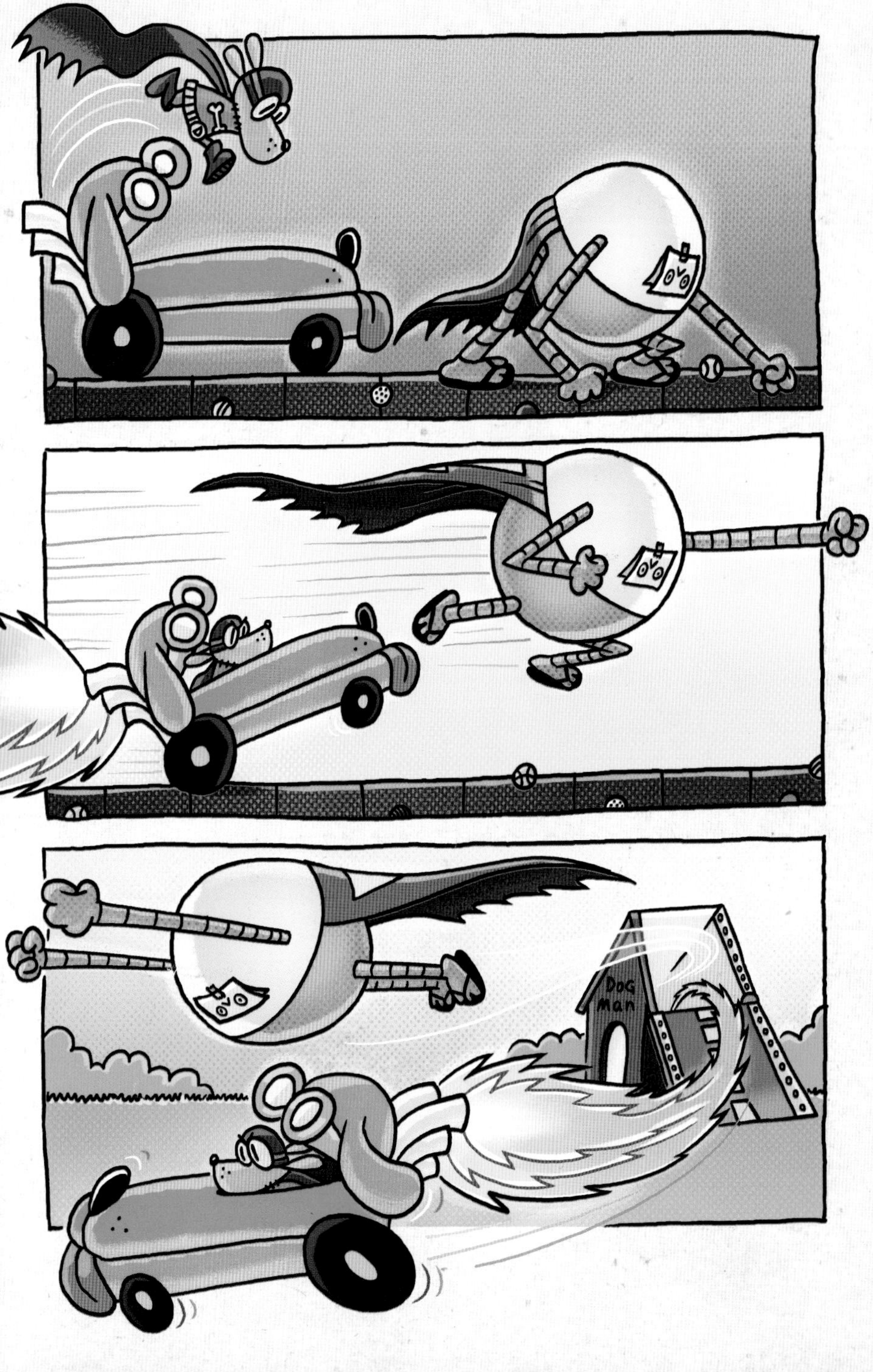
DOG
Man

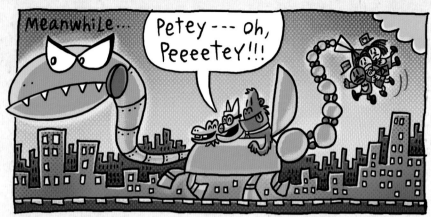

Meanwhile...

Petey --- Oh, Peeeetey!!!

Come out and Plaaay — aaay!!!

Come out, come out, wherever you are!

Alright, kid. Listen up!

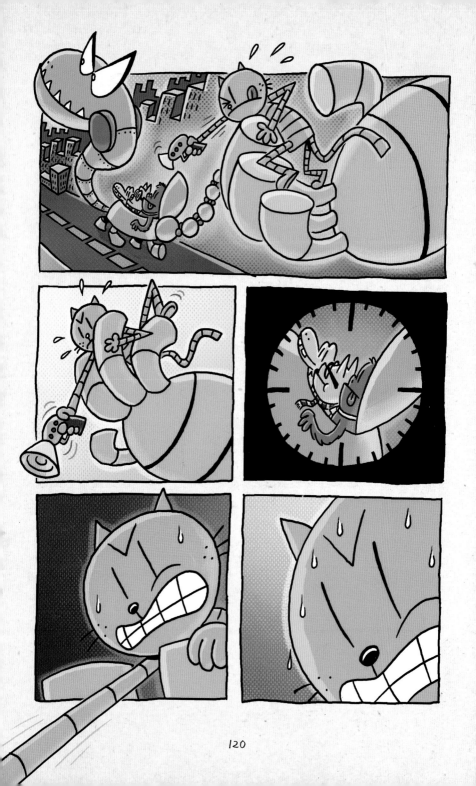

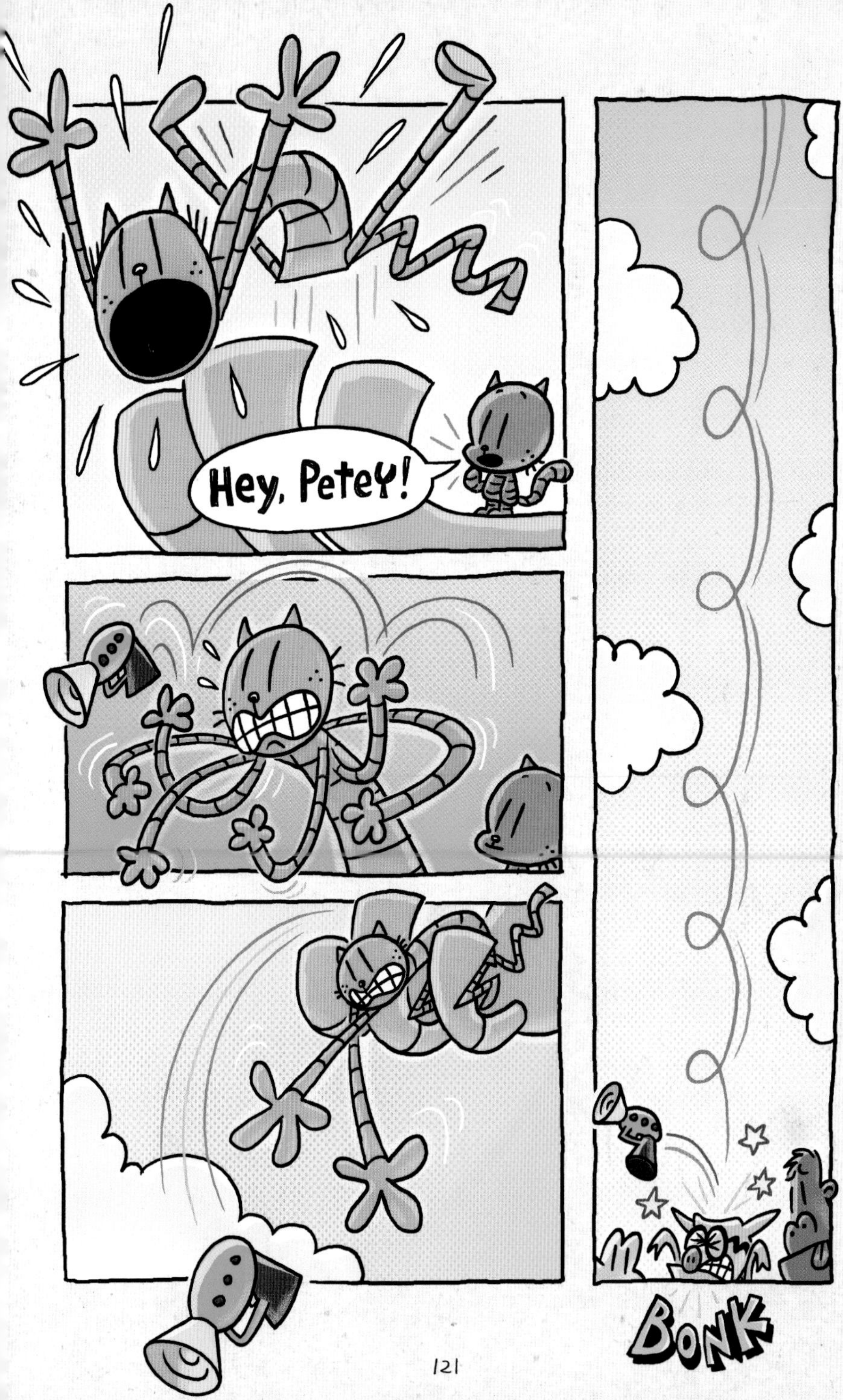
Hey, Petey!
BONK

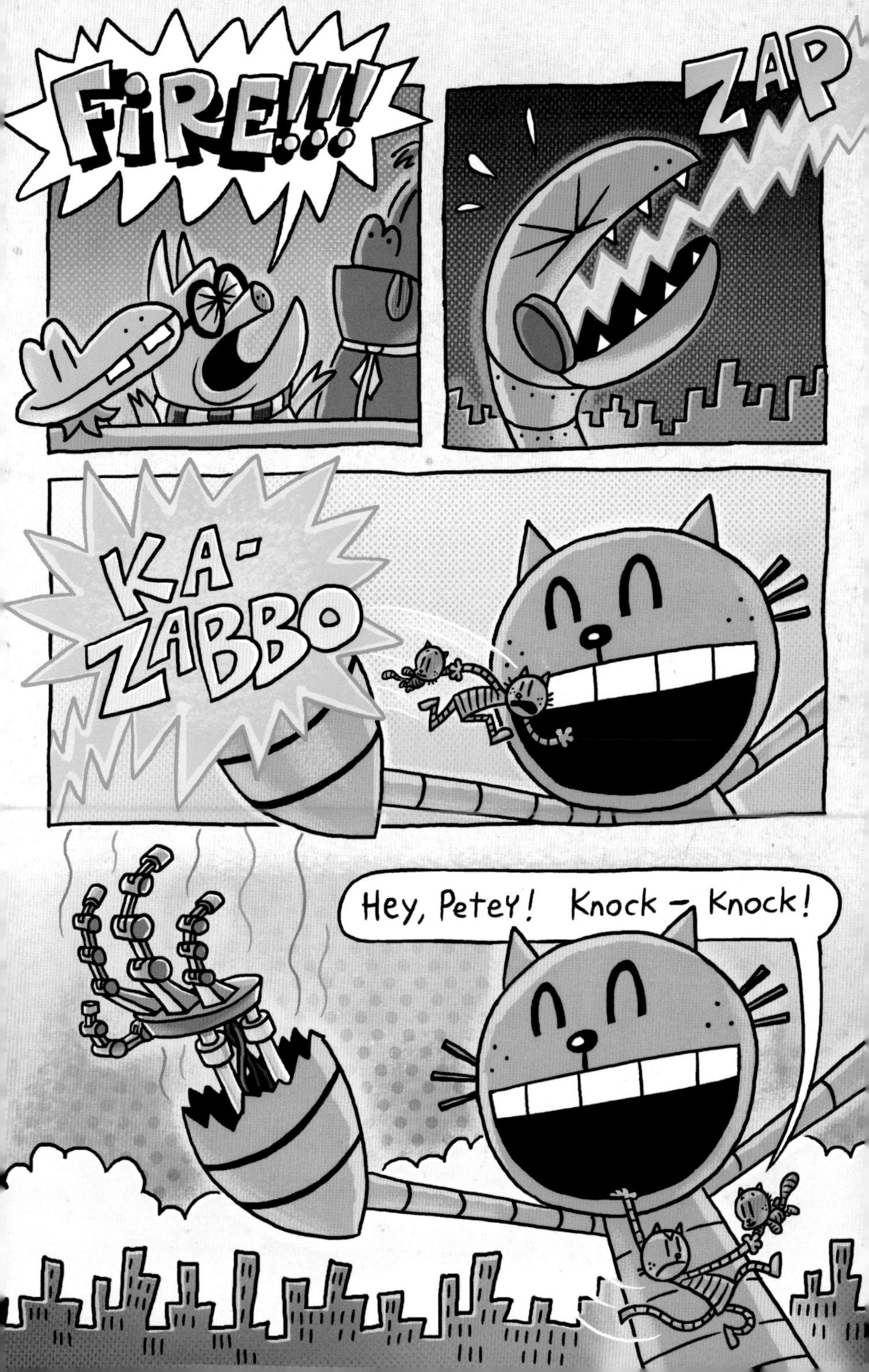

FIRE!!!
ZAP
KA-ZABBO
Hey, Petey! Knock-Knock!

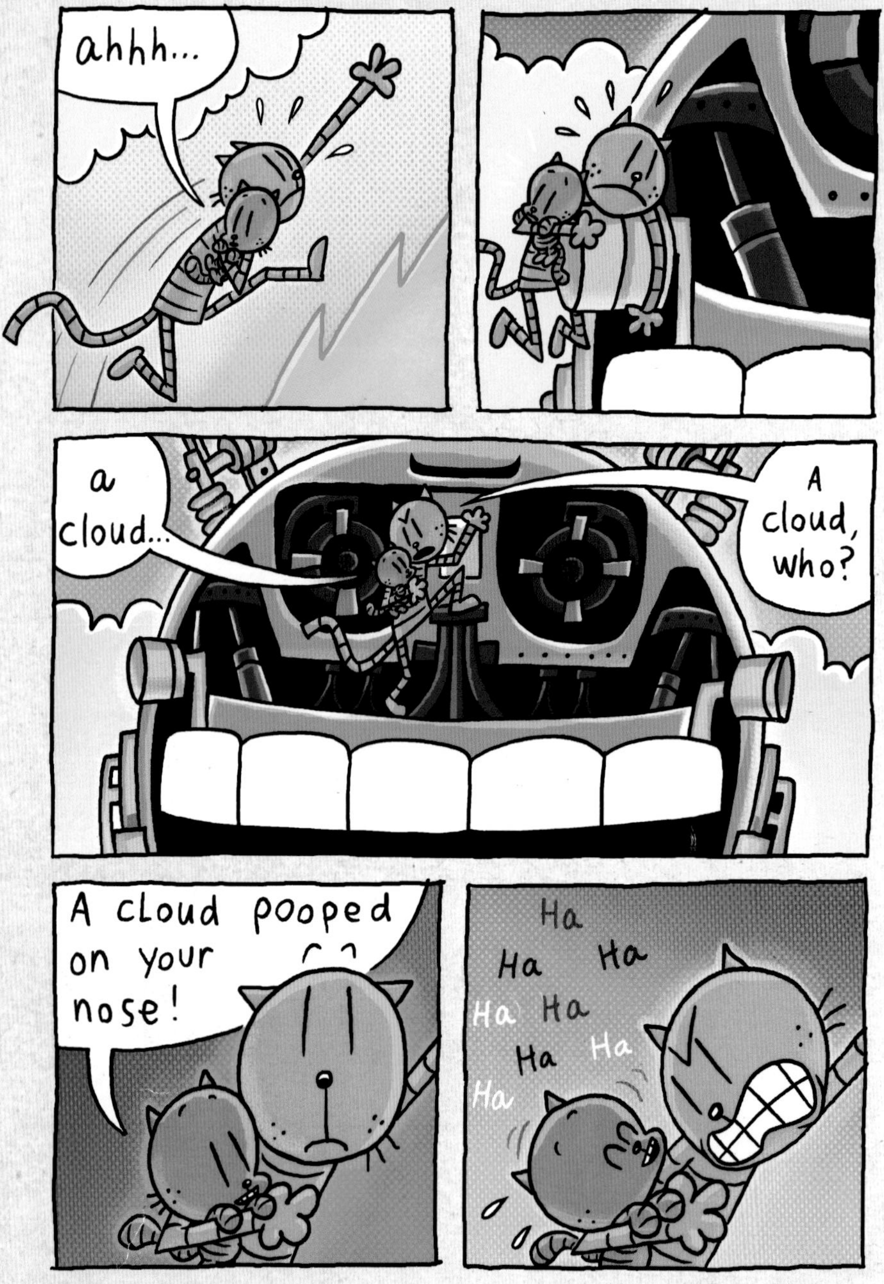
ahhh...
a cloud...
A cloud, who?
A cloud pooped on your nose!
Ha Ha Ha Ha Ha Ha Ha Ha

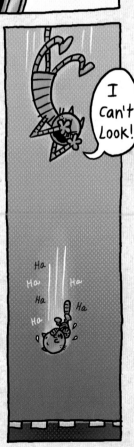

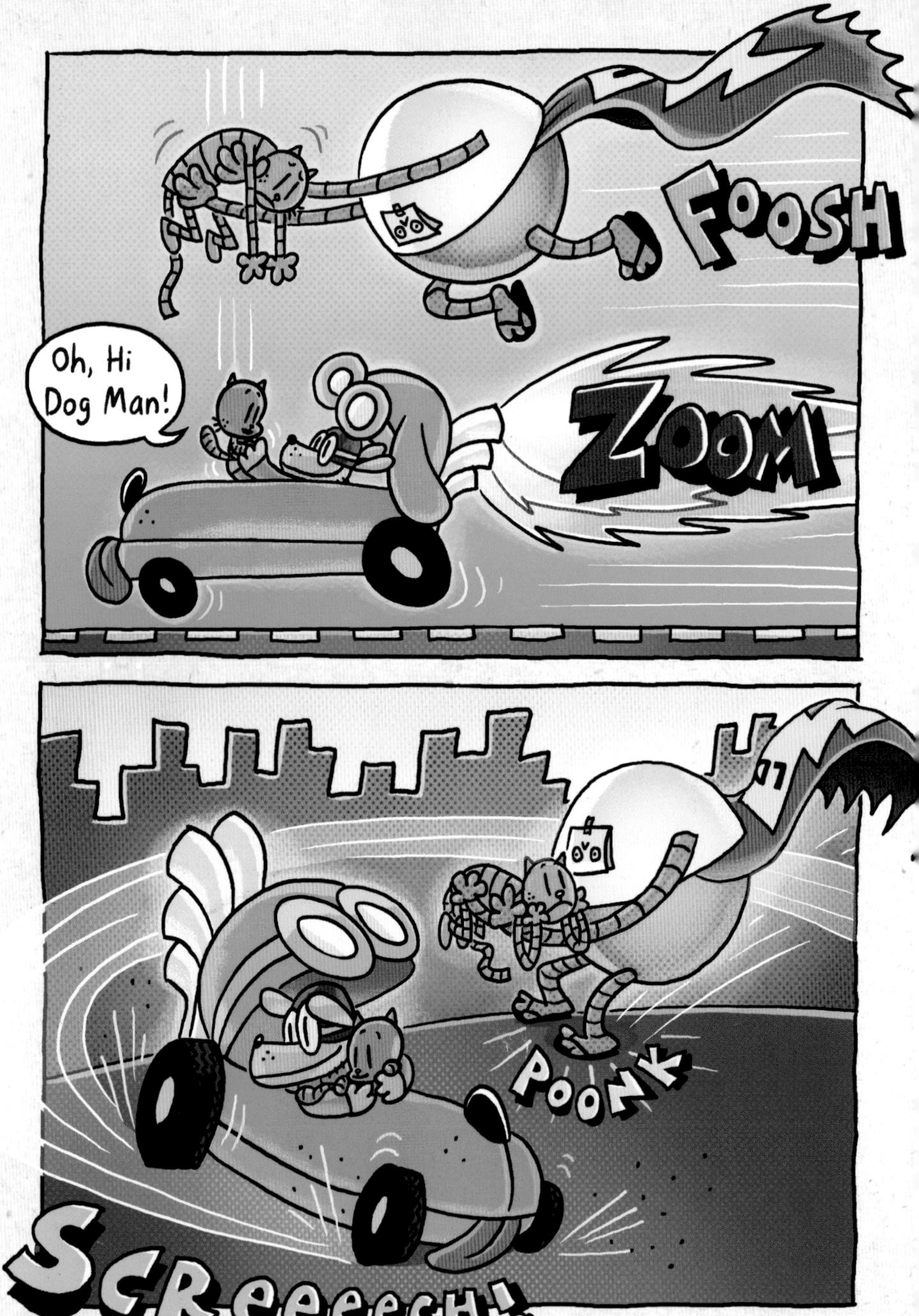
FOOSH
Oh, Hi Dog Man!
ZOOM
POONK
SCReeeeCH!

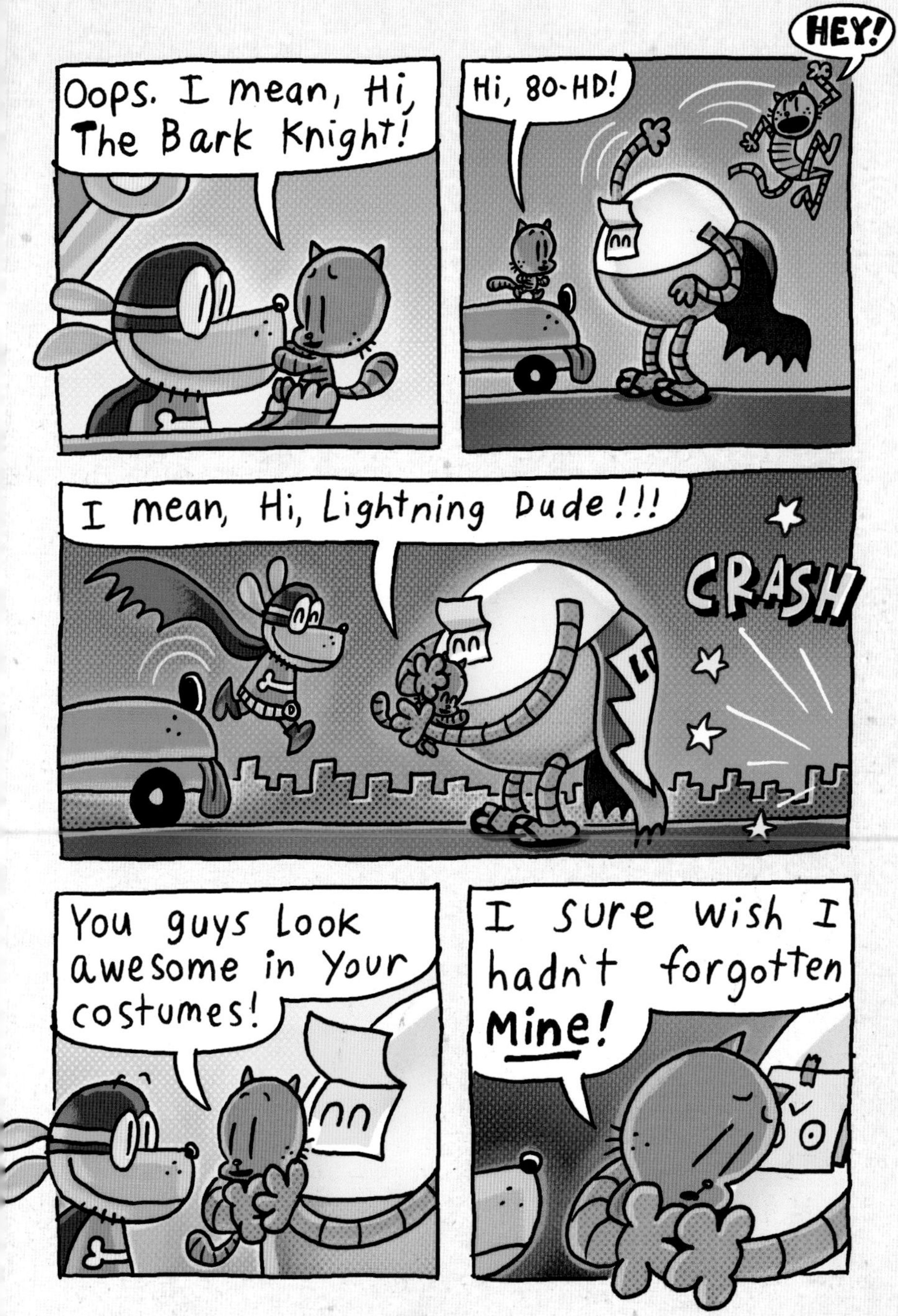
Oops. I mean, Hi, The Bark Knight!
Hi, 80-HD!
HEY!
I mean, Hi, Lightning Dude!!!
CRASH
You guys look awesome in your costumes!
I sure wish I hadn't forgotten Mine!

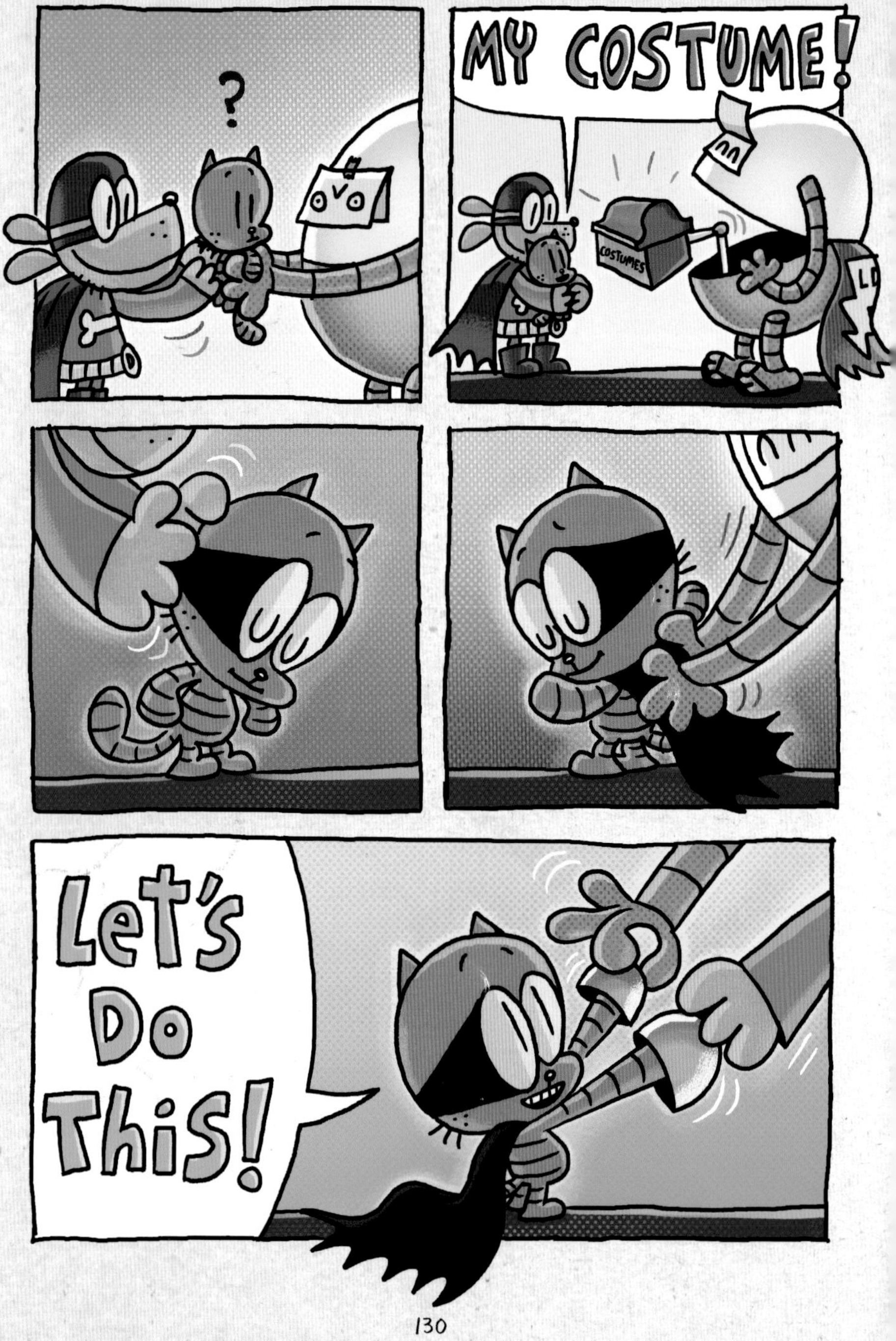
?
MY COSTUME!
COSTUMES
Let's Do This!

CHAPTER 6

SUPA BUDDIES

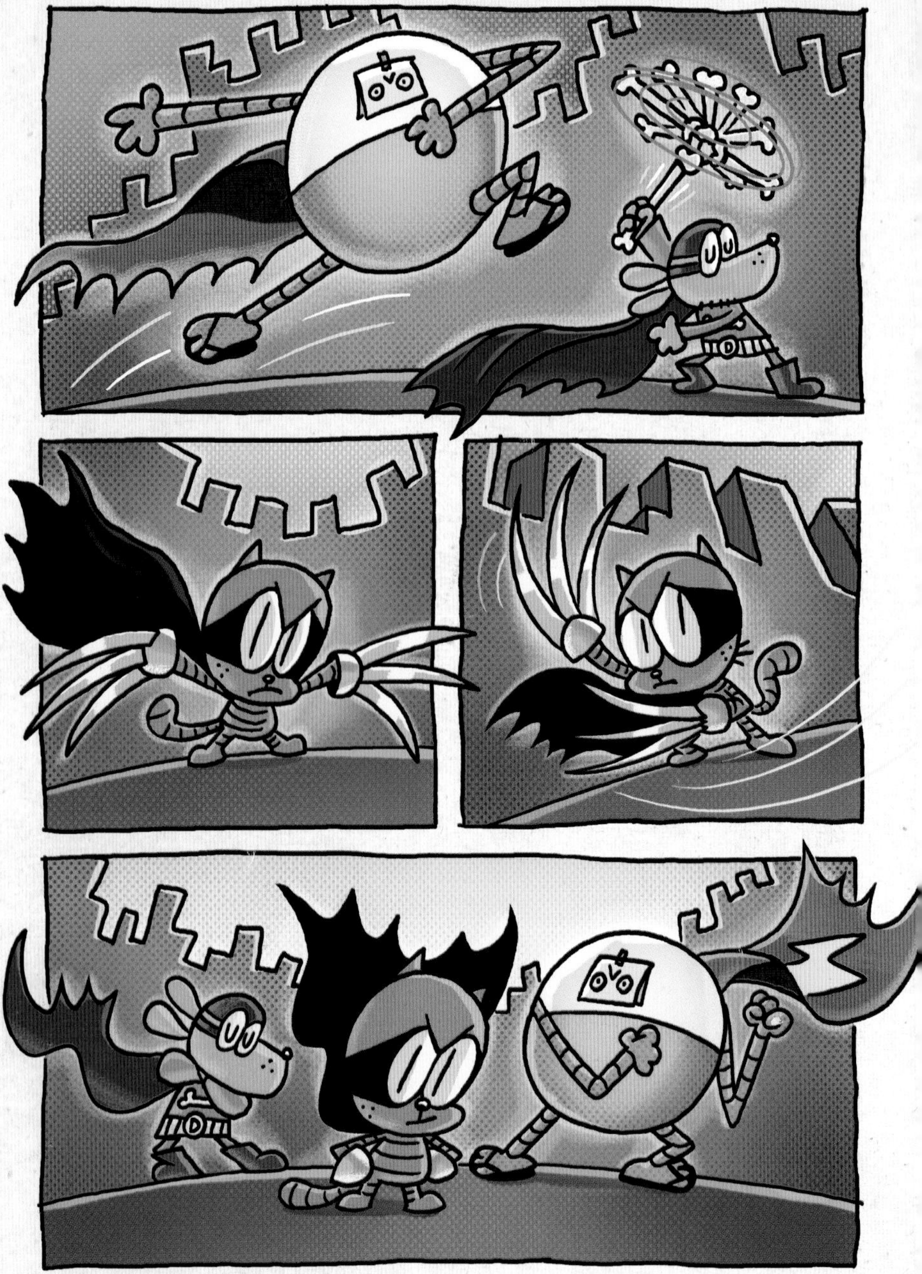

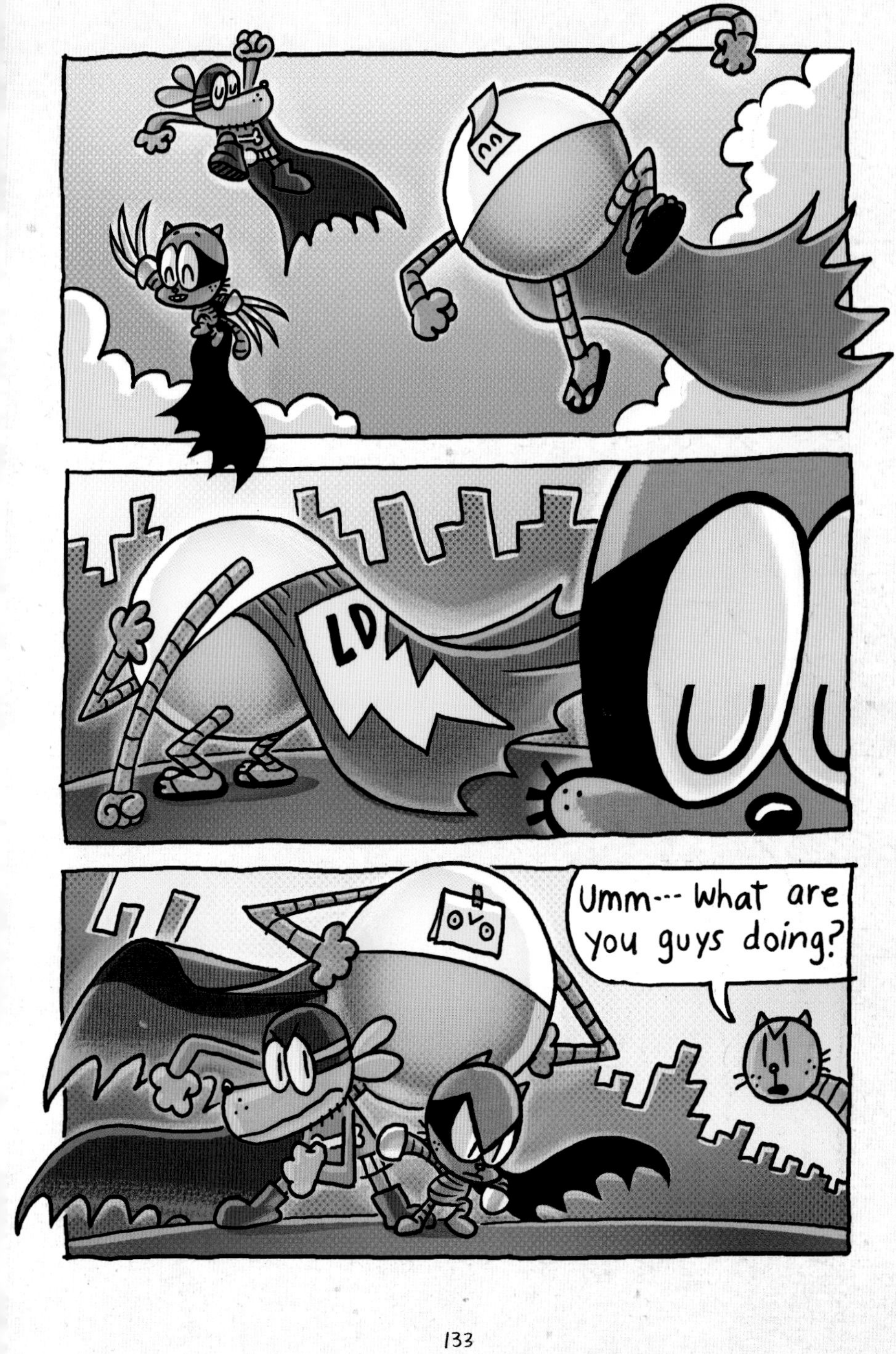
LD
Umm--- What are you guys doing?

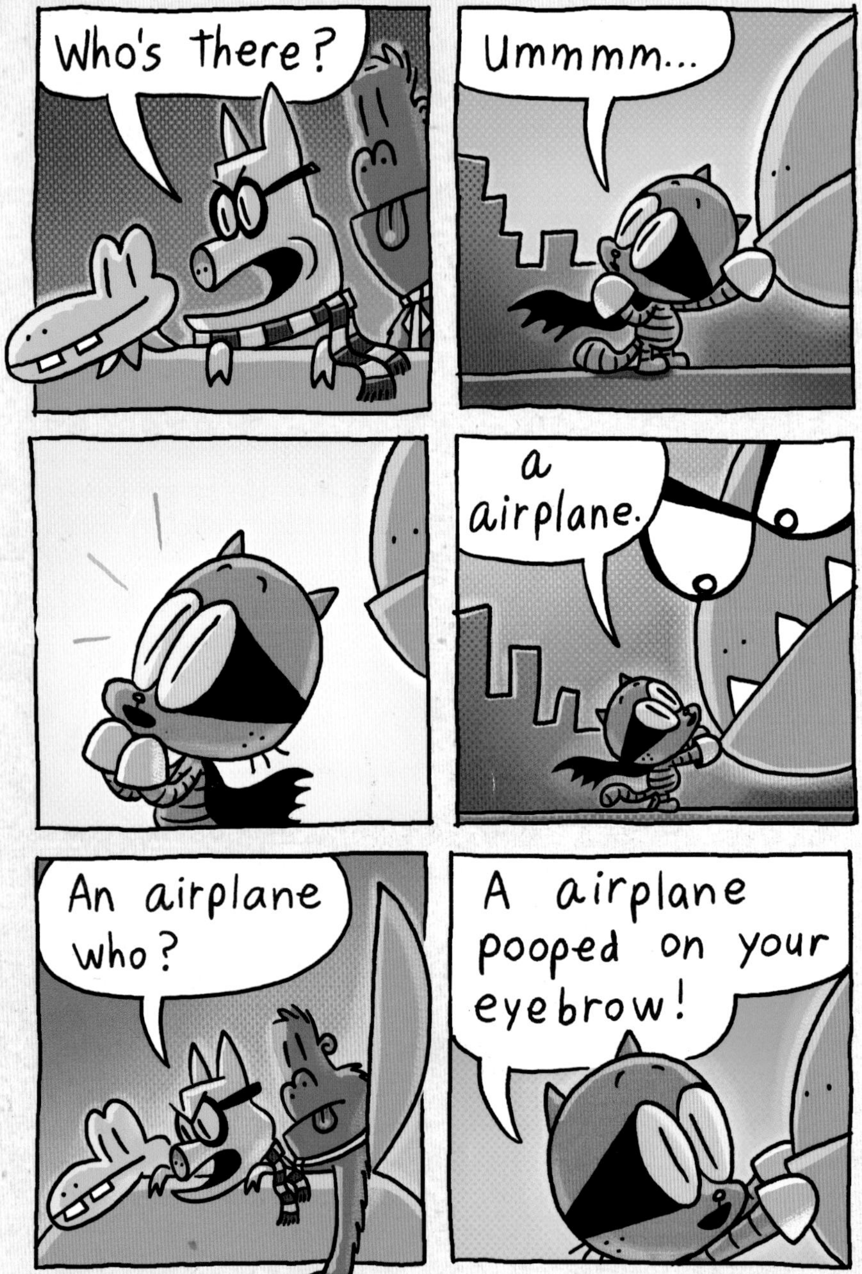
Who's there?
Ummmm...
a
airplane.
An airplane who?
A airplane pooped on your eyebrow!

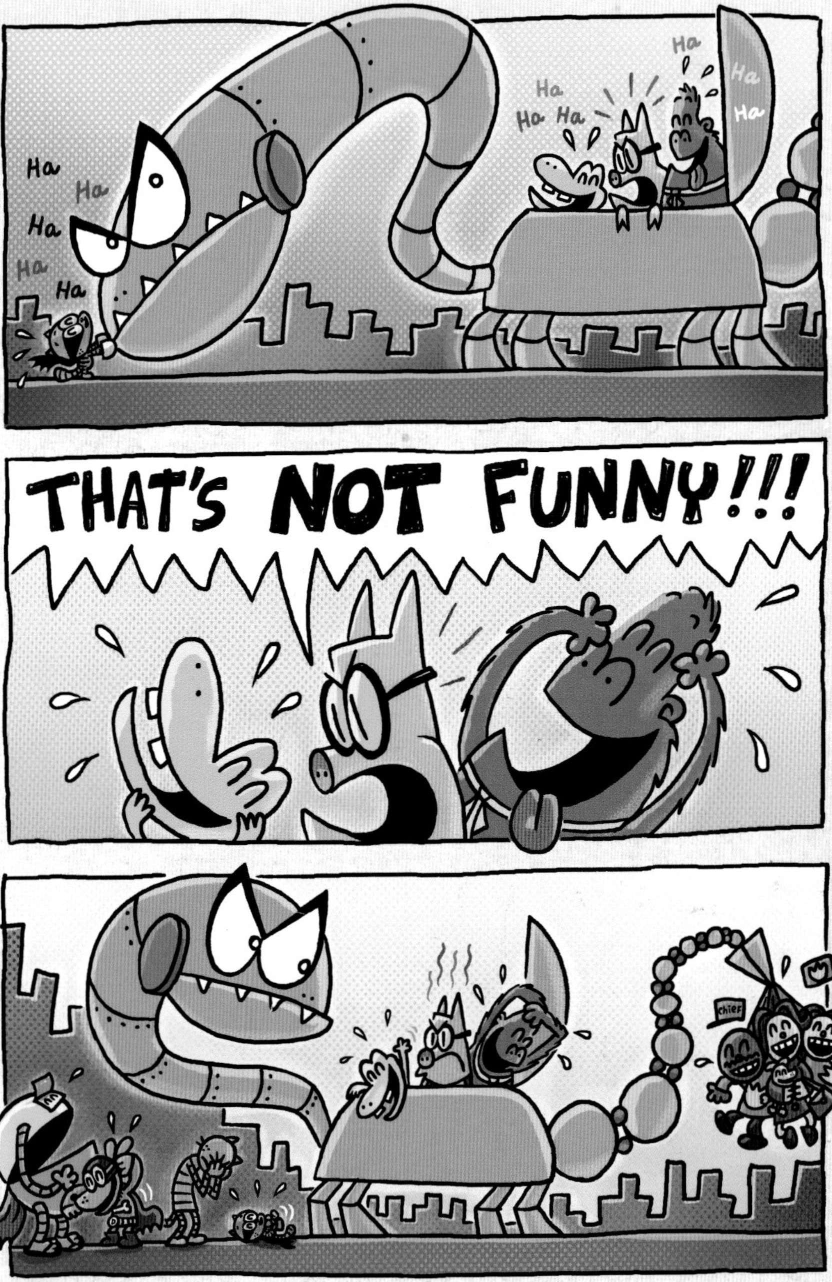
Ha
Ha
Ha
Ha
Ha
Ha
Ha Ha
Ha
Ha
Ha
THAT'S NOT FUNNY!!!
chief

Hey, you were right!

That **WAS** a funny story!

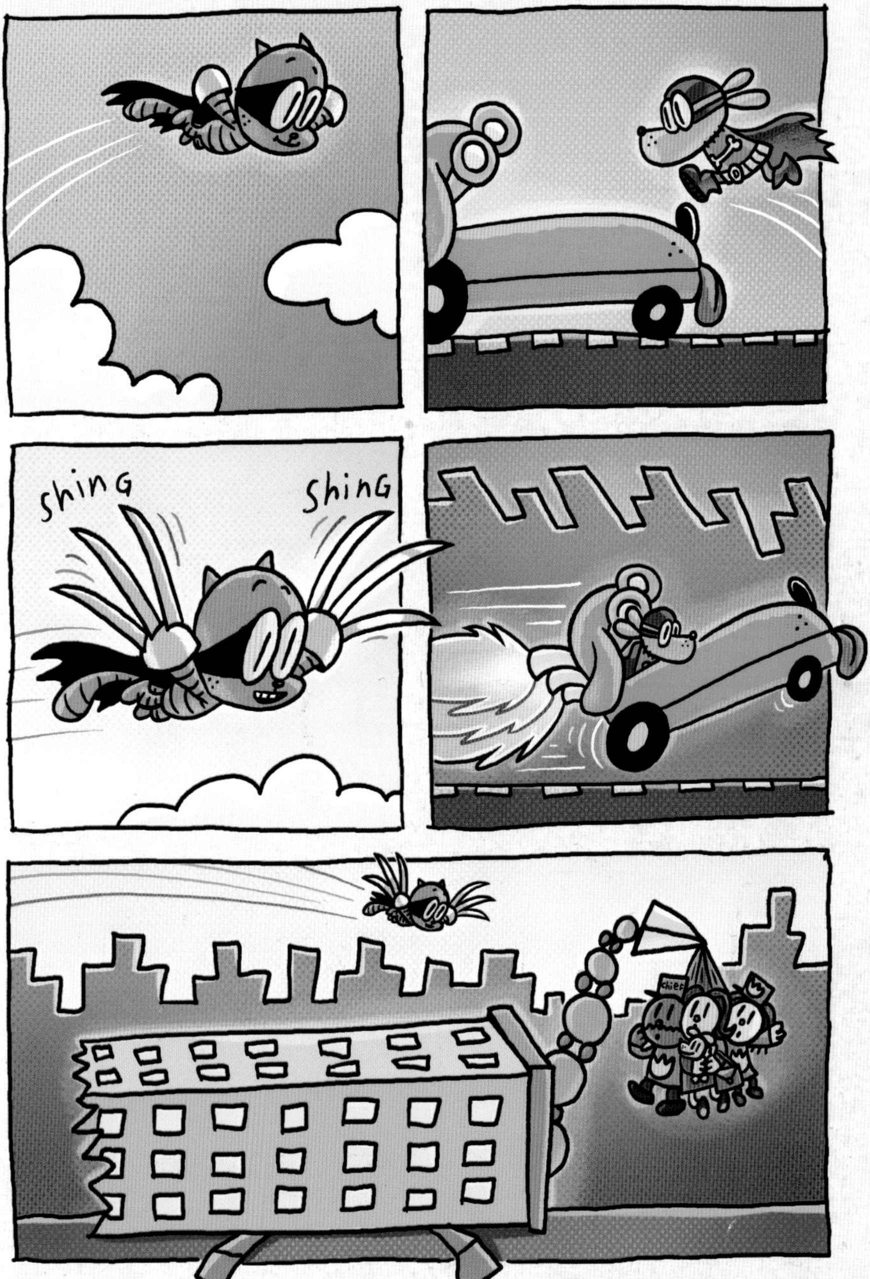
shing
shing

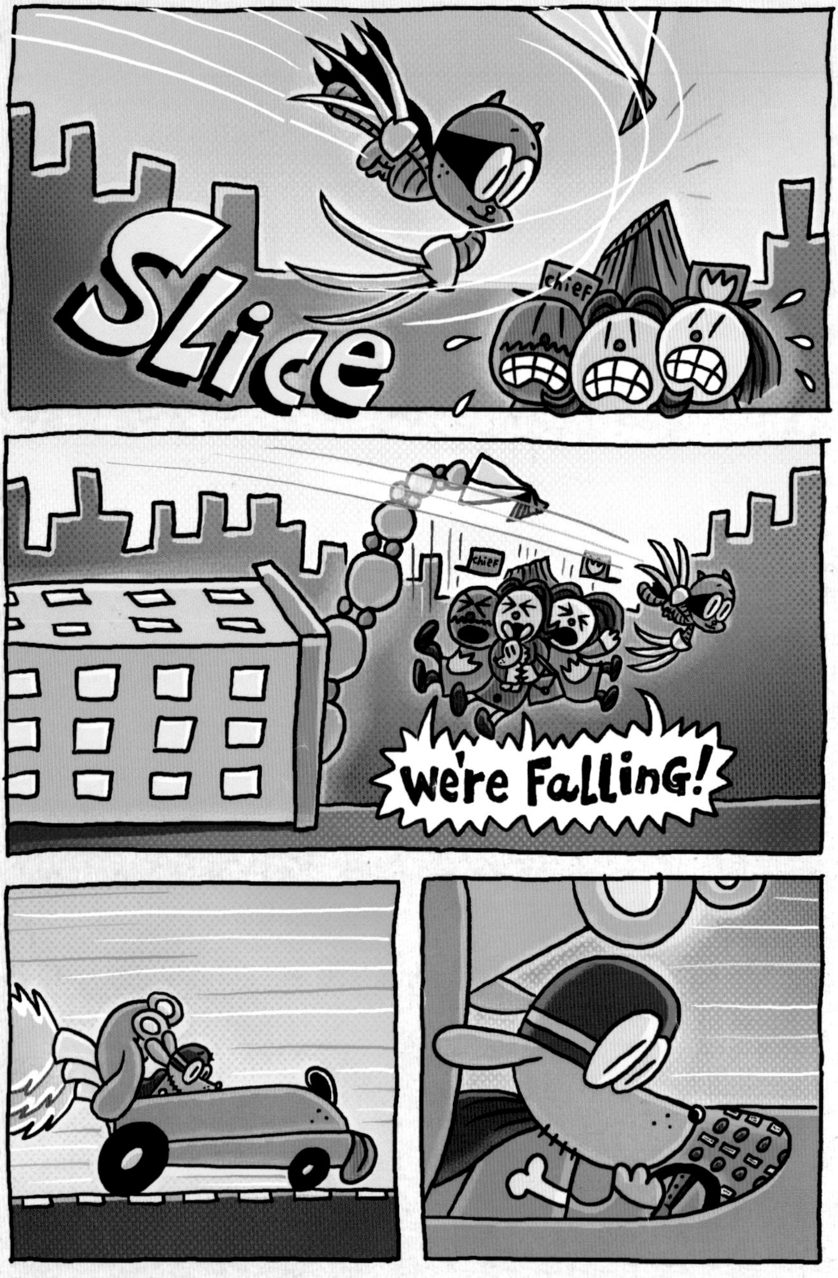
SLICE
CHIEF
CHIEF
WE'RE FALLING!

We're STILL FALLING!

And I'm about to crash into the ground!!!

PLOOF!

Good catch, the Bark Knight!

Well, when you think about it...

None of us existed for trillions of years **BEFORE** we were born...

..And we didn't seem to mind it then!

Yeah--- I didn't even notice!!!!!

True dat!

Let's not cry 'cuz we're Gonna die. Let's Laugh 'cuz we Got to **LiVE!!!**

Ha-Ha!

Yeah! Ha-Ha!

FACTORY

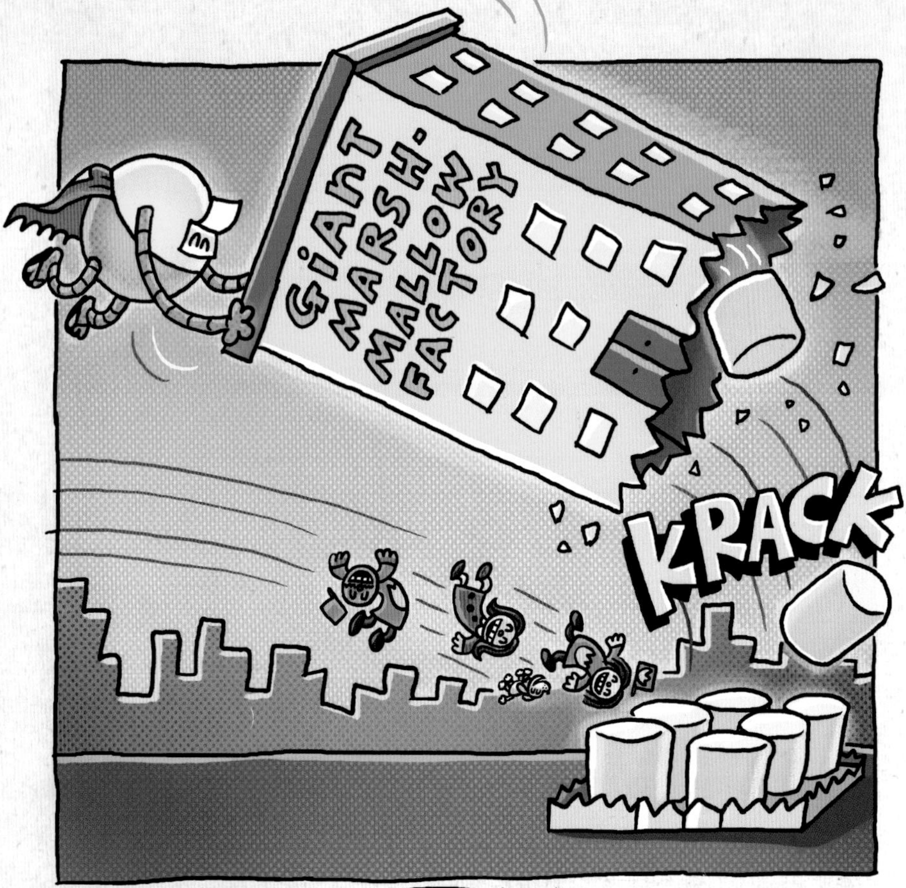
GIANT MARSH-MALLOW FACTORY
KRACK

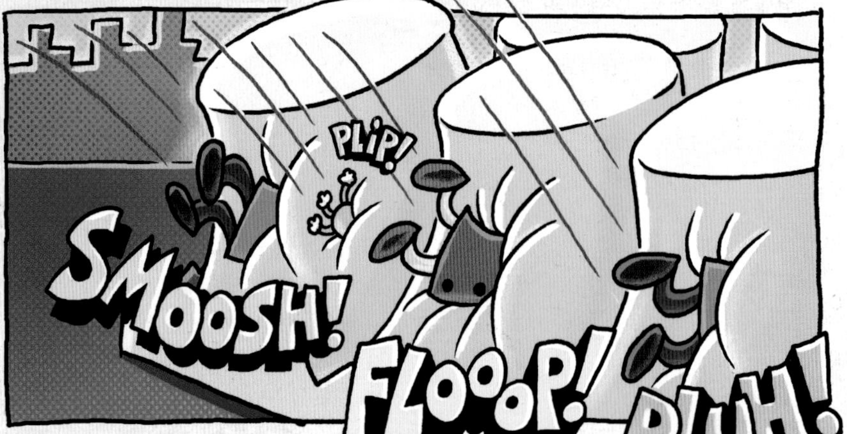
PLIP!
SMOOSH!
FLOOOOP!
PLUH!

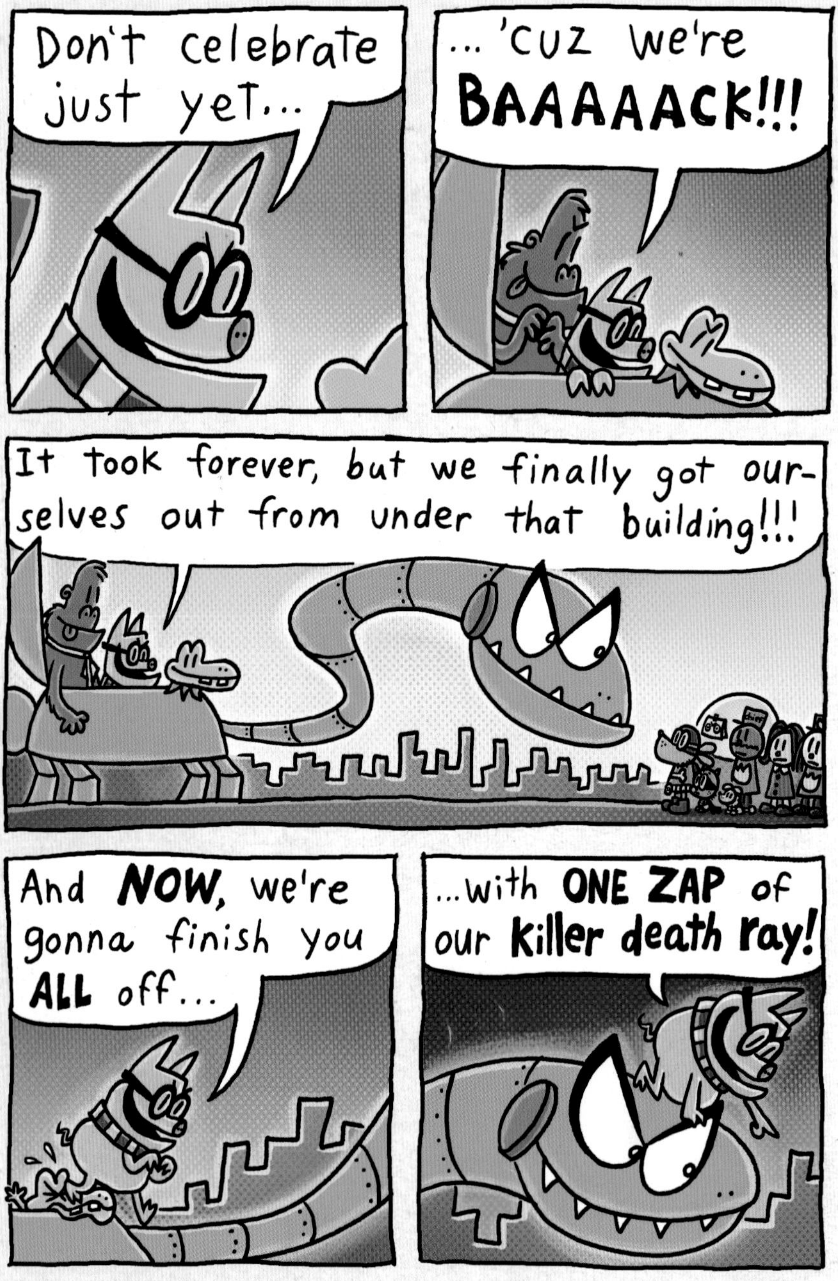
Don't celebrate just yet...
...'cuz we're BAAAAACK!!!
It took forever, but we finally got ourselves out from under that building!!!
And NOW, we're gonna finish you ALL off...
...with ONE ZAP of our Killer death ray!

So you'd better say "Goodbye!"

Bye-bye, Dog Man!

So Long, Sarah!

Au revoir, Zuzu!

Adiós, Milly!

We love you, 80-HD!

WOULD YOU GUYS STOP BEING SO PLEASANT ABOUT EVERYTHING?!?

GO ON, ZAP 'em!

ZAP

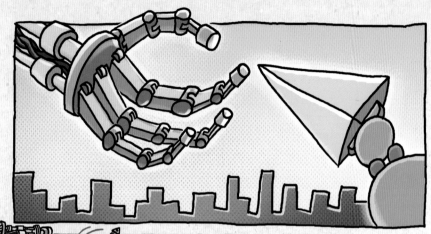

YANK!

Looks like we're gonna have a Giant Robo-Battle...

...IN FLIP-O-RAMA!

Left hand here.

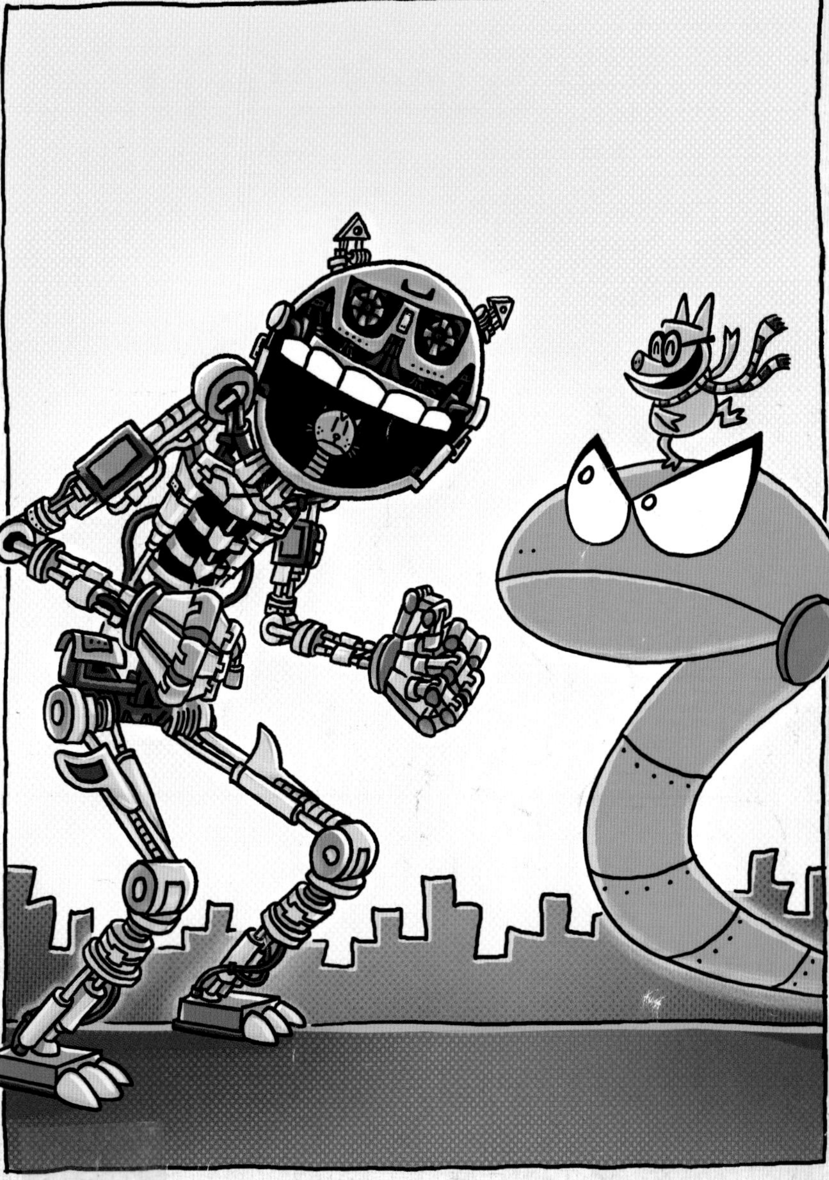

Right Thumb here.

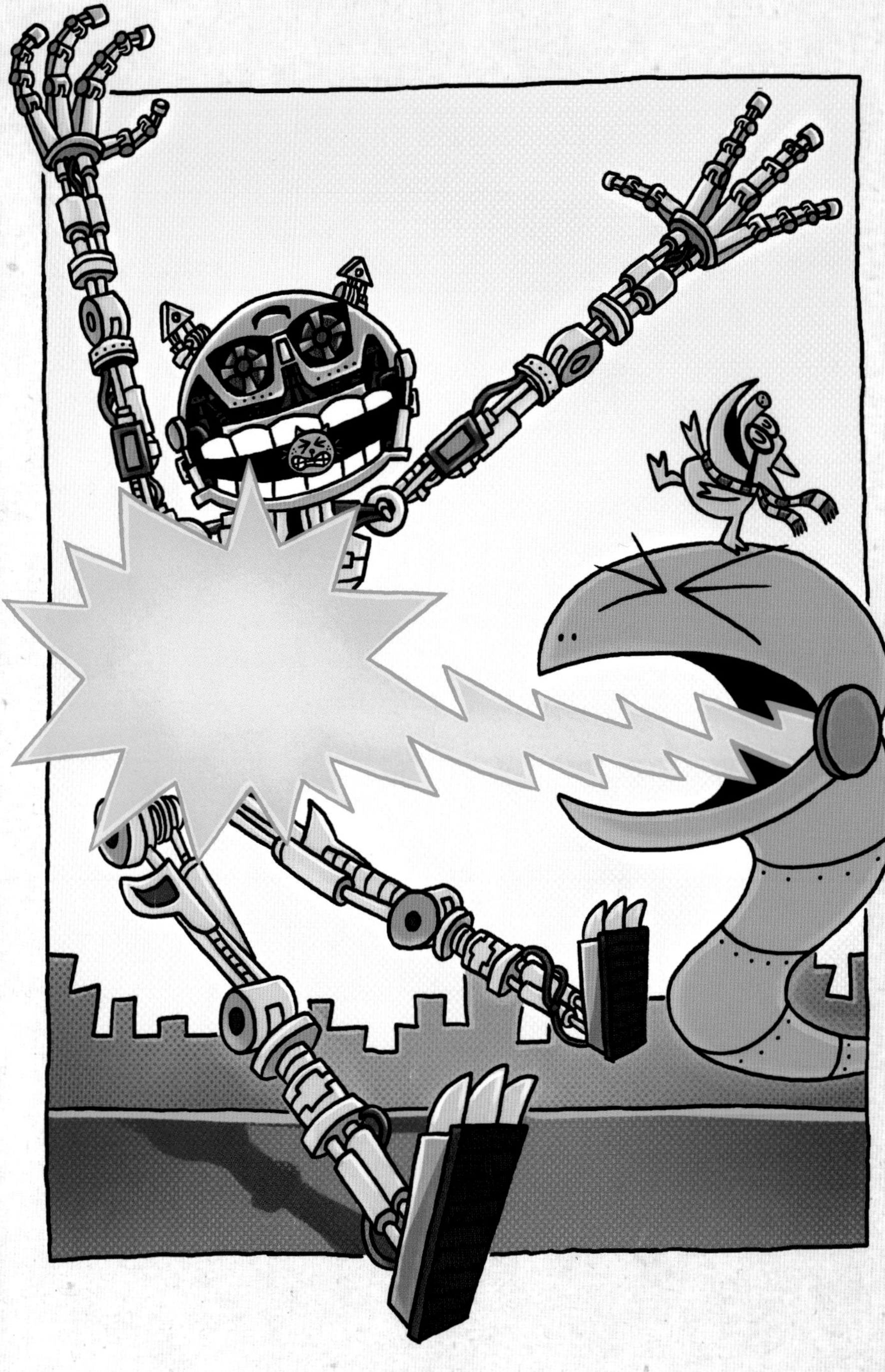

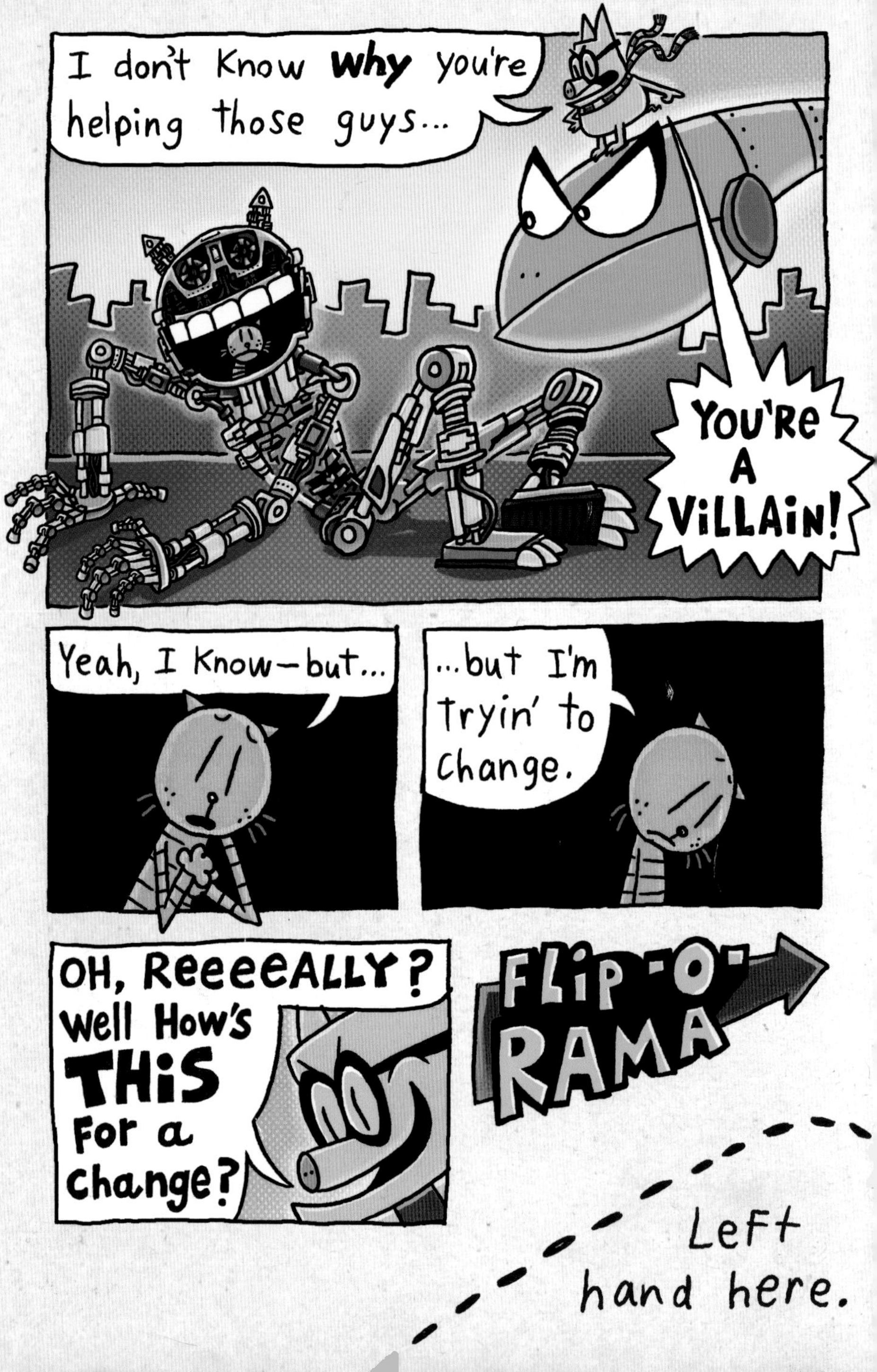
I don't know why you're helping those guys...
YOU'RE A VILLAIN!
Yeah, I know—but...
...but I'm tryin' to change.
OH, REEEEEALLY? Well how's THIS for a change?
FLIP-O-RAMA
Left hand here.

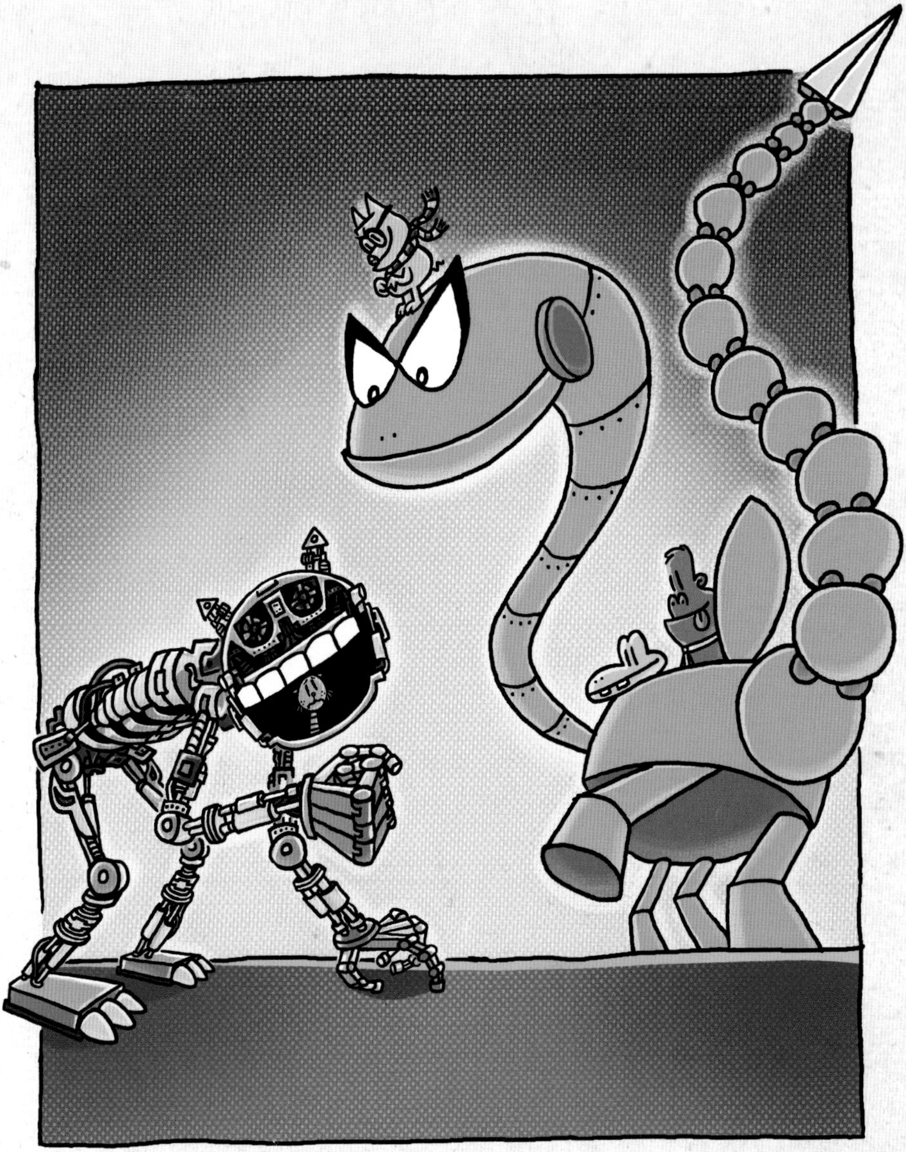

Right
Thumb
here.

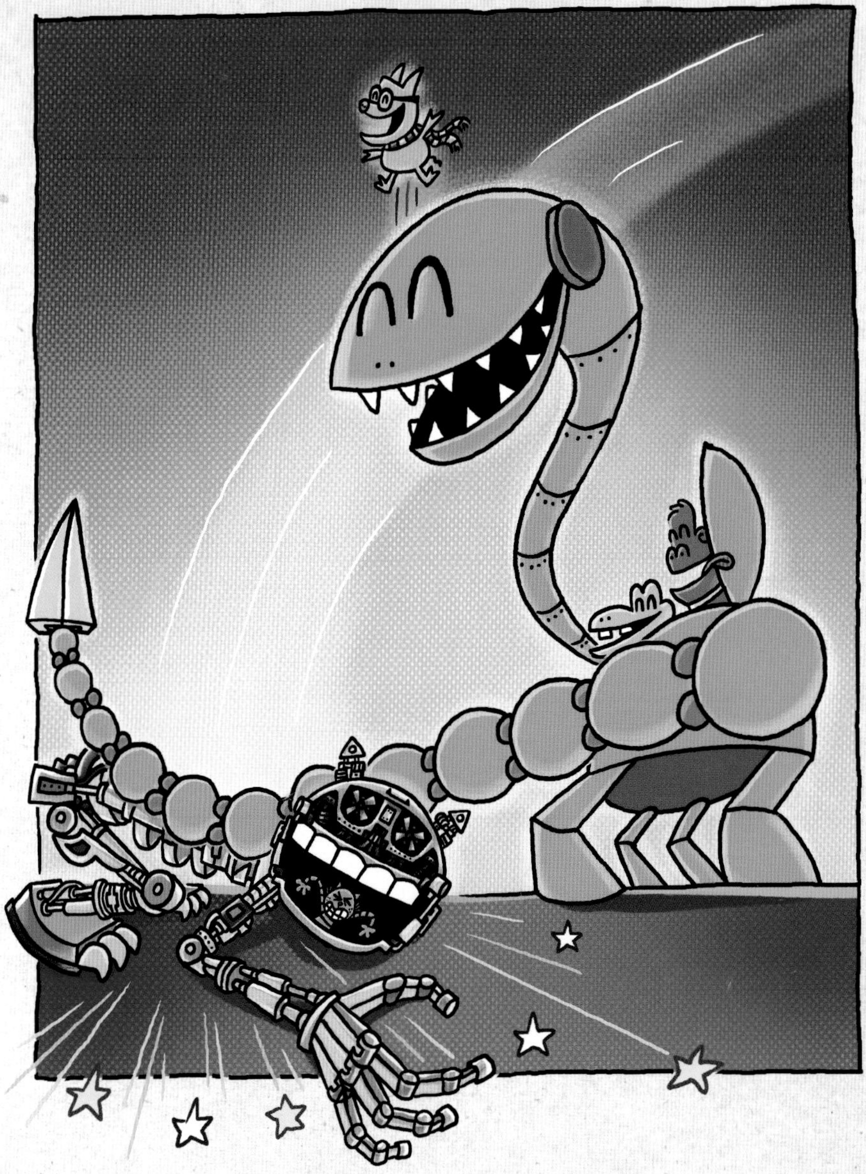

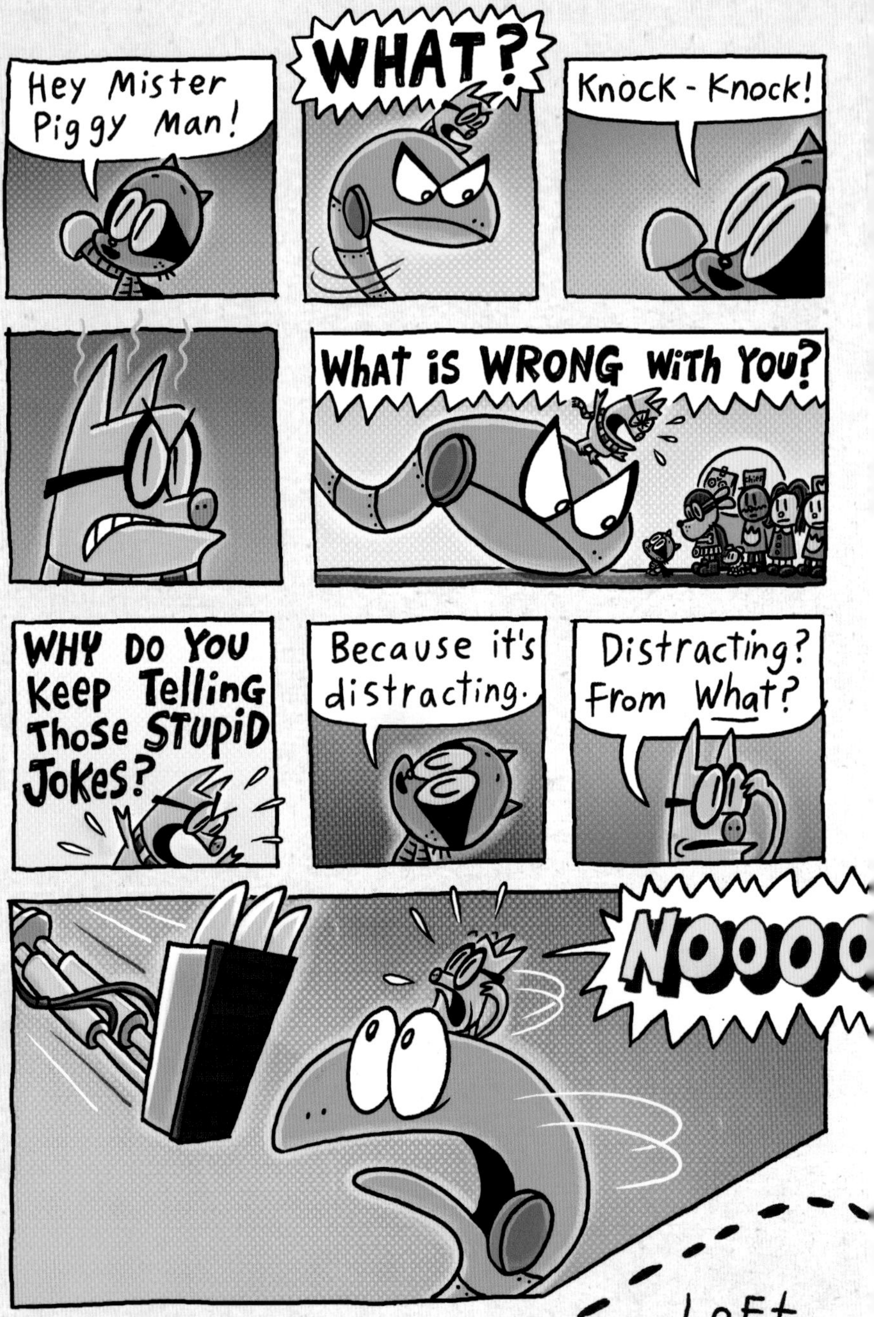
Hey Mister Piggy Man!
WHAT?
Knock-Knock!
What is WRONG With You?
WHY DO YOU Keep Telling Those STUPID Jokes?
Because it's distracting.
Distracting? From What?
NOOOO

Left hand here.

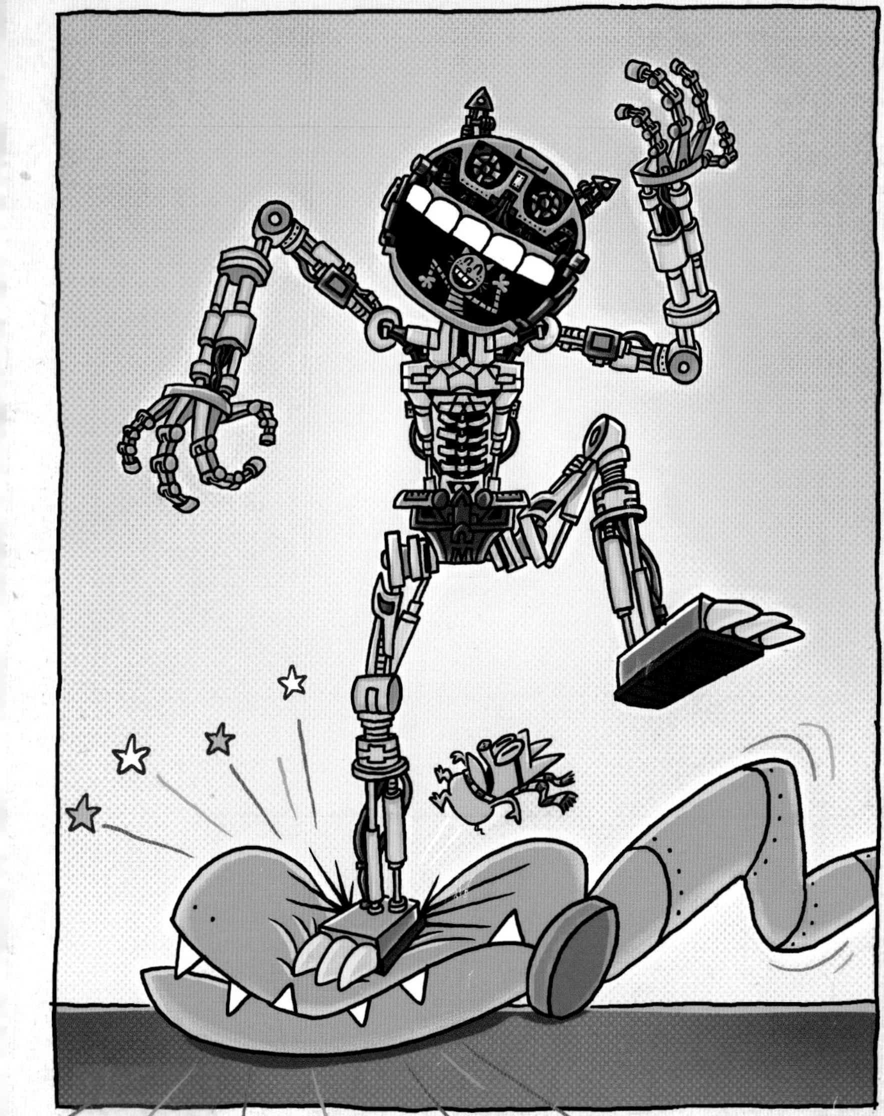

Right Thumb here.

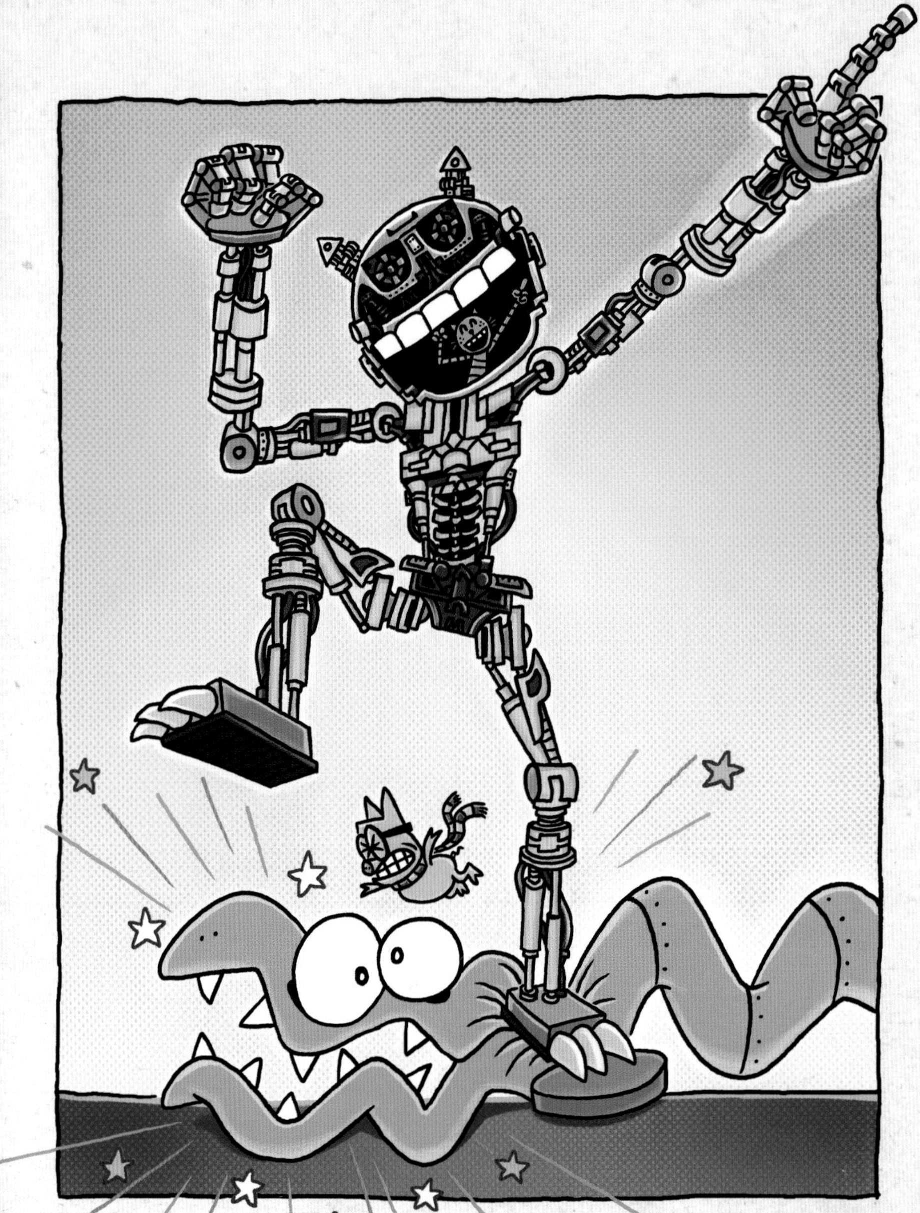

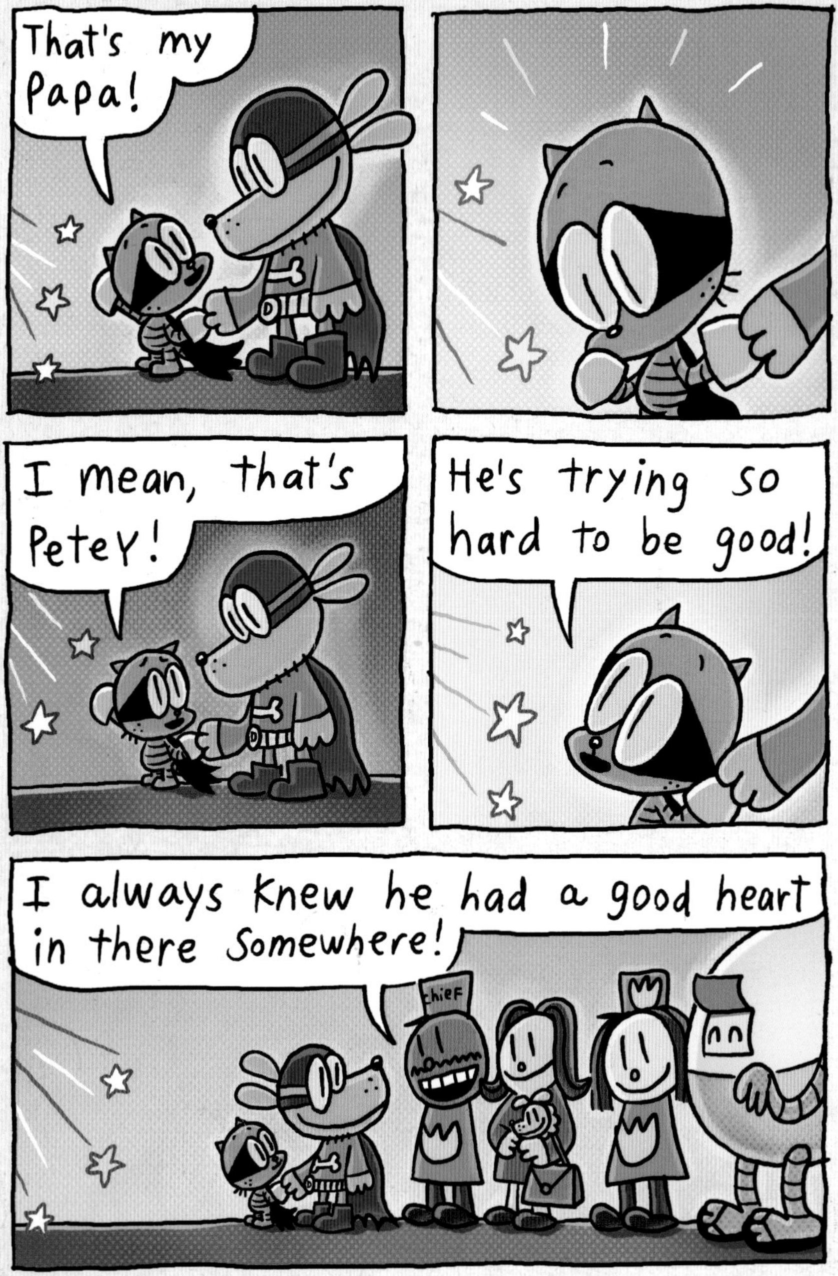

That's my Papa!
I mean, that's Petey!
He's trying so hard to be good!
I always knew he had a good heart in there Somewhere!
chief

Chapter 7
The Darkness

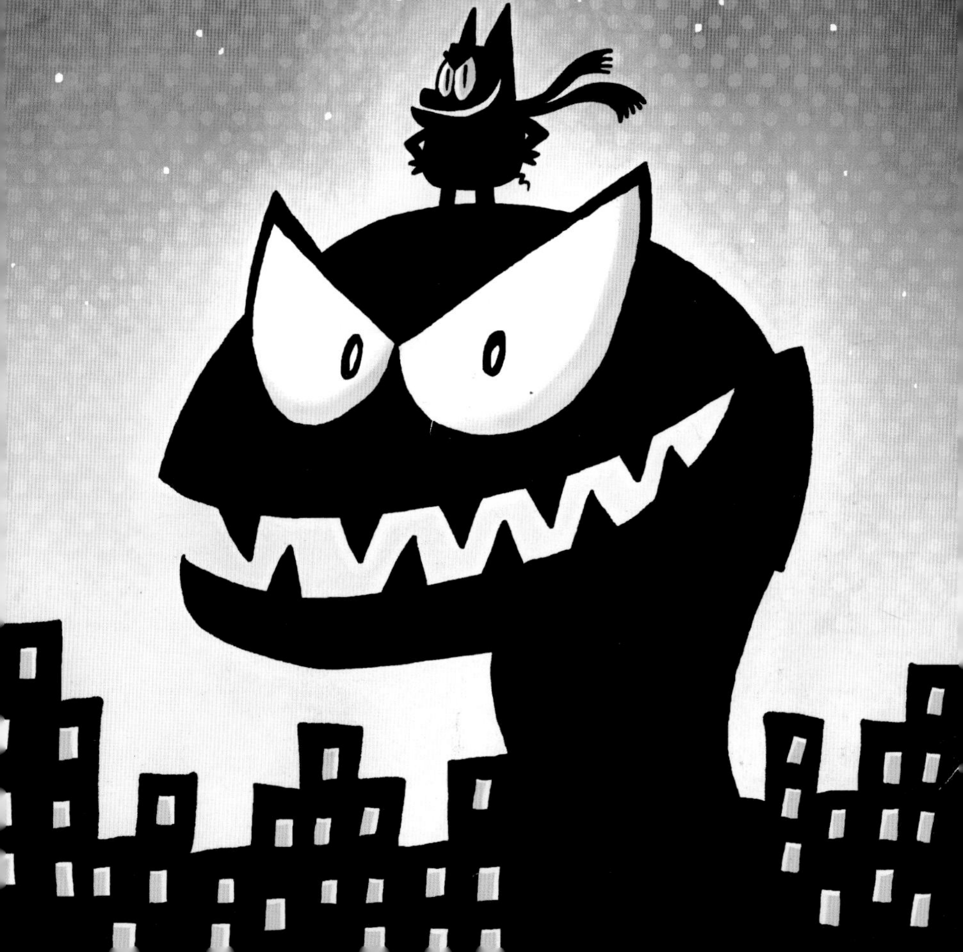

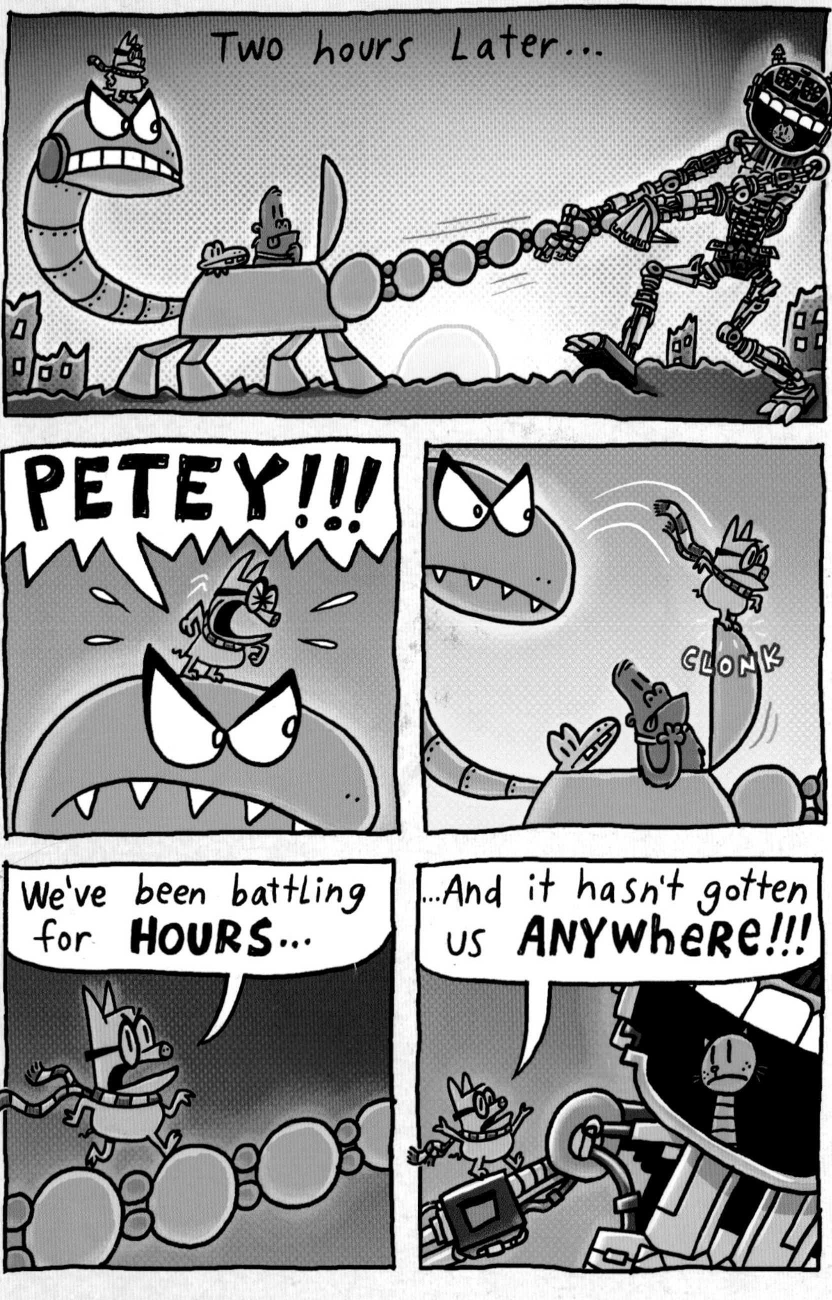
Two hours Later...
PETEY!!!
CLONK
We've been battling for HOURS...
...And it hasn't gotten us ANYWHERE!!!

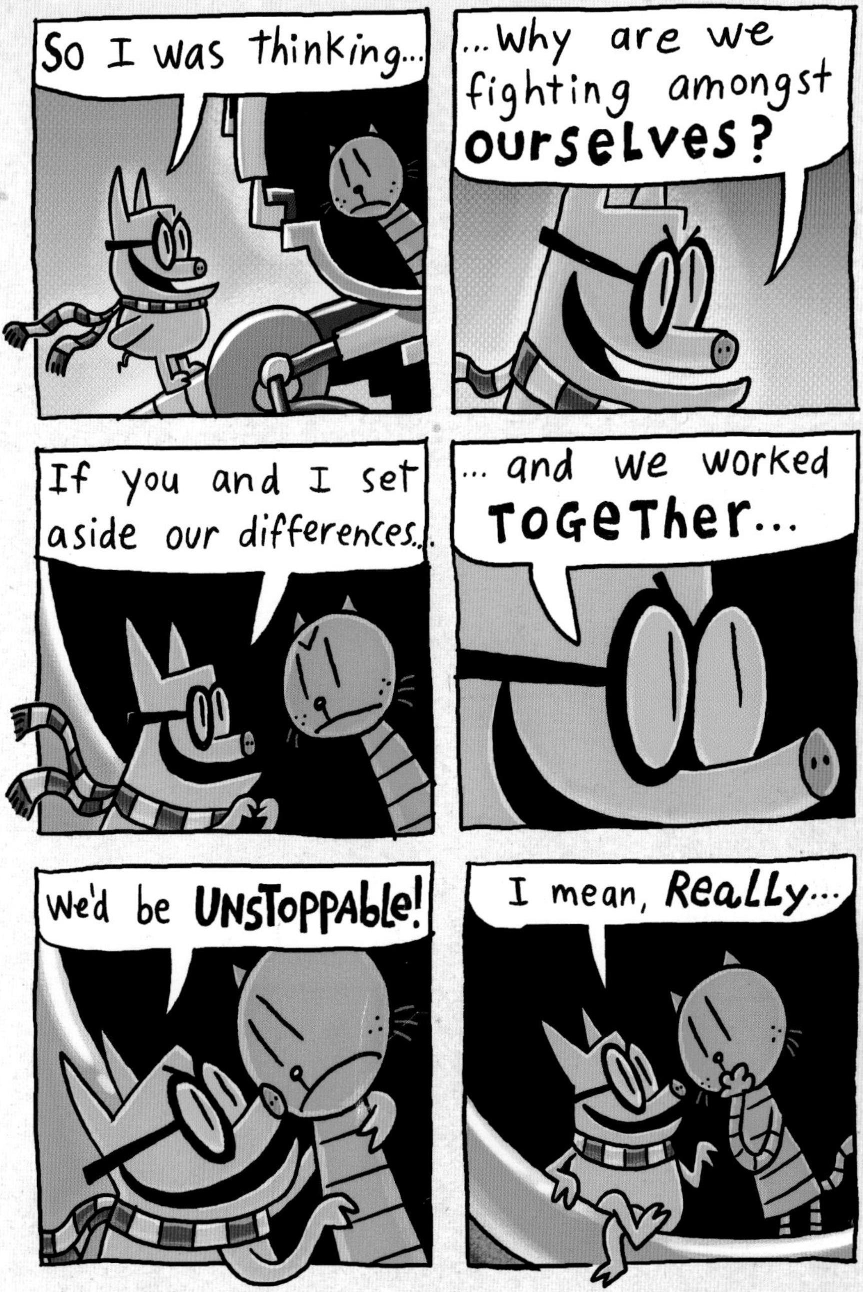
So I was thinking...
...Why are we fighting amongst ourselves?
If you and I set aside our differences...
... and we worked TOGETHER...
We'd be UNSTOPPABLE!
I mean, REALLY...

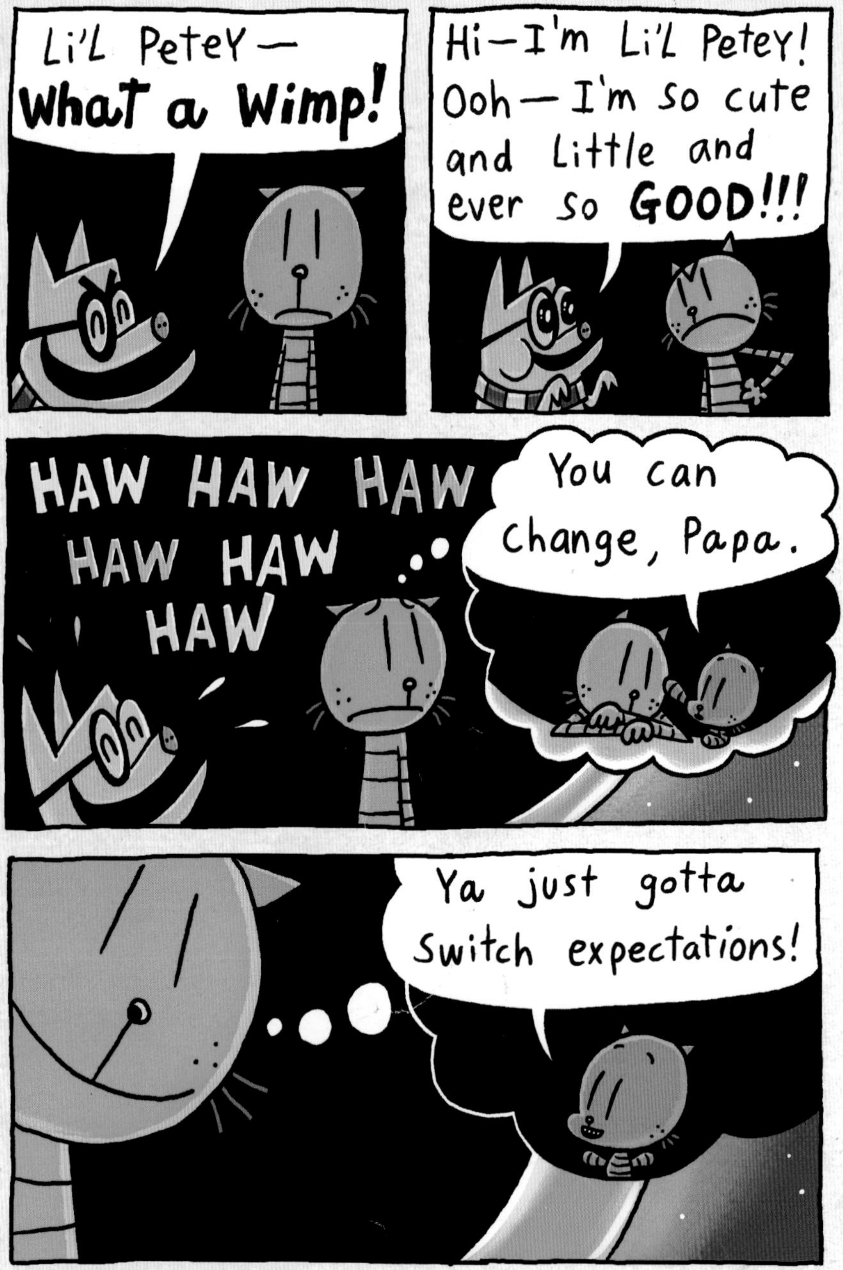
Li'L Petey—
What a Wimp!
Hi—I'm Li'L Petey! Ooh—I'm so cute and Little and ever so GOOD!!!
HAW HAW HAW HAW HAW HAW
You can change, Papa.
Ya just gotta switch expectations!

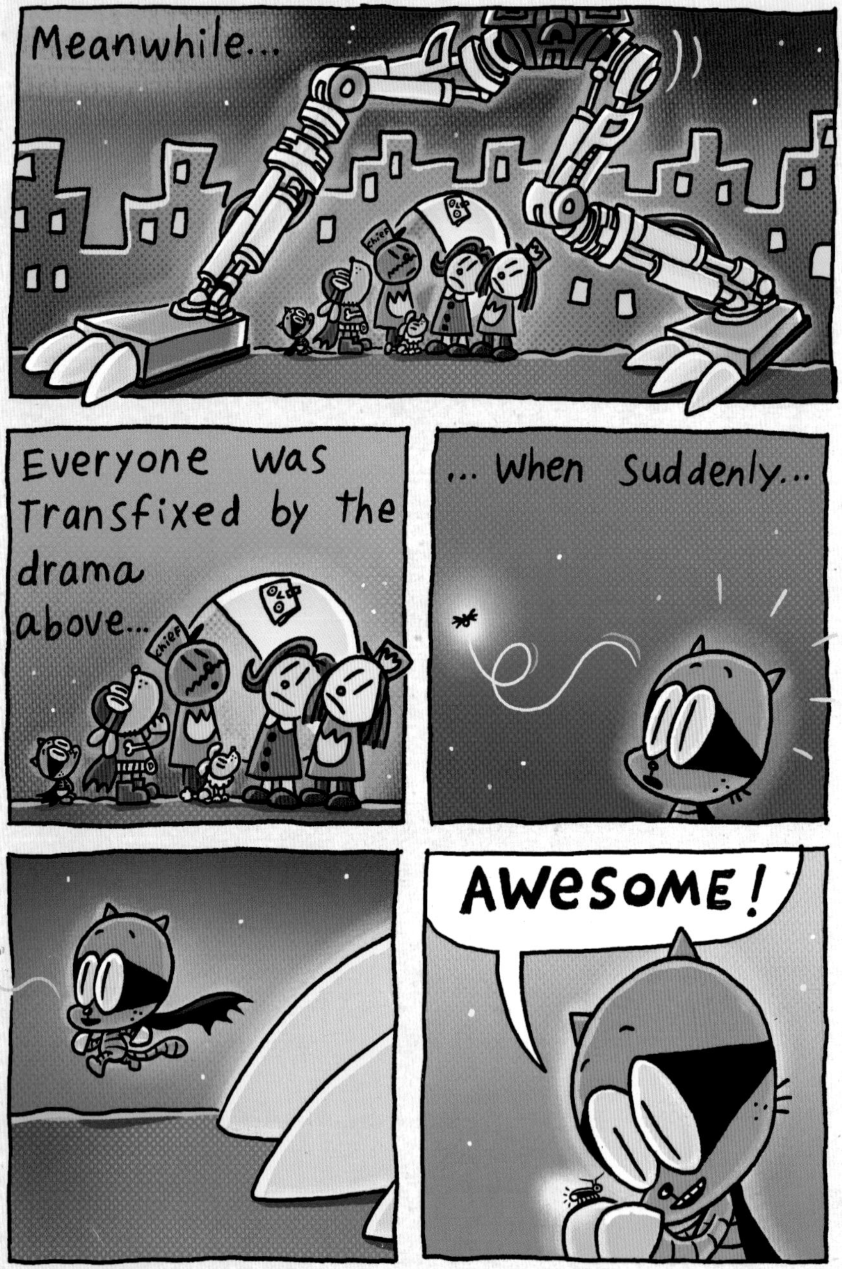
Meanwhile...
Everyone was Transfixed by the drama above...
... When suddenly...
AWESOME!

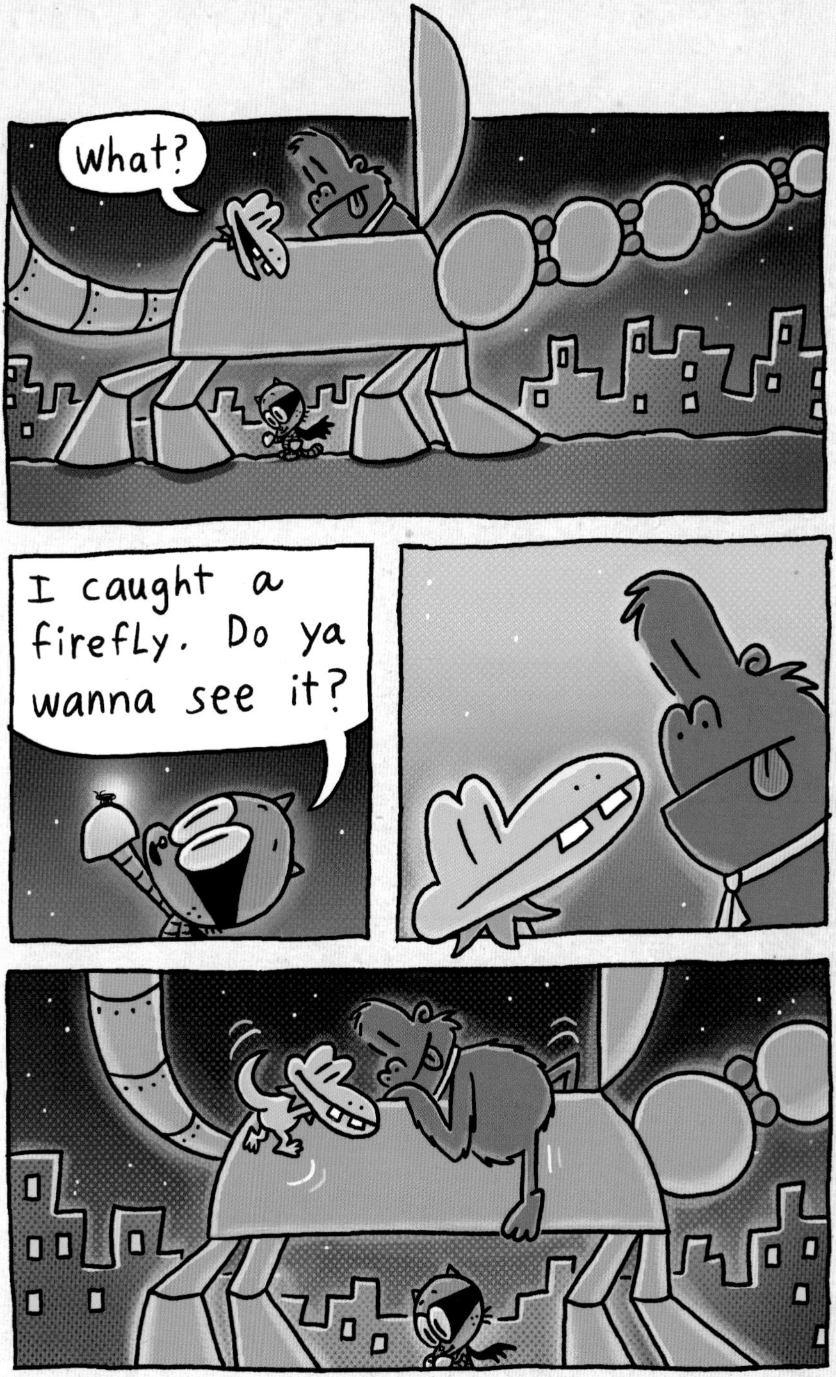
What?
I caught a firefly. Do ya wanna see it?

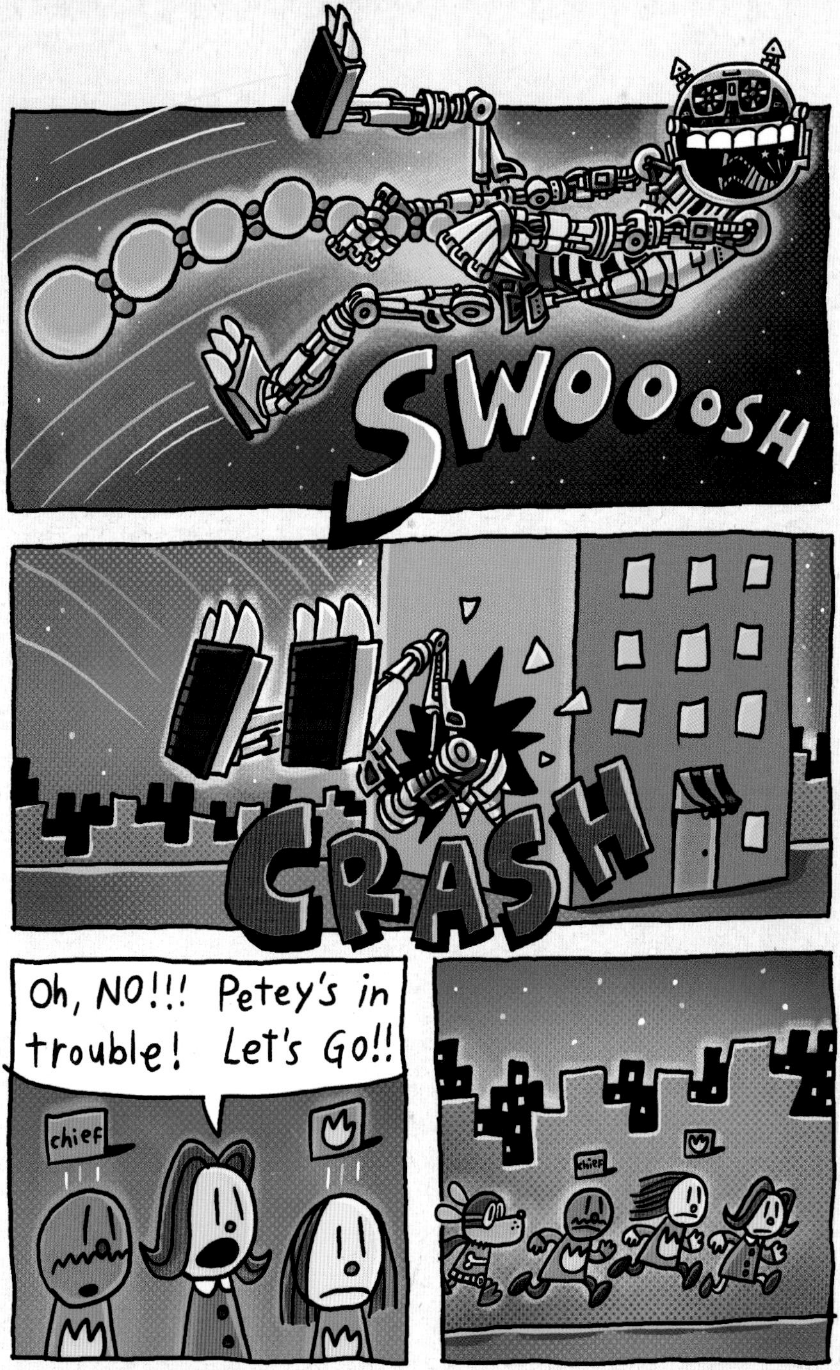
SWOOOOSH
CRASH
Oh, NO!!! Petey's in trouble! Let's Go!!
chief
chief

Well, well, Well...

All of my **Enemies** Are together in **ONE PLACE!** How **CONVENIENT!!!**

OH, **CRUNKY!** OH, **BUB!!!**

CRUNKY! BUB!!!

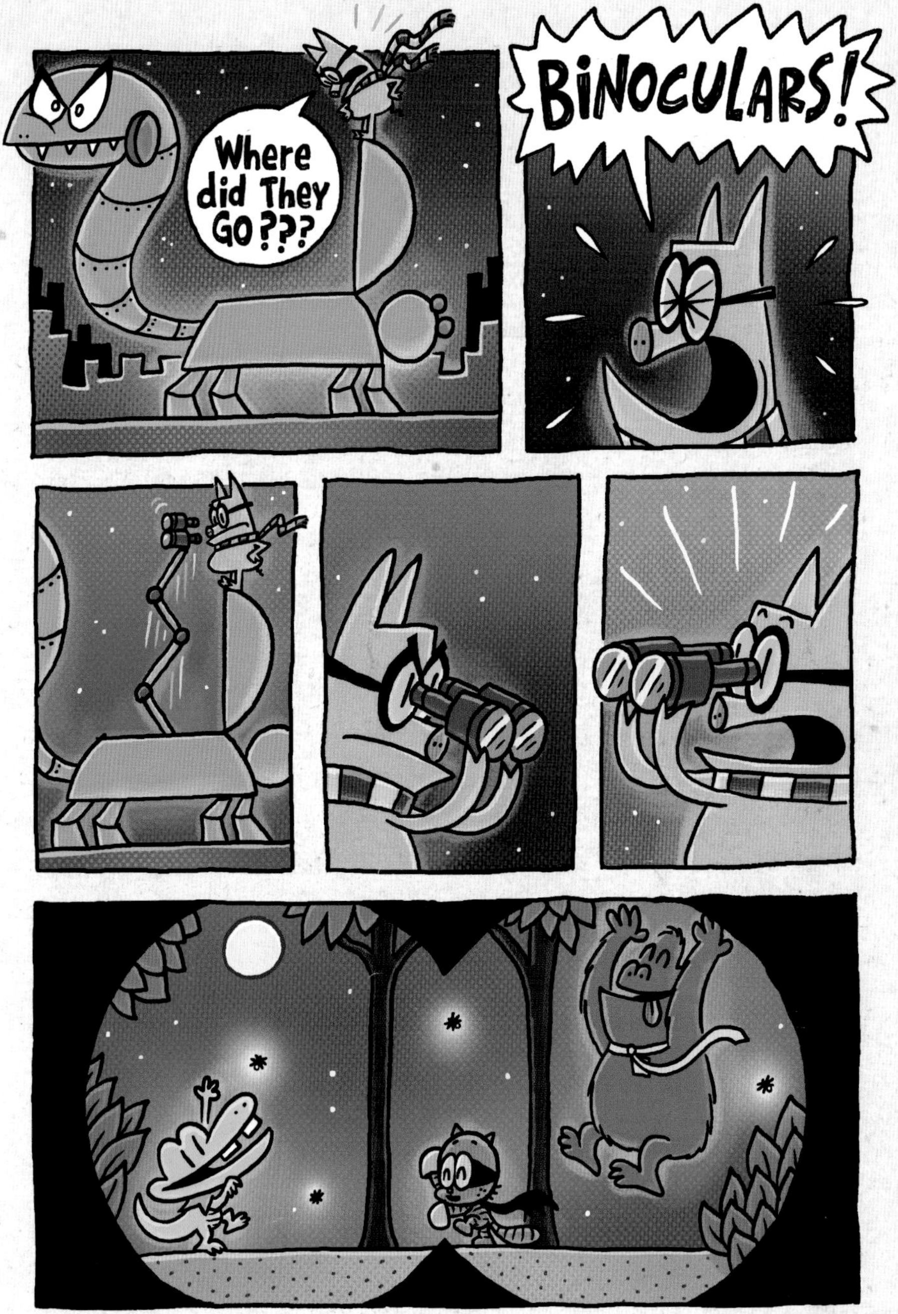
Where did They GO???
BiNOCULARS!

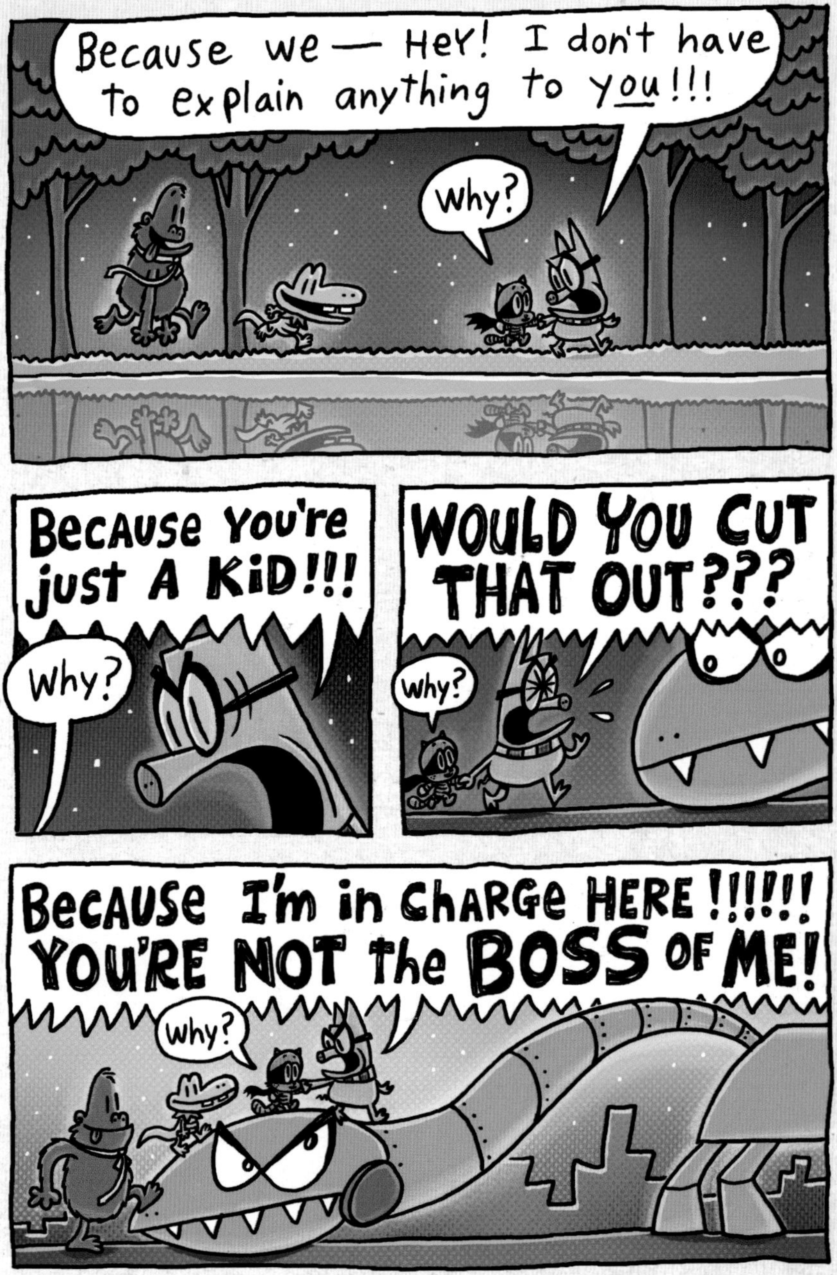
Because we— HEY! I don't have to explain anything to you!!!
Why?
Because you're just A KID!!!
Why?
WOULD YOU CUT THAT OUT???
Why?
Because I'm in CHARGE HERE!!!!!! YOU'RE NOT the BOSS OF ME!
Why?

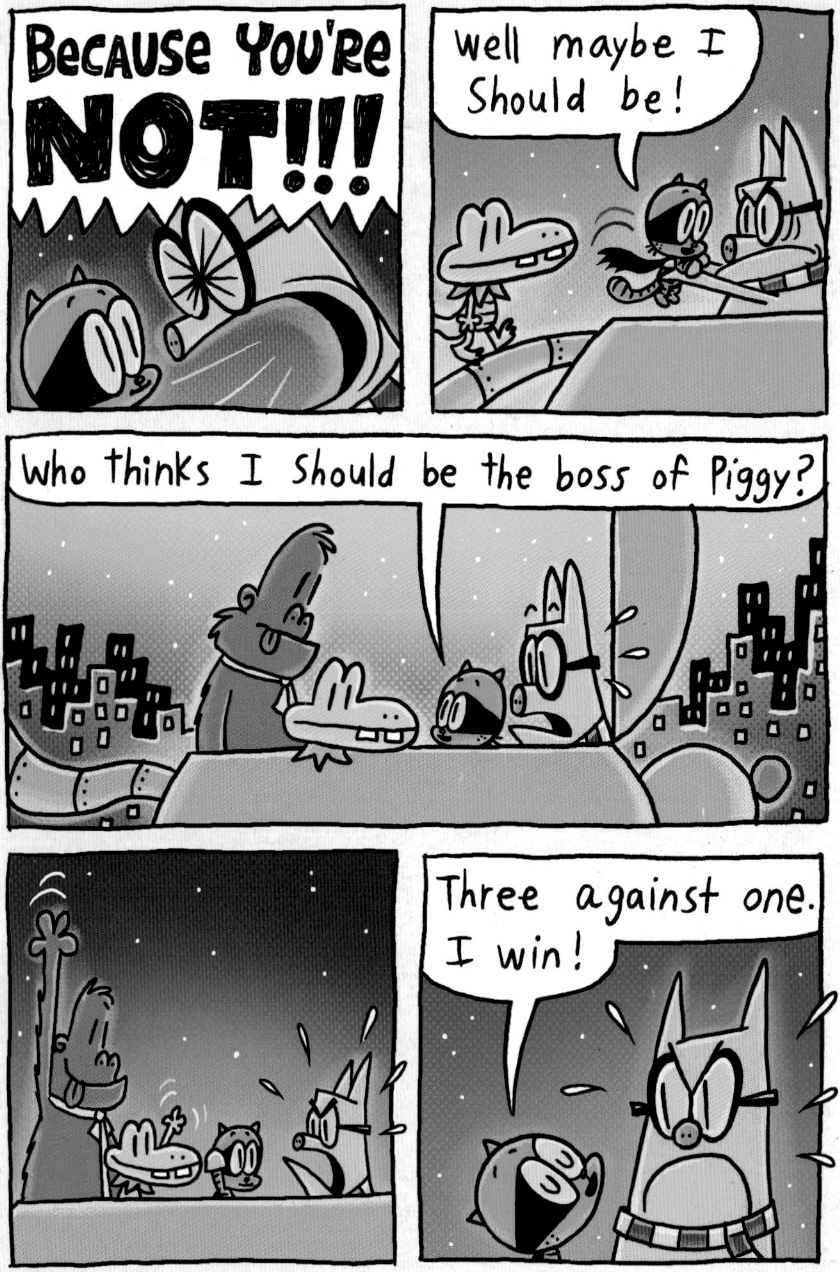
BECAUSE YOU'RE NOT!!!
Well maybe I Should be!
Who thinks I Should be the boss of Piggy?
Three against one. I win!

I – I can't believe you guys saved me!

We're the good guys, Petey!

That's what we do!

But...

...Where's the Kid?

WHERE'S Li'L PETEY?

I'm up here, playin' with the bad guys!

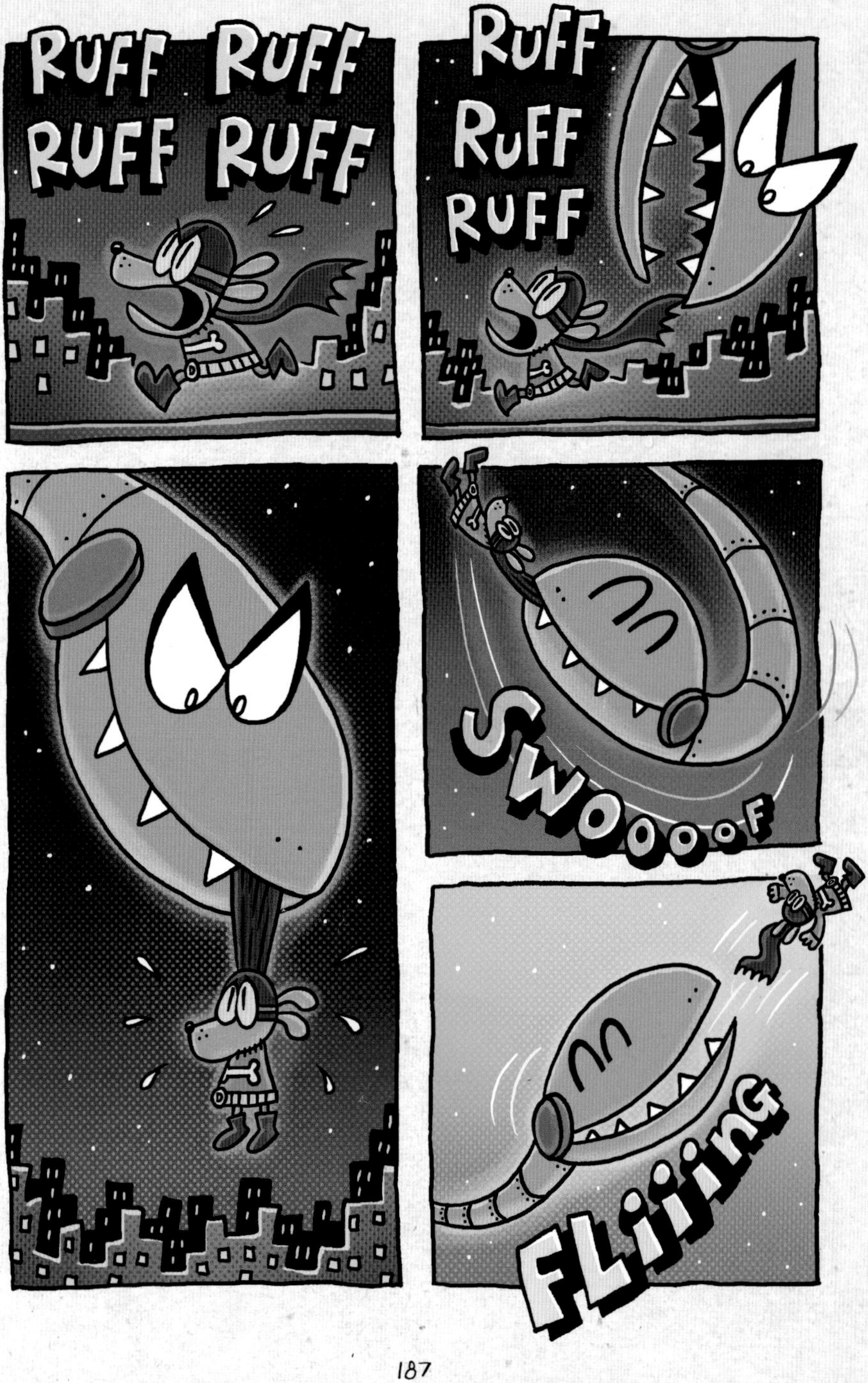

RUFF RUFF
RUFF RUFF
RUFF
RUFF
RUFF
SWOOOOF
FLiiinG

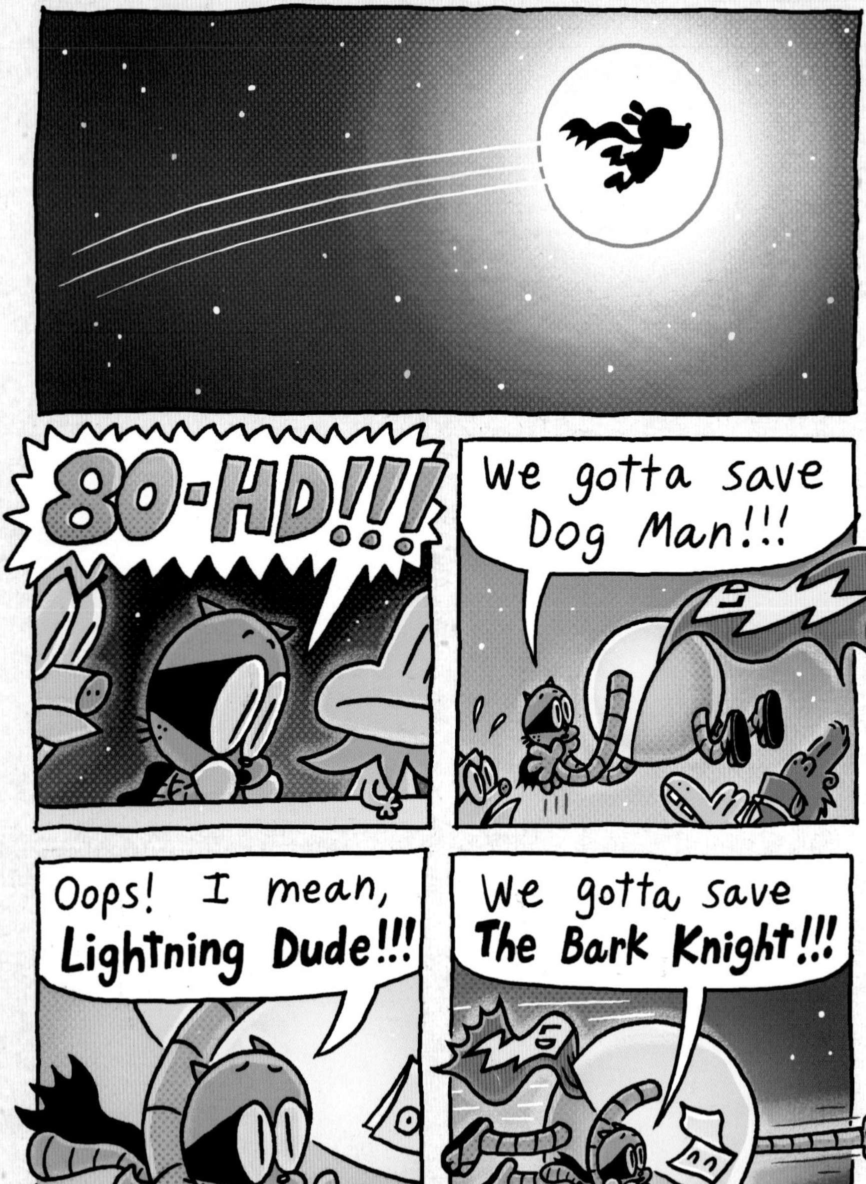
80-HD!!!
We gotta save Dog Man!!!
Oops! I mean, Lightning Dude!!!
We gotta save The Bark Knight!!!

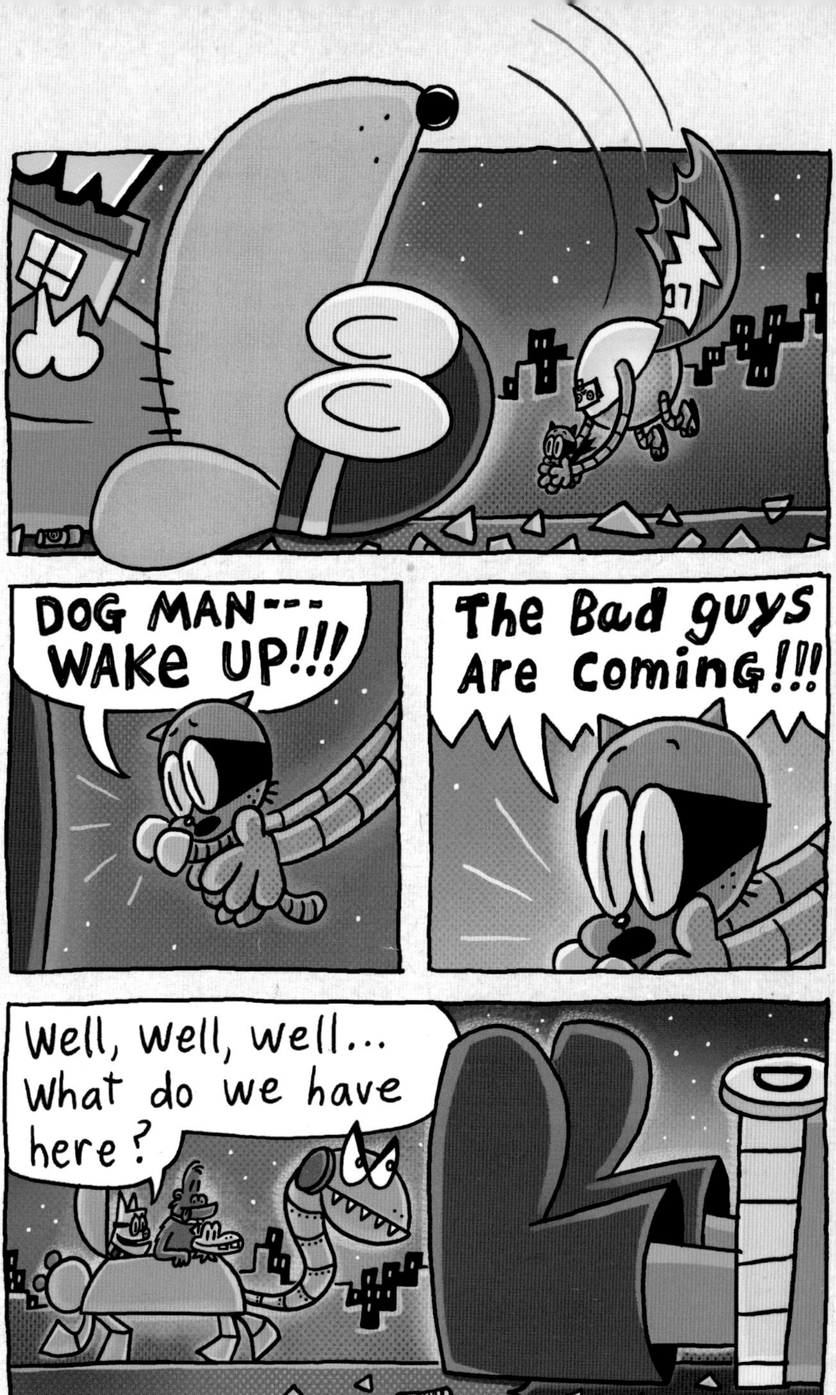
DOG MAN---
WAKE UP!!!
The Bad guys
Are Coming!!!
Well, well, well...
What do we have
here?

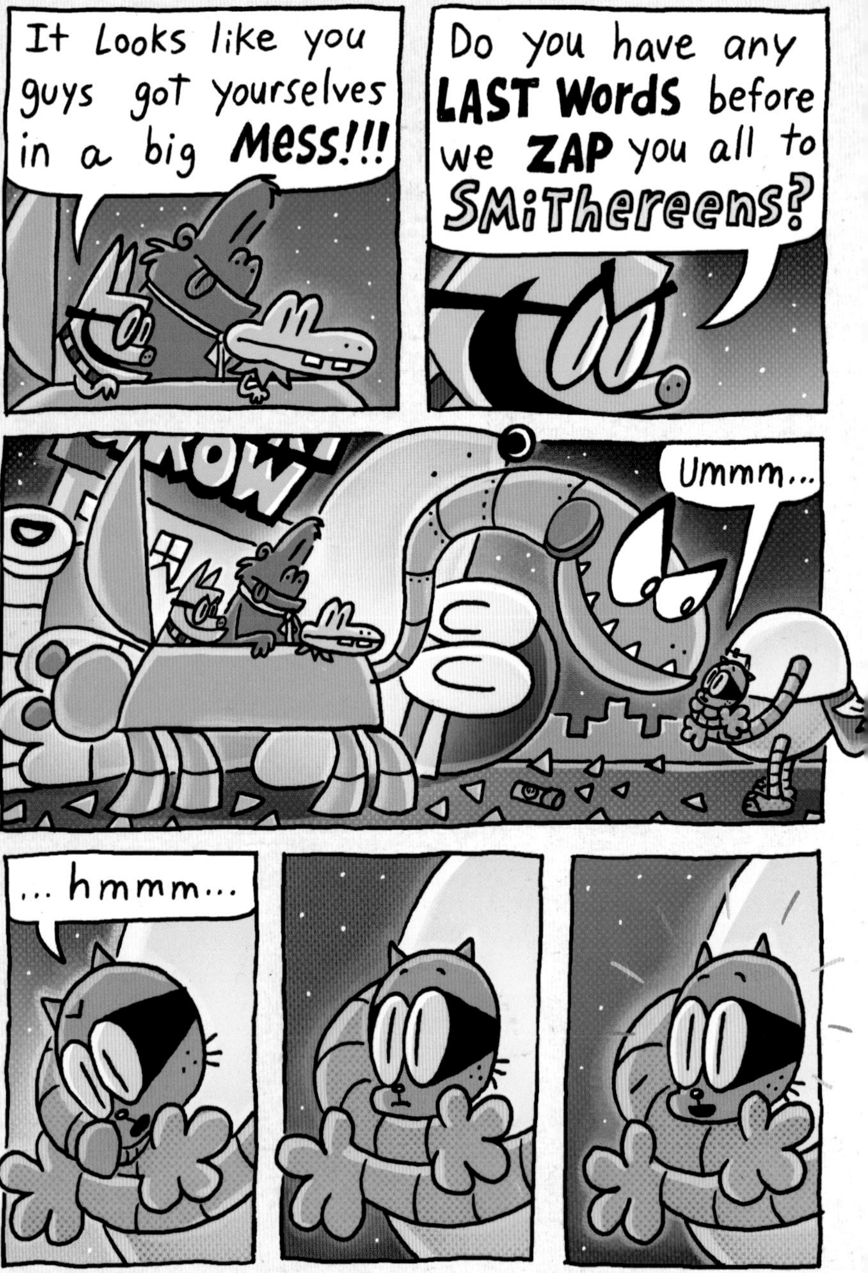
It Looks like you guys got yourselves in a big MESS!!!
Do you have any LAST Words before we ZAP you all to SMiThereeens?
Ummm...
... hmmm...

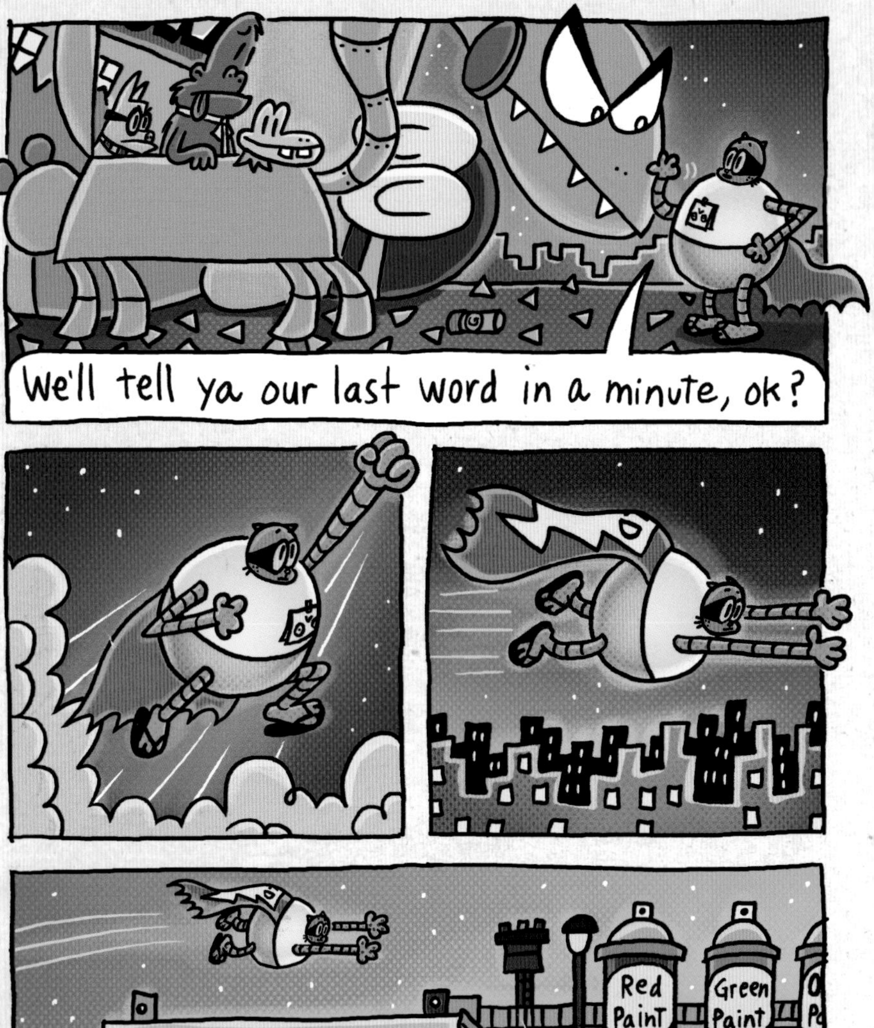
We'll tell ya our last word in a minute, ok?
MR. SQUIRTY'S SPRAY PAINT FACTORY
Red Paint
Green Paint

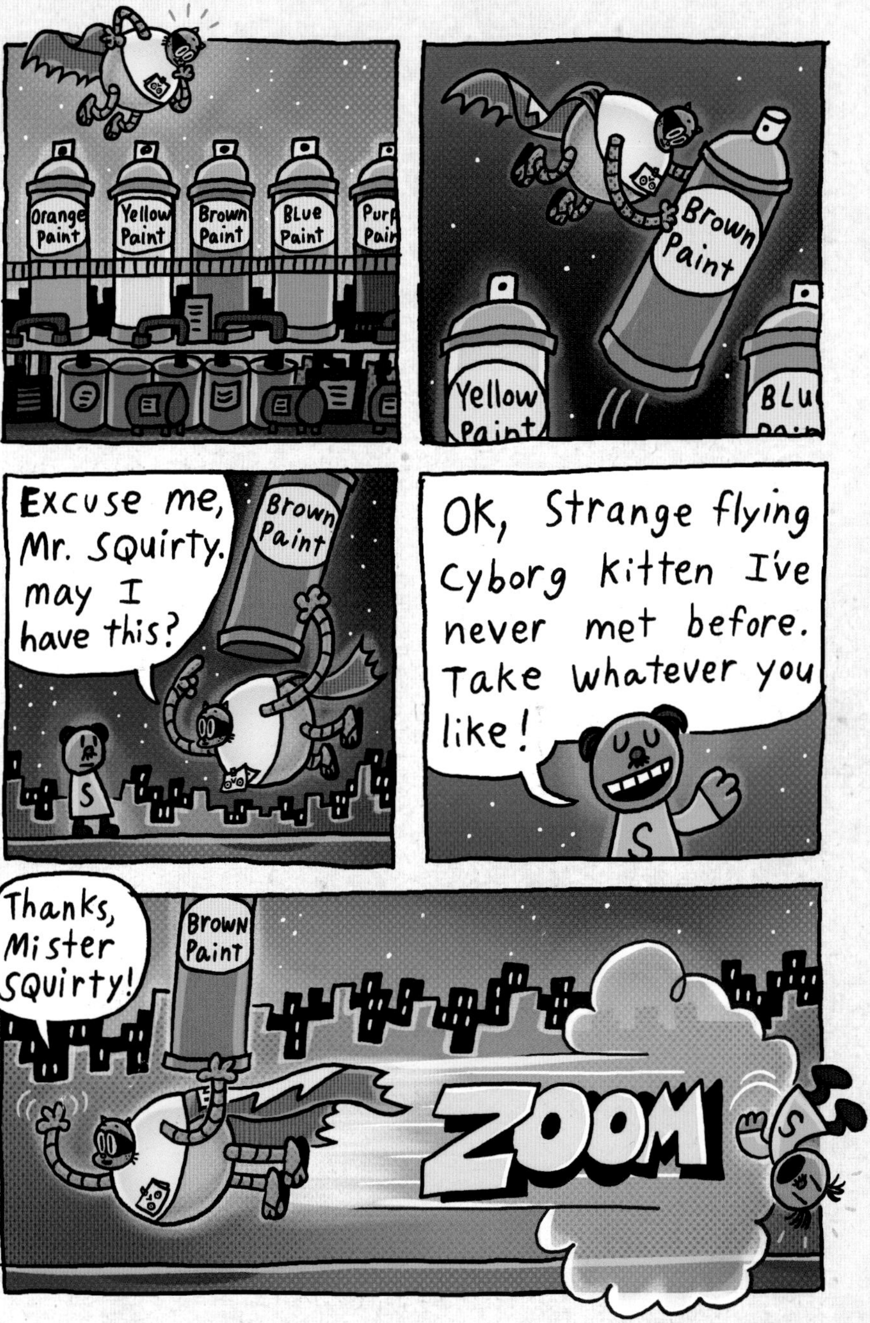
Orange Paint
Yellow Paint
Brown Paint
Blue Paint
Brown Paint
Yellow Paint
Excuse me, Mr. Squirty. may I have this?
Brown Paint
OK, Strange flying Cyborg kitten I've never met before. Take whatever you like!
Thanks, Mister Squirty!
Brown Paint
ZOOM

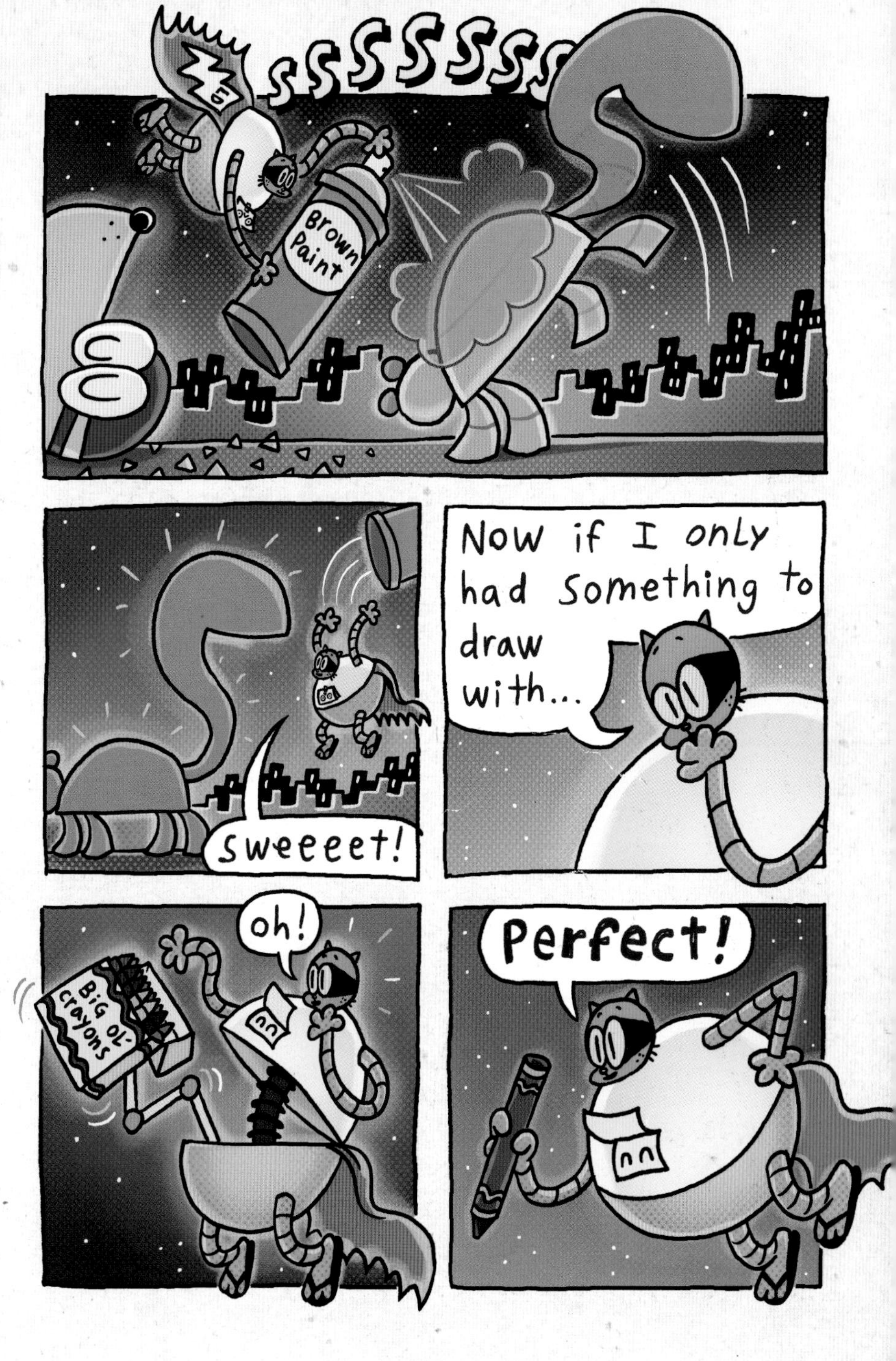
sSSSSSS
Brown Paint
sweeeet!
Now if I only had Something to draw with...
oh!
BiG OL' crayons
Perfect!

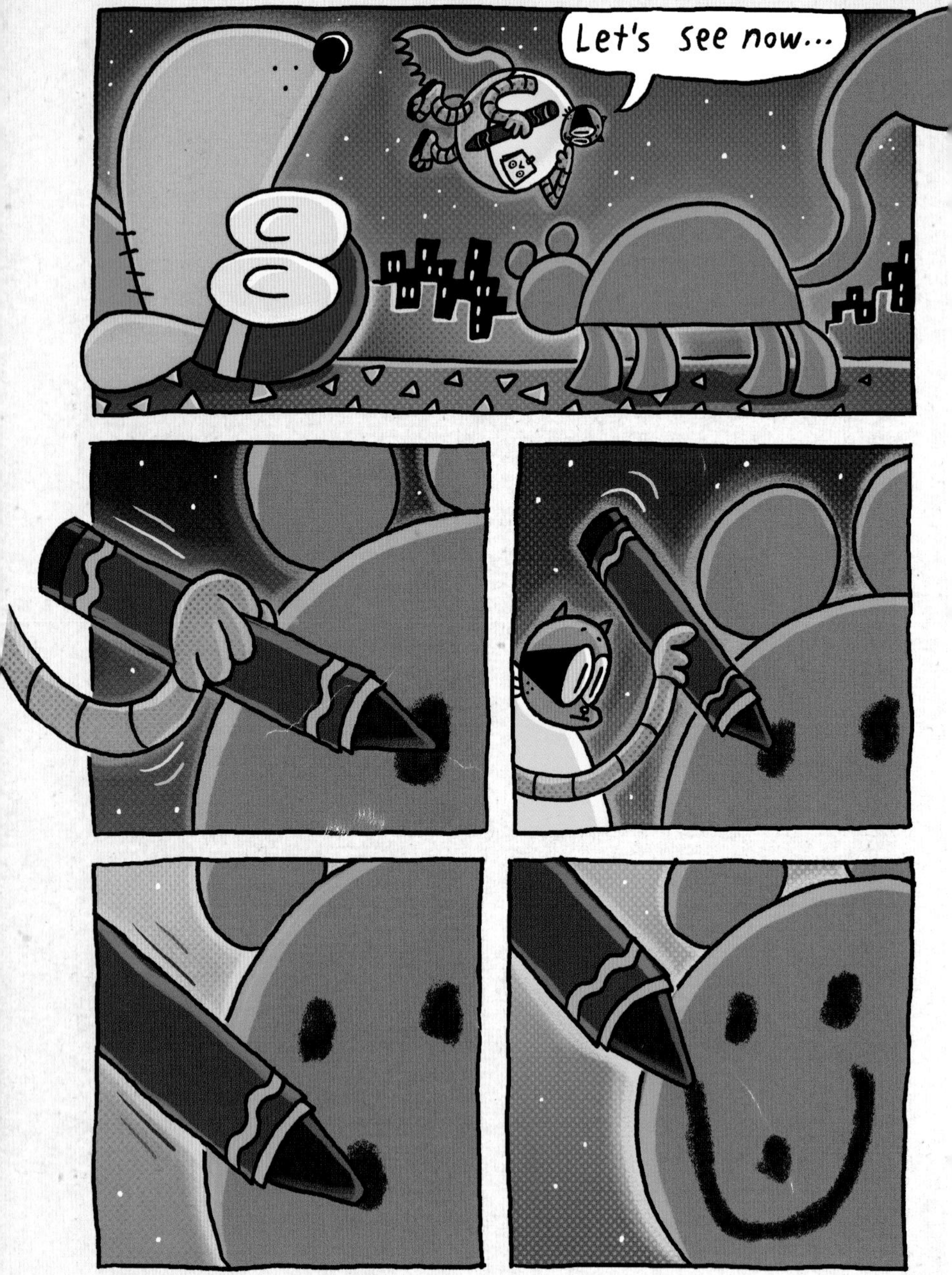
Let's see now...

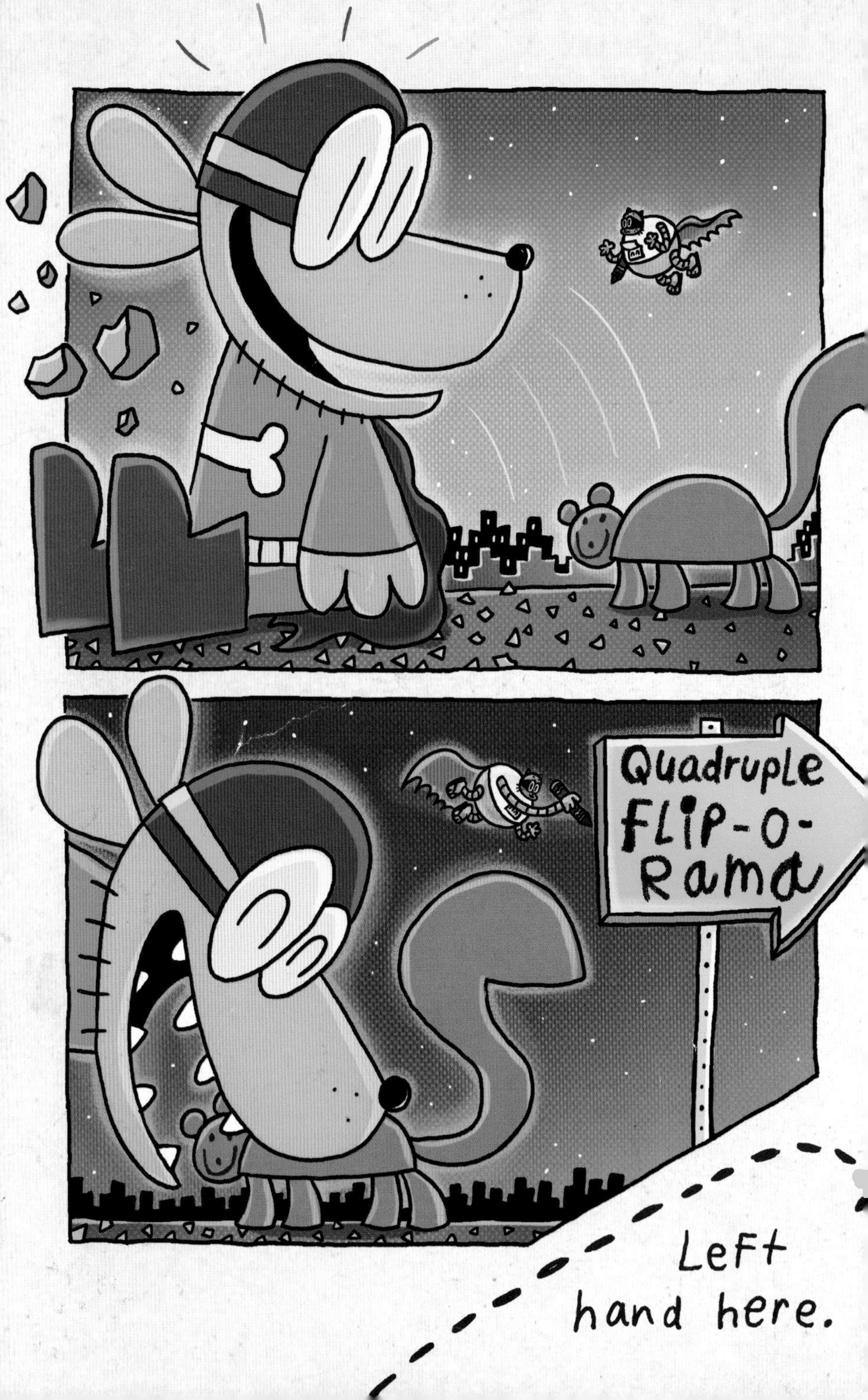

Quadruple FLIP-O-Rama
Left hand here.

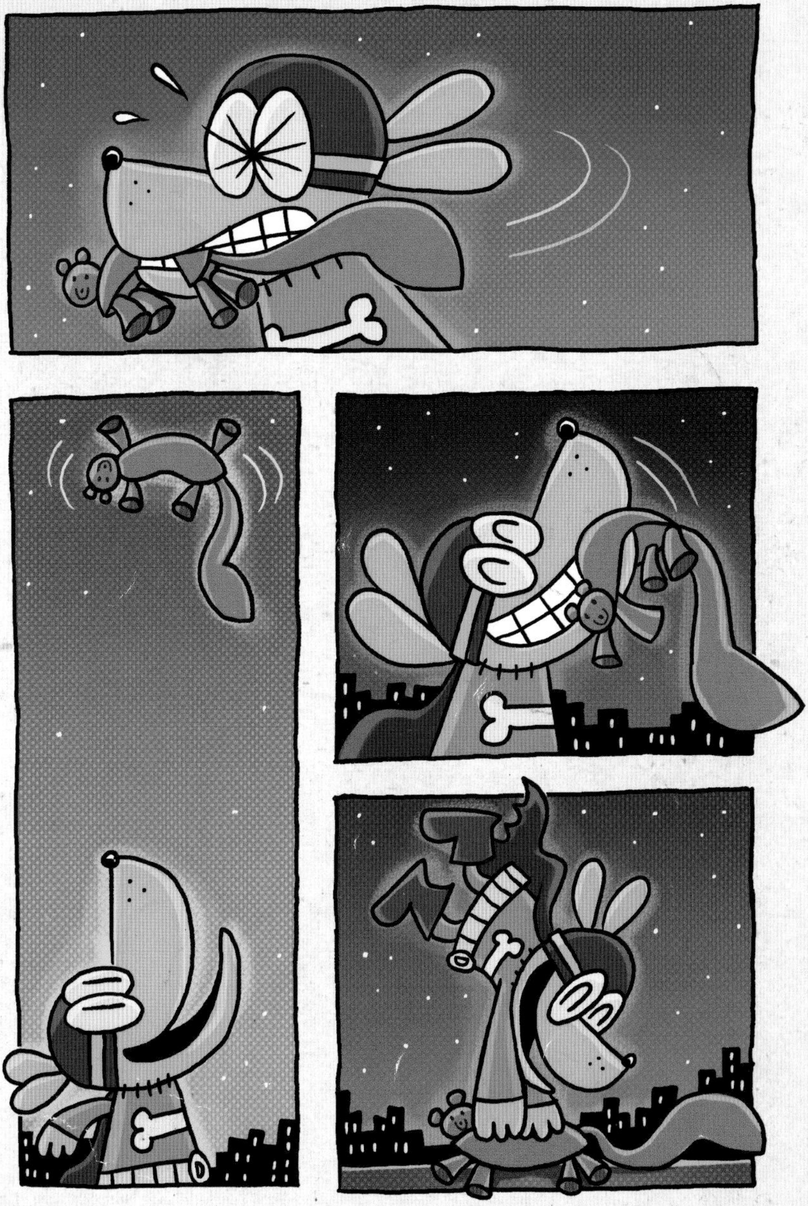

Right Thumb here.

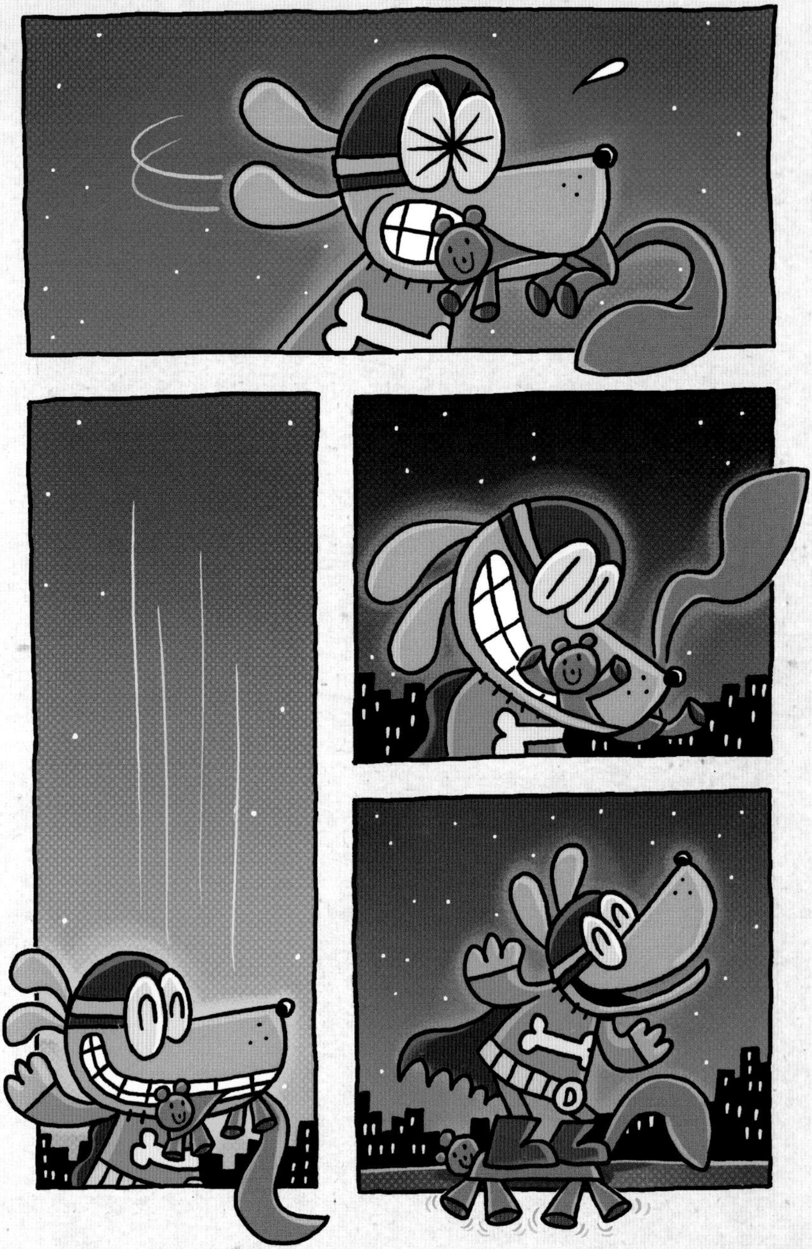

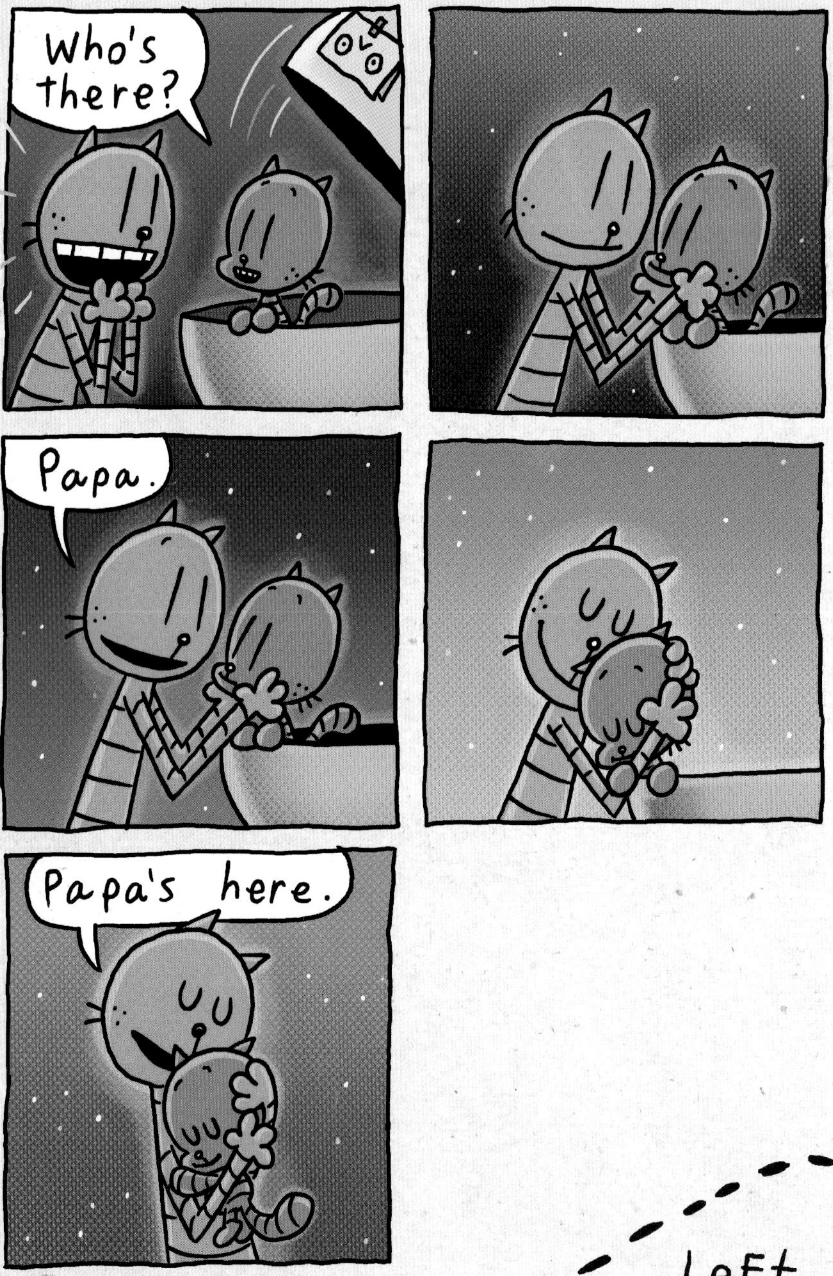
Who's there?
Papa.
Papa's here.

Left hand here.

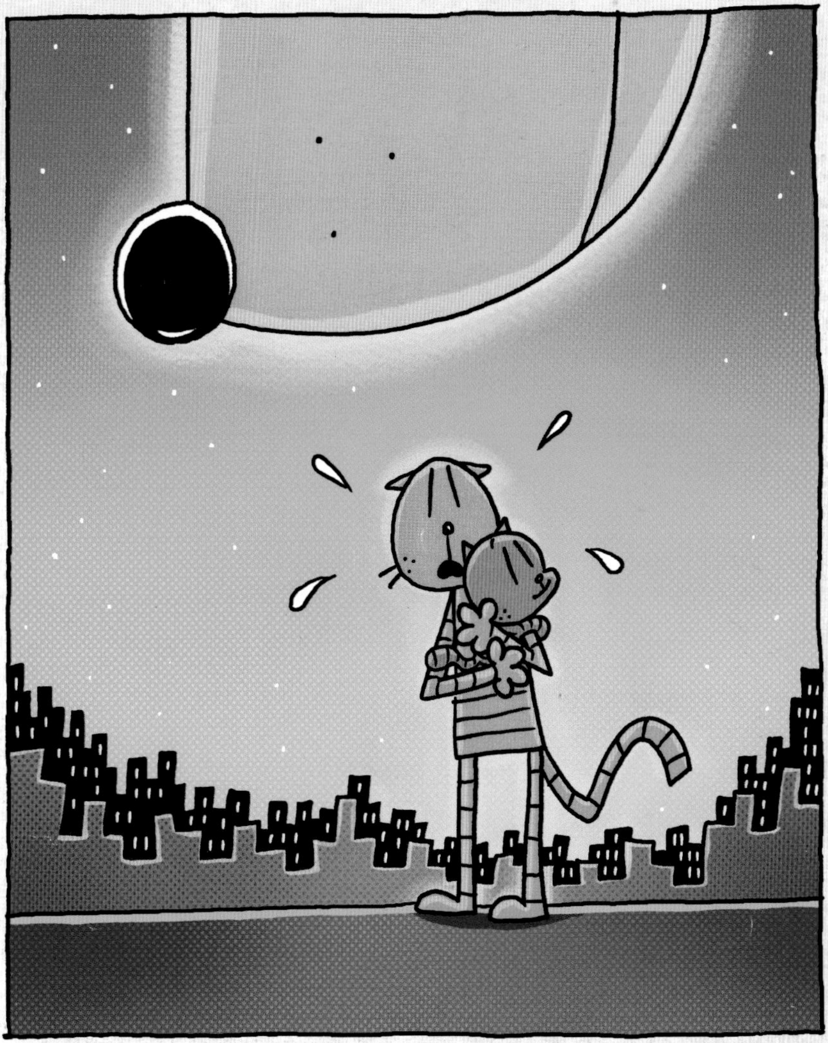

Love, Sloppily

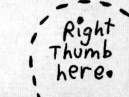

Right Thumb here.

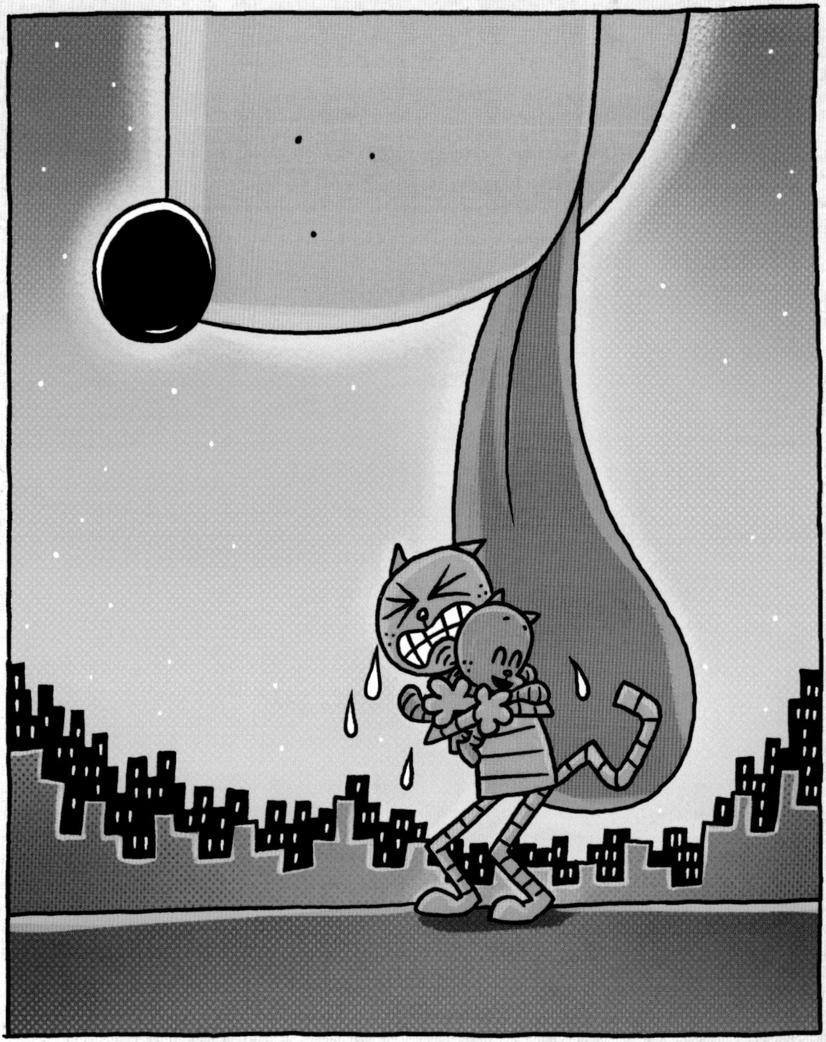

Love, Sloppily

Hey Papa, Look!

Dog Man Kissed us!

Yeeeeeeeah...

...Lovely.

HOORAY FOR DOG MAN! ...oops, WE MEAN The BARK Knight!

CHAPTER 8

MY DOG MAN HAS FLEAS!

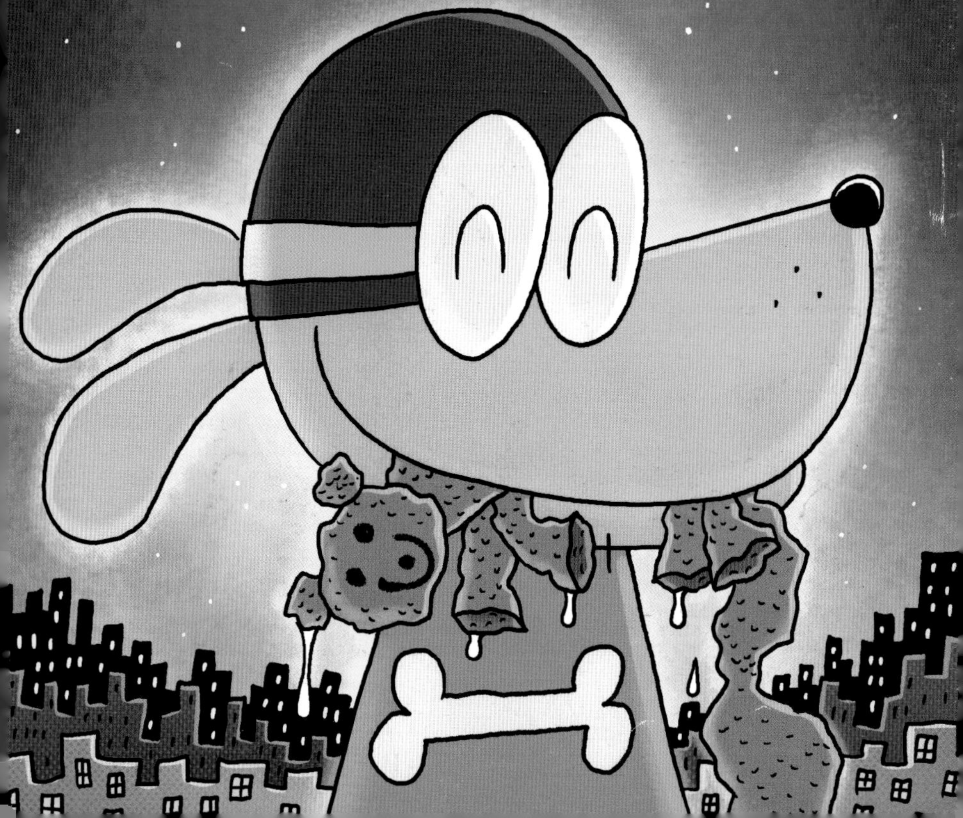

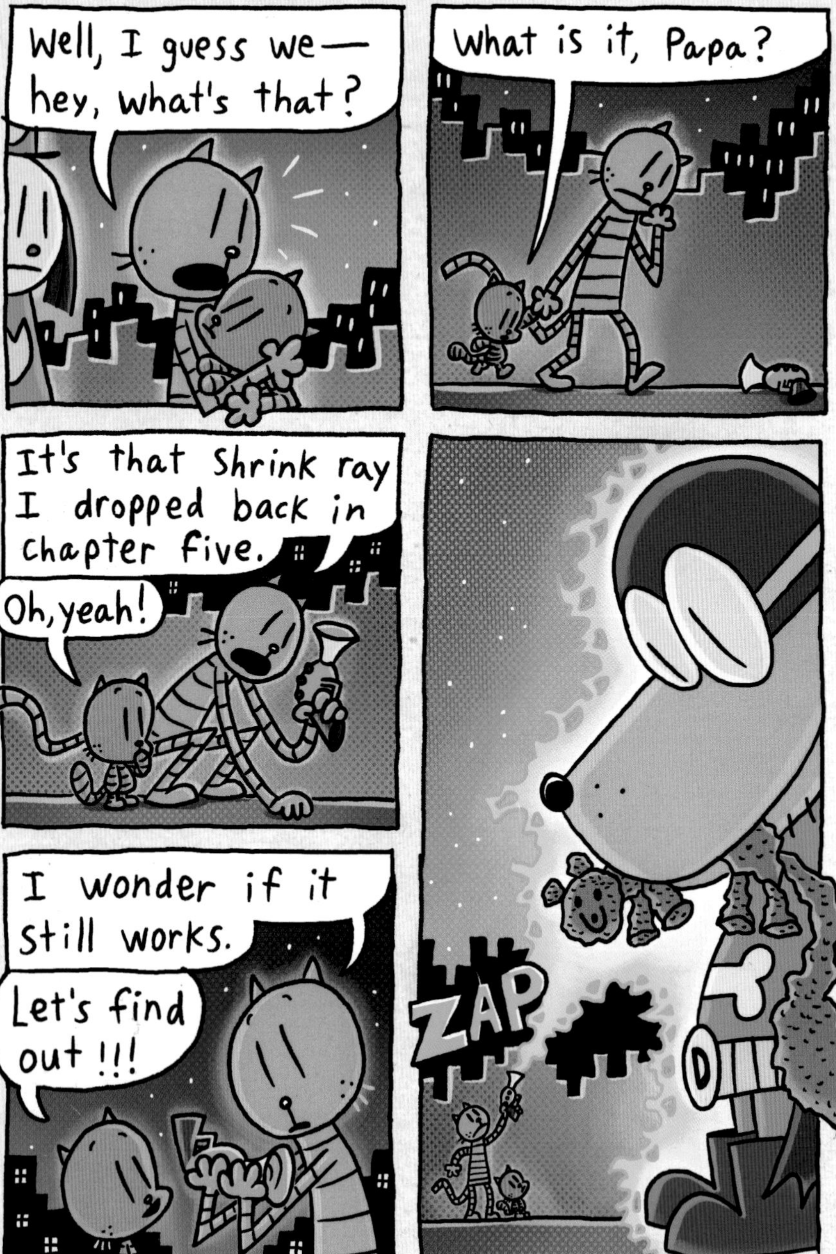
Well, I guess we— hey, what's that?
What is it, Papa?
It's that Shrink ray I dropped back in chapter five.
Oh, yeah!
I wonder if it still works.
Let's find out!!!
ZAP
D

But I'm a good guy now!!!

I know. But ya still gotta pay for the crimes ya did yesterday...

...and the day before that, and the day before that, and the...

Well THAT'S JUST GREAT!!!

I WAS GOOD for, like, THE WHOLE BOOK!

AND iT DiDn't MAKE ANY DifFerence!

Dog Man, I'm gonna go with them, okay?

Don't worry. Chief will walk me home.

scratch scratch scratch

G'night everybody! Let's all play again tomorrow!!!

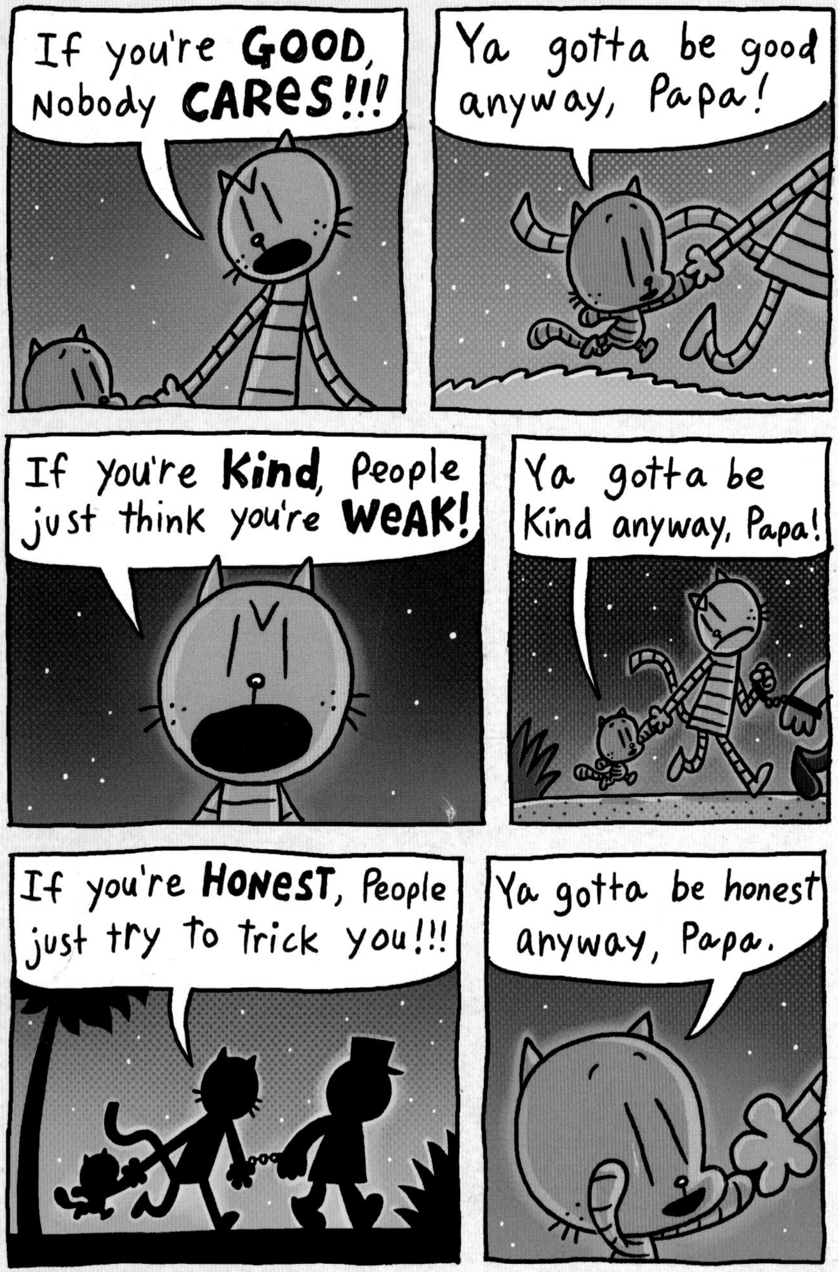
If you're GOOD, Nobody CARES!!!
Ya gotta be good anyway, Papa!
If you're Kind, People just think you're WEAK!
Ya gotta be Kind anyway, Papa!
If you're HONEST, People just try to trick you!!!
Ya gotta be honest anyway, Papa.

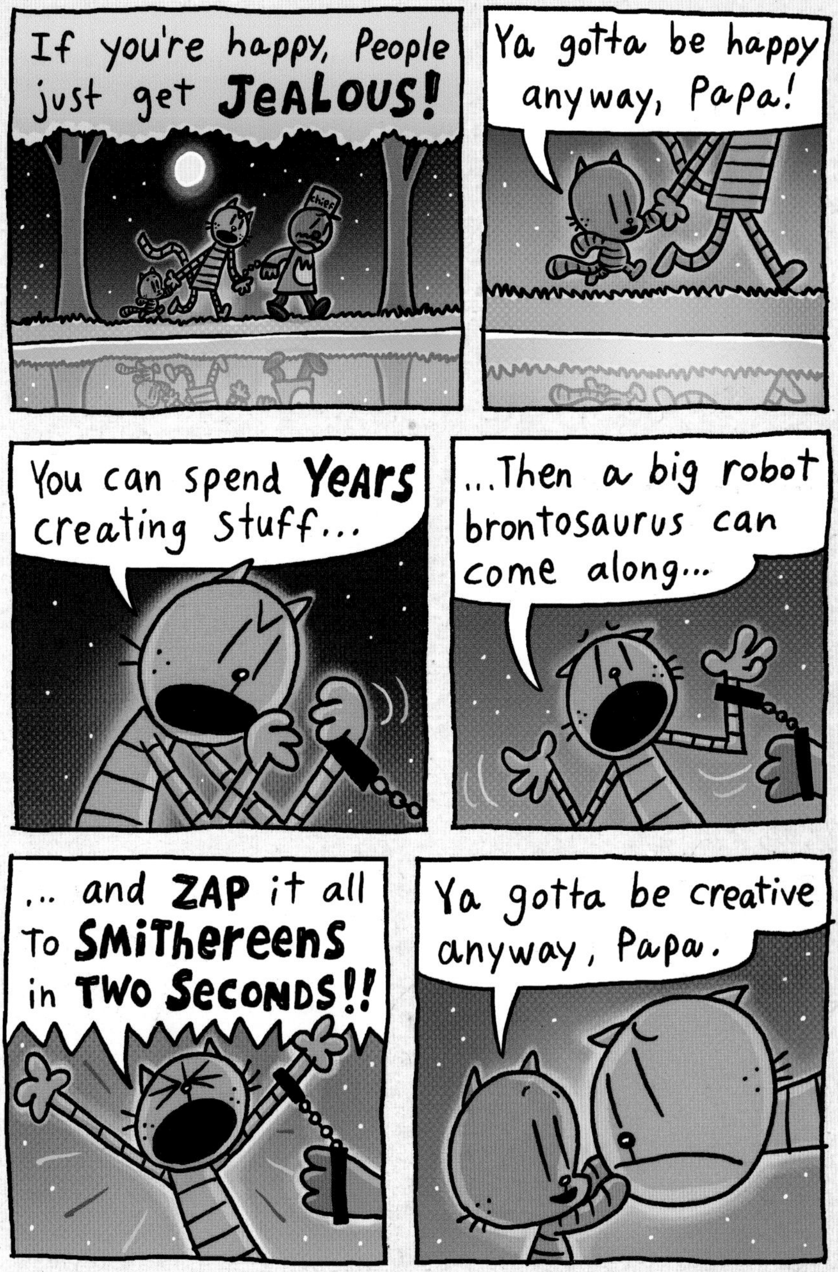
If you're happy, People just get JEALOUS!
Ya gotta be happy anyway, Papa!
You can spend YEARS creating stuff...
...Then a big robot brontosaurus can come along...
... and ZAP it all To SMiThereens in TWO SeCONDS!!
Ya gotta be creative anyway, Papa.

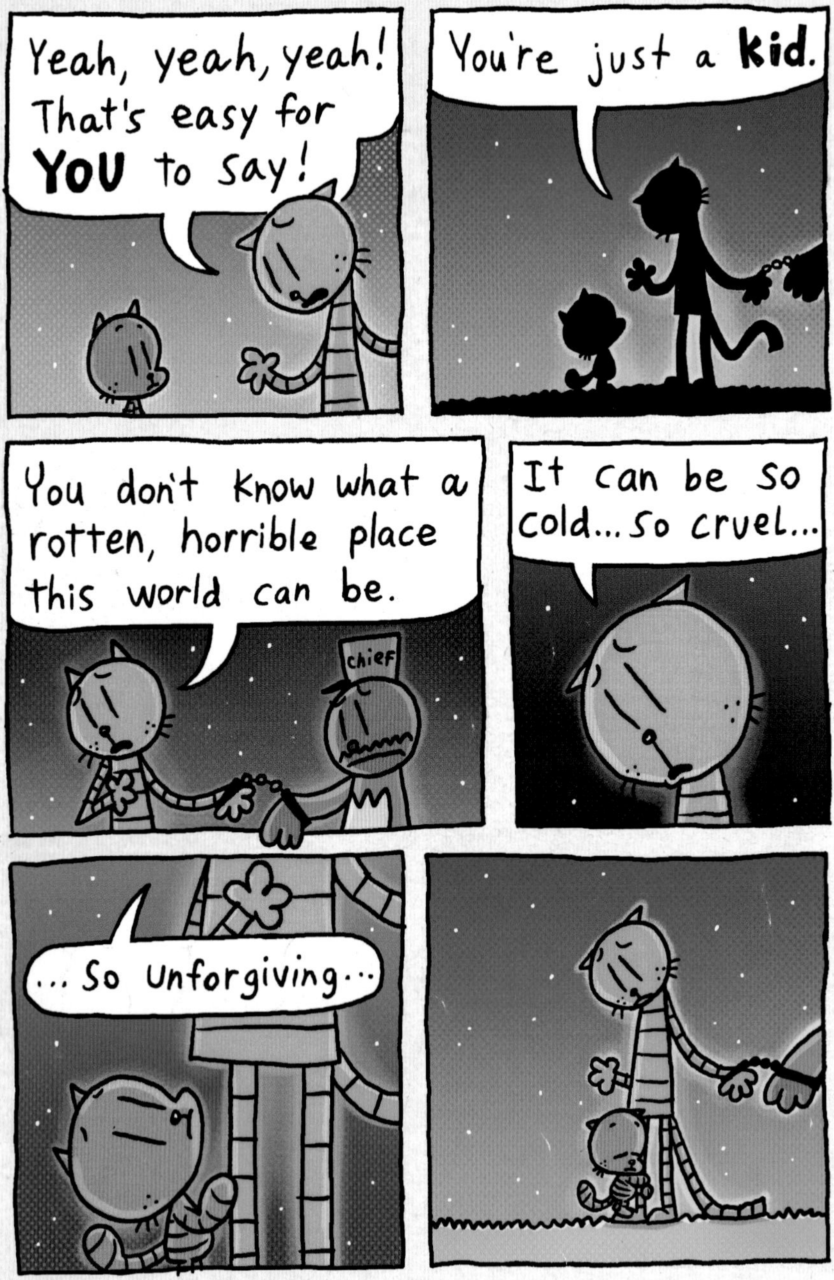
Yeah, yeah, yeah! That's easy for YOU to say!
You're just a kid.
You don't know what a rotten, horrible place this world can be.
chief
It can be so cold... so cruel...
... so unforgiving...

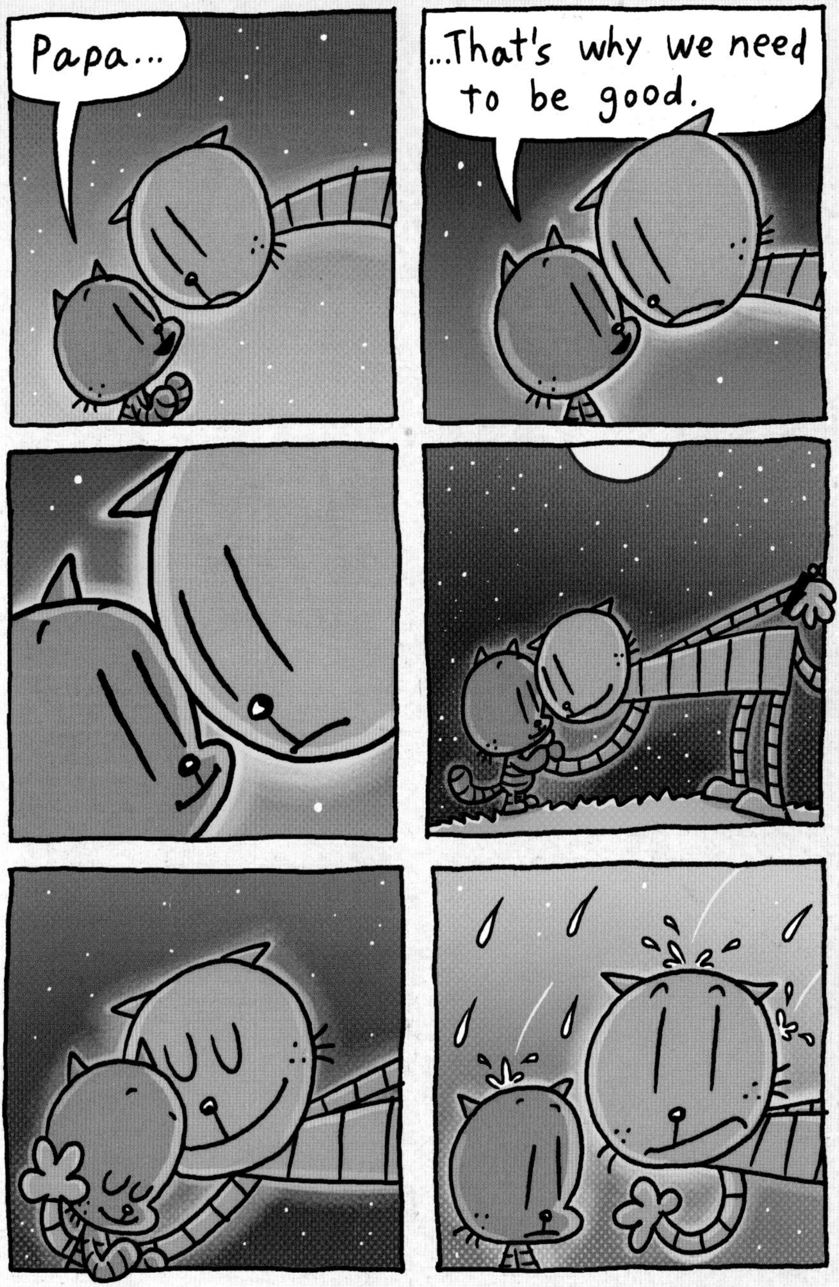
Papa...
...That's why we need to be good.

Hey Chief, what's gelato?

It's Like ice cream.

Oh.

sweeeet!

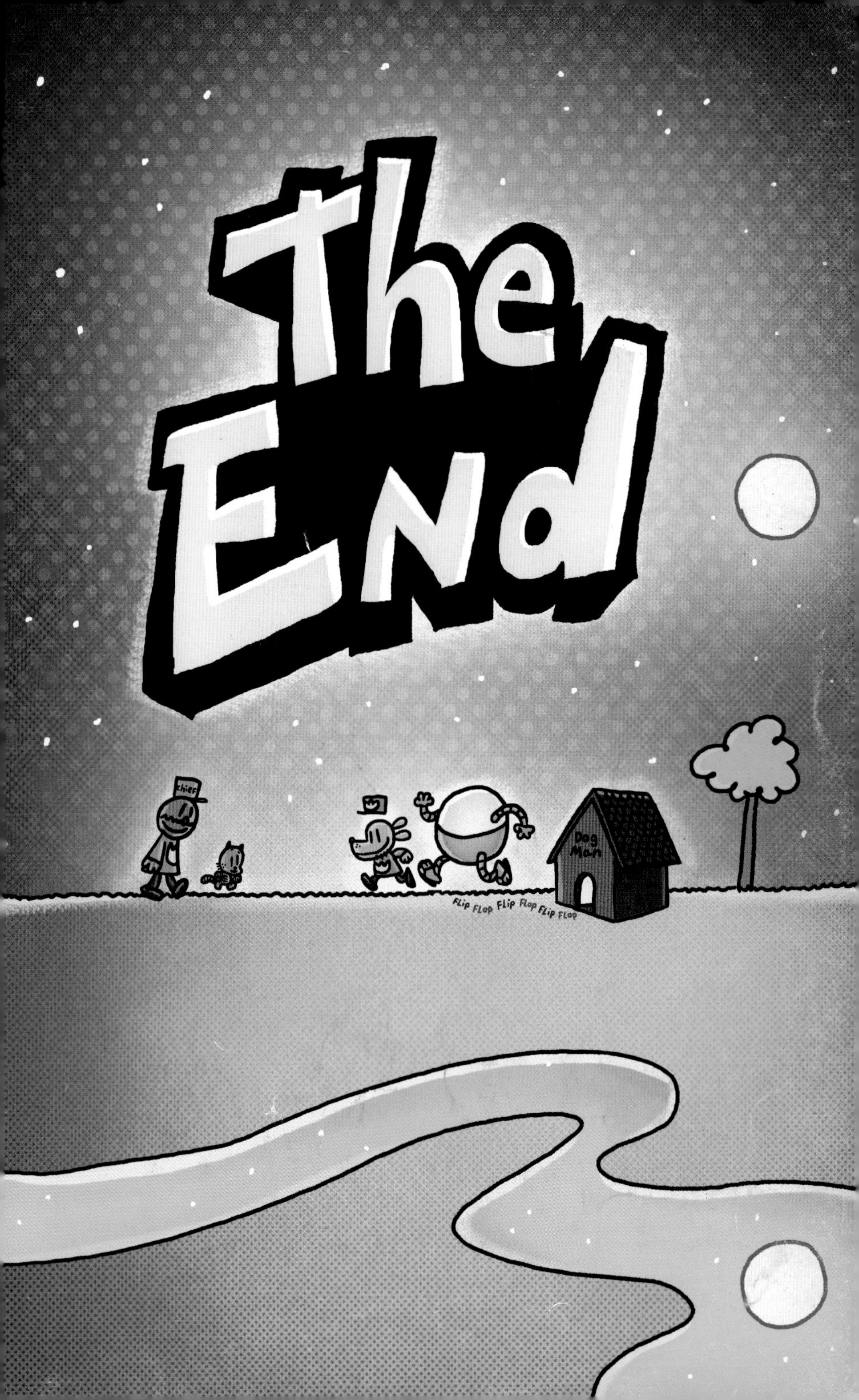
The End
Chief
Dog Man
Flip Flop Flip Flop Flip Flop

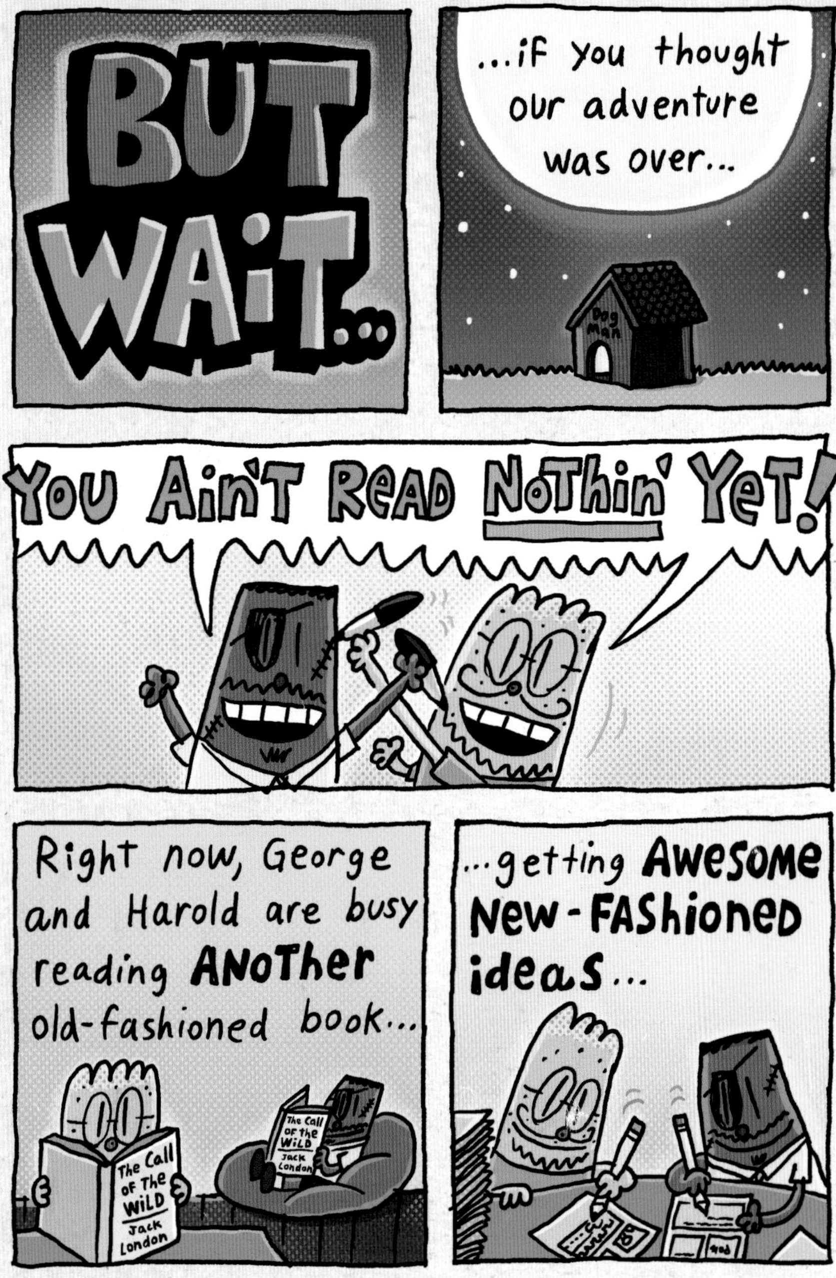
BUT WAIT...
...if you thought our adventure was over...
Dog Man
YOU AIN'T READ NOTHIN' YET!
Right now, George and Harold are busy reading ANOTHER old-fashioned book...
The Call of The WILD Jack London
The Call of the WILD Jack London
...getting AWESOME NEW-FASHIONED ideas...

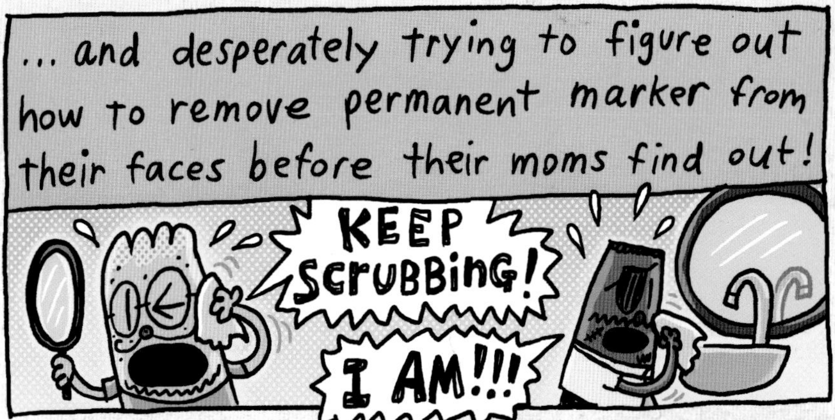
... and desperately trying to figure out how to remove permanent marker from their faces before their moms find out!
KEEP SCRUBBING!
I AM!!!

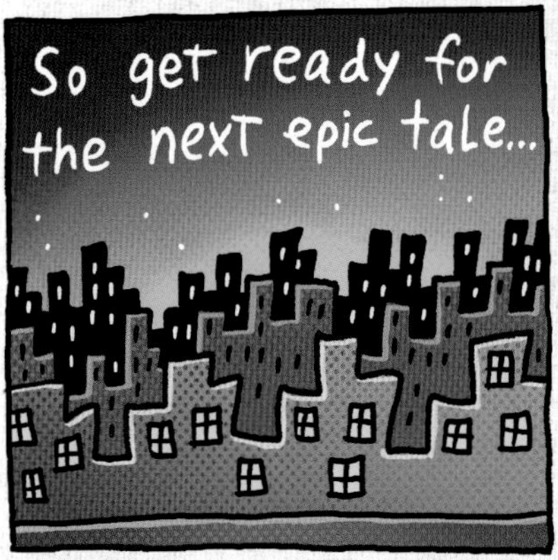
So get ready for the next epic tale...

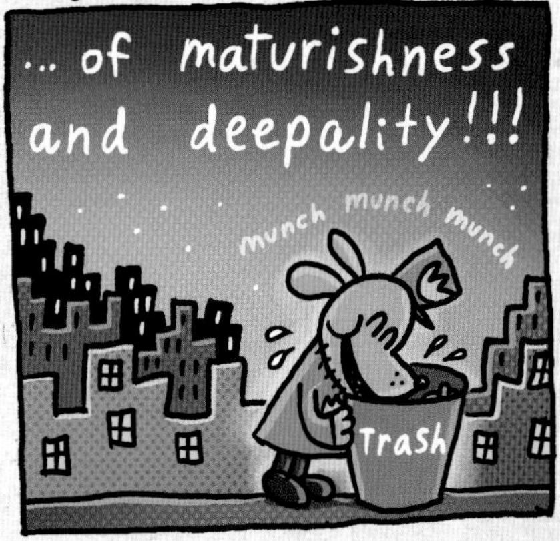
... of maturishness and deepality!!!
munch munch munch
Trash

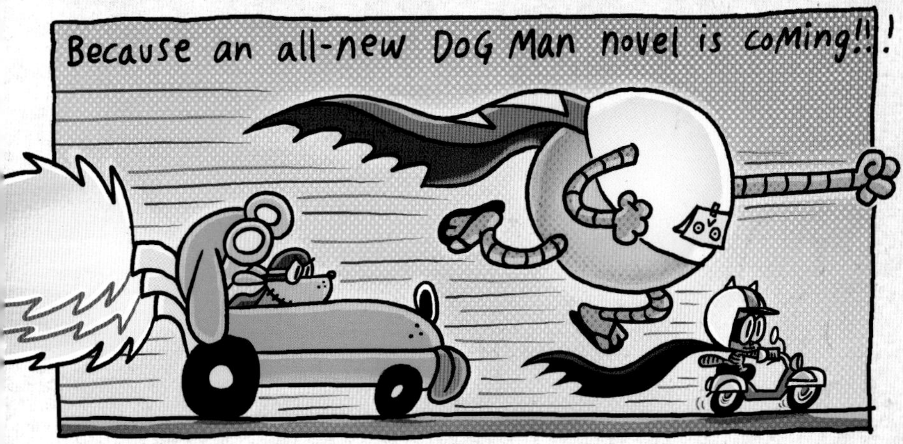
Because an all-new DOG MAN novel is coming!!!

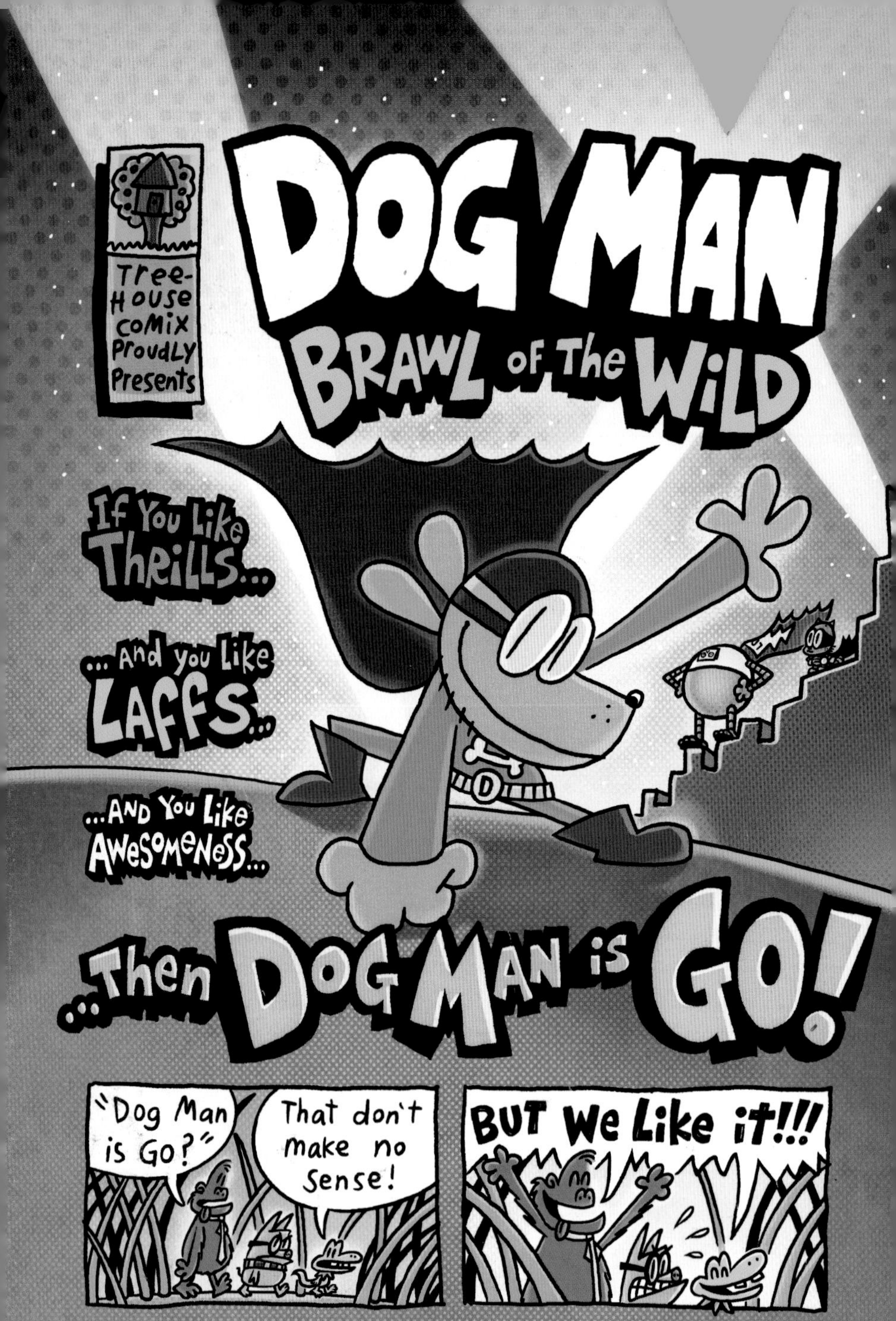
Tree-House Comix Proudly Presents
DOG MAN
BRAWL of The WiLD
If You Like THRiLLS...
...And you Like LAFFS...
...AND You Like AWESOMENESS...
...Then DOG MAN is GO!
"Dog Man is Go?"
That don't make no Sense!
BUT We Like it!!!

HOW 2 DRAW

The BARK KNIGHT

in **42** Ridiculously easy steps!

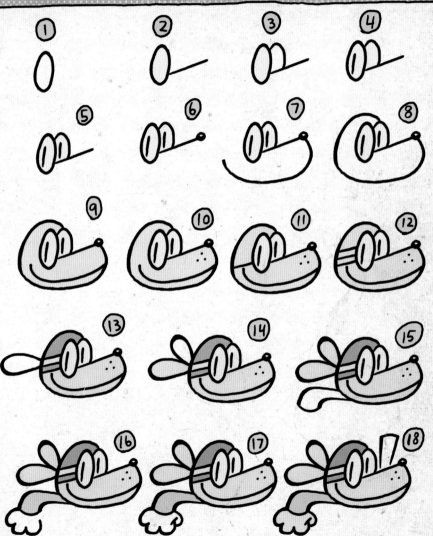

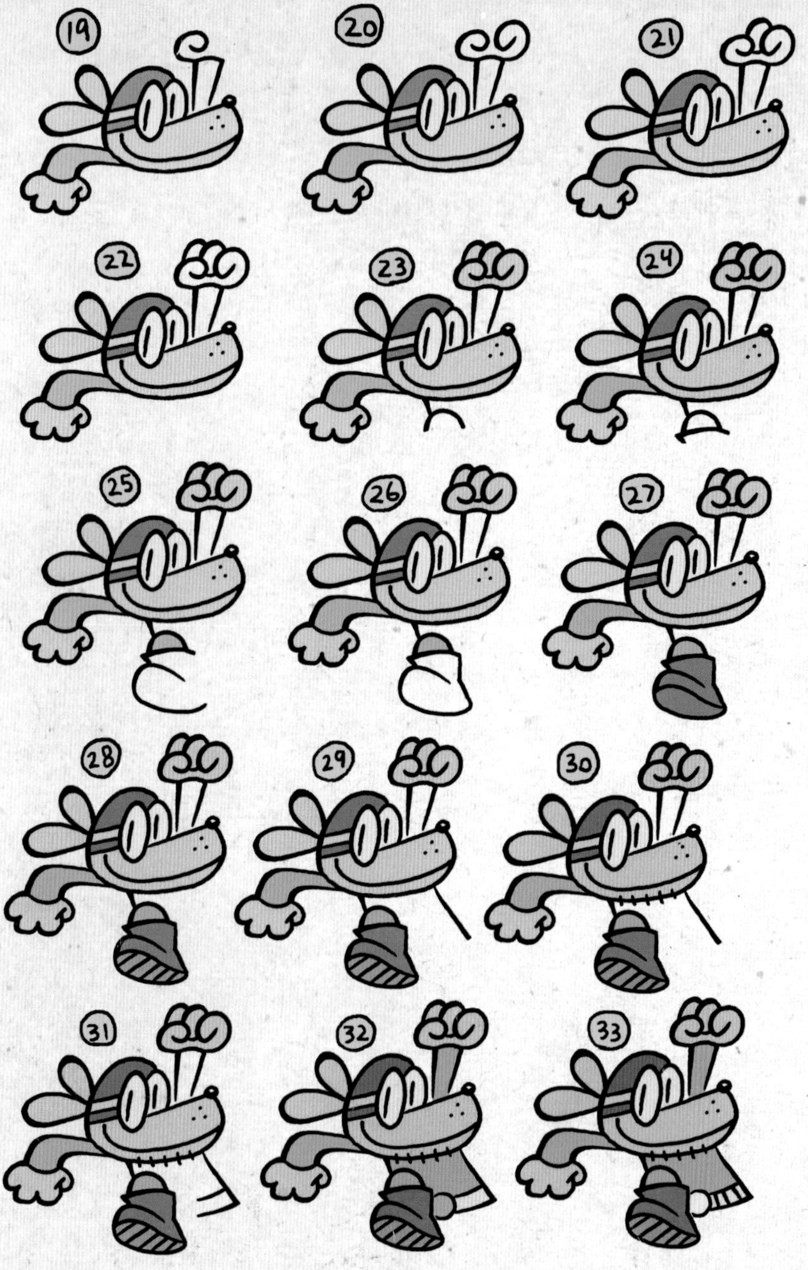
19
20
21
22
23
24
25
26
27
28
29
30
31
32
33

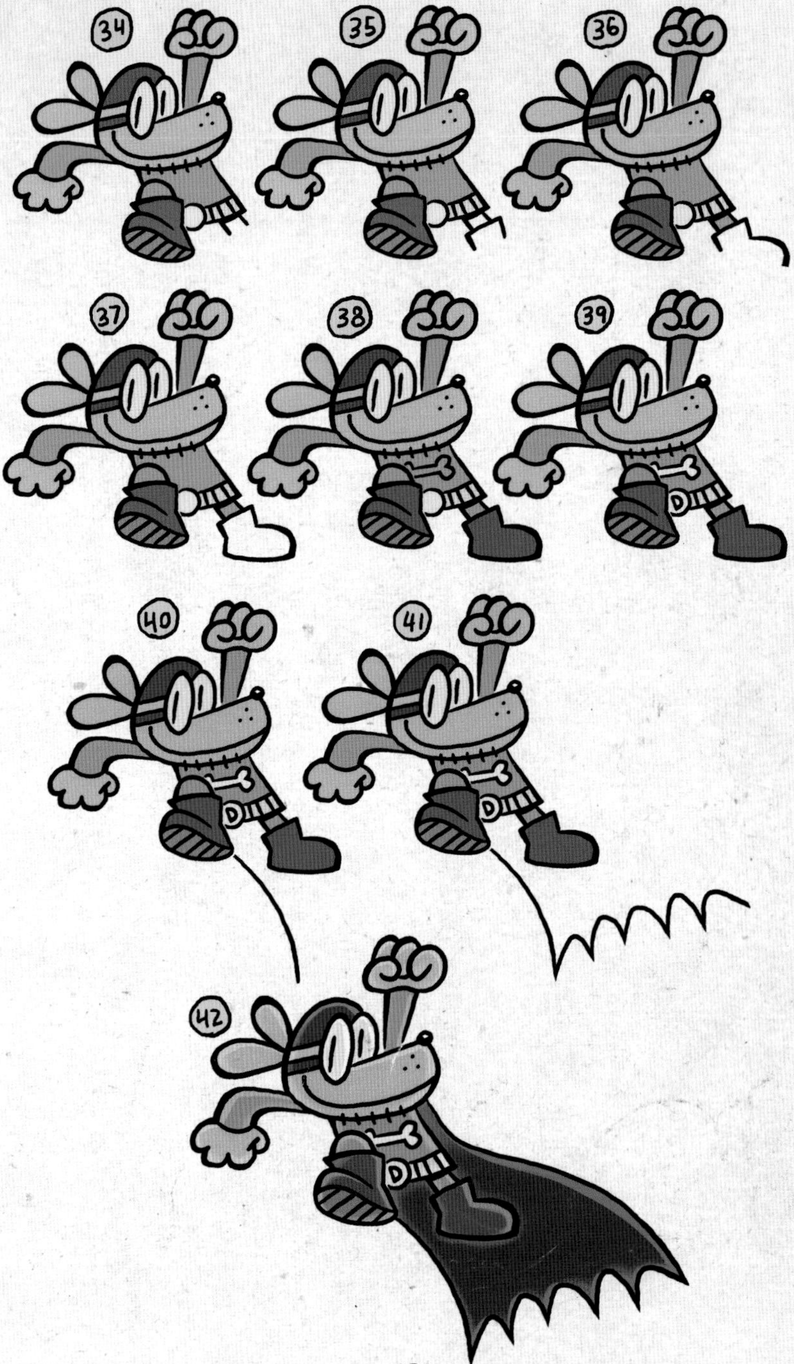
34
35
36
37
38
39
40
41
42

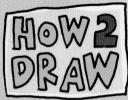

CAT KiD

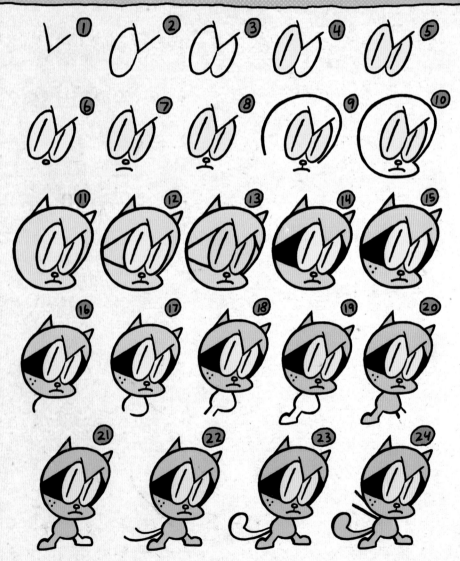

HOW 2 DRAW CRUNKY

in **26** Ridiculously easy steps!

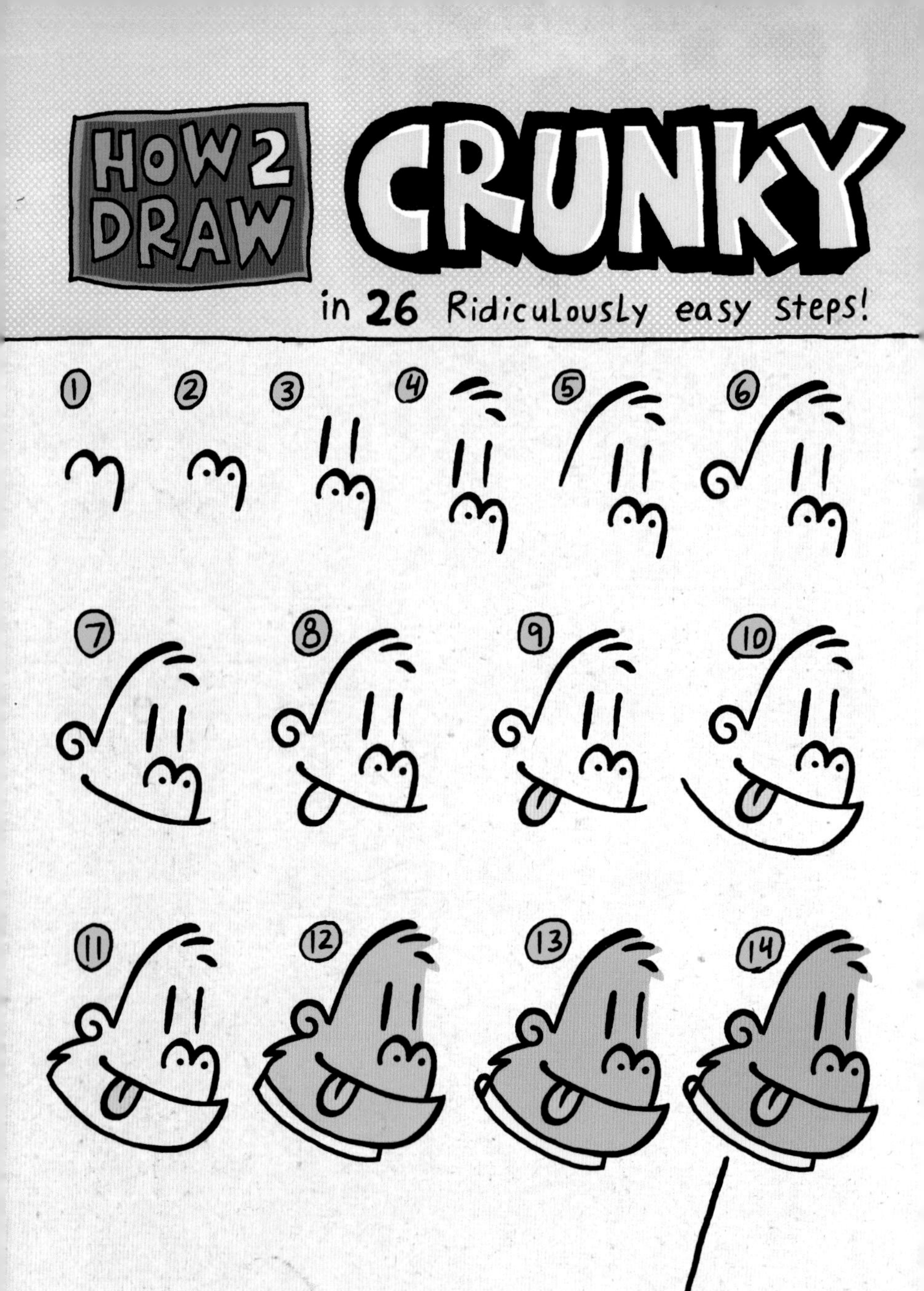
1
2
3
4
5
6
7
8
9
10
11
12
13
14

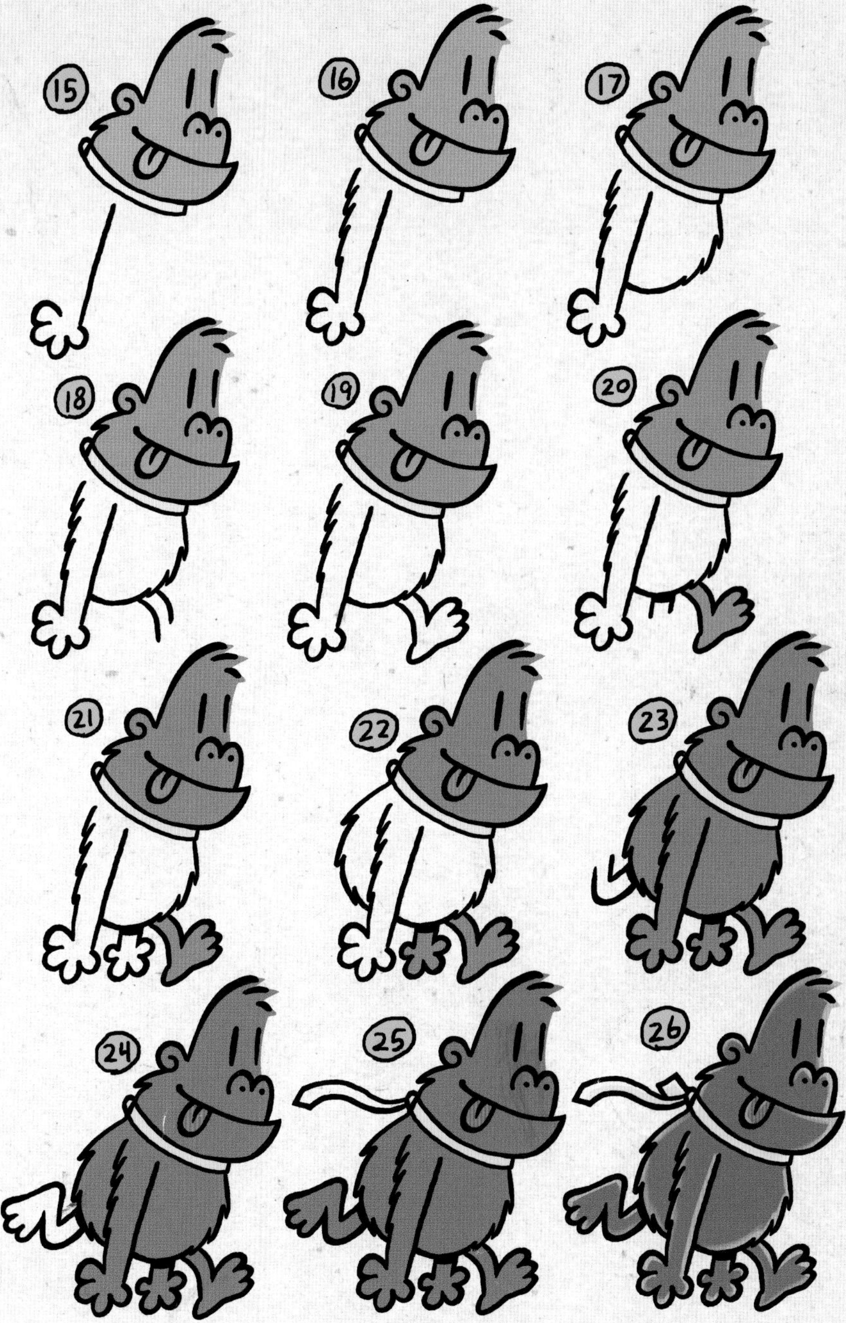
15
16
17
18
19
20
21
22
23
24
25
26

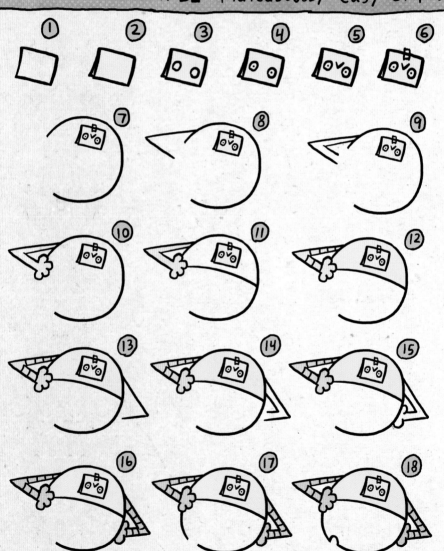

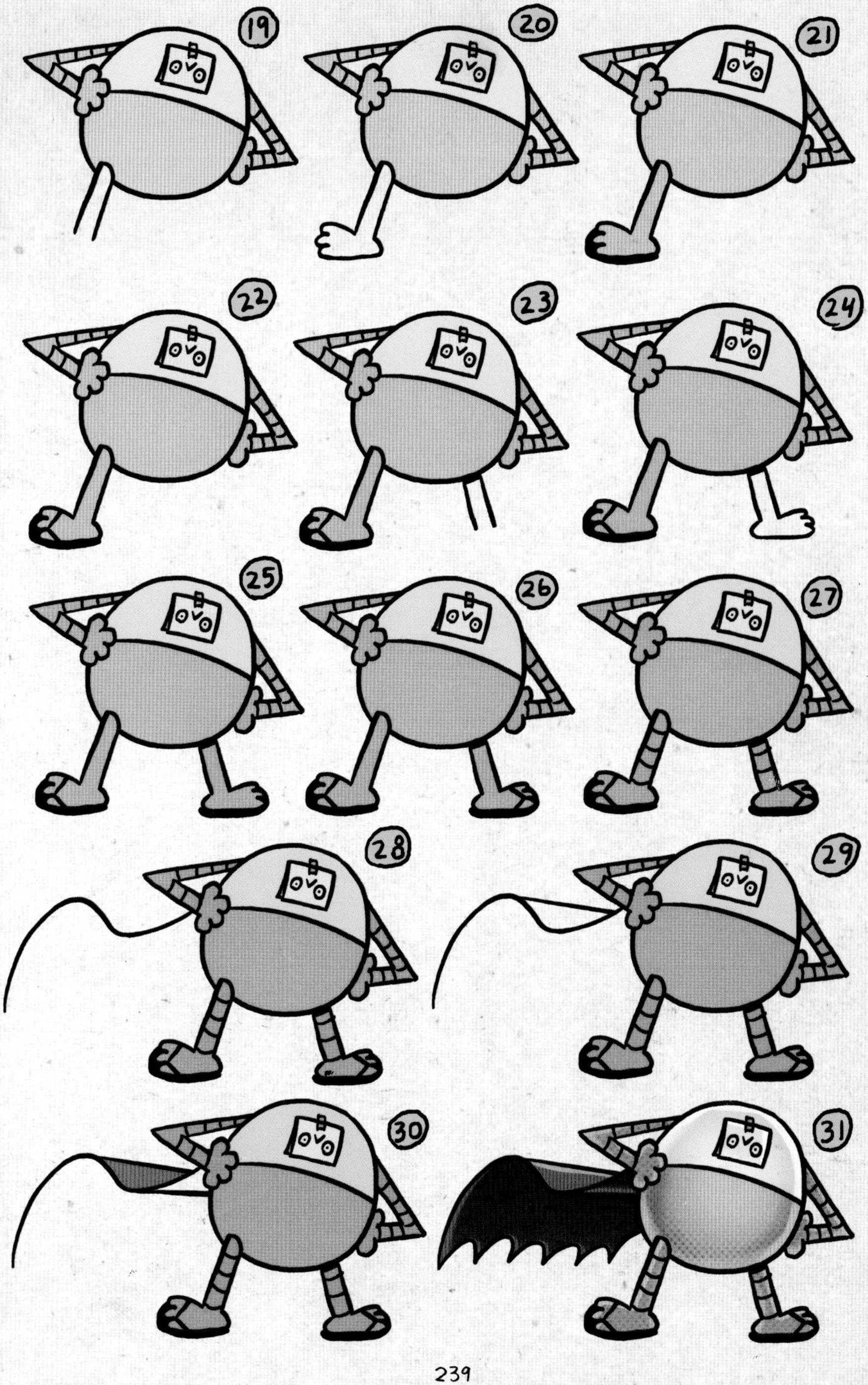
19
20
21
22
23
24
25
26
27
28
29
30
31

HOW 2 DRAW PIGGY

in **33** Ridiculously easy steps!

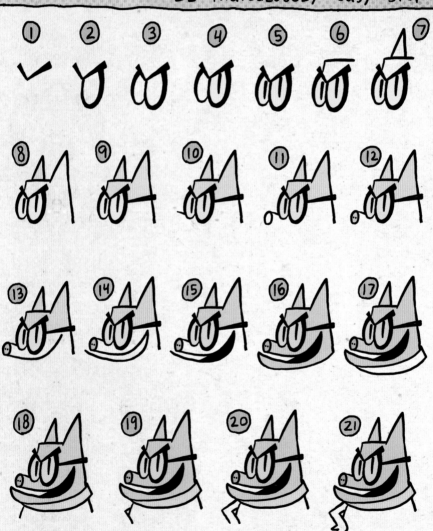

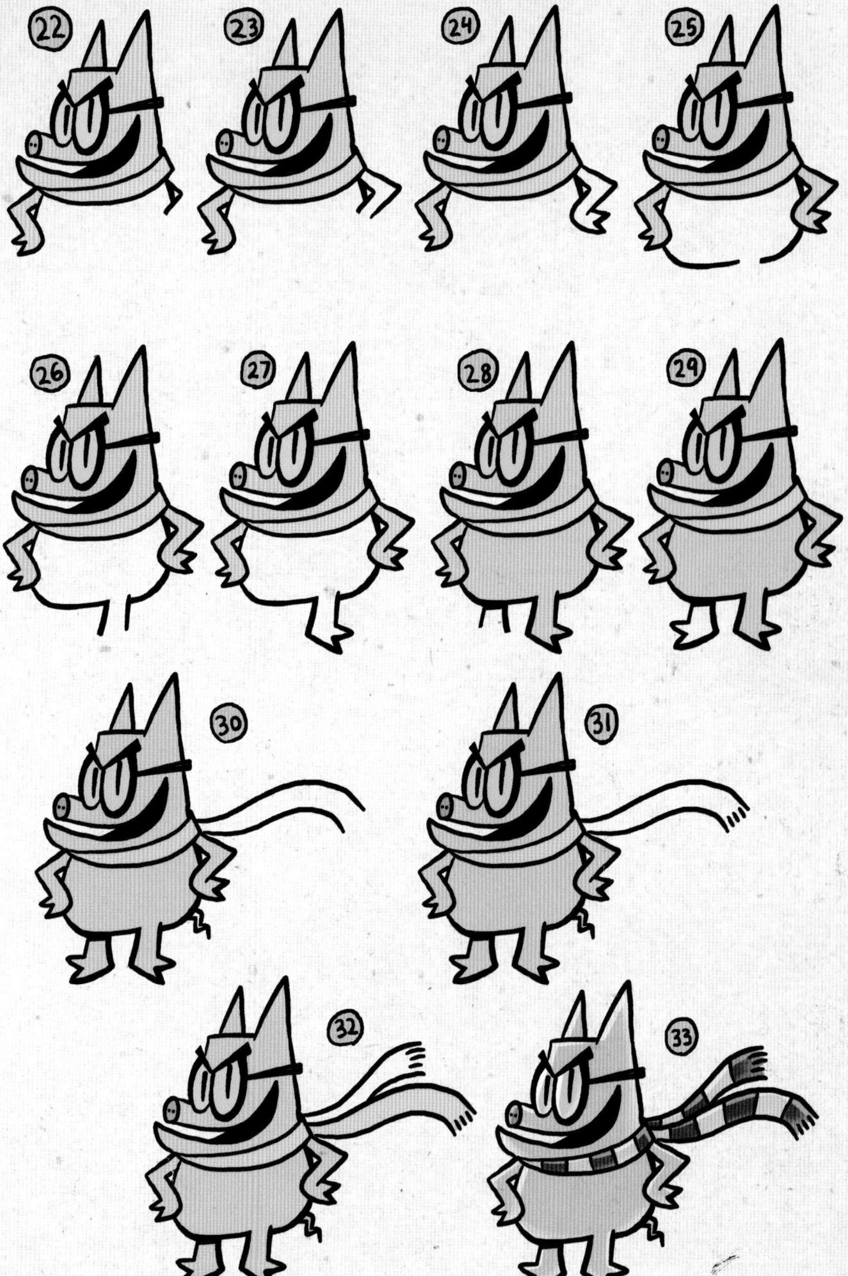
22
23
24
25
26
27
28
29
30
31
32
33

HOW 2 DRAW BUB

in **21** Ridiculously easy steps!

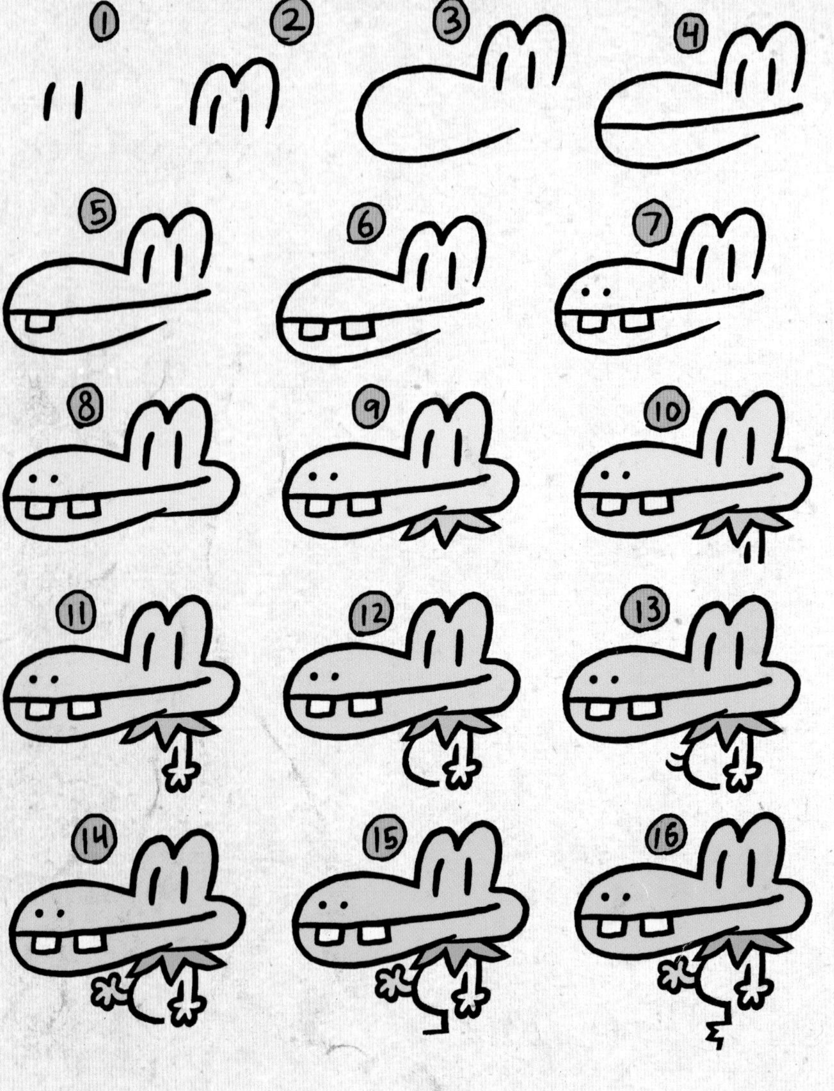
1
2
3
4
5
6
7
8
9
10
11
12
13
14
15
16

NOTES

by George and Harold

⭐ Our favorite character from William Golding's <u>Lord of the Flies</u> is Piggy. The Piggy in our book is a bad guy, though.

⭐ The dialogue on page 147 was inspired by quotes commonly attributed to Mark Twain and Dr. Seuss.

⭐ The conversation on pages 220-221 was inspired by the poem "Anyway," by Kent M. Keith. A version of this poem is inscribed on the wall of Mother Teresa's home for children in Calcutta, India.

⭐ "I finally finished reading <u>Lord of the Flies</u>. It was awesome." — Harold Hutchins

Read to Your CAT, Kid!

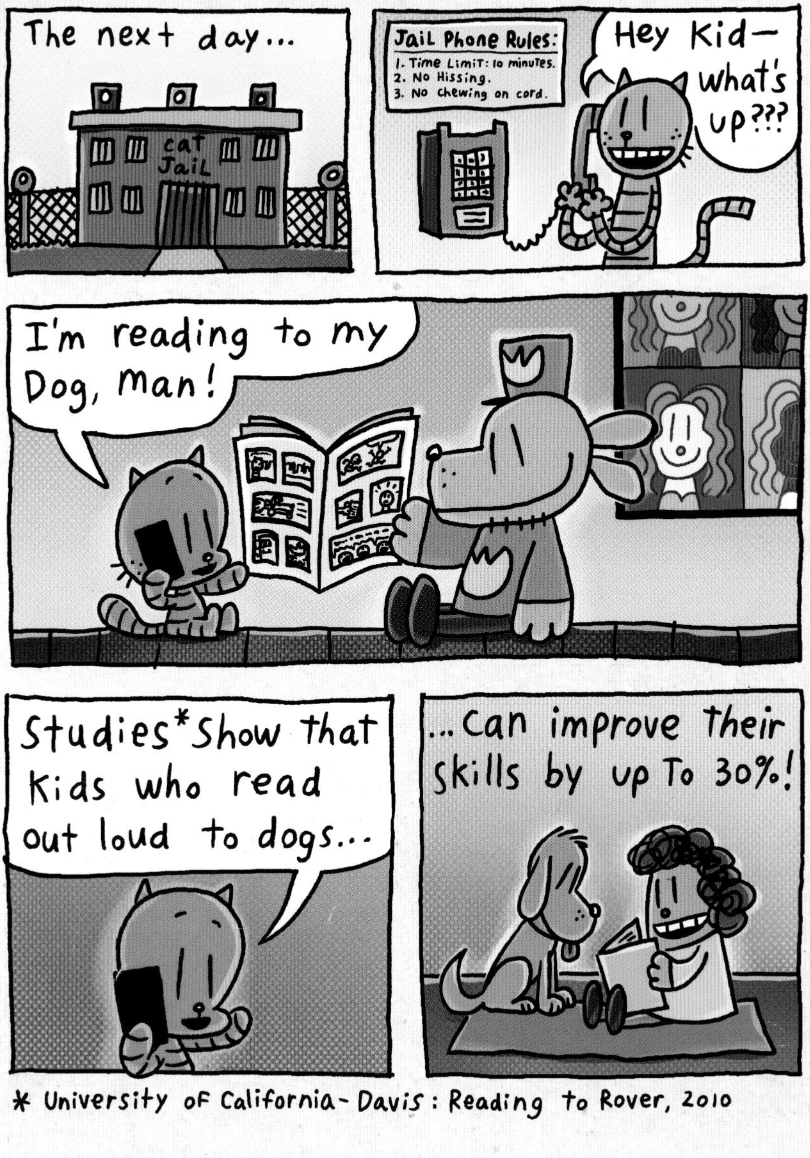
The next day...
cat Jail
Jail Phone Rules:
1. Time Limit: 10 minutes.
2. No Hissing.
3. No chewing on cord.
Hey Kid— what's up???
I'm reading to my Dog, Man!
Studies* Show that Kids who read out loud to dogs...
...Can improve their skills by up To 30%!

* University of California-Davis: Reading to Rover, 2010

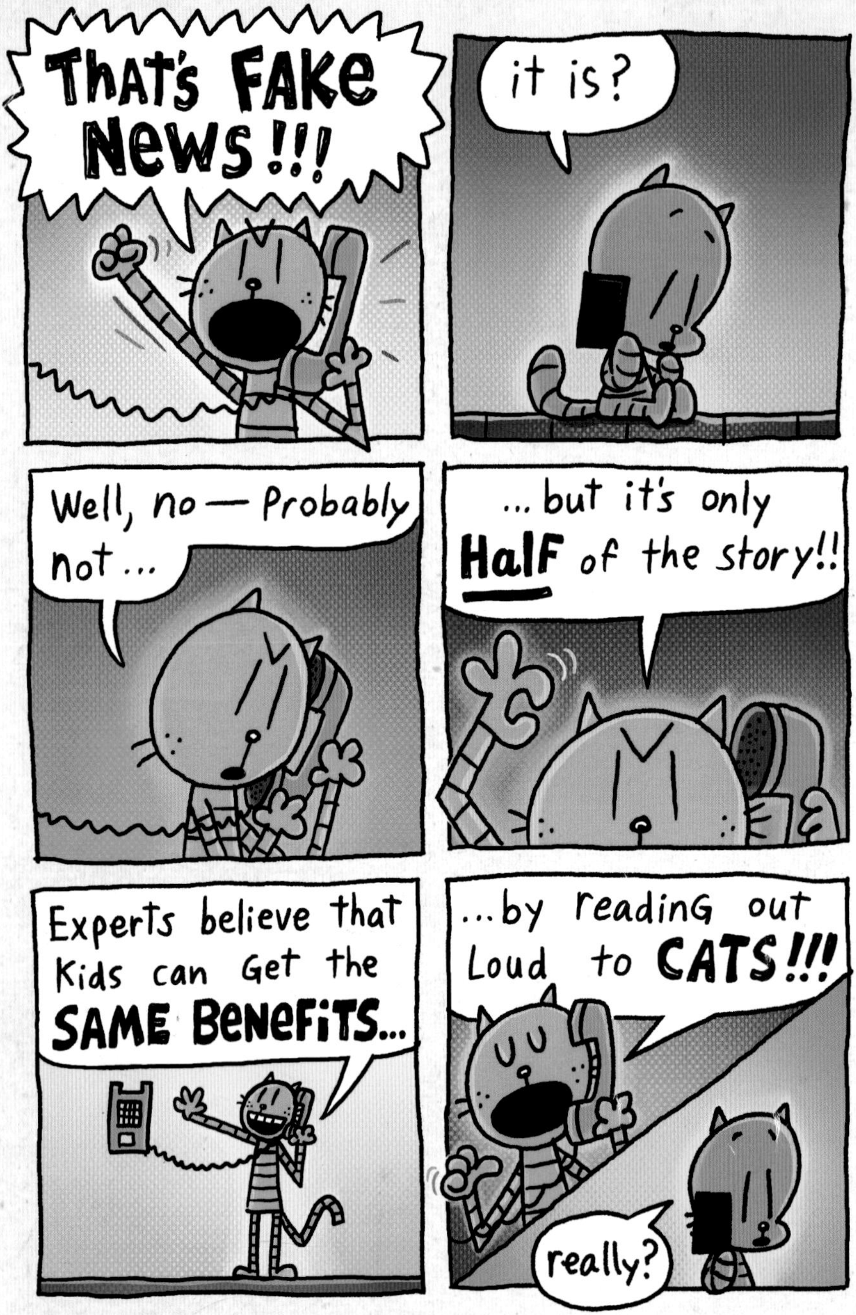
THAT'S FAKE NEWS!!!
it is?
Well, no— Probably not...
...but it's only HALF of the story!!
Experts believe that Kids can Get the SAME BENEFITS...
...by reading out Loud to CATS!!!
really?

Sure! Kids who read out loud to cats can improve their skills _AND_ their confidence!!!

I'm getting better by the minute, Kid!!!

Me too, Kid!!!

They become better communicators, and participate more in class!

Yo! I got MAD Communicatin' Skillz, Kid!

Me too, kid!!!

And they have reduced stress levels because cats don't judge 'em!

He accidentally skipped a word.

She didn't even notice.

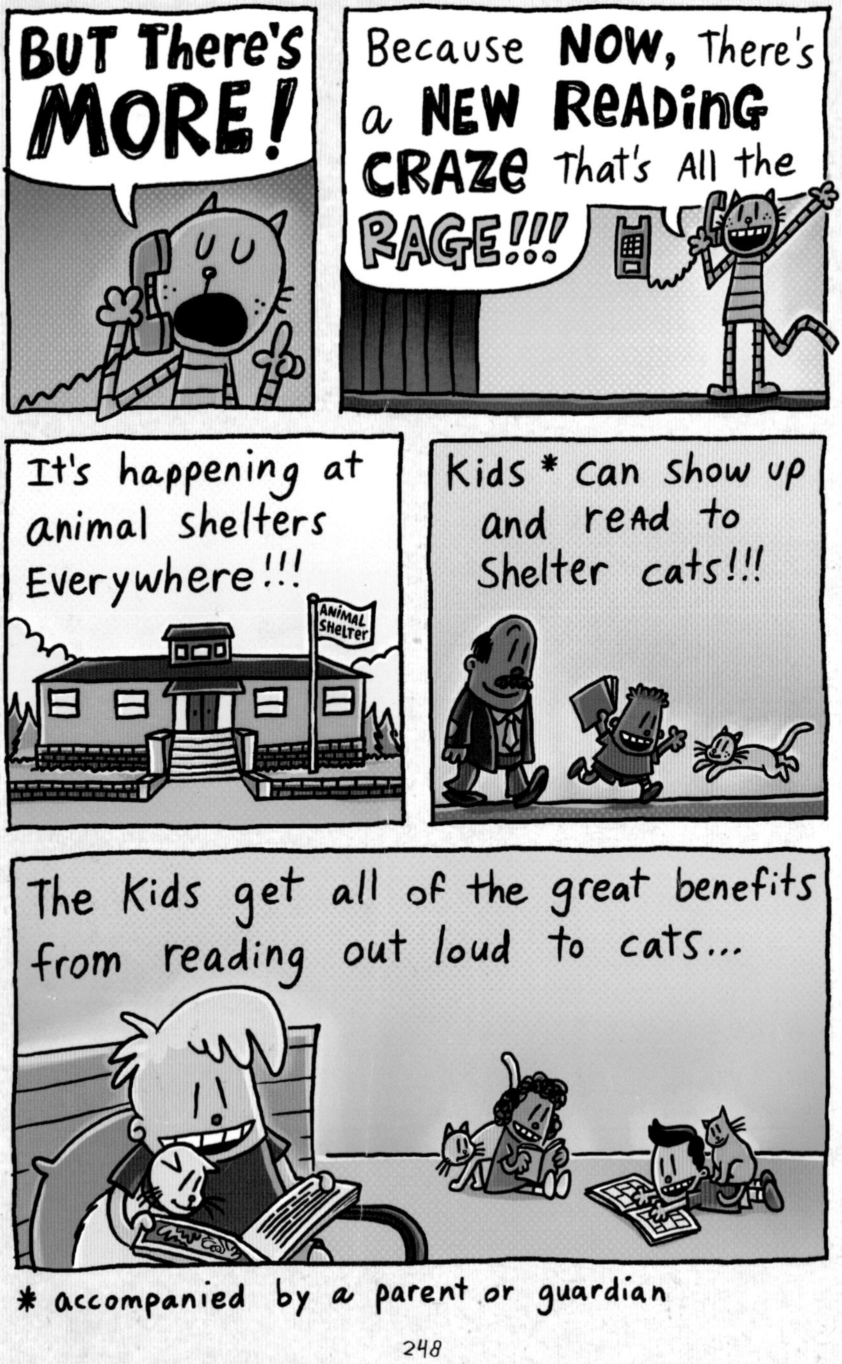
BUT There's MORE!
Because NOW, There's a NEW READING CRAZE That's All the RAGE!!!
It's happening at animal shelters Everywhere!!!
ANIMAL SHELTER
Kids * can show up and read to Shelter cats!!!
The Kids get all of the great benefits from reading out loud to cats...

* accompanied by a parent or guardian

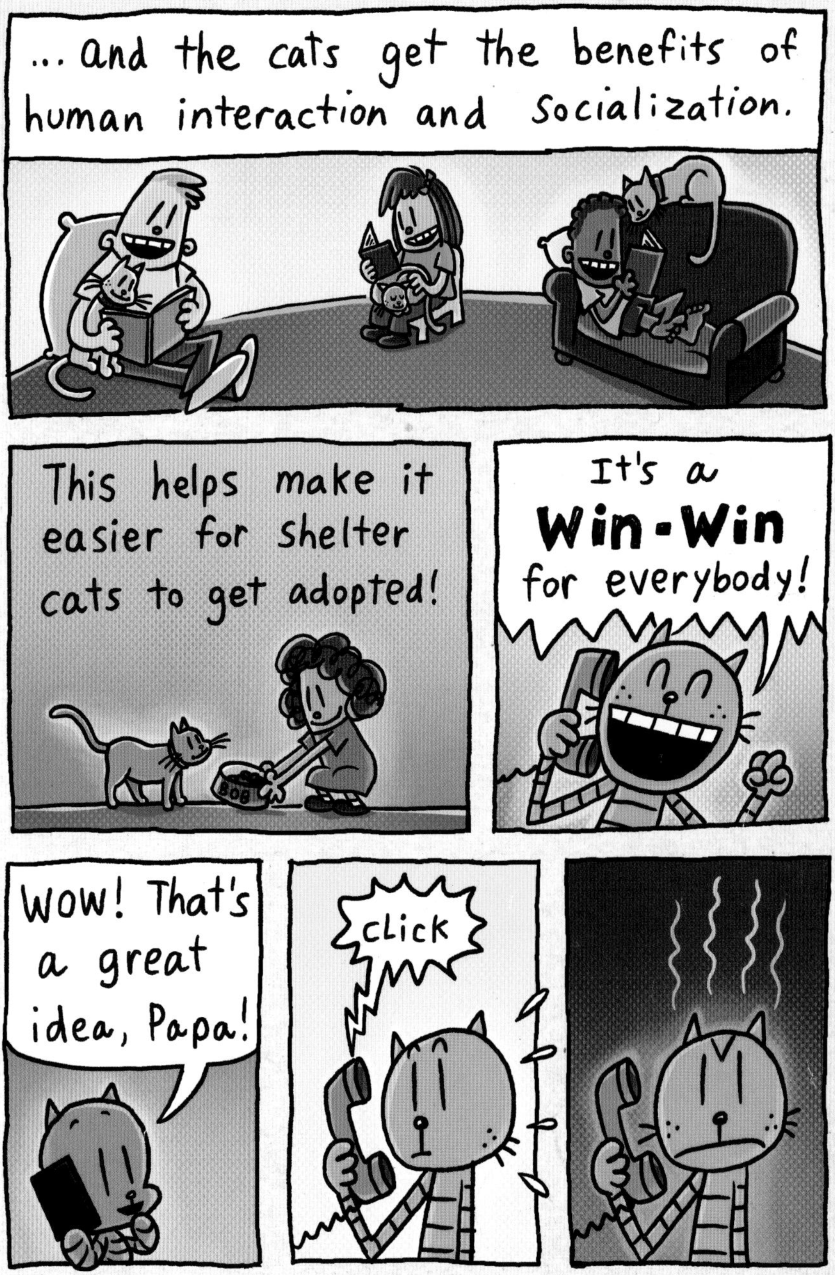
...and the cats get the benefits of human interaction and socialization.
This helps make it easier for shelter cats to get adopted!
BOB
It's a Win-Win for everybody!
WOW! That's a great idea, Papa!
CLICK

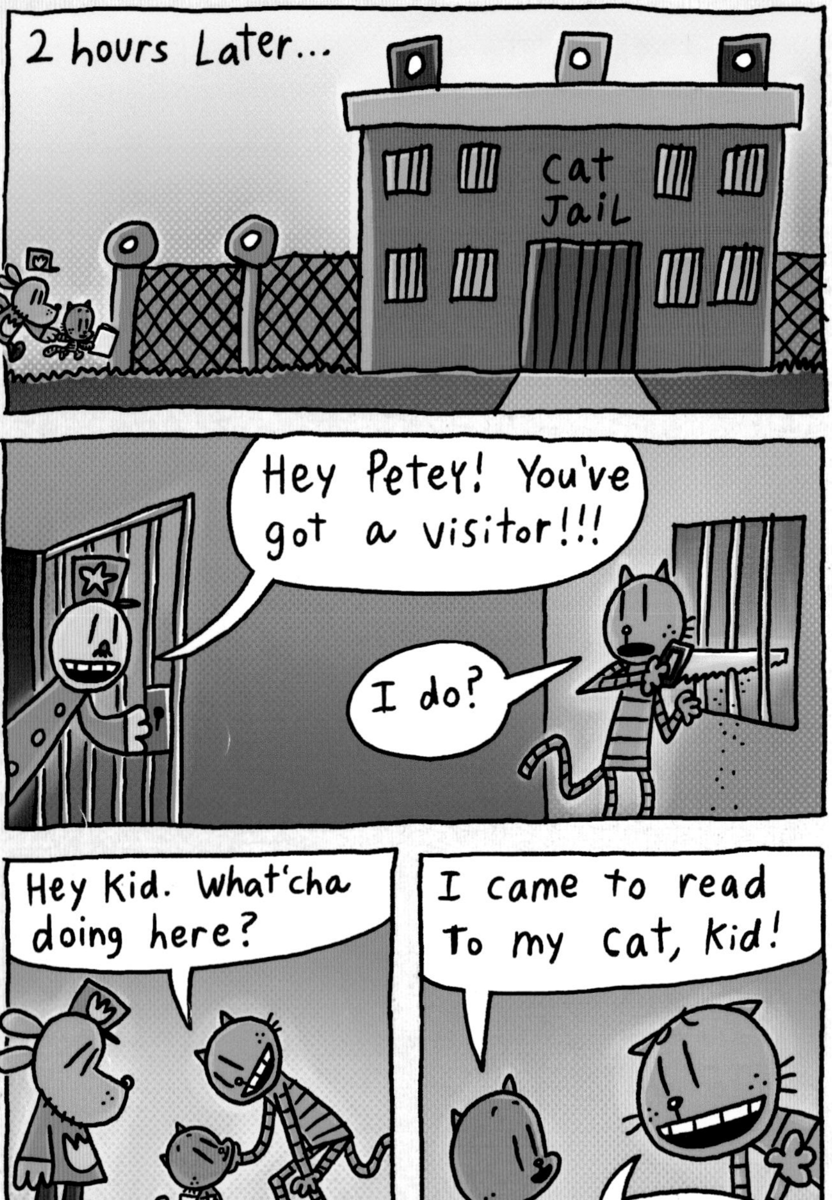
2 hours Later...
Cat Jail
Hey Petey! You've got a visitor!!!
I do?
Hey Kid. What'cha doing here?
I came to read To my cat, Kid!
Really?

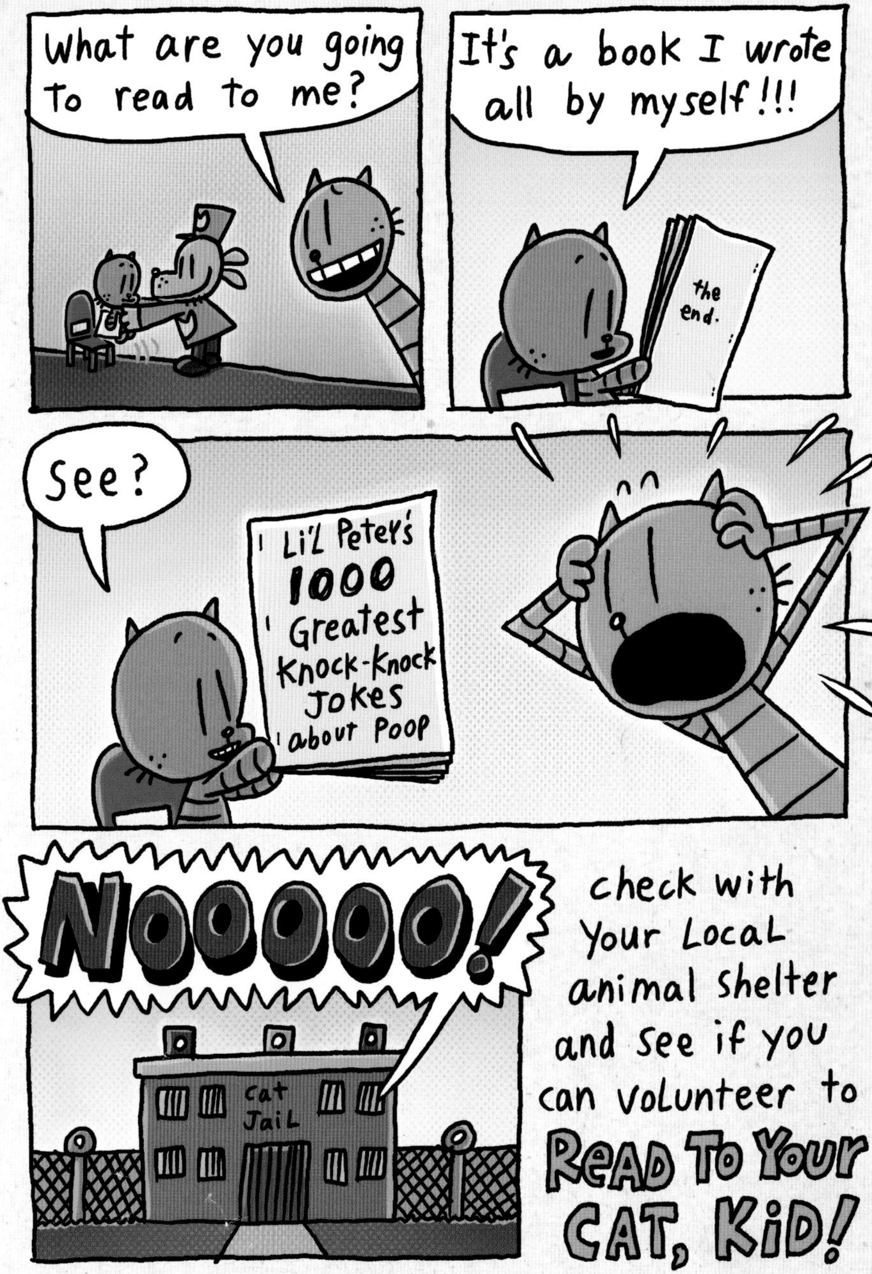
What are you going to read to me?
It's a book I wrote all by myself!!!
the end.
See?
Li'L Peter's 1000 Greatest Knock-Knock Jokes about Poop
NOOOOO!
cat JaiL
check with your Local animal shelter and see if you can volunteer to
READ TO YOUR CAT, KID!

READING TO YOUR CAT IS ALWAYS A PAWS-ITIVE EXPERIENCE!

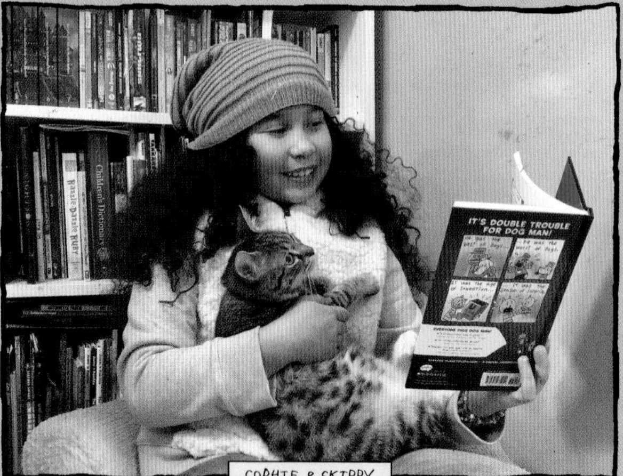
IT'S DOUBLE TROUBLE FOR DOG MAN!

SOPHIE & SKIPPY

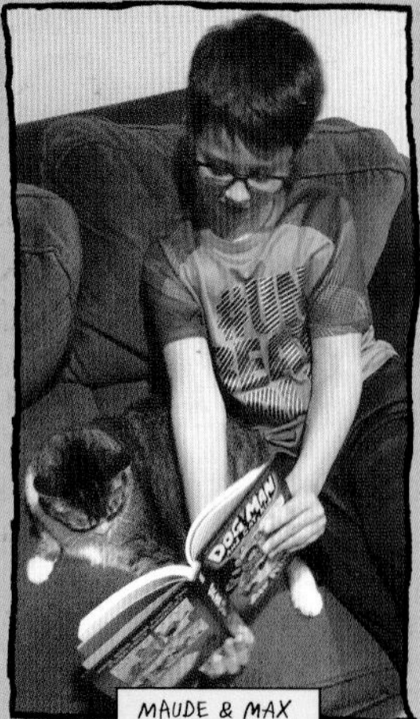

MAUDE & MAX

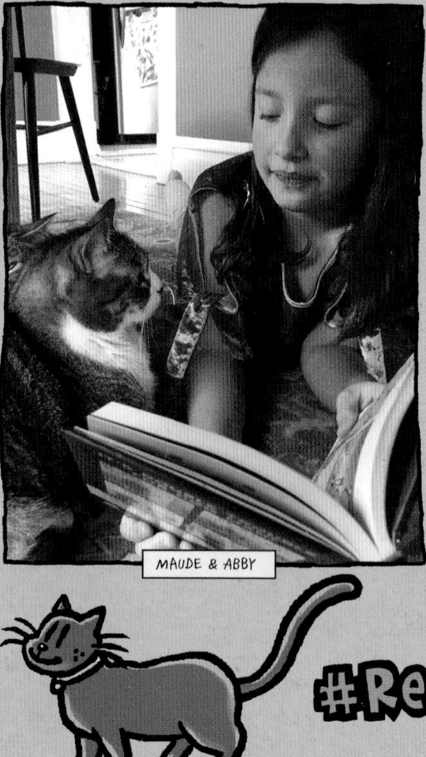

MAUDE & ABBY

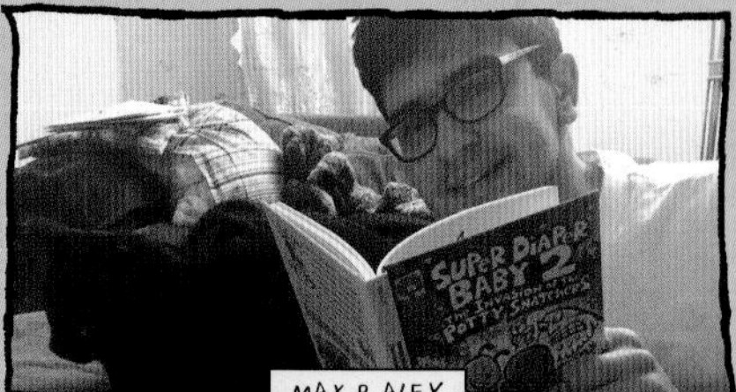

MAX & ALEX

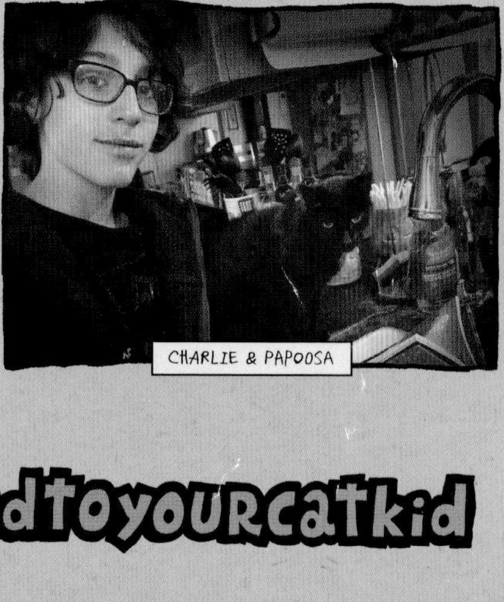

CHARLIE & PAPOOSA

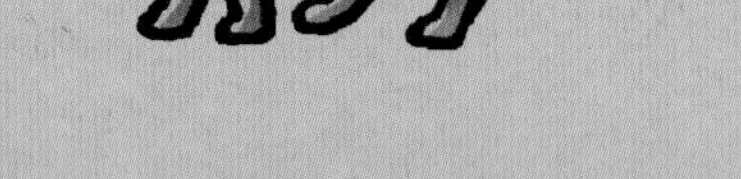

#ReadToYourCatKid

AARON & PAPOOSA

JAC, KATE & DELILAH

KOUME, RINKA & YUMA

SOPHIA, ISABELLE, SCOOT & NINJA

GALEN, FINN & RUCKUS

LEARN MORE AT PILKEY.COM!

THE CUTE LITTLE SQUIRREL

ABOUT THE AUTHOR-ILLUSTRATOR

When Dav Pilkey was a kid, he suffered from ADHD, dyslexia, and behavioral problems. Dav was so disruptive in class that his teachers made him sit out in the hall every day. Luckily, Dav loved to draw and make up stories. He spent his time in the hallway creating his own original comic books.

In the second grade, Dav Pilkey created a comic book about a superhero named Captain Underpants. His teacher ripped it up and told him he couldn't spend the rest of his life making silly books.

Fortunately, Dav was not a very good listener.

ABOUT THE COLORIST

Jose Garibaldi grew up on the South Side of Chicago. As a kid, he was a daydreamer and a doodler, and now it's his full-time job to do both. Jose is a professional illustrator, painter, and cartoonist who has created work for Dark Horse Comics, Disney, Nickelodeon, MAD Magazine, and many more. He lives in Los Angeles, California, with his wife and their cats.